The Horror Zine Magazine

Spring 2021

THE HORROR ZINE

Since 2009, The Horror Zine has published exceptional horror fiction by emerging talent and today's leading authors. Editor Jeani Rector selects only the most inventive, captivating tales, provocative poetry, and amazing art for each issue. In addition to short fiction, The Horror Zine features horror-themed poetry and artwork.

"I have seen the future of horror—and so has Jeani Rector. In fact, she's publishing it. Amazing stuff." – Bentley Little, author of *The Disappearance* and *The Haunted*

"The Horror Zine is one of the very best horror sites online." – Graham Masterton, author of *Blind Panic* and the *Manitou* series

"The Horror Zine is a gloriously rich feast of images and text. Truly a banquet of delights for the discerning horror fan." – Simon Clark, author of *Whitby Vampyrrhic*

"A terrific zine of horrific delights!" – the late Tom Piccirilli, author of *Shadow Season*

"The Horror Zine is a great online magazine that recognizes good work by new and established writers. I think highly of it." – Joe R. Lansdale, author of *Cold in July* and the *Hap and Leonard* series

"The Horror Zine is the genre's Ground Zero where horror legends merge with the talents of tomorrow." – Scott Nicholson, author of The *Red Church*

"Short fiction is the beating, bloody heart of the horror genre, and The Horror Zine has consistently presented startling and superb short stories, poetry and art." – Lisa Morton, multiple Bram Stoker Award-winning author and co-editor of *Hallow's Eve*

"Wired Light" by Marije Berting

THE HORROR ZINE

MAGAZINE

The Horror Zine's mission is to provide a venue in which writers, poets, and artists can exhibit their work. The Horror Zine is an ezine, spotlighting the works of talented people, and displaying their deliciously dark delights for the world to enjoy.

The Horror Zine accepts submissions of fiction, poetry and art from morbidly creative people.

Visit The Horror Zine at
www.thehorrorzine.com

Staff:
Jeani Rector, Editor
Dean H. Wild, Assistant Editor
Bruce Memblatt, Kindle Coordinator

Bat art logo created by Riaan Marais
The Spring 2021 issue cover and Kindle formatted by:
Bruce Memblatt

THE HORROR ZINE MAGAZINE

Dark Delights from the ezine

Edited by Jeani Rector

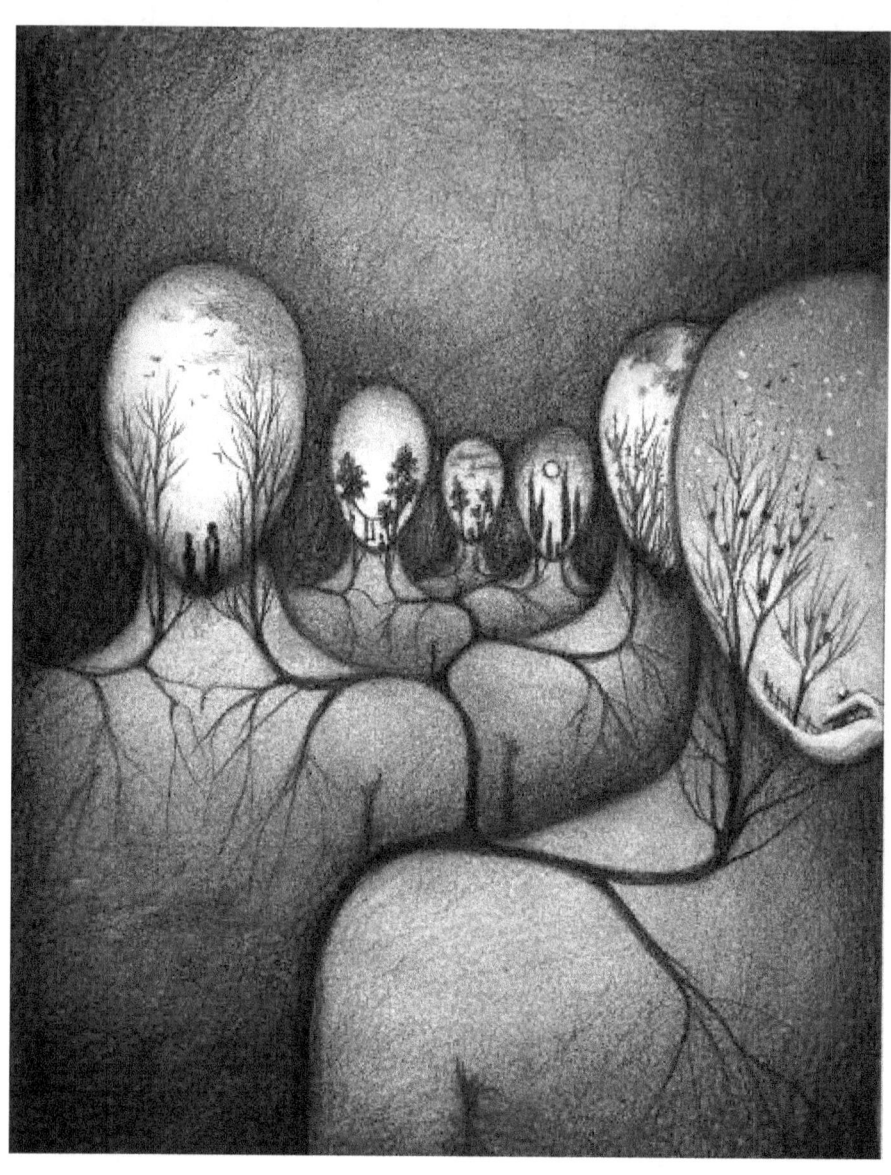

"Vein" by Maksim Alimetov

TABLE OF CONTENTS

Fiction

Poetry

Niloufar Behrooz
Ed Blundell
Donna Dallas
Yuan Hongri (Translated by Yuanbing Zhang)
Paul Sohar
Tony Daly
J.B. Toner
D.J. Tyrer
Mark Powers
Juan Perez
Norbert Hirschhorn
Judson Michael Agla
David M. Hoenig

The Artists

(Artist bios at the back of this magazine)

Cover artist: Jean Sarnay
Marije Berting
Maksim Alimetov
Adam Plant
Bobby Cooper

"Nyx" by Jean Sarnay

FICTION

THE FRIDGE
by Gina Easton

"Ugh!" Jane wrinkled her nose at the sight which greeted her as she peered into the fridge. She'd just bought those strawberries yesterday. And now look at them. She gazed in dismay at the fruit in the basket, the berries now sprouting greenish fur.

Mold! If there was one thing Jane hated, that revolted her to her core, it was moldy food. Mould itself was bad enough wherever it grew, but when it invaded food, especially her food, it was positively disgusting. The very idea of any sort of fungus was an affront to her peace of mind.

The berries had looked perfectly fine yesterday at the grocer's, ruby gems of luscious flavor just waiting to be enjoyed. And now this. She'd refrigerated them right away so the mould growth obviously wasn't her fault. Sighing as she dumped the strawberries, basket and all, into the garbage, she decided she'd have to let Mr. DeMarco know. He should be made aware that his so-called "fresh" organic produce wasn't all that fresh.

No time like the present. Besides, she was really craving some fruit. If the strawberries weren't up to snuff she could always try something else.

Jane walked the short distance to DeMarco's Fresh Fruit and Vegetable store. It had been a fixture in the neighborhood for many years and the proprietor knew most of his customers by name. Mr. DeMarco (Just call me Frank) was a round, jovial man in his mid-fifties, proud of his thriving family business at which both his wife and teenage son worked.

Jane glanced at the array of tempting fruit and vegetables on display outside the store. Each row of fruit looked invitingly free of mold. The small bell above the door tinkled as she entered the cool interior of the store. Mr. DeMarco beamed at her from behind the counter.

"Jane. How nice to see you again. What a glorious day! One of the best we've had all summer."

Jane smiled tightly as she replied, "Yes it is. Mr. DeMarco...I don't want to complain but...the strawberries I bought yesterday were moldy."

The proprietor's smile wavered. "Moldy? But I check my stock carefully. I would never put moldy produce on the shelves."

"No, no," Jane hastened to explain. "The berries seemed fine when I bought them. But when I went to eat them today, mold was growing on them. And that's not all—it's the second time this has happened. Last week the blueberries I purchased went bad the next day too."

DeMarco frowned. "I...I don't know what to say, Jane. Did you refrigerate them? In this weather, you know, if you leave them out..."

Jane said a bit impatiently, "Of course I refrigerated them."

"Why didn't you bring them back for a refund?"

Jane shrugged. "Well—I thought it was just an aberration. I mean, I've been buying your produce for a long time, and always been satisfied with the quality."

DeMarco looked perplexed. "That's strange. I've not received any other complaints. You're the only customer who's reported finding mould."

"I don't know about anyone else. I can only tell you my experience."

"I'm very sorry, Jane. Like I said, I check all the fruit and vegetables for any imperfections, bruises and, of course, mold. So I'm at a loss to explain what's happened. I'll check with the producers and see if they've had similar complaints from other vendors. In the meantime, please accept any fruit you like, free of charge."

"Thank you, Mr. DeMarco. I hope the issue is resolved soon. You've

15

always sold the best fruit and veggies around."

*****

Oh no. Not again. Jane couldn't believe her eyes. She'd opened the fridge door to get some of the delicious cherries she'd enjoyed last evening after returning from DeMarco's, a bushel of the fruit under her arm.

She'd eaten a bowlful and they were ripe and juicy, as tasty as cherries should be. But now…a fine layer of mold coated the remaining berries. Jane cursed in dismay. What was going on here? How could the cherries have gone bad overnight in the fridge?

She glared at the fridge. Could it be the culprit? Maybe it wasn't regulating the temperature properly, thus allowing the fruit to spoil. She peered at the control panel. It was set at moderately cold and the temperature inside the fridge felt sufficiently cool. She turned the dial up anyway, just to make sure.

The fridge couldn't be the problem, she decided, even though it did make strange noises at times. Which, now that she thought about it, seemed odd for a new fridge she'd had less than a month.

In fact…it was only since she bought this fridge that she'd encountered the problem of mold. But her old fridge had died suddenly and she'd had to scramble to find a replacement. The salesman at the warehouse assured her that the fridge was indeed "new" in that it had been returned, apparently still in its original packaging, by a previous customer. No, the customer hadn't said why he returned it, and had, in fact, refused a replacement. The salesman shook his head and shrugged. This was a great model, he said, and at an even greater discount, if she purchased it that very day.

Jane had figured it for a bargain too good to refuse, but now, looking at the ruined cherries, she wasn't so sure. The fridge could be defective; if so she was stuck with it because there was no warranty and she couldn't afford to buy another.

16

She grabbed the bushel of remaining cherries and placed it on the counter-top. She would return the fruit to DeMarco later today, show him first-hand the evidence that his produce was sub-standard. She grimaced in disgust at the cherries, wrapped in their blanket of green fungus. It looked like there was more mould than when she first took them out of the fridge only minutes ago, but that couldn't be. Her eyes must be playing tricks.

Jane shivered slightly. She couldn't help it. Mould gave her the creeps. Fungus of any kind, if truth be told. Her stomach turned whenever she encountered it. That's why she was admittedly a bit of a clean-freak. Her kitchen and bathroom fixtures were spotless as she waged a daily battle against mildew. Not one fungal spore was allowed to exist in her domain, and Jane was not about to let some rotten fruit get the better of her.

Towards the end of the afternoon, Jane decided she needed a break. Working from home was great, but hours in front of a computer screen were often more than her body could handle. It was actually her job as editor of an online science magazine which had contributed to her abhorrence of fungus. She'd learned a great deal about the disgusting organism, which was one of the most adaptable and pernicious of parasites. Abounding in nature it thrived in nearly any kind of environment.

It reproduced in spores which, depending on the specific fungus, if inhaled, ingested, or absorbed through the skin or bloodstream, could wreak terrible and permanent damage on its human host. An insidious predator, fungus was difficult for the human immune system to destroy completely. Sometimes, especially if it infiltrated the body's vital organs, it could cause fatal infections.

No wonder then, Jane reasoned, she held a healthy respect for (and fear of) this microscopic yet formidable enemy.

She pushed her chair away from the computer, yawning as she stood. Despite getting her usual amount of sleep, she noticed that she was more tired these days. She seemed to fatigue more easily and just didn't feel her normal energetic self. She shrugged, trying to shake off the sluggish feeling in her muscles. Glancing at the clock on the wall she decided she should return the cherries and give Mr. DeMarco a piece of her mind...selling rancid produce was just not acceptable.

She entered the kitchen and stopped short, frowning. The counter-top was bare. But she'd taken the basket of fruit out of the fridge and placed it on the counter. She knew she had. She looked at the fridge and saw that its door was slightly ajar. Her frown deepened. What the hell was going on? She marched over to the fridge and pulled open the door.

The basket of cherries was there.

On the second shelf.

Where they'd been before she deposited them on the counter.

Jane stared in consternation. Not only were the cherries back in the fridge, but the coating of mould was like a blanket now, sickly green with black tinges. She sniffed, detecting a subtle odor of decay which seemed to emanate not only from the fruit but the fridge itself. She recoiled, stomach clenching in revulsion as she noted smudges of black mould on the wall of the fridge nearest the rotting fruit.

"Shit, shit, shit," she muttered, backing away from the fridge. Black mold. The kind that wreaked disaster on immune systems and caused a number of horrible and potentially deadly syndromes. How did this species of fungus come to be in *her* kitchen? She was always so diligent in her efforts to maintain a clean environment in her home.

She quickly gathered her cleaning supplies, plastic apron and mask. It was imperative that she not inhale any spores. Donning her rubber gloves she gingerly lifted the basket of cherries from the fridge. Her gorge rose as she saw that the mould had seeped right through the bottom of the basket and now stained the fridge shelf with its slimy, fetid presence. She hastily carried the basket over to the garbage bin.

A nasty, pungent smell greeted her when she opened the bin. Jane gagged, cursing her oversight. The strawberries she threw away yesterday were festering in the garbage, the dark, dank space an ideal breeding-ground for the abominable fungal spores.

"Uggh! Ick! Oh yuck!" Jane cried, teeth clenched tightly behind her mask. She had to discard the putrid mess before her stomach heaved its contents all over her spotless kitchen floor. She grabbed another garbage liner and dumped the first one into it, then sealed it tightly. Carrying it to the back entry she opened the screen door and threw the bag out on the deck. She would deposit it into the outside disposal bin later. For now…she needed to tackle the fridge.

*****

Jane sighed as she put away the cleaning supplies and removed her apron, mask and gloves. She'd scrubbed every last bit of revolting fungus from the wall and shelf of the fridge. Now it gleamed like new again.

But she was so tired. Looking at the time, she saw to her surprise that it was going on ten p.m. She'd been so preoccupied, obsessed even, with getting rid of the mold that she'd lost track of time. She even forgot to eat dinner. And now after looking at and smelling that fungus, she completely lost her appetite. Besides, she was so weary she might as well just go to bed.

Later in the night, Jane awoke to the sound of the fridge droning and gurgling loudly. *Now what?* she thought groggily. *It sounds like it has indigestion. Hopefully it isn't the motor.*

Sighing in annoyance, she got out of bed and walked into the kitchen.

Stopped in her tracks.

The fridge door was wide open. Most of the contents were strewn around the kitchen floor. Bottles and jars shattered. A carton of eggs was smashed, yellow yolks oozing sticky puddles. Packages of

19

cheese, various containers of left-overs…as though the fridge, in the throes of a mad frenzy, had suddenly disgorged its innards everywhere.

Jane gasped. A sob of disbelief escaped her.

The solitary light bulb inside the fridge glowed brightly, revealing the large, irregular patches of black fungus which covered the fridge's walls and shelves. Long streaks, jagged cracks of mold, like a grotesque parody of Chistmas decorations, festooned most of the interior.

"No, no, no!" Jane exclaimed, shaking her head. This had to be a nightmare, right? It couldn't be real. She was still asleep in bed, not standing before this monstrosity of a fridge, staring at the malignant growths festering inside it. It was the only rational explanation.

Jane pinched the skin on her forearm so hard she cried out in pain. But the scene before her didn't waver. She didn't suddenly wake up in bed. Then she actually *was* awake and this was really happening? Stifling another sob, Jane bit her lip and straightened her shoulders. Only one thing to do at this moment…

She trudged off to find her cleaning supplies.

*****

First she was indignant. Then outright angry.

"Yes, of course it's defective," she shouted at the salesman on the phone. "That's what I've been telling you. All my food is spoiling. Do you know how much food has gone to waste?" She listened as the man interrupted to say something.

"I know there's no warranty. I don't care about getting my money back. Why can't you give me another fridge in exchange?"

The salesman replied.

20

"What do you mean that was the last one in stock? What am I supposed to do? I need a fridge!"

The salesman murmured something suitably soothing.

Jane exclaimed in exasperation, "You know what? I don't care. Just come pick it up."

Another brief response.

"Of course you have to pick it up. I'm returning it! Don't you understand, you moron? I don't want the fucking fridge! It's possessed!"

A shocked silence greeted her outburst. After a moment, the man said something.

"Please," Jane begged, her voice breaking. "Honestly, I'm at my wit's end." Listening. "I see. Well, thanks for nothing!" She slammed the phone down so hard her hand tingled from the impact "Asshole!" she yelled, jumping to her feet.

After spending most of the wee hours of the previous night scouring the fungus from the fridge and cleaning up the mess on the floor, she'd crept back to bed, exhausted. Then, once the supermarket was open she'd gone shopping, buying fresh groceries as test subjects. She'd come home, unpacked the groceries, made herself a cup of tea and attempted to return the cursed (and she meant that literally) refrigerator back to the warehouse.

A futile endeavor, as it turned out. Which meant that she was on her own when it came to dealing with this problem. Fleetingly, the thought occurred to her that she might be insane, trapped in a weird hallucinatory psychosis. But she really didn't think so.

Time to go check on things. Jane had decided to conduct an experiment. The fridge had remained spotlessly clean today, no trace of fungus within its pristine interior. However, it had also been empty—until she recently re-stocked it with fresh grocery items.

That had been what—five hours ago now? Time to see what the fridge had been up to.

She stealthily approached the fridge, girding herself to do battle. The door was closed. With a flourish born of false bravado, Jane flung open the door.

Her eyes registered the clean walls and shelves. She released a breath she hadn't realized she was holding. She reached for a jar of fresh pasta sauce and unscrewed the lid.

Her eyes widened in horrified dismay at the skim of green mold resting on the surface. Next she grabbed a container of milk, the sour smell assailing her nostrils as she removed the cap. Emptying the contents down the sink, she gagged at the sight of greenish-brown chunks which clogged the opening of the drain. She reached for the casserole of beef stew she'd cooked a few hours ago. And lifted the foil wrap to discover a thick, crusty coating of mold.

Jane reeled as a wave of dizziness assaulted her. She was drained of energy, limbs trembling uselessly, unable to support her weight. Seized by a profound fatigue, she sank to the floor, her back propped against the counter, facing the gaping interior of the fridge. Her vision swam out of focus as her eyes closed.

*****

Jane's eyes snapped open. It took a few seconds to adjust as the kitchen was in shadows. How long had she been...asleep? Why was she half-sprawled on the kitchen floor? Her head felt fuzzy, her thoughts sluggish. It was evening, judging from the darkness outside the kitchen window. The sole light in the room came from the fridge, whose door was still agape.

Jane straightened up from her slumped position and gazed at the scene before her. For some moments she was unable to register what had transpired. Containers of food once again scattered everywhere, mostly empty of their contents. She looked down at the beef casserole on the floor beside her. It was half-eaten, a thick layer of

22

fungus oozing through the chunks of meat and vegetables. Where was the other half of the casserole? Inexplicably gone.

As was most of the jar of pasta sauce, tell-tale lumps of black-green mold nestled amongst the tomatoes and mushrooms. A carton of vanilla yogurt, seal newly broken, the dairy product demolished, just a few swirls of green and black at the bottom.

Jane burped loudly. Wiped her mouth with the back of her hand. Looked at her hand, at the smeared remnants of stew, pasta sauce and yogourt.

She gagged as revulsion filled her. Just as the awful, horrible truth hit her like a punch in the gut. *She* had ingested this rancid, tainted food. In some altered state, a fugue, a trance, whatever, she had *eaten* the fungus-infested food.

She gasped as a memory jolted her. Sitting on the kitchen floor, casserole container in both hands, tipping it to her mouth. Avidly devouring the slimy, gelatinous reeking stew. Followed by the pasta sauce. Fingers digging into the spongy, pungent mixture, cramming the putrid mess into her greedy mouth…

Bile, burning and acrid, rose in her throat. Staggering to her feet she stumbled towards the sink. Head bent, waves of nausea crested in her gut as she waited for the sickness to hit. Normally she hated to vomit; it disgusted her almost as much as mold. Now she welcomed it. But despite the roiling greasiness in her stomach nothing happened. Steeling herself against the unpleasantness of the task Jane lowered her head and stuck her fingers down her throat.

No matter how much she wanted it, willed it, all she could manage was a few paltry retches, stomach dry-heaving and clenching painfully.

Panic started to bubble inside her. She had to get rid of the repulsive fungus she'd unwittingly ingested. How many millions of spores were now multiplying in her digestive tract, biding their time before absorption into her bloodstream? Once there, it was game over. The fungus would destroy her, organ by organ. She could almost feel the deadly spores burrowing into the tiny alveoli in her lungs, eating away at the lobes of her brain...

Crying in distress, Jane ran into the bathroom. Flipping on the light switch, she gazed at her reflection in the mirror. Wild eyes red-rimmed, lids encrusted with green gunk. A thin stream of greenish-brown fluid the consistency of pus emanated from both nostrils. She opened her mouth wide. A black fuzzy layer coated her tongue and the inside of her cheeks.

In mounting terror, Jane screamed and careened back into the kitchen. For the first time she noticed that the back door was open and a trail of garbage led from the deck into the kitchen. Throwing up her hands in abject fear she saw the streaks from the torn garbage bin which stained the floor like so much blood. Strawberry juice like bright arterial blood. Cherry juice like darker venous blood.

Oh, God, no. Surely she hadn't scavenged through the garbage as well? Shoveling rotten berries down her throat, too? She couldn't bear the thought. Have to stop the fungus. Have to stop it.

She couldn't let any more of the noxious spores be absorbed from her digestive system. It might already be too late.

She ran to the gleaming set of kitchen knives, grabbing the longest and sharpest one in the block. She felt her eyes being drawn to the fridge, her body and mind growing cold. She was mesmerized by the spotless interior. The fridge taunted her with its pristine quality, so different from her own filthy, defiled body. Didn't she want to be all purified and cleansed on the inside, too? No more loathsome fungus.

Only one way to accomplish that.

Sobbing desperately, mad with fear, she plunged the knife into her abdomen, savagely lacerating the layers of dermis, sawing through thick fat and sinewy muscle .Blood spurted copiously as she continued to hack down to her intestinal wall.

Finally able to glimpse the shiny coils of intestines, she severed the mesenteric artery, watching the bright geyser of blood erupt.

And at last, a glimpse of the glistening viscera throbbing with the presence of millions of fungal spores. Both hands slick with blood and gore, she struggled to maintain her grip on the knife.

As Jane sank to the floor, consciousness quickly ebbing, the final thing she saw was the cold mocking light from the fridge.

About Gina Easton

Gina Easton is a former registered nurse who decided to pursue her long-time dream of writing as a profession. To date she has had twelve short-stories published in horror anthologies and magazines.

She also has two novels (both in the horror/fantasy genre) scheduled for release in 2021.

She adores the weird, mysterious and magical aspects of life, which she explores through her writing.

She lives in Toronto, Canada, with her husband.

WHEN THE CARNIVAL CAME TO TOWN
by Theresa Jacobs

Christopher kept to the back of each ride, sure to stay out of sight of the carnies. Twilight lay a blanket of darkness to the shadows where he hovered. Behind the constant whir, bang, hum, loud rock and roll, along with kids hooting and hollering, he never had to worry about making a sound. Tonight, marked his third night spying on the traveling carnival, and he hoped his last.

Following the Ringmaster was easy. The man had to be near seven-feet tall; he wore black silk pants with a blazing red stripe down the outer leg, and he was never without his top hat. The oddest thing was he was never without sunglasses either, even at night. His attention was drawn from his mission as two teenage girls, leaning into each other giggling, moved to the counter at the ring toss. He pressed between the concessions, careful not to trip on the thick rubber wires, as he tried to hear what was being said.

"Ah, lovely young ladies!" A carny working the book had greased back hair, too toothy of a grin, and wrinkles for days. "Step up, try your hand and catch a prize!" With a wink and smile, he placed the rings in the one girl's hand.

Even from Christopher's nook, he saw the young girl flinch from the carny's touch. Crouching down to his knees, he leaned against the booth, aiming to see the thin, blonde girl's face as she tossed the rings. He hadn't yet been able to sort out how people approached the games: normal, laughing, happy, having a grand ole time, only to walk away in a dumb state. As though their heads were empty of self-thought.

The teen's hand rose and the yellow ring left her fingers; it floated across the space, hit a bottle, tinged, bounced and rolled away. The carny gave a low *tsk*, but didn't shout out or entice her to try harder. He was watching her eyes. Even the waiting friend had grown quiet. Around them, lights flashed, danced and sparkled as darkness grew deeper. With the last ring tossed, the girls turned, dumb-struck now, and walked away.

Christopher watched them go, then looked back to the ring toss. The carny gathered up the errant rings, returning them to his pouch, and sat. Not needing to see more—he'd already watched the exact same oddity transpire countless times over the last three nights—he moved on.

What he needed were answers. What were these guys doing to people? Could he find any authority that wouldn't lock him up and think he was crazy? Was there a way to reverse it? Whatever, it, was?

*****

Four days prior, the carnival had come to his town of Blue Springs. On the night of the family outing, fifteen-year-old Christopher was feeling under the weather. His family had traipsed off to enjoy the thrills, take in the junk food, and play games, leaving him behind because of his illness.

But when they came home, they had changed. They continued to go through the motions of life, but in a quiet, zoned-out state. They didn't talk, or interact with each other, or him. He'd yelled at them and even went so far as to punch his older brother in the stomach. Only a short time ago this would have elicited a good beating. But now there was no reaction, not even a raised eyebrow.

At any time in the past, he would have said his family was a nuisance; his brothers were mean, his father demanding, and his mom too emotional, he longed for those people back. Fighting back tears—no fifteen-year-old guy in his right mind would cry—he stalked the carnival instead, looking for answers.

*****

He blended back into the shadows, searching for the Ringmaster again.

27

Glancing up and down the midway, looking beyond the naïve marks, past the calling carnies and ignoring the tanned, leggy girls, he spotted a tall shadow disappear into the fun house. Eye on the prize, he took considerable strides after the man, avoiding people like a pinball down an inlane, when a sandpapery grip jerked him to the right and nearly off his feet.

"Where you rushing off to, sonny? You look like a strapping young man. Why not try your hand at the ten-in-one." The carny chewed out his spiel, still holding Christopher's arm while rolling three baseballs in his other mitt of a hand.

For the briefest of moments, he thought, *And what if I did? It's one way to see what happens. I can pull away before my mind gets melted.*

He looked into the carny's dark eyes and didn't like what stared back at him. There was something not right about the man. He had no whites to his eyes, at least none that could be discerned in the darkness. They appeared as blind pits of tar.

Christopher pulled back. "Sorry, my sister is waiting to go on the teacups. I'm already late." He was surprised at how easily the lie tumbled from his lips.

The carny's nose crinkled oddly and his eyes narrowed as if he was sniffing out the lie. "Just three tosses boy. Ya sis can wait I'm sure."

"Nah, I'm already in good with my ma, but thanks for the offer."

As another unsuspecting mark took up the carny's attention, Christopher spun and took off at a light jog. Sweat dripped down his back as the funhouse grew closer. The attraction was set up off the ground in what appeared to be tracker-trailers lined up in rows, with metal stairs leading to a giant, open clown mouth.

Turning and looking back at the raucous carnival, this end of the field had an abandoned feel to it. There were no overhead lights. No crazy, pumping music, and it was a good twenty feet or more away from the rest of the games. He checked to ensure no one was watching and hurried into the darkness under the iron stairs.

"What am I doing here?" he asked himself, not for the first time, as he waited to make sure no one was coming after him. After a few minutes on his knees in the grass, he decided what he must do. Go inside the funhouse.

His heart picked up the pace as he moved from under the stairs and tiptoed up them. The large round O of a mouth did not appear fun. The clown's eyes were downcast, staring in a peeling royal blue at all that entered. The lips, once red, had dulled to salmon pink, and he felt like they'd close around him the minute he stepped onto the red-carpet tongue. Knowing that he had to follow through, he gulped and took a fast leap into the attraction.

The door remained open behind him, as he knew in his mind it would, but his clenched sphincter still told him otherwise. The hallway was one person wide and lined with small, round pot lights along the floor. From this angle, they cast long, dancing shadows around him.

All the hair on his body stood on end. Despite the heat of the July, chills ran up his spine. He walked slow and quiet, listening for any sounds from within, and wondered what direction he should take. He had never been in a funhouse before and had no clue what to expect. What was so fun about it anyways?

Suddenly the floor beneath his feet tilted. Stretching out his arms, he teetered like a drunken sailor from side to side, and inadvertently cried out. He braced himself from tumbling over when the floor tipped the other way. The next section was convex and as he stepped down it began to spin beneath his feet.

"Shit!" The idea of sneaking in was lost to his unexpected reaction. As he staggered off the rolling barrel, puffs of air shot out with loud, compressed bursts. He realized that each section was like an obstacle course. Passing the skirt blowing portion, the next ten feet were

29

oddly shaped mirrors. As he moved, they distorted and contorted his features.

Seeing himself all misshapen gave him the willies again. He heard loud voices echoing from ahead. Finally seeing a t-off in the hallways, he paused, listening.

Turning left, he followed the voices to an open room. His heart fluttered again, his stomach churned in knots, and his palms grew cool with sweat. There was nowhere for him to hide and watch. He bent down to his hands and knees, stayed tight to the wall, and crept quiet as a mouse along the hall until he could see partially into the room.

It appeared to be a makeshift office, with a single person wood desk upon which the Ringmaster half perched. A younger man, his face pale and tight with fear, sat in one of the two worn purple guest chairs, the Ringmaster hovering above him.

"I'mmm sssory, Vasilica I..." the young man stuttered, wringing his hands red in his lap.
"Sorry? You sniveling rot! I expect at least two feedings a night. You've been here three months. Three months!" The Ringmaster seethed, hissing through his teeth.

Christopher's heart went out to the guy who appeared to be only a few years older than himself. He looked away as a tear fell from the man's eye, and wondered how long this dressing down had been going on for. But he didn't have to worry because it didn't last much longer.

"Really Vas...no! No! please..."

The Ringmaster lifted the young man from his chair.

The man's legs flailed ineffectually against the Ringmaster's shins as he was lifted effortlessly into the air. The Ringmaster's lips pulled back in a wide, face-splitting grin, revealing row after row of tiny, pointed teeth stacked one upon another. With his free hand, he reached up, sliding his dark sunglasses down his nose. The young man writhed side to side, gurgling nonsensical noises but not speaking, or screaming. His own eyes fixated on the Ringmaster's. The young man's bladder let loose and his jeans darkened with wet.

Christopher bit his tongue as he held back a cry of his own. Even from his vantage point, he could see the voluminous round eyes of the Ringmaster, bulging outward as though too big for their sockets. They shone, illuminated from within, and altered colors, akin to a kaleidoscope. They turned from all shades of blue to light brown, to green, to grey, to hazel, to white, to black, to dark brown, to violet, and altered faster and faster.

As the young man went limp in the large man's grip, Christopher couldn't restrain a gurgle of fear from escaping his lips this time.

The Ringmaster's head swivelled to the hallway to spot Christopher, a clear form cowering on the floor. He released the young man, who fell into a catatonic heap on the floor.

Christopher didn't hesitate. He pushed himself up, turned back the way he came and bolted. Praying that the speed of youth was on his side, he dared not look back as he took the turn back into the funhouse.

He jolted at the sight of himself when he stepped into the mirrored hallway, then realizing it was his own refection, pushed on. Before he reached the last mirror, the Ringmaster's reflection melded with Christopher's, creating a grotesque amalgamation of the two.

"What are you?" Christopher screamed as he ran on.

Air puffed at him in the skirt blowing lane, but it would not slow him. He hit the barrel roll at such a high rate of speed that the barrel barely spun. He had a thought that if he could turn his foot as he hit the end, he could get it spinning, slowing the Ringmaster down.

But that was a childish thought; there was no time for any tricks. The man, or beast, or demon—whatever the Ringmaster was—with his crazy long legs would be on Christopher before he could hit the outside. And sure enough, as he entered the tilting hallway, the Ringmaster came right behind.

As he tilted right, the weight of the other man began the tilt left, jarring him across the short hall and bouncing him into the left wall. Now with both their weight holding the floor down, they were rammed up on an angle.

"Hold up! Stop," a deep voice called out. Multiple forms darkened the hallway.

Christopher's legs gave out, and he fell forward, landing pinched between the wall and the tilted floor. His breath came in short hyper gasps, his heart pounding like a snare drum in his chest.

The Ringmaster shuffled up to Christopher's feet. "How'd he get in here? Get him up. To my place, now," he ordered.

Whether from extreme fear or plain exhaustion, Christopher didn't have time to ponder as he passed out cold.

*****

In the darkness under Christopher's eyelids, he imagined he was curled in his bed, dreading the new day. As he moved to stretch out, his length was impeded with a clang, only then was he aware of being balled up in a small space. Suddenly recalling he'd been captured by the Ringmaster at the carnival, his eyes flew open.

"Well, it lives," Vasilica chuckled.

Christopher gasped, taking in his predicament. He was locked in a cage that might be large enough for a Rottweiler, but certainly not large enough for him. He pressed against the back of the cage, stretching his legs out as straight as he could to relieve the cramping. He said nothing, only glanced warily from carny to carny. Four of them surrounded him, and he avoided the alien gaze of the Ringmaster.

32

Vasilica leaned over the open wire cage, plucking at the bars as a musician to a guitar. "And just how long were you following us, boy?" he cooed in a soft, eerie voice.

Christopher stared at the cage door, already trying to sort out an escape rather than give in to the intimidation of the creeper.

"Oh." Vasilica straightened, holding his excessively long arms out to his sides. "We caught ourselves a toughie here, fellas. Why, just look at him concentrating on that lock." His lips peeled back revealing his pointed, glistening rows of teeth.

Moving faster than his large frame should allow, the Ringmaster darted back over the top of the cage. Now above Christopher's head, Vasilica's hot, fetid breath washed over the boy's downturned face. "Well then, perhaps this will entice you to talk." The Ringmaster spun and grabbed the arm of the carny that had mesmerized the two girls at the ring toss earlier and brought him closer to the cage.

Christopher didn't want to look, but curiosity was his Achilles' heel. He wished he'd never come to this infernal carnival. He wished he'd stayed home with his placid zombie-esque family and did his own thing. He could have too. He could have quit school and lazed around the house all day. He could have had any life he wanted.

The Ringmaster tore open the carny's plaid shirt, revealing a horror worse than the sights Christopher had seen as of yet. The man's stomach—although there was no possible way this thing was a man—was a cavern that traveled to a distance farther than human eyesight. The gaping hole roiled blood red with countless souls trapped and screaming inside.

Christopher could not look away even though his mind was screaming at him to. He watched as people clawed at the opening, their screams echoing around the room. Their faces and sex were indiscernible. He pissed his pants, then leaned forward and vomited between his legs.

The Ringmaster closed the carny's shirt. He knelt before the cage. "Look at me."

Christopher looked up and stared into the eyes that shifted colors. As a soft blue rose to the surface, he knew they were his mother's, they blended to black, and she was gone. Tears formed in his own eyes and he began to cry in earnest, whether from hunger, exhaustion, or pure terror, he no longer cared.

"You have a choice here, boy. You can be fed to Ungunnolth here and live eternally in that hell. Believe it or not, the souls I eat, while tormented, are not as much so as those are." Vasilica clicked his teeth and waggled his tongue.

The rest of the room remained silent, either they knew not to interrupt the Ringmaster, or they were eagerly waiting for a bite of Christopher.

The Ringmaster resumed, "We always need regular men like yourself to run some of the rides. As you saw, I had to dispose of one such boy earlier."

Christopher gulped and nodded. "H-h-h," he stuttered, cleared his throat and tried again. "How do I take the souls from the marks?"

Vasilica tossed his head back, a deep, rumbling laugh erupting from his gut. His chest rose and fell, causing the silver buttons on his vest to flash blindingly. Then, just as abruptly, his laughter ended and he leaned close to the bars, his teeth bared in warning. "This is the real-world, boy. Not some fantasy novel, or action flick on the big screen. You will work for me behind a booth. You'll eat and sleep in this cage! You'll be my slave until you get old and feeble. Or anger me and I eat you. No hero is going to ride in and save you."

Vasilica angled his head so that one eye bulged its prismatic dance at Christopher and then he continued. "You're still young enough to believe in tripe. But guess what, buddy boy, we've been doing this carnival for thousands of years."

34

Christopher began crying. His eyes darted from man to man—or demon to demon. He didn't know what they were, but they weren't men. He knew the Ringmaster was right, he was too inexperienced in life to know anything. He was surprised that he'd gotten as far as he had without being caught. Now his life, if it would be a life, was in the hands of evil. He had no options. "Yes, sir," he mumbled.

Vasilica clapped and stood. "Ah, I knew you'd choose my way over the tortured soul highway. Tomorrow's a big day. We tear down and move to a new spot. Sleep now." Finished, he led his troupe out the door, flicking off the lights as he went.

Plunged into darkness, Christopher pulled his legs up to his chest away from the vomit. "What am I going to do? I can't work for him. I just can't." He broke down and cried harder. When the tears dried up, he tried shifting to a better position and felt his belt buckle dig into his stomach. As he pulled to loosen it, the tine jabbed his finger.

"Ohh," he gasped, as a thought came to him. He wriggled around painfully as the cage bars dug into his back and butt. With little elbow room, he unlatched the buckle, yanking the belt out of the loops. Belt in hand he squirmed, maneuvering himself to turn around. He knew the cage was backed up to a wall, now he could only hope it was near an outlet. He had to squint and focus his eyes up close in the dark. At least the walls were white, and that helped to pick up shapes. He made out a dark cord, draped from an end table a mere two feet from him.

Now he had to figure out how to shift the cage. The bars were already killing his knees, but he had to try.

Pressing himself as far right as he could, he bounced up. The cage rattled louder than he expected and his breath caught as his heart leaped into his throat. He sat, holding his breath for the count of ten, then waited silently ten seconds more. When no one came bolting through the door, he bounced again, and again, and again.

The cage moved a few inches at a time. But it *was* moving. This gave him hope. He paused to rest, but not too long, and began bouncing again.

Eventually, the cage butted up to the plug in the wall. He reached through the bars, feeling the outlet with his fingers. Sure enough, the only thing plugged in was a single lamp. The bottom was clear.

Not wanting to lose where the outlet was in the dark, Christopher prayed this would work. Taking his belt in hand, he held the buckle tight and pressed the tine between his thumb and index finger.

"I'm sorry, Mom and Dad. I thought I could save you somehow. I hope someday, someone smarter and braver than me can. I love you."

He hocked a wad of warm spittle on the belt tine and his fingers. Gripping the bars tight with his left hand, Christopher leaned his forehead against the cage. Using his free fingers, he felt for the plug, then below it, the receptacle. Thinking 'god, I hope this works,' he rammed the wet metal tine into the open socket.

*****

Outside the huddle of carny trailers, one of the electrical poles sparked a flash of blinding white-blue, popping the transformer. All the trailers whirred to silence as they lost power. If anyone had been looking at the Ringmaster's trailer at that exact moment, they would have seen the inside light up orange as the interior caught fire.

But at that moment, everyone was busy shutting down the midway for the night. They didn't suspect anything until plumes of acrid, poison filled smoke billowed towards the moon. Everyone, including the demon-kind, rushed forward with fire extinguishers.

The Ringmaster's trailer was lost to the fire, all other trailers survived.

The next morning when the ashes cooled, the Ringmaster pulled a still hot belt buckle from outside the locked, melted cage.

Vasilica tipped his hat to the pile of blackened bones and gave a bow to his first-ever escapee.

About Theresa Jacobs

Theresa Jacobs shocks her readers with her versatile style, from kids' books, to horror, to crime, she'll never let her creativity be stifled, and after writing eleven books in six years, nothing will stop her now. She still works full time in the real world and spends every free moment either writing new stories or binge watching popular shows. She lives in Canada with her handy husband and goofy dog, both of whom vie for the rest of her time.

BEHIND THE DOOR
by Eric Neher

The door was locked. My older brother Dave slammed his shoulder against the panel, the panic in his eyes contagious. Even now, I can still hear the explosion that had wrenched us away from our afternoon cartoons.

"Was that a gun?" I asked.

"Stay here," said Dave.

I waited as he rushed out of the back door and made his way around to our father's bedroom window. The shattering glass caused me to flinch, and within moments the handle began to turn.

Dave cracked the door open, careful not to allow enough space for me to see inside of the room.

"Get back, Jake," he said, nudging me away and pulling the door shut behind him. I followed him into our kitchen, my knees feeling as if they had suddenly become disconnected and slid down against the wall as he picked up the phone.

That was a long time ago, but I never forget.

*****

Strange how one act can influence the lives of so many. At first, the outcry was overwhelming with feigned offers of *If there's anything we can do, just let us know.* What would they have done if we had called their bluff? Could they have saved our mother from the bottle? Could they have stopped the nightmares that soon infested our sleep like monstrous invaders? Most likely not, and even if they could, would they have?

Our father's legacy was much too well-known for such a conclusion. His tragedy swept through the community like a spring breeze, allowing those who dwelt within his darkness a momentary reprieve, a chance to laugh at their own demons in a squandered celebration of life.

This was the road that Dave and I suddenly found ourselves thrust upon, paved with shame, lit only by the haloes of guilt and loathing. Our father was the creator; the architect whose own resignation had designed a merciless pit both cold and without hope, and it was from here that our lives truly began.

Where does one go when all of the doors have been shut? There was no magical savior, no spiritual guide that would appear upon command like some kind of Holy Cab. When in the dark, you reach for anything that might help light your way.

For my brother, that beacon was found in the reoccurring jabs of a needle. The felonious liquid muffled the screams that he had yet to release. Never once did I see him cry, even after he was forced to step over our father's body. It was as if a part of him had split, had agreed to hide away in forgotten seclusion just as long as it remained fed.

One would think that the enveloping darkness would begin to brighten at some point, that time would eventually heal even the deepest of wounds, but that is not always the case. Instead, the years only widened the divide, and soon where once stood, a comrade was a stranger. Dave's skin had aged; his bright eyes dulled into a reaction-less stare void of emotion. Had I not been so consumed with my own fight for survival, I might have been able to help him.

The ramifications of our choices are not clear. We all teeter on edge hoping that yesterday's decision doesn't lead to today's disaster. Each precaution that we take based on fear that our past has produced. Within our shattered brotherhood, we had made a sacred pact. There would be no more guns in the house, and all doors would remain open, except for our father's. That door would be forever closed.

It now seems like a humorous slant on our tragic slide from the truth. We both had embraced our agreement, clinging to it like a buoy as the water continued to rise, and yet we were content to tread, unaware that exhaustion was already setting in. We had created a sanctuary of lies, a blanket of artificial perceptions fueled by toxins and buffered by shallow promises.

Still, we chose to linger in the house, ignoring its warnings, pretending that the opened doors and weaponless rooms would be enough. And yet, there were nights when I swear I could hear the floors creak, would catch a glimpse of shadows, there and then gone.

Discussing this with Dave would have been pointless. By then, the hidden section of himself had ballooned into addiction. Often I would stop at his doorway and watch as the sheets covering his comatose body hitched their way up and then slip back down in timing with his breathing. But if he was breathing, then at least I knew he was still alive.

*****

On one occasion, I was awoken by the sound of whispering. I sat up and quietly crept out of my room into a hallway illuminated by dust infected beams of silver moonlight. I made my way down the hall, pausing briefly at Dave's room, sure that what I was hearing was nothing more than my brother's hidden half trying to make a brief appearance. But the only sound from his chamber was the rasping storm of his narcotic slumber.

And yet the unintelligible voice continued, and a sudden chill flooded through my veins as I realized that there were words melded in this whispering; consonants tripping into long, anguished vowels but I couldn't make them out.

A sudden thought struck me like a hammer: Perhaps this was madness! Perhaps I had been mad all along! It was then that a spine-tingling grind of a rusted hinge echoed throughout the hallway. I looked into the weak glow and saw that my father's door had opened. I stood there, my skin constricted, my heart pounding.

Did terror accompany madness? For a moment, I again felt like the child from all those years ago who could do nothing more than helplessly wait as his older brother confirmed what we both already knew. I gazed over at Dave's doorway and considered calling out to him but decided against it. Not because I was afraid, although there could be no denying that. It was because of the sudden anger that had washed over me.

Dave had already crossed this line, had already gone into the unknown to protect me, and it had cost him everything. Could I expect him to do that again? Was I that much of a coward?

Yes, you are, was the immediate response. I closed my eyes, took in a deep, shuddering breath, and made my way down the hallway. My father's doorway stood just a couple of feet away. The posts of his unmade bed cast thin roads of shadow across the dark carpet, winding their way towards me.

Across the room was the very window that my brother had climbed through. Under its sill was the throw rug that had been placed over the burgundy stain. I stood there motionless, my gaze darting from one relic to the next like a patron at a freak show. All of these things I had seen before and yet in the low light, they appeared oddly new. Each one holding the memory that I had for so long been trying to forget.

The low wind of the whisper continued, garbled words lost in an eerie moan. I could feel my legs shaking, and despite the cold that seemed to be emanating from everywhere felt a layer of sweat form across my brow. A sudden motion drew my attention to the dark corner just beyond the bed. A shadow was rising from the floor like a trickling creek. The blurred stream of nonsense began to slow, articulating itself into carefully timed syllables. I found myself drawn to it; my eyes never leaving the image that had appeared.

Come to me, Jacob, it whispered.

An explosion of pain erupted from my shoulder, and I felt myself pulled from the room.

"Get back, Jake!"

Dave slid passed me, seemingly lucid as he reached for the handle of the door, slamming it shut just as the shadow from the corner rushed forward.

"Did you see it?" I said. "When you went into the room, did you see it?"

Dave looked at me, his watery eyes narrowed.

"You saw nothing," he said.

"Someone was in there!" I said.

Ignoring that, Dave asked, "Why did you open the door?"

"I didn't. It was already open. Didn't you see it?"

"Stay out, Jake," he said. "There's nothing in there for us." He then erupted into a sickening cough. I reached out for him, offering what little support I could give. He brushed away my hand and stumbled back towards his room.

Strange that a man at my age would adhere to a command from someone just a couple of years older, but Dave's wisdom had always been unquestionable. It had come from the true knowledge of his sacrifice.

There are ghosts. I genuinely believe that, although they may not be the wayward spirits of those who have died, more like manifestations of our past that refuse to go away. And for me, that is much more terrifying, for one can always leave a place that is haunted. But where does one go when you are the one haunted?

I turned back to the door, expecting it to burst open, but it remained closed. The whispering had stopped leading me to believe that what had happened was nothing more than a sleepwalker's dream. How else could I explain the rising shadow in the corner or the jumbled voice that had called my name?

I turned to make my way to my room when I heard something like sandpaper slowly scraping against the laminated finish of my father's panel. I did not turn back.

Sleep abandoned me for the rest of that night. I lay there staring up at the cracked ceiling fighting the urge to investigate further. *Come to me, Jacob,* the voice had said as if it had been waiting. Had it been the shadow that had spoken? I nestled my eyes within the crook of my arm and again told myself that it had only been a dream.

*****

That morning, I found Dave leaning against the kitchen counter, staring into the coffee pot as it slowly filled. His thinning hair stood like desolate clumps of weeds on a desert floor. Yellow stains ringed the pits of his dirty white t-shirt. He looked up at me as I walked into the room.

"Do you want a cup?" he said.

"Please," I answered. I watched as Dave poured the coffee with a trembling hand. He then shuffled his way over to the table, placing the cup in front of me, then went around to the other side and collapsed in his chair. We sat there for a while, quietly sipping. Dave placed his cup down on the table, slowly spinning it, his brow furrowed.

"I want to talk to you," he said finally.

"I know it was only a dream, Dave," I said.

"Just shut up and listen," he said with a sternness that left me mute. "I have to tell you about *that day*. The day when I went into our father's room. I think it's time."

"Okay," I said.

"I ran into the room and almost fell over his body. He had shot himself by the window." My brother's face was a portrait of misery. Never had he spoken of that day, at least not to me, and I could see the memories assaulting his mind like invading hordes.

"I couldn't help but look down," he said. "I didn't want to, but I had no choice. I knew what he had done, even before I came through the window, I knew."

"I think we both did," I said.

"Yes," he snapped. "I suppose we did; only it was me who had to check."

"I was only seven," I said.

"And I was only ten!" Dave shouted. "Ten years old and standing over the corpse of my father."

"I'm sorry, Dave. I would have gone if I could have."

He looked over at me with disbelieving contempt. I sat back in my chair, crossing both arms over my chest in defiance, but it was a feeble gesture.

"None of that matters," he said. "It's not you that I'm made at. It's not what I want to talk to you about, anyway."

"Then what?" I said.

"Last night, you said that you saw something in the room...a shadow."

44

"Yes," I said. "I also heard a voice, but it went away as soon as you woke me up."

Dave let his gaze wander back down to his coffee cup, his hand again slowly turning it. "That day I went into the room, I heard scraping against the wall. At first, I was far too shocked to notice, but then something moved. I looked over and saw a black shape in the corner. It was like someone had suddenly appeared."

"That's what I saw!" I cried, my hand now clenching my cup.

"I know it is," he said. "And it scares me."

Dave shook his head and continued, "There's more. A couple of nights before he died, I woke up to voices coming from his room. At first, I thought that maybe it was his television, but then I heard his voice, and it sounded like he was talking to someone, so I snuck over to the door and put my ear against it."

I found myself now leaning on the table, my jaw hanging loose and my eyes wide. Dave was opening up in a way that he had never done before, and I was terrified.

"What were they saying?" I said.

"I'm not sure," said Dave. "The other voice was so low that it barely sounded like a voice at all. But Father sounded worried, and I did hear him say *But you already have her,* and then I swear the other thing began to laugh. Jake, it sounded like snakes, and I almost screamed."

"What did you do?"

"I went back to my room," said Dave. "I covered my head with my blanket and put my fingers in my ears. I didn't want to hear any more."

"Maybe it was our father talking to himself," I said. "He was obviously losing it."

"I told myself the same thing," said Dave. "And I would have believed it had I not heard it again."

"Wait," I said. "You've heard it since father died?"

Dave looked up from his cup, his eyes narrowed. "Listen to me, Jake," he said. "There is something in there, and it knows us. I think that it wants us. It took our mother and our father, and now it wants us."

"That's crazy," I said. "Mother drank herself to death."

"Did she?" said Dave. "And do you think that I shoot myself up with heroin because I enjoy the ride? I'm right next door to it, and it knows that. But I can't hear it when I'm high."

"You think mother heard it too? That's why she was always drunk?"

"Maybe," said Dave. "Maybe it already had her. Maybe it already has us."

I knew then that we were in trouble. Not because of some hideous creature lingering in a corner but because we had let our habits take control. We had both become junkies standing on the edge of suicidal delusion. His weapon of choice was the needle, and mine was whatever bottle of pills I could find that day. We were two codependents in free fall, and there was only one thing for us to do.

"Dave," I said. "We have to get out of this house."

"And where would we go, Jake?"

"Anywhere but here," I said, reaching for his paper skinned hand. "This place is killing us. Our addictions are killing us. Maybe a rehab?"

"This house is all we have," said Dave. "It's free and clear. We couldn't afford anything else. And we certainly cannot afford any rehabs."

"Who cares about the house?" I said. "What good is it if we're dead?"

Dave shook his head and stood up. The thought of leaving seemed to fill him with as much dread as whatever he assumed the dark thing in the corner was. I understood his mindset: it was scary being an addict, but trying to quit…the unknown was even scarier. But could anything be worse than this?

I watched my brother exit the room, his stride matching the withered gate of an old man. For a moment, I considered calling out to him, imploring him to at least consider my proposal. If his fantastic story about the house was correct, then why would he want to stay? Could we not sell the house and use those funds to start over? Why was he so reluctant? I decided to wait until later to approach him.

Of course, that would prove to be my worst mistake.

*****

That evening found us deep within our own devices. Dave was once again swimming in hypodermic euphoria while I plummeted down a Valium slope. I lay in bed watching out my window as the fading orange of the setting sun devolved to black. Even in my modified state, I couldn't escape the conversation from earlier that day. We had to get clean, and to do that, we would have to leave this house and all of the nightmares that it contained. I would have to convince Dave. I decided to try again.

I rose from the bed, and made my way to his bedroom. The hallway again held the trespassing silver rays of the moon. I stumbled my way through his doorway, flipping on the light as I entered. It was empty.

A moment of unexplainable dread seized me. I stepped back out into the hallway and felt my heart freeze.

My father's door was open.

Slowly I crept my way towards the threatening void, my head slightly tilted, listening. Dave was standing near the corner where the shadow had been, his hands hanging loose at his side, his dirty t-shirt draped just past his boxers. My brother suddenly began to shake in place, his hands clenching and then releasing.

"Do you promise?" he cried out. "Will it be over?"

I had seen enough.

"Dave, you're sleepwalking," I said gently.

He turned his grief-stricken face toward me and said, "I wish that were true."

I threw my arm around his waist and led him out of our father's room, shutting the door behind us. He came with me quickly enough, his head lowered, his breath hitching like a child recovering from a fit.

"It's okay," I said. "You were just dreaming."

We made it to the threshold of his room when he suddenly stopped.

"You were right," he said. "We need to leave this place."

"We can talk about it in the morning,"

"No," said Dave, tossing my arm off. "I want you to pack and be ready to go."

"Are you serious?"

"Do it, Jake," he said. "Be ready when I get back."

"Where are you going?"

"I need to get supplies," he said.

I knew then that he was serious. Dave was ready to leave, but he wouldn't go cold turkey. I considered trying to talk him out of his 'supply' trip but realized this was something that we would have to deal with one step at a time.

At least we were leaving. We could confront the getting clean part after we had gotten to wherever we were going. And just where were we going? Did Dave have a plan? For me, it mattered little as long as it was far from here.

I barely noticed the front door closing as I pilfered through my closet and drawers hastily cramming clothes into the suitcase I had laid out on my bed.

Once I had everything that I wanted, I placed the case on the floor and stretched out on the mattress. The pills had gone into overdrive, and I felt my eyelids struggling to remain open.

And then something jolted me awake. I could feel my heart thrumming as cold sweat trickled into my half-opened eyes. The room felt chilled, like winter had found its way inside. I looked up and saw Dave standing at my door.

"That was fast," I managed to mumble.

"Are you ready to go?" he said.

I was able to sit up on my second attempt and pointed at the clock. "It's two-thirty in the morning."

"We either go now or not at all," he said, and his tone acted like a sudden shot of adrenaline. I found myself reaching for my suitcase and following him down the hall toward the front door.

"Where are your bags?" I said.

"I already put them in the car. Come on. We have to hurry."

Dave moved as if fifteen years had been washed away, and I found myself struggling to keep up. We neared the end of the hallway and were about to turn into the living room when I suddenly stopped.

"Dave, it's open." Our father's doorway sat like a gaping mouth, its dark chasm seeming to devour what little light the hallway could provide. A sudden sound like rolling wind surrounded us, whispered screams filled with anguish and regret. I felt my stomach clench, and for a moment, I was sure that I would be sick. Dave grasped my arm and pulled me into the living room.

"Go," he said. "Get out of the house."

I made my way to the front door, turning the handle, and noticed that I was alone. Dave was still standing by our father's door and in his hand was a pistol.

"What are you doing?" I said.

"You have to go, Jake," he said, and I could see tears now streaming from his eyes. "It's the only way."

"What are you talking about?" I said, feeling frantic.

"It's a trap, Jake," he said, his voice rising near hysteria. "It claims everyone who witnesses. It killed our father to get to me. You'll be next. Don't you see?"

I stood there, my heart drumming in my head. "I don't understand," was all I could say.

"Don't go into the room no matter what you hear," said Dave, the gun now trembling in his hand. "Just get in the car and leave." Dave then turned and stepped through our father's doorway, pausing just long enough to say, "I love you, Jake."

50

I darted forward as if released from a spell just as the door slammed shut. The whispering moans intensified, and I could hear ghostly sighs of warning hidden within. I grabbed the doorknob, twisting it. The door was locked. It would not allow me inside.

I felt myself again cringing like a child. A sudden blast sent a wave of pain through my skull, decorating my vision with a brief moment of red.

"Dave!" I screamed. But there was no answer, nor would there be. The whispering warnings were now shrieks with hideous cries of *FLEE! RUN! IT IS COMING!*

I let out a shriek of my own and dashed for the front door. The Toyota that Dave and I had shared sat idling in the driveway. I raced to the driver's side door, flinging it open and tossed both bags into the back seat. From behind, the wails of misery continued, but I did not look back. It was only after the sign for the I-35 on-ramp appeared did I dare gaze into my rearview mirror.

*****

I admit now that only the shade of night lingered. But within it, camouflaged in that darkness hid a timeless killer, a destroyer of dreams. My brother knew this, perhaps had always known it, and had sacrificed himself in a selfless attempt to save his younger brother. A span of fifteen hundred miles now separates me from the origin of this story, and yet I still feel the darkness. And even now, so many years later, I sleep with the light on and with one eye open.

About Eric Neher

Eric Neher is an award-winning author who lives in Newcastle, Oklahoma with his wife Tammy (The Traveling Nurse). He is a continuing contributor to *Uniqelahoma Magazine*, as well as having numerous short and flash fiction stories published.

Notable works include "Permian Remorse," "The Bane of Dave," "Fractured Frame," "The Cycle," "A Haunted Cemetery," and "Horrific Separation."

His debut horror novel titled *The Killing Pledge* will be released in June 2021.

Follow him on Twitter: @ENeherfiction
Email: ericneher3@gmail.com

SQUIRREL PLAY
by K. Marvin Bruce

I should've left when I saw how they'd destroyed The Predator. It was gashed and slashed and gnawed to pieces. I was afraid even to touch the heavy plastic casing. Their attack had been vicious. I'd been trying to be humane, but they wouldn't. Now it's too late.

Home ownership had always been a fantasy. Given my career trajectory, it seemed impossible. Gary, the financial advisor, scratched his head. "You can afford a house, but not in New Jersey or New York. Have you considered Pennsylvania?"

Connectivity is essential, but what sold me on the property was the converted barn. Set a hundred feet from the house, the barn had been reconstructed on a freshly poured concrete slab. "Made into a garage, and wired, by the previous owner," Tom the realtor had said. "It has an upper floor that can be used for storage."

Storage. That's what a packrat needs. Having grown up poor, I learned two big lessons: you never know what'll appreciate in value, and if you throw something away you'll quickly learn what had. The movers groaned and complained. Their job is to move people's stuff—why do they always complain? I wouldn't keep it if I didn't need it.

On closing day, we inspect it again, Tom and I. "Did they do the repairs you requested?" He scratches his ear.

"I asked for the animal access to the barn to be sealed. They just used expanding foam. Won't keep the squirrels out for long. I need this space for storage."

Tom looks dyspeptic. "Mr. Weeks," he sighs, "it's been a seller's market all year. The inventory hasn't been this low since the recession. There just aren't that many houses available. If you back out now you'll lose your deposit and you can't recoup the inspector's fees. Do you really want to walk away because some critters can get into the garage? You'll lose money on this if you do."

"Gary says I should buy." I say. I quote him, "If you want to retire, you'll want equity."

In my mind I've already become a remote worker. No more daily commute to Manhattan. No more getting up at 4 a.m.

I sign the damn paperwork. The seller says no more than he absolutely has to.

*****

The squirrels took just a week to chew through the expanding foam. My plans for making the upper story of the garage into my library falls apart.

I value the books. I can't have brainless rodents snacking on them so I keep those in the house now. Instead, the seasonal and seldom-used stuff goes up here.

I watch the grays all summer. They are abundant and, I thought, playful. Not very afraid of people. If a morning's suddenly rolled-up shade frightened them, they'd pause a moment—head up, paw mid-air. Noses twitching, they'd fix me with their black eyes, stare a moment, and get back to squirrel business. I don't feel threatened. Yet.

I find walnut shells on the porch.

Carelessly left or a peace offering?

Winter comes, and they keep to themselves in the garage ceiling.

When spring sends me upstairs in the garage, my jaw drops. The wood-plank cathedral ceiling has been knocked in here and there.

I heard their feet scrambling out as I opened the door. My storage items are covered with debris that's fallen from their messy nests.

Bits of styrofoam food containers slip between the planks. The wires for the ceiling lights are chewed through; the fixture is smashed on the floor. The curtains—I always wonder why there are curtains in a country garage—torn down.

The squirrels have taken over. This is war.

"The squirrel's need to chew is overpowering. Their teeth continually grow and they must gnaw incessantly to prevent over-growing. If they stop chewing, they'll die." So the internet informs me. They're chewing machines. "They will gnaw concrete, and have chewed through cinderblocks in desperation." Not comforting words.

I don't like hurting animals. A memory still haunts me:

Out for a drive one autumn day along a wooded road, a squirrel darts out in front of my Miata. I swerve, but feel the thump as my front tire hits. In the rearview mirror I see it thrashing its tail in agony as it drags itself off the road with a smashed leg. I didn't sleep that night. The squirrel was only doing what animals do. Why hadn't I been going slower? Why couldn't I have reacted faster? I was responsible for some poor animal's suffering. It had crawled off alone to die because of me.

I've been more vigilant ever since.

The next morning I head to the garage. The sudden scrabbling of claws startles me as a squirrel jolts up the planks and into the hole chewed through the foam. It sticks its head out and scolds me. Chattering angrily, it wants me to leave its home.

I hate to admit it, but I'm intimidated. I forget what I came out for. Besides, it's time to start work—my deadly-dull internet job.

Right now, I have a more immediate problem. Squirrels are destroying my property. My options are limited. Capturing them by humane traps will only result in more moving in. Where could I release them far enough away? Philadelphia?

Squirrels are everywhere! I can't reach the roof of my two-story barn-garage to properly repair it. I can't afford to pay a contractor to do it. Rodent repellent may be the answer. I have to buy a hundred-foot hose. There's an Agway a few miles down the road.

I unroll the hose and screw on the repellant bottle. Water pressure reaches where I'm not able. Ghost peppers, the label says, will deter just about anything. I soak the holes they've chewed. If they're trapped inside, I realize, they'll chew another way out. I have to wait to see if it works.

Suddenly I notice that squirrels begin to regard me with some intention. One morning I open the shades. Four squirrels on my back porch look a little startled, but not afraid. They stare at me through the glass, noses twitching.

Something in that stare frightens me. I feel it in the center of my chest. I stare at them as an animal lover. Their gaze says something far different. Then one of them swishes her tail. The others, obviously males, immediately follow her. They are multiplying.

I turn on the coffee maker and wonder. Property ownership's a strange idea. We can drive in yard spikes to frighten away moles. Spray repellent to keep out most mammals. There's nothing we can do about birds, though. Animals were here first, after all.

Winter is coming again. In the fading light after work, I go out to the garage to see if the spray has worked. A squirrel scrambles up the boards, heads to the hole and then scurries around it, up onto the roof. Inside I hear them. More styrofoam containers.

I haven't solved the problem. The hose doesn't reach to the far end of the garage. They've chewed a hole on that side. A dead squirrel on the floor makes the place smell putrid. I don't want to touch it. Trying to cover my face with one arm, I grab a shovel and slot it under the rotting corpse. Toss it outside.

That's when I found The Predator. The ultimate in human superior thinking. It's a device that can run on electricity or batteries. It has high frequency sound that drives squirrels away. It also has a predator setting with recorded wildcat calls. And a strobe light. The instructions say that after about a week most squirrels will leave, not standing the irritation.

"Warning," it says, "under extreme conditions, survival pressure on an animal becomes great enough to overcome any deterrent."

These are squirrels—what can they do? They've got the whole woods to survive in. Pennsylvania's got enough space to keep everyone happy.

The Predator's a sleek machine. Sturdy plastic case. Approved for outdoor use. It can take abuse. I walk to the garage. Up the wooden stairs. I'm afraid to plug things in because they've been chewing wires. But I feel compelled to do this anyway.

I set the volume to max, although I can't hear it. Put on the strobe just to make sure it's working. I'm not hurting anything. Just encouraging them to go elsewhere, right? They're animals. They evolved to live outdoors.

The next morning, The Predator's destroyed. They've attacked it. I look up at the plank ceiling where they've knocked the boards down. I see their heads with their eyes peering down at me. I don't like the feeling. I back away to the stairs, shutting the door behind me.

I want to ask the neighbors if they have this problem too. I've never met them. Their lot's a mile from mine, backing into the same Bucks County woods. Do you just pull up in someone's drive, knock on their door and say "Are you afraid of squirrels?"

Afraid. There it is, out in the open. Squirrels can be tamed, to a degree. They're prey, not predators. Timid. They rely on their speed and amazing climbing ability to escape. They run from people.

I look up from my computer screen. A squirrel sits on my window sill. Sitting up on its haunches, I see the little chest rising and falling.

Its black eye bores into me. It has a paw on the glass, as if testing it. I fling my hands up in a sudden move. It doesn't move until I round the desk and approach the window.

*****

Tonight I hear them on the roof. Rampaging around in the dark. I can't even count how many.

Farm houses, Tom told me, follow no particular plan. Built to meet the needs of the individual or family, they are idiosyncratic—not following a standard plan. Although only two floors, mine has a full attic and reaching the roof is something that requires a thirty-six foot ladder. But ladders cost over $300 on Amazon. Maybe next year.

Noises, the website says, frighten animals away. I'm a quiet guy. I live alone. How much noise can I make?

The former owner had the garage loft set up as a rock studio. I assume so, anyway, from the guitar brackets left on the walls, and the quiet room for recording. That'd keep squirrels away.

The sudden silence when he moved out was their formal invitation. I don't know how far they're carrying the styrofoam food containers, but it's got to be a distance. They've chosen my barn. They own it.

It's my name on the deed, but that only means others of my species recognize my ownership. Logically we might argue people built this structure so people own it, but that's not really true either, is it? We made those rules. We build our houses where other creatures lived first, and we make laws saying we own it. What about animal laws? The laws of nature?

The stuff in the garage is getting ruined. I can't afford to move again. And the squirrels seem too intelligent for me to handle. How'd they figure out The Predator was making the noise? How'd they know to destroy it? Under extreme conditions, survival pressure on an animal becomes great enough to overcome any deterrent. What extreme conditions? They have the entire Bucks County woods.

Work gets in the way of solving such problems. Long hours in front of the screen turn into a week and soon I realize the rodents have had all this time to make their own plans. They don't rely on paychecks to stay in their chosen home. They don't need the internet to stay connected. They don't awake by alarm clock and eat on cue. Theirs is the day. Theirs also is the night. Somebody else owns my time.

Now that winter's approaching once again, it's nearly dark by the end of the work day. I fear going out to the garage after dark, but I grab a flashlight anyway. The summer insects are gone and the night is silent. Country silent.

The path to the garage is well worn. The quiet is unnerving. The hasp on the door is down at the bottom and I have to squat to dial the combination. I need both hands. Light held under my chin. Rustling in the tall grass behind me. I'm not alone.

"Who's there?" I instinctively call out. The flashlight falls. Goes out.

Rustling in the weeds. My ears prick up. I left the back porch light on. I run for the house, small feet behind me. Slam the door. The porch is flooded with gray squirrels that squirm and almost undulate. I can't count them. Their eyes are staring. Knowing. I pull the shade.

Tomorrow's Saturday. I'll drive to the neighbors' place, although I don't even know their name. Ask them what they do about squirrels.

Tonight I hear them on the roof again. Tiny claws above as I try to sleep. "If they find exposed wood," The Predator website said, "squirrels can get into your house." When had the roof last been replaced?

Awake in my bed, I'm thinking about ownership. Could other animals develop a sense of it? We call some animals territorial. Isn't that a form of ownership? We took the land from large predators by driving them near extinction. Had smaller creatures filled the void? Do squirrels think they owned my garage? That I, who paid for it, am the interloper?

The irrationality of sleeplessness haunts me. I need to think clearly. The night is very long. Is that chewing I hear above my head?

First light. The squirrels appear to have vanished. I see none at all. A quick breakfast. *I'll drive to the neighbors' place*, I tell myself. *Ask if they've seen what I have.*

It's chilly enough for a jacket. I examine the space outside the door. No sign of squirrels. Some walnut husks on the porch. Outside I glance around cautiously. Nothing.

The garage is just a hundred feet away. Of course, it's their property. I solve the combination. Slide open the door. Lift the aluminum car port door. No squirrels. Get in. Try the ignition. Nothing happens.

Try again. Pop the hood. I dread to look.

The wires have been chewed through. Anything plastic has been gashed to pieces.

I feel the hairs at the back of my neck stand up. I slowly turn around to look. A squirrel appears at the garage door. Sits up. Stares.

I run to the house. Squirrels are inside!

The spare bedroom, with my computer, is clear. I slam the door, but they can chew through mere wood.

Open a chat app. I need help! Just as long as I can let someone know before they find the mains. No mains, no electr

About K. Marvin Bruce

K. Marvin Bruce is a self-taught writer who makes a living as a nonfiction editor in New York City. He has published twenty-eight fiction stories in a variety of venues. His work has been nominated for a Pushcart Prize, the Write Well Award (Silver Pen Writers Association), and the Best of the Web Award, and has won prizes from *Calliope, Danse Macabre*, and *Typehouse Literary Magazine.*

A ROOM OF HIS OWN
by Kristen Houghton

It was remarkable, thought Lucien as he surveyed his home from the front yard, that he was able to buy this stately old house in this quiet, beautiful neighborhood. The fact that it was perfect for everything he needed and wanted in a house never ceased to amaze him. That basement room for example.

"It's a perfect find, Lucien," said his oldest friend Marco when Lucien had shown him the room. "I wish I had a place like this. You're lucky to live here. It will make it easier when you have to, uh, I mean when you're, you know—away—for those monthly business trips."

And Lucien did indeed consider himself lucky for finding and purchasing this house, even considering the indisputable fact that he was cursed.

He had taken the morning off from work so that he could be home for that delivery from Home Depot. He'd been meticulous about what materials he had needed. A heavy steel door, double dead-bolt locks, thick steel rings and chains, and sound-proofing materials for that room he'd refurbished in the basement. His quiet room so to speak. A deep sigh escaped him when he thought about how he would use the room but still, it had to be done. Had.To.Be.Done.

As he screwed the heavy metal rings into the cement wall, Lucien knew that he had to be quick and secretive. He couldn't take the risk that his wife of just one year, a beautiful woman named Skye, would find out what was going on. She was gone for the next two weeks visiting and nursing her brother who had broken his leg in a soccer match. All to the good. Lucien didn't want her to know what he was doing, not yet. She might be repulsed, might get hysterical about the cruelty of it all, might spoil all his carefully laid plans. The place, *that room*, had to be kept a secret. Soundproof. No one would hear any sounds coming from there, no one would know what he was doing.

He'd found out about that hidden room when they'd toured the home during an open house. While Skye had been checking out a pottery shed in the backyard, he'd wandered into the basement. Plain, unfinished, and empty, it was nothing to see really. But then, as he'd walked around the room touching the foundation near the walls, looking for any sign of the mold usually found in basements, he'd bumped into a wall that didn't feel solid. It looked like the other three walls but it wasn't like them at all. Intrigued Lucien had inspected it and found that the wall slid into a hidden pocket on one side. Pushing it open he was amazed to see that, behind the wall, was a small room, an obviously long unused, hidden room filled with dusty jars for canning. After carefully inspecting the room, he met his wife in the backyard.

"Oh Lucien, the potting shed is a real gem for me. There's even an attached greenhouse. I can really attend to my plants there. It's absolutely perfect and, best of all, it has a lock and key. I won't have to worry about any thefts."

Lucien smiled indulgently. Skye and her plants! Most of them looked as if they should be in a jungle setting. She was passionate about her plants and she had some rare, expensive ones. Lucien assumed that it was a good thing that the shed and greenhouse had a lock and key. Believe it or not, there were some people who would actually steal the rare plants and sell them to the highest bidders. Who knew that plants could be so lucrative? Suddenly he was glad that Skye had this interest in growing huge displays of tropical vegetation. It was a time-consuming hobby that would keep her distracted and out of his way.

"It's so beautifully secluded too, Lucien. I like that. We'll have all the privacy we've always said we wanted. No one for miles around. I can attend to my planting business in peace."

Privacy, thought Lucien. *All the privacy I need.*

After they bought the house and moved in, he kept the knowledge of the room's existence from Skye. Luckily his wife hated basements—

she wouldn't come into the basement of her own accord. She called them "musty, smelly, spider-web-filled horrors". She'd hated doing laundry in the basement of their old house and was thrilled that she now had a laundry room equipped with a new washer and dryer on the first floor next to the kitchen. Plus, she was busy cleaning and refurbishing the potting shed and greenhouse. That took a great deal of her time.

That dirty little room was his and he set about cleaning it up whenever Skye was not at home. He wanted the quiet room to be as comfortable as it was secure. To that end he had painted the walls in soft pastel colors, colors that were soothing and peaceful, and installed a Bose system that would, among other things, play the sounds of nature—gentle summer rain, the chirping of crickets, and soft noises of a forest at night. "These peaceful sounds will help soothe the savage soul," said the cheery advertisement he had seen at the store.

Soothe me! Oh God, if only something *could* soothe my fevered, tortured soul, the soul that compels me to act out in the vilest ways imaginable.

After the delivery from Home Depot, Lucien got to work and worked feverishly through the night. When he was finished he went outside for some air. Glancing at the cloud-covered night sky, he sighed deeply. Soon. What had to be done, had to be done. He was compelled to do it.

Cruel or not. Torturous or not. Screams and all.

*****

Everything was secured. The sliding wall was firmly in place. It looked like the other walls in that empty basement. There was no sign of the heavy door hiding behind it. Lucien had tested the soundproofing by playing a *Creedance Clearwater Revival* song on the Bose at full blast, shutting the steel door, and going upstairs. He walked quietly around the house stopping in each room to listen; just listen for any sound from the basement.He heard absolutely nothing.

64

No sounds could be heard coming from that room. His quiet room. No sounds at all. Lucien breathed a sigh of relief. No one would hear the cries.

He walked in the backyard late that night, glancing, always glancing, up at the night sky. Night sky. His wife had told him that she'd been named for the night sky that loomed majestically over Big Sur. "The night I was born, the moon was full and there were so many brilliant stars out. My father told me that the stars spoke to him and he just knew that I had to be named for the sky. His divine night sky, he said."

The night sky, Lucien's nemesis. How ironic that his wife was named after the very thing that contained something having the power to torment him.

His own Skye, his beautiful unsuspecting wife, so trusting, so innocent—she was a gift from the gods. A special, tantalizing gift so to speak because in some strange way she was an enigma to him. There was a subtle age-old mystery about her. At the beginning of their relationship, Lucien had spent many nights trying to figure out what made her mysterious. Finally, he had put her mystery down to a shyness and reserve that was rather old-fashioned, qualities that made her all the more enchanting.

Lucien had met her at a museum where they had both attended a show on Western Asian art. The art was exquisite if not a bit frightening in its detailed sketches of ancient Mesopotamian demon gods destroying humanity. Skye had been fascinated by it all. Lucien had been fascinated as well but also sad and just a bit repulsed by the horrible nature of those demon gods. He knew all too well the horror of his own nature.

Ah, my beautiful wife. Lucien dreaded when he had to tell her the truth about—he sighed—the truth about that *quiet* room and—everything he was going to do there. Everything his nature compelled him to do.

*****

His cell phone buzzed and he saw it was a call from Skye. Watching the clouds drift slowly past the moon, Lucien answered, making his voice sound as if he didn't have a care in the world. "Hello my love; how are you doing? How's William?"

"Lucien, I love hearing your voice. I miss you. I'm okay—finally got William's apartment straightened out. He takes bachelor life to a whole new level of messiness! Anyway, he's fine and lying on the couch watching some horror movie. I'm hoping to return next week. William's fiancée should be back from her business trip by Tuesday. I have to be here when she arrives."

"Of course you need to be there. I understand. I miss you too, Skye."

"And speaking of business trips, I know you have one coming up soon, so I want to make sure I'm home before you leave. I want to make that special dinner you love so much. You always seem to be ravenous the night before going on a trip."

Ravenous, yes, ravenous. Lucien held his breath for a second. "Yes, of course, but listen Skye, I...um, I wanted to talk to you about my uh, well, my future trips."

He'd often wondered how Skye passed the time when he was away. She did have her plants and all. Still, he imagined she was lonely and missed him as much as he missed her. When he'd ask her how she spent her time she always smiled mysteriously and told him not to worry about her. She had things to do; things that needed her attention.

There was a soft laugh. "Why Lucien! Are you suggesting that I accompany you on those trips that you say are oh, so boring?"

"Well, not exactly but, listen we'll, we'll definitely need to talk about—about everything when you come home next week. It's very important to me that we talk."

"Everything?" Her voice sounded strange—too alert as if she already knew his secret. Lucien shook his head. *No, no, of course she doesn't know anything. I've been careful.*

"Should I be concerned, Lucien? Is there a problem? Have I done something to make you angry with me?"

Her hastened to reassure her. "Oh no, my love, of course not. I simply meant that we should talk about everything that's important to you, to us—everything that's needed for us to have a good life together." Lucien found that he was sweating profusely.

There was a pause and then a deep sigh of relief before she answered him. "Lucien, you are so sweet. We *are* going to have a wonderful life. Okay, when I return we'll sit, snuggle, and talk." She laughed again and began to talk about what it was like staying at her brother's condo. "Guess what I did yesterday?"

Lucien sighed and listened to her talk. He adored the sound of her voice, a combination of breathless excitement and girlish innocence. He had truly believed that with her he could have a semblance of a normal life, a peaceful existence—but he was what he was. He could not deny his true self.

They talked for a few more minutes about ordinary things and then Skye had to hang up to give her brother his meds. "Bye, Lucien. Talk soon. I love you."

Loves me, thought Lucien returning the sentiment as he clicked off. *How much would you love me if you knew what a monster I am? Oh Skye!*

Thinking of his wife, Lucien went to the quiet room to check the steel rings in the wall to make sure that they were strong enough to hold the heavy chains he would attach to them.

*****

Skye had been home for two days when Lucien spoke to her about his 'business trips' and what he now wanted, needed to do. How he had decided that he had to do what he did at home, had to take care of his needs, attend to his business, so to speak, here where it was safer.Where no one would know what was happening, where there was no chance of anyone discovering the truth about what he was compelled to do. Skye sat and listened quietly, wide-eyed at first, and then surprisingly calm as Lucien described what he needed.

"Show me, Lucien," was all she had said when he finished talking. "Show me what you want from me."

Gently, silently he led her to the quiet room and stood back as she examined it. His sweet, innocent Skye surprised him. She showed more compassion and more understanding than Lucien had any right to expect. With interest and curiosity but no revulsion, she inspected the chains hooked by heavy metal rings embedded in the cement walls of the quiet room. Turning to Lucien she said, "They're strong. They will hold no matter how hard one struggles."

She walked around the room as he explained to her that it was thoroughly sound-proof. What went on here would not be heard by anyone else. He told her what to expect. The pain, the agony, what his needs and wants were. How he had to do what his mind compelled him to do and how she had to be a part of it.

She wasn't disgusted by what he told her as he had feared she would be, and—here Lucien had to breathe a sigh of relief—nor was she afraid of him as she had every right to be. She accepted the situation as it was. As. It. Was. No one…no one had ever done that.

She was truly his mysterious gift from the gods.

That first night they were to use the quiet room, Skye walked hand-in-hand down to the basement with Lucien. It was empty of any furniture. The only items in the room were a large container of water near the wall where the shackles were to be used and a pile of blankets.

She fitted her slim wrist into the shackle as Lucien watched, then she cried softly for a few agonizing minutes. *How horrible to be shackled*, she thought, *how awful to have to fight against one's own natural instincts.*

Finally, she looked at her husband and whispered, "I'm ready now."

"My dearest love," said Lucien as he approached the chains. "You have no idea what your willingness to do this means to me."

Wrists were shackled to the thick chains, each one kissed gently before the locking mechanism was clicked.

"It's time," whispered Lucien. "Are you sure you're ready?"

"Yes. Now I know what you are." She kissed him and held him for a long time. "We can begin."

*****

Standing in the doorway, Skye watched as Lucien began his change into a fierce, enormous wild-eyed wolf. He struggled mightily against the heavy chains to no avail. His breath came in gasps and his eyes—oh, his lupine eyes still had a look of humanity in them as he looked pleadingly at her. Skye's own eyes watched calmly at his frenzied desire to break free.

Break free. Freedom. One's own nature. She knew, oh she knew!

She turned on the Bose and played the song Lucien had requested. Giving him one more loving look she said, "I'll be back for you in three days, Lucien. I will be back and then we'll talk again about the new path of our life together."

A howl escaped from Lucien and then another and another. She was grateful that he had the quiet room and no longer had to hide in a dirty old root cellar in the woods on his monthly 'business trips.' Here, in their own home, he was finally safe.

69

But still—the horror of having to hide one's own natural self. That was always the hardest thing to do in life. Hide one's true self from the world. She sighed. Lucien's fevered werewolf's brain would cause him to struggle and howl in agony in his quiet room. His curse. Her gentle Lucien a raving, tormented creature during the full moon, hiding what he really was.

Ah, Lucien. I have always looked forward to your business trips, always treasured those few days of the month when I was alone to do what I had to do, what I needed to do. Skye shut the door behind her and bolted it closed.

It was time now for her. She had to attend to her own—business.

*****

Standing in the back yard, Skye watched the moon rise to its majestic fullness. The moon: the mysterious full moon. *Funny how it affects all creatures*, she thought. She moved to the shadows by a tree and began her monthly chant to the night sky.

"Hear me, night stars, hear me as I stand now under your canopy of light and speak my truth. All humankind must fear me for I am Lamashtu, the ravenous hunter, the most terrible of all female demons, the daughter of the thunderous sky god Anu and Ki, the fiery lightning goddess of destruction.

"I, who hunt humans to drink their blood and eat their flesh, praise the night sky in all its glory. Hear my call and witness what I do this night. I am Lamashtu, the sky demon to be feared by all. Under the full moon of night, I give free rein to my own nature."

Giving a fierce cry, Skye began her own change. A thick and glorious mane began to surround her head as her teeth grew long, pointed, and savage. Her skull moved agonizingly as her bones changed shape and her face morphed into a lion's head. A loud roar escaped her lips as she gave one last look to the stars. A full moon, a bad moon. She growled with delight as the words to the song Lucien had requested she play for him sang in her mind.

70

I see the bad moon arising.
I see trouble on the way.
Well, don't go around tonight,
'Cause it's bound to take your life,
There's a bad moon on the rise.*

"A bad moon indeed, Lucien. A bad moon for you but not for me. For me the full moon is a time to be my true self. To satisfy my strong needs."

Purring deeply, the lion-headed woman walked slowly to the potting shed where her brother's fiancée awaited her surrounded by large plants native to old Mesopotamia and the old gods. Awaiting her, bound and ready, to have her blood drunk and her flesh eaten. Lamashtu salivated in expectation.

Tonight her hunger was great and she, Lucien's sweet, beloved Skye, was her true self: Lamashtu the ravenous one.

*Written by John Fogerty

About Kristen Houghton

Kristen Houghton is the author of nine novels, two non-fiction books, a collection of short stories, a book of essays, and a children's novella. The first four books in her best-selling series, *A Cate Harlow Private Investigation*, are now available in a box-set. The series has been voted one of the top five mystery/thriller series by International Mystery Writers. She is also the author of the Horror Book Club award-winning Quick-Read, *Welcome to Hell*.

Her latest book, *Lilith Angel*, was released in April, 2019. A sequel is slated for release later this year. "Her parents are vampires, her boyfriend's a werewolf, she has untried witchy powers of her own—but teenager Lilith is just trying to live a "normal" life and pass advanced calculus! Life can be difficult for the otherworldly."

71

Kristen Houghton has covered politics, news, and lifestyle issues as a contributor to the *Huffington Post*. Her writing portfolio includes *Criminal Element Magazine*, a division of Macmillan Publishing, *Hartford Woman, Today*, is head writer and senior fiction editor for *Mused Literary Magazine*, performs interviews and reviews for HBO documentaries, OWN, The Oprah Winfrey Network, and The Style Channel.

THE VOICE OF SOURIS
by Harrison Kim

A tiny voice squeaked behind my ear. "Your lost keys are behind the woodpile."

I stared up at the cracked cabin ceiling as the room swirled.

"Behind the woodpile," the voice chittered.

I reached for my rum bottle.

"Hey, take a shot for me," said the voice.

"Who are you?" I could barely speak. I quaffed down a big gulp of the alcohol.

"I'm one of the mice," said the voice. "The cousin of the one you freed, O merciful Jackson."

"A mouse," I slurred. "How do you know my name?"

"We read your mail, my friend," said the tiny voice. "Before we eat it."

Then I noticed the little head poking out from behind my coffee stained pillow. As soon as I looked, it disappeared. I sat up. My head pounded. I held my cranium in both hands.

*****

A couple of dozen little rodents lived in the walls of my current home, a deteriorating orchard picker's cabin in the Okanagan Hills. They scrabbled under the floorboards, in the walls, and they skittered over my butter dish and ate my porridge oats.

I put out live traps, and yesterday, after I'd pulled back a couple of rum, a sallow grey animal lay quivering in one trap. I had a glow on

73

and couldn't bring myself to throw the tiny creature outside in the freezing winter. So I set it free. Then I lost my keys as I staggered around arranging my equipment for tomorrow's tree pruning.

I answered the tiny vice. "The keys are behind the woodpile, eh?"

I pushed myself out of bed and crawled across the freezing room to light the stove. Sure enough, my keys lay behind several blocks of wood.

"Wow, thanks!" I said out loud.

I recalled tiny feet moving along the back of my neck during the night. That was real. But mice don't talk. I thought about that as I worked all day, pruned bare branched apple trees under January skies.

"Could be just the rum," I mused. "Between dream and reality. Maybe I subconsciously knew where my keys were."

I walked wearily back to the cabin after my day's labor, and set up my painting easel. I hadn't taken it out for months. I felt tired, but also inspired. I'd draw that little creature I'd imagined.

I opened a bottle of wine, and looked at the empty canvas. Then I started to sketch a mouse head. I drank a lot, and drew a little. I heard a movement over by the kitchen area, walked over and saw another mouse in the live trap. This one was a mottled grey color.

"Do you talk?" I asked.

The mouse cowered in the box.

"I could use some genuine friends," I said, lifting up the trap. "Ones that won't betray me."

The mouse skittered out, and darted across the floor.

"This time," I asked, "Could you ask your English speaking doppelganger to find my odd socks?"

I laughed and took another swig of rum. I'd have to go to town tomorrow and buy some more. I didn't like being around people, but sometimes it became unavoidable. I finished some more drawing and went to bed.

*****

That night, I awakened to feel familiar tiny feet skitter across my sleeping bag. I stayed still, half asleep. The feet stopped right on top of my head. I opened my eyes. Like the previous night, the room-rum swirled again.

"Thanks for setting another of our sisters free," announced the squeaky voice. "We appreciate your mercy."

"You're welcome," I mumbled, then giggled. "What's your name, is it Mickey?"

"My name is Souris," said the voice. He sounded louder than before, and clearer. "You asked about odd socks. But we can help more than that. We know there's some money in a package under the floorboards. My compatriots have been reading your correspondence and we know you owe people."

"Yeah," I mumbled some more. "I have bad debts."

The mouse pawed my cheek. "It's under the third plank from the door."

I felt something pitterpat over my ear. Then Souris was gone.

I opened my eyes wide. "That's crazy!" I said out loud as the room swirled again. I got up and took a few aspirin and made myself ready once again to go pruning for the day.

"Is this all there is to life?" I asked myself. "I really have no purpose."

I took a good look at my mouse sketch from yesterday. I'd concentrated mainly on the pupils of his eyes.

"That's funny," I said, looking at my face in the mirror. "I haven't even seen Souris's eyes."

I forced myself out into the snow and pruned six rows of trees, thinking all the time about the tiny voice. At noon I returned, took my crowbar and hammer and kneeled down by the third plank from the door. It didn't take long to pry the board loose.

At first, I didn't perceive anything different underneath. I lay down with the floor at eye level; saw mouse droppings in the hole along with hard, brown dirt. Then I noticed something square wedged further back. I reached for it.

It was some kind of package wrapped in faded cloth material, a few holes in it here and there. I reached and grabbed it, unzipped the top. A sheaf of twenty dollar bills lay inside. I pulled out at least a few hundred dollars, limp and dusty.

I got up, feeling light headed, and laid the money on the table and did some more work on the mouse painting, examining the bills from time to time to see if they were counterfeit. All the time I drew, the voice of Souris squeaked through my head. I reached for some peanuts in the cupboard, and noticed far more mouse droppings than usual. They'd eaten a hole in my porridge bag.

I guess the little creatures are hungry, I thought.

That night I took a chunk of cheese out of the fridge and set it carefully on the table with a note: "Thanks, Souris. Eat all you like."

*****

Before bed, I drained the remainder of my rum. I rubbed the money between my fingers and grinned. "Inspiration," I said out loud.

I hadn't been able to work at my art hobby for years, so much on my mind with my divorce, not being able to see my kids, and all the alimony bills. I'd borrowed a lot of money from Murphy Reid, a full-patch biker and loan shark, to pay my child support, and to obtain my alcohol and marijuana. My rusty van broke down and I borrowed a few thousand more off him for another used vehicle. Reid couldn't reach me by phone. I didn't have one. I liked it that way.

I sketched out the mouse's face, paying special attention to the whiskers. Before going to bed, I wrote some more on my note. "Hey, Souris, maybe we could talk tonight?"

It felt funny, but somewhat comforting to think of his friendly voice. People could not be trusted. This mouse, on the other hand, might be a true friend. He looked out for me, because I looked out for him. I'd drive into town and test out the money in the morning.

I didn't hear anything that night. "Perhaps I wasn't drunk enough," I thought as I woke up. I'd only imbibed a couple of rum swallows. I felt let down, but I pocketed the mouse money and wheeled my van down the road to buy more supplies and liquor. I passed Ron Patel, my dreadlocked orchard owner boss, as he picked up his mail.

"Hey, Jackson, some rough looking guy was asking for you," he said.

"Did you tell him I was at work?"

"You know I wouldn't do that." Ron rubbed his long black beard, which was tied with little knots.

"Thanks," I said.

I hadn't made any payments to Murphy Reid for awhile.

"I have some mouse traps for you if the little critters are getting too bothersome," Ron offered. "Stan, the worker last winter, told me they became quite aggressive. He told me they bit him at night."

"Hasn't happened to me," I said. "The little animals are actually good company."

"Company? Well, be careful," said Ron. "Stan came down with some kind of Hanta virus."

"What the hell is that?"

"He kinda turned into a giant mouse. Last time I saw him at the beach, he had grey hair all over his back. When he saw me he ran for his hole." Then Ron laughed, he guffawed and slapped his knee. "Gotcha," he said.

*****

I drove into town, musing about the mice. I treated them well, so being bitten wouldn't be a problem. I pushed some of the found money through Murphy Reid's trailer letterbox.

"I'll pay the rest soon," I wrote on the envelope. "Please be patient."

Then I bought several bottles of rum and packages of porridge oats, eggs, powdered milk, and slabs of bacon. I looked at the cheese section of the deli. "I'll get some of this," I said, "and some of that." I handed my dusty bills as payment. The store clerk didn't look twice.

Back at the dilapidated cabin, I quickly made a good fire in the stove. I cooked up some bacon and eggs, and devoured a big meal washed down with plenty of rum. I left my unspent money on the table to count later. I worked at my art, filled in the mouse's eyes with charcoal, then dropped into bed, awaiting the voice of Souris.

"We are happy you are feeding us," came the sound, right in my ear and not a whisper now, a soft spoken voice, like a mellow radio announcer. "We very much enjoy your art process."

"Oh, yeah," I replied, my pounding head and nausea somewhat relieved by Souris' vocal tone.

"We've told many of our friends about your hospitality and they are moving here," the mouse continued. "This is much appreciated."

"Well," I said. "That's sorta good to hear."

I'd noticed more droppings everywhere, even in my porridge oats. "Could you tell your friends to be more careful in their bathroom habits?"

"I could tell them," said Souris. "But mice will be mice." I could feel his little snout in my earhole. He sounded a bit peevish. "I hope you spent that money wisely."

"Uh huh," I said. I felt comforted, with his furry whiskers there. "Can you give me any advice? I need some life advice."

"You've got to keep drinking," Souris said. His voice sounded louder now. "Keep with the rum, chum. That is the way to become a true mouse communicator."

He pulled his snout back. I heard him chitter once or twice. Then he skittered over me and disappeared. I stumbled from my sleeping bag and heaved towards the bathroom.

"Yeah," I said to myself. "Keep drinking."

I went back to bed. Winter light woke me up, and a pounding on the old cabin door.

"Jackson, open up!"

Murphy Reid's thin, fidgety face showed through the icy windowpane. He was grimacing and holding up my delivered envelope.

"Okay," I said. The pounding on the door matched the hammer sound in my head. I unlatched the tiny hook.

"Hey, Jackson!" Reid's skinny frame slipped through the doorway. "Thanks for the money!"

"You're welcome," I said.

"But you're still two payments behind. And you know there's a vig."

He handed me a steaming hot cup of coffee. "That's the carrot," Reid grinned. "Here's the stick."

A large man with puffy hair and a handlebar moustache strutted in. With his dominance walk, he resembled a big tom cat.

"This is Vern," said Reid.

Vern swung his arms over and grabbed the money I'd left on the table last night. "Partial recompense," Vern said.

"Hey," I told him. "I was going to buy more cheese with that."

I don't know how that came out. I couldn't stop myself.

"Are you a freaking rodent?" said Vern. He poked me in the belly, very hard, then smiled just like his boss, very wide and white-toothed.

I gagged and sat back in my chair, the breath knocked out of me .

"You're lucky" said Reid. "Now you only owe me two thousand bucks." He smiled sardonically. "There's a two hundred dollar vig. For now. Interest is compounded daily."

He peered at my mouse sketch on the easel. "Hey man, I hate mice, but you're talented. I'm an artist myself." Then he chuckled. "Remember what happened to Van Gogh's ear? You better bring in the cheese, man."

Vern chuckled back and the two shakedown guys slipped out the door as fast and slippery as they'd come in.

I took several aspirin after they left, then forced myself out to do more pruning. Ron paid me by the row, and I had to earn more money. I worked efficiently, but couldn't get the talking mouse out of my head. I could forego my child support payments, and save a bit of cash to pay Reid, or I could ask Souris for advice. One thing I didn't want was more pokes in the stomach, or a severed organ.

I came back into the cabin to a strong rodent odor. Mouse droppings lay all over the kitchen, and even on my bed. A few mice scampered away from the kitchen area, and I felt tiny eyes watching from the cracks in the walls. I opened my porridge cupboard to see mouse excrement dotted within the burst porridge bag. They'd also got into the bread.

I brushed off a bun and shoved it in the toaster, then jumped to the fridge. At least they hadn't got in there. I cooked up a bacon and egg sandwich, and drank my rum, while studying my artwork. I needed to shade a little more aggression in Souris' eyes.

I took out a few of my paints. I pictured a clear image of Souris in my head. As I drank, I heard chittering from under the floorboards. It seemed that the mice were cheering me on as I brushed and shaped the painting. I painted til my hands felt too ill coordinated. I fell into bed without brushing off the mouse droppings.

"You forgot to put the cheese out," said the loud voice in my ear.

"I'm sorry, Souris," I mumbled. It was good to feel his muzzle grazing my sideburns, but he sounded demanding. "I'll do it tonight," I said.

"Do it before you go to work," Souris commanded.

"Listen," I told him. "I need some more money. Are there any more packages under the floorboards?"

I felt Souris moving around. "You've been remiss in your tributes this evening, but we can arrange that," he said. "How much do you need?"

"At least two thousand dollars."

"That's going to be a lot of cheese," Souris said. "I don't want any more complaints about the droppings."

"Okay," I agreed. Then I asked. "Where are all your friends coming from? There certainly are a lot."

Souris sat on my sideburns and blew into my ear. His breath smelled like plum ice wine. "We come from all the fields and orchards," Souris said. "From far beyond this cabin. You might call us the winter *diaspora*."

"Thanks, Souris," I said, feeling a bit apprehensive but not wanting to anger him. "I'll put the cheese out as soon as possible."

*****

That day, all I could keep in my mind were mice, and the scent of that ice wine. I didn't go pruning; I stayed and worked at my painting. The whiskers and the nose were coming along fine.

There's a lot of detail in a mouse's sensitive nose.

About mid-morning, I saw a couple of rodents watching me from the kitchen counter.

"Are either of you Souris?" I asked.

82

They kept staring. I kept painting. When I glanced towards the counter again, the mice were gone, and only a couple of droppings remained.

I turned towards my bed. What were those black lumps on my pillow? Yes, more mice were watching me work. They skittered away as I held out a piece of banana. I went to the fridge and cut off some cheese and a bit of bacon, put it discreetly under the bed, so they could dine in peace.

I swallowed some rum as I worked, but not too much. My ex-wife told me I had an alcohol problem.

"I'm only going to drink half a bottle today," I told myself. "That's not a problem."

The room swirled a bit by mid afternoon. I lay down for a nap, happy with my work. I dreamed of holes in the walls, crumbs in a dish, and a comely lady mouse squeaking to me.

I awakened to hear Souris. "There is a package under the fourth plank to the right of the bathroom," he said, his voice sounding quite urgent. "We worked very hard to obtain this."

I felt many feet running over my sleeping bag.

"We've come from far across the fields and woods, and we now expect your food and hospitality."

It sounded like dozens of mice speaking at once. Souris must have bought his whole army.

I felt a nibbling at my ear, first rather pleasant, then irritating. "Please get up and feed us now."

I rolled over. "Watch out!" yelled some voices.

I sat up to see tails disappearing off the bed and dark forms running across the floor. It was night already, the moon shining in through the winter ice on the windows.

I got up, took my crowbar and hammer, crawled over to the fourth plank to the right of the bathroom and with some effort, heaved it up. The moonlight spilled across the floor. I could see everything. My head pounded as I opened the faded package, and yes: there were crumpled, crinkly hundred dollar bills in there.

I counted twenty-one. "They gave me an extra!" I said. "Thank you, Souris."

I stood up and heard a rustling as feet pattering away to the corners. My mouse portrait lay bathed in the silvery winter light. It looked so real, so alive. I felt very proud at my painting prowess, and at the dedication it took.

I walked to the cupboard to celebrate with a drink. I opened the porridge cabinet drawer.

A not unpleasant old cheese odor wafted out. I saw nests and heard the squeaks of little baby mice.

"Wow, those creatures work fast," was my first reaction. Then I closed the door. "They need privacy."

I put a whole block of cheddar on the counter, then walked by the bathroom, glanced at myself in the mirror, surprised to see flecks of grey in my hair and a white whiskered moustache.

My eyes, though, were the biggest shock. They were no longer brown, but black, and huge, like the eyes of the mouse in the portrait. I'm not sure how much time went by as I stared at myself, but again there was a pounding at the door.

I looked out to see Murphy Reid, with Vern right behind him.

"I'm coming, guys," I said, tucking the money into my back pocket. "I've got your cash."

"Jeez, this place stinks," Reid said as I opened the door.

"Smells like mouse piss," Vern agreed, padding around looking at everything. "You're missing some floorboards."

"Here's the money," I said, putting it down on the table. "It's all there."

Reid counted it. "You're looking a little rough," he said. "Bad debts keeping you awake? You still owe another hundred for the vig. Two hundred, actually, since interest is compounded daily."

I noticed a couple of mice watching us from the bed.

I looked away quickly, but Vern turned and grabbed my crowbar.

"Gotcha, you little bastards!" he yelled, and smashed the crowbar down on the bed.

I saw his triumphant face. "You shouldn't have done that," I said in a high-pitched voice.

"You sound like a girl," Vern chuckled. "I can't stand mice."

The outside door slammed shut. I heard a skittering and a chittering.

"What the hell?" Reid shouted.

We watched as mice came running out of the walls and the floor, dozens, no, scores of them, the complete *diaspora*. They ran up Vern's pant legs; they jumped off the table and landed on his face. They crash-landed from the ceiling, onto his head.

He screamed, knocked my chair over, and he bounced against the refrigerator. I saw a particularly large mouse tearing at his eyes. He pushed open the door and staggered out, fell over in the snow. The

85

mice swarmed all over his body, biting and scratching, then scattered back towards the cabin.

Reid looked at my face. "Shit," he said. "You're the mouse master." He yelled at his enforcer. "Are you okay, Vern?"

"I'm not going back in there!" Vern yelled. He sounded like a stuck pig. Flecks of blood dripped off his face. "Pestilence! That place is crawling with it! I'm gonna have to get a shot, man!" He zig- zagged down the driveway, blood streaming from his face and onto the snow. I heard him jump in his truck and slam the door.

Reid shook his head. "I saw a thing like that before," he said. "But it was with bears. Not pretty at all."

He took a bottle from his pocket and shook out several pills of odd shapes and sizes. "I'm gonna have to take Vern to the hospital. I'll send you the bill."

He tipped back his head and swallowed the pills dry. "We're square on the cash for now." He held out his hand. I shook it. He took another look at my mouse portrait.

"Hey," he said. "If you finish that, I'll erase the two hundred bucks. That creature looks alive. Like I said, you've got talent." He sniffed the air. "You need to fumigate this place, though," he yelled as he threw the door shut behind him.

I dashed over to the bed and used a fresh hand wipe to pick up the remains of the two little mice.
I rolled them up in tissues and buried them in the dirt beneath the floorboards. As I did so, I sensed dozens of small rodents around me, watching from the cupboards and the shelves, some on the dresser and the old TV that never worked.

I said a few words. "They were small, but they gave their lives as warriors."

I covered up the bodies in the turned over ground, and replaced the floor plank. Then I went to the fridge and took out all the cheese, cut it up and placed it all round the cabin.

"We shall have a wake," I announced. "All who wish to participate may come to eat now."

I picked up my rum bottle, gazed at the writing. "Captain Morgan's," it read.

"A swig for our friends," I declared, and raised the bottle to my lips.

I drank and painted and drank and painted some more. Then I fell on the bed and slept.

*****

In the middle of the night, I awakened with the room swaying about me once again. I held my head and sat up. All stayed quiet.

"Where's Souris?" I moaned out loud. Silence remained for a moment, and then I heard rustling. Suddenly there was a clear chorus of voices squeaking from out of the darkness. Dozens and dozens of tiny voices, raised in unison.

"Souris is dead, killed by the Vern creature. But you will take his place, for you have been good to us, and this is our highest honor." They repeated, "This is our highest honor."

The moonlight fell through the window and onto the big mouse portrait, and I stared at the big black eyes I'd painted. "Souris will live on through my art," I told the chanting chorus.

I'd never trusted people, they'd always betrayed me. My wife, my divorce lawyer, the loan sharks and the car mechanics, the whole shit-show. The mice came into my cabin domain to escape the cold. They sheltered under the floorboards and in the walls and ate the crumbs I could share with them. I had enough.

I lived alone; I would always live alone because people always do something disappointing, or irritating, or stupid. But these mice, they did not let me down. They found my keys and came through with the packages of money. I paid my debts.

Now I have a lot of responsibility: to provide for my friends, and yes, family. I'm sure my compatriots, my rodent posse, will come up with the money, whether under the floorboards or elsewhere. I will buy them whatever they wish.

The cabin smelled sweet to me, as I filled in a few more details of the mouse portrait. I breathed in deep the friendly air.

"I'm not an alcoholic," I said to myself, reaching for my bottle. "This is my way of communicating with the rodent world."

As I said this, I heard the chorus of mice chant in answer, "Indeed, O mighty provider. As long as you care for us, we shall care for you."

"I expect to find some drinks under the floorboards tonight!" I laughed, and rushed into the bathroom to check the length of my front teeth, which I sensed were growing out right over my lower lip.

I had found my purpose in the world at last.

About Harrison Kim

The idea for this story came about when Harrison stayed at an orchard picker's cabin overrun by mice. His friend, at first, treated them as pets because he wasn't big on people. Their numbers grew and he got rid of them, but then giant furry marmots showed up and ate under the cabin's foundation. Out of the frying pan…Mice, though, have more charm and can whisper, or at least squeak, in your ear, so Harrison chose them for the story theme.

Harrison Kim lives and writes in Victoria, Canada. His stories have been published in *Spadina Literary Review, Fiction on the Web U. K., Storgy, Siren's Call, The Blue Lake Review, Horla, Bewildering Stories* and others.

His blogspot is here: https://harrisonkim1.blogspot.com

A MAN AND A DOG
by Tina Marlene Goodman

It took him a while to notice the dog.

The man squatted in the dirt road, careful not to rub against his dusty Lamborfari, and examined his back tire. It was flat and several jagged shards of glass were in the treads.

He stood and was about to run his fingers through his hair when he remembered something his therapist had said at their last session and stopped himself: "Perhaps you should consider cutting back on your habit of excessive grooming." It was the word 'habit' that dug into the man. To his mind, it suggested a lack of self-control, which was incorrect since he had that in abundance. He walked to the rear of the car and tried to ignore the small mushroom clouds of dust that bloomed from each step he took in his cap-toe oxfords.

He opened the trunk and admired the personal hygiene station that was built into the top panel. It appeared that all the shaking caused by driving on unpaid roads for the last few hours, and then the wobbling of the flat tire, hadn't disturbed a thing. And he had many things.

He fought the urge to take out his shoe-shining kit, his suit brush, and his hairbrush, even though any fool, including his therapist, Mr. Owen, would agree that he needed a thorough tidying up. He'd wait to clean up after he'd changed the tire, that was reasonable.

Then he noticed something, and it wasn't the dog. It was a sort of swath stuck on the cuff of his khaki tan trousers which would've blended in better if it weren't for the red specks of blood. And hair.

Now, being assaulted, in a way, by part of a stranger's body should be enough to justify his need for the mobile grooming station. But he was sure that at their next session, Mr. Owen would listen while he recounted this latest incident and then remind him that actions create consequences. Then the man would nod and say that he is truly the master of his own destiny. After that, Mr. Owen would let out a long sigh and make another note in his file.

He grabbed his longest pair of tweezers from the trunk, and carefully plucked the skin off his pants. He flung it away, as far as he could, and it almost reached into the field of tall grass that was next to the road. Then he used a moist towelette to blot at his cuff, although it was of little use, he knew from experience, since blood leaves a stain. He tossed the towelette onto the road and watched as it was picked up by a breeze, flown over to the field, and lowered into the grass.

That's when he noticed the dog sitting in the field.

"Looks like we have an audience," he whispered and quickly took a tire iron out of the trunk. "A big, shaggy one. At least this one's not a barker."

His next-door neighbor used to have a barker. It takes a firm hand to train a dog to mind its master, but his neighbor hadn't been fit for the task. And, she had been either too proud, or too stupid to ask for help. So, the man had been forced to take care of the problem himself. Then the ingrate had reported him to the authorities which led to mandated sessions with Mr. Owen.

"Stay," he yelled to the dog and held up the tire iron. "Be good, or this is what you'll get."

The dog remained still, like a large golden statue, probably perched on something hidden by the grass. Now, looking at its eyes, the man wondered if the dog even knew he was there, it seemed to be looking past or through him.

"Dumb, lazy dog. It's no wonder they dumped you out here."

The man chuckled then propped the tire iron against the car's bumper. He took another look at the dog before reaching into the bottom of the trunk and grabbing his spare tire with both hands.

Right away he could tell it was flat. "Dammit! Those dirty squirrels."

A few days earlier, the man hadn't been able to get his Range Rover to start. A check under the hood had revealed chewed wires and a squirrel's nest. So, he had driven off in the Lamborfari, and after only a few miles, had spotted a squirrel on the side of the road. Just as he had swerved to run it over, a tire blew out, which he had replaced with the spare. Then he had forgotten about it.

He took his phone from the inside pocket of his jacket and commanded it to call an automotive service.

"Hello, this is Car Care," a robotic voice said. "How may I help you?"

"Bring me a tire and change my flat. It's a Lamborfari XL."

"Okay. I can do that. What is your location?"

"How should I know? The GPS was acting up."

"What are the nearest crossroads?"

"Just track this phone."

"What are the nearest crossroads?"

"Are you so incompetent that you need me to do your job for you?" The man's hand started to shake so he gripped the phone tighter and yelled into it. "Put your manager on the line!"

"What are the nearest crossroads?"

The man forced himself to calm down before replying in a firm, confident tone. "I was driving down Darwin and turned onto Charon. Then, I heard a loud bang, followed by car alarms, so I drove toward the sound. I didn't pay attention to any signs; I was in a hurry to get to the crash site."

"Naturally, sir. Are the emergency vehicles with you now?"

"No. There was barely enough time to take a few pictures before I smelled gas and had to get out of there. I drove as fast and as far away as I could. Track my phone and you'll find me."

"Did you report the accident?"

"Well, no, but everyone was pretty much beyond help. One of them tried to tell me something but I couldn't understand because of the noise. There were the car alarms, like I said…and a baby. Lots of screaming. Track this phone and tell the driver to—"

An eerie guttural sound came from his phone. "Hello? Are you there? Did you get that? Bring me a tire and change my flat."

A spark shot out of his phone and he dropped it onto the road. "Jeez!" He kicked dirt over it. "Lousy service and now this! Are you kidding?"

His trembled and looked across the sky and down the road, as if searching for an answer. After he regained his composure, he turned back to the dog and yelled. "What! I suppose you think you're better than me, huh? Well, let me tell you, you're nothing but a bottom of the barrel, mangy mutt!"

He positioned himself before the open trunk, pressed the timer function on his Rolex, and reached into his grooming station. He grabbed an ashwood handled brush and stroked his hair. Its hornbeam pins massaged his scalp. Then he exchanged the hairbrush for a luxurious Italian neck duster that he twirled and flicked lightly against his skin. Next, he took off his jacket and draped it across a satin covered rod that hung from the trunk door. He cleaned the jacket with an antique suit brush, stroking gently with the grain of the wool, then he did the same to his pants while wearing them, careful of the bloody smudge on one cuff.

He swept a horsehair brush across his oxfords to remove the dust. Then he took two yack-bristle brushes out of the trunk, one in each hand, and polished both shoes simultaneously. When he was done, he tossed the brushes into the air, crossed his arms, and caught them. He placed the brushes back into their compartments, slipped on his jacket, stopped the timer on his watch, then smiled. He had set a new speed record.

A flash caught the corner of his eye. It had come from the field. He studied the dog for signs that it had moved, but, as far as he could tell, it hadn't, and everything else looked the same. He was about to turn back to the trunk when he saw the flicker of light again. He looked back at the dog and this time he discovered the source of the sparkle.

Of course, he thought, *a dog with a collar is a pet; a pet has a master, and the master has a home. With a working phone or an extra tire.*

He closed the trunk and grabbed the tire iron. He kept it at his side as he walked into the field and stopped near the dog. Closer up, he was able to see that the dog wasn't mangy or neglected. It was a pampered pooch. And its collar was paved with gemstones that looked real.

"Steady, now." He held the tire iron up and stepped closer to the dog. "I just want to look at your collar. Your very, very expensive collar." He peered at the collar but couldn't find what he was looking for. The tags. "Hmm. Where do you live? Where's your master's house? Be a good dog and show me."

The dog yawned.

He saw the dog's teeth. They were immaculate and probably in as good of shape as his own, which was extremely, excessively good. "My, don't you have nice teefers? Yes, you do. They're all polished and flossed. Who's the poor sucker that's been paying for that service? He must be rich. Where is he? Huh? Where's your master? Go."

The dog lifted a shaggy leg and slowly scratched his chin with manicured claws.

The man had never seen that breed of dog before and thought it was probably exotic. He knew someone who would pay well to get his hands, and other things, on a dog like that. And he wanted that collar. He decided to come back later, with a rented van, and lure the dumb beast into it with some raw hamburger that was laced with a tranquilizer.

The dog stood up, then turned and raced across the length of the field and into a row of poplars. The man hurried after it, but when he entered the copse, he couldn't see the dog and there weren't any prints to follow. The trees were much taller than they had seemed just seconds before and the man suddenly felt insignificant among the massive columns. He decided to go back to his car to groom himself again.

Then he heard a dog barking.

"Is that you, boy?"

There was another bark. The man moved toward the sound and stepped out of the trees, onto freshly cut, lush grass that stretched as far as he could see. A magnificent, gilded pavilion gleamed in the sunshine and almost blinded the man. The dog was there, waiting, wagging its tail.

"Wow, these are some digs," the man said as the dog ran up to him and dropped a ball at his feet. He picked up the ball and tossed it. The dog ran after it and brought it back. Then he tossed it again, and the dog brought it back. "That's enough for now. I don't like touching your ball; it's dirty like you. Where's your master's house? Home. Go now, dog!"

The dog nudged the ball closer to the man's shoes.

He held the tire iron up to show the dog he meant business. "I said that's enough. You've got to learn to mind. Your master must be very weak. And rich. Now, where's the big house? Home. Where's home? Go!"

The dog turned away and walked up the marble steps of the pavilion, then sat on a cushion.

The man looked around and saw a shabby structure off to the side of the pavilion that was probably a small maintenance shed, or a doghouse. There were no other buildings in sight.

"Come on, you spoiled, lazy dog. Take me to your master, and his mansion."

The dog ignored him and sat like a golden statue once again.

Then he saw something crawl out of the shed. When it stood up, the man saw that it was a filthy, emaciated, naked man with a large black sack hanging from his neck.

The man stared, frozen with disgust as the hunched creature limped toward him and stopped in front of him. The naked man took the heavy sack from his neck and dropped it. It fell to the ground and the contents spilled over the man's oxfords.

"Pick that up quick," the naked man whispered.

"You pick it up. You dropped it."

Then the naked man grabbed the tie iron and hit himself in the head.

"What are you doing?" the man shouted. "What's going on?"

"Pick up the stuff. Everything has to be neat," the naked man said before he turned and limped toward the trees.

The man decided it was best to do as he was told. Without taking his eyes off the naked man, he bent down and felt for the things that had fallen on the grass. He could pretty much tell what the objects were by touch. After he was sure that he had returned everything to the bag, he stood up and yelled, "You forgot your bag!"

The naked man stopped in front of the trees and didn't turn around. He began hitting the trees with the tire iron.

"Hey!" the man shouted as loudly as he could but still got no response. As he watched the naked man pound the trees with the tire iron, it occurred to him that perhaps the naked man couldn't hear him. There was something strange about the acoustics in that place. He, himself, could hear the naked man grunt and pant as he beat the trees, but he couldn't hear the sound that must have occurred when the tire iron made contact with the trees."Hey, can you hear me? You left your grooming supplies!"

He finally looked away from the naked man and inside the bag.

Then he looked back at the naked man who had stopped hitting the trees and had started hitting his head with the tire iron until he fell onto the well-manicured lawn and was still.

A great wave of panic threatened to overtake the man and he felt extremely fortunate for already having just what he needed to control the tide: the new bag of grooming supplies. He reached into the bag with a trembling hand and pulled out one of the brushes. It wasn't a style he was familiar with, so he examined it. He noticed a strand of yellow hair that was caught in the bristles.

That's odd, he thought, *that man wasn't blonde. He had dark hair, what was left of it, anyway. If he were an animal, I'd swear he had mange. And*, he couldn't stop himself from thinking, *and... not an inch of him was groomed...not in the slightest. Yet he had all these grooming supplies. But they were different...were they for animals?*

Then the man slowly turned to look at the dog, with its golden fur, sitting regally in the pavilion. It had grown to the size of a woolly mammoth. He shook his head. "No, no!" Then his head continued to shake, uncontrollably, along with his entire body.

About Tina Marlene Goodman

Blood of the Chitwood-Crawford clan throbs through Tina Marlene Goodman's veins. Her ancestral land, Chitwood, Oregon, once a thriving community, is now a decaying ghost town. Sometimes, a misguided soul will venture into Chitwood to gawk at its red covered bridge which is at risk of disappearing into heavy, moist-laden air, or being sucked down into rain-saturated sludge.

THE DARK
by Logan Fourie

Jessi sat on her bed and stared out the window. The rain pelted down and the rumbling of thunder interrupted the silence. Thin blades of lightning sliced through the inky blackness, bathing the darkness in flashes of sterile white light only to fade away, leaving the world drowned in blackness once more.

As the glow of the lightning slunk away, the dark flowed back in to fill the spaces in her room with shadows. The movements of the shadows made them seem almost alive as they stalked and slithered in the corners of her bedroom.

The electricity had gone out an hour earlier. She sat in the dark, jumping every time the thunder boomed and the lightning flashed. She cringed every time the dark oozed back after the light receded.

Jessi hated nights like this. It reminded her of all those fears and anxieties she had buried deep inside. It made her feel as though the darkness was a living, breathing thing that was always waiting to swallow her whole.

She chastised herself at her thoughts. She knew the darkness wasn't really alive. It couldn't be. It was just a state of being where light had vacated leaving only darkness behind. It wasn't like it was a sentient beast hunting her and stalking her every move, waiting for the right time to pounce and devour her.

She yelped at the latest crack of thunder, as if the storm was replying to the absurdity of her thoughts and fears. She hugged her knees and wished the darkness would leave her alone.

She decided to get something to drink, at least to warm her up a little, if nothing else. She got up and headed towards the bedroom door, being careful to avoid the dreaded shadows that reached out for her. She twisted the handle slowly. The door groaned as it slowly swung open. *Why is it that the dark always makes everything sound so much louder?* she wondered as she stepped into the dark corridor.

All the lights were out, and the house was silent. She softly padded on the pale, gray carpet, the soft thickness muffling her steps. Irrationally, she wanted to be as quiet as possible so nothing would know she was there. She logically knew nothing was there; monsters didn't exist. But she felt that maybe...maybe, something *was* lurking somewhere in the house.

She gingerly took each step as to avoid the creaking groan of the steps as she made her way toward the cupboard downstairs. She reached the foot of the stairs without incidence and avoided being caught by the shadows. She crept silently to the cupboard door and slowly opened it. She reached in and took out a flashlight...and a bottle of vodka.

She needed juice. She turned on the flashlight, which made the shadows run to the room corners and that almost made them worse. She moved towards the refrigerator and took out a carton and poured herself a glass of orange juice and carefully added the vodka. She was slowly sipping when something caught her eye.

She heard the sound of the kitchen door opening. She slowly set her glass down on the smooth, quartz countertop, leaving a wet ring on its flawless surface. She sat on a barstool, willing herself to turn around to look at the door, but finding herself frozen instead.

She shivered as the temperature dropped suddenly. She realized that somehow, the window in front of her, over the sink, was open. The breeze coming from the window must have blown the kitchen door open.

Jessi felt dismay as the rain poured in from the open window, unimpeded, and the cold wind tugged and pulled at the curtain. She knew she needed to close it immediately, but still remained frozen in irrational fear

She sat on the counter barstool and watched as the rain began to form a dark puddle between the sink and the kitchen counter where the knives stood.

Her gaze fixed on the wooden block that held the knives and she pointed the flashlight beam I that direction. One of them was missing. The Butcher Knife—the one with the large heavy blade.

Finally she got up from her stool. Her eyes followed the trail the dark rain-puddle left behind, all the way to the corner. There she saw a shadow that was thicker than the darkness that enveloped it. The shadow 'looked' at her menacingly. She yelped and spun around away from it and began to run up the stairs.

The Dark. It had finally come for her. It had finally come to claim her.

She ran back down the corridor towards her bedroom but stopped suddenly as she reached the door. The door was open. *I know I did not leave the door open. Why was the door open?*

She backed away from the door slightly, pressing her back against the wall behind her. She noticed wet footprints on the carpet.

She looked back down the corridor towards the staircase. There, at the landing, the shadow was thicker than everywhere else. Somebody(thing) was waiting. The Dark was waiting for her.

She bit her bottom lip as she weighed up her options. The shadow at the end of the hall was not moving, yet, but she needed to make a plan. She needed to figure out what she was going to do. She couldn't go into her room because there may be somebody(thing) waiting for her just beyond her door. She couldn't run towards the stairs because the shadow was waiting for her there. The only other option was going into the second bedroom. But why was she so scared to go in? She glanced back toward the end of the hall. The Dark was still looming there, waiting for her to decide.

She edged back toward the door to the second room, always keeping her eyes glued on the shadow, making sure it was not crawling closer. It wasn't. It stood dead still, and seemed to watch her.

She stepped inside and shut the door quickly behind her, locking it, and let out a sigh of relief. *Was she safe now?* she wondered. She felt safe, even if it was just for a little while.

She looked towards the bed. She could crawl in and huddle under the blanket until the storm ended. Surely there had been no shadow watching her. She figured her previous nervous breakdown could explain everything. All of this was in her mind and not reality.

The lightning crashed again, shedding slated light into the room. She sobbed quietly, trying hard not to make a noise, hoping that The Dark wouldn't find her and claim her as it claimed the only family she ever knew. Images of her past flashed in her mind.

*****

Games played in the sun, dinners eaten in the family dining room, being tucked into bed at night, the bedroom door closed…and locked from the outside. Half smiles and nervous glances. Timid and fearful hugs. Explicit warnings and instructions from a child therapist. Cautionary words as the doctor glared at 6 year-old Jessi. Reassurance from Jessi's Daddy that everything would be fine.

Visions of dark halls in a storm-filled night; flashes of lightning dancing over the silvered-steel of the large knife in a small pale hand. Memories of slender feet padding over pale-grey carpet to a door. The door slowly creaking open and the stalking to the edge of the bed.

Images of a small 6-year old girl standing over the figures in the bed (a looming shadow behind her), knife-wielding hand reaching out and drawing a thin line of red over the exposed throat and the strained gurgle of pain and surprise.

The knowing look from a father killed by a stranger he thought he knew. The terror of a loving mother who felt nothing but love…and fear…for her own progeny. The sadistic glee of the child reflected in the crimson blade.

But they had treated her and released her. She was better now, right? There were no shadows, and The Dark was simply the night.

With these thoughts comforting her, she finally fell asleep in the second bedroom, the one that had once belonged to her parents.

*****

She gasped as a flash of bright white light split the darkness and woke her. She felt wet and sticky. She grabbed the flashlight from the nightstand and lifted the covers. She saw that her soft blue nightie was soaked red, her hands too. And her feet.

She started. Her feet! The dark footprints of bloody red, leading from the pools of blood puddling on the floor at the bed to the bedroom door and out into the hall. She let out a long animalistic scream, like a wounded beast howling in the dead night. She curled up into the fetal position and softly sobbed into her knees.

The door of the wardrobe swung open. She looked from her huddled position to see a shadow crawling out. It pulled itself up, tall and lithe, with locks of fiery red danced in an ethereal wind. Its face was clothed in darkness but (and it might have just been her imagination) it looked beautiful as it smiled down at her in knowing sadness. It leaned down and kissed her softly on the forehead. Jessi felt a sharp jab in her ribs and warmth seeping out her chest and down her waist and hips and pooling beneath her.

Jessi's last moments were spent finally being able to see The Dark's face. She saw herself. She saw the knife protruding from her own chest and knew her madness had returned.

The Dark had finally claimed her. She was The Dark.

About Logan Fourie

Logan Fourie is a 40-year old English teacher from Pretoria, South Africa. He has great passion for reading and loves novels with dark and gothic themes. A lot of his inspiration comes from the works of HP Lovecraft and Edgar Alan Poe. Logan enjoys writing as a form of release and expression. He dreads the day the written word is no more.

A LONG WAY TO…
by Ed Nobody

We were sitting in a field, and the sun seemed to be setting in the wrong direction. We were speaking but I couldn't hear a sound. We talked in perfect silence until you whispered my name. At last, the world slid open and the sun shot a blazing halo. My gaze tangled with yours, and the world spun…and your empty words spun…and my head swirled downwards out of the dream.

Expelled from my bed, I fell into total grief: into a world composed of heartbreak, more remote from the comfort of sleep than the moons. I opened my eyes and found myself outside. Perhaps I had not woken up from my dream after all.

I began walking, bearing this deep pain like a charred black cross. I stumbled on aching legs across a shadowy, gust-raped plain—my steps ringing out on the hard ground as I traveled.

The sound of a faraway car closed in, growing louder and louder, then vanished into nothing.

I stood upon a bleak moor, among patches of tousled heather and black, slimy water. I dragged my burden across that dead land, under a starless sky, shivering and sweating in belligerent wind.

I no longer felt as if I was walking, but rather tumbling forward towards a pit of sinister truth. Underneath me, a deep brown bog of sorrow bubbled and burped, greedily tasting my shadow, waiting for any misstep into that fathomless muck, sitting there waiting to drink me down in an instant.

Where had the sun gone? Where had my love gone?

*****

Someone should have seen it coming. I certainly should have.

I was staring into the brilliant ochre of her sunlit eyes. As we walked, we left clear-cut shadows on a ripe green paddock, trailing the darkness behind us. On my tongue tickled the taste of sweet almonds or chocolate; I knew it was your taste—which only came in sweet, always hopping in my mouth and licking between my teeth and gums.

Your breath rushed around my neck. Your voice flapped in my ear like tiny butterfly wings. The foliage of the trees pattered under a late winter shower, like the low growl of a faraway car...the fuzzy rolls of your hair brushed like sheepskin against my exposed neck; you leaned into me, lightly touching my torso, pinching my guts—I was rotted by you. Rotted to the core by vacuous hope.

A flock of disturbed sparrows suddenly shot out from under the grove—the leaves still pattering below. We were standing at the edge of the street, about to head home.

Then fire and darkness whirled across the road. And it happened. And it was over.

You left like a lamb, like a doe.

Yet to me you were always a wildcat—your voice thick like milk and your soul red as meat.
With you it was life and life and life, and then nothing.

*****

I kept rolling on from dank shelter to murky marsh, tracing the curdling waters, the pale moon falling in slick shiny waves over its black cloak. I felt the night clasping over me and couldn't escape its stubby, frozen fingers. It was here for good—as if the sun was always yours, and you had taken it with you.

The sound of the faraway car closed back in, growing louder and louder, then vanished into nothing. The rumble of Death's engine broke the sky from afar; but when would it ever come for me? My blood had grown too cold for living without her, and I needed to be with her soon.

Once, your breath never ceased to swirl in my mouth, your voice kept fluting in my thoughts. But now there was nothing but dust and dirt and the swirling of the night's raw wind, trying to call me away from your memory.

I kept walking through smoky mists and banks of fog and wisps of dewy vapor. I kicked over every dark corner of the gloom until at last I came across an old town. It had been caught in a strange state of frozen animation: soundless streets, still shadows behind dim-lit windows, pets stiff and strewn in the road. Time was slowly trickling out of the town in the intermittent flicker of bare electric bulbs, in the brief surges of water from broken taps, in the crumbling of the walls.

I felt the Devil dancing over the earth, catching souls and letting them go again, like a cat teasing a mouse without his own destiny.

The wind howled and cursed outside like the nagging of an old crone. I found myself entering one of the secluded houses; its cold yellow light had attracted me inside like a starving moth. Its owner eyed me with tired incredulity.

"I'm sorry to just barge in here," I said. "I'm lost you see, and..."

"Don't you know where you are?" He curled the ends of his face as if to smile.

"Look, just answer me something truthfully," I told him.

He raised his eyebrows genially, waiting for whatever stupid question I had brought pointlessly along with me.

"Are we...in Limbo?"

"No, but close enough: Tipperary."

"Where in Tipperary?"

"Close enough."

I tried not to snarl at the man; he seemed to be in enough distress. I didn't quite believe his story, but I did think *he* believed in it. Why couldn't people just deal with reality? The indignant thought slipped over my mind, then caught—wait.

Hadn't I myself traipsed around in the pitch-black bogs of God knows where, for who knows how long, just to escape my own despair? Was that reality, or…?

The cottage, barely furnished, was a low large room with bare, stone walls, a crooked bed with misshapen posts, and a short kitchen table branded by kettle-shaped rings. The old man sat at this table on an uncomfortable chair, stooping over, icicles hanging from his purple, swollen nose.

On the wall hung a dirty, sacred heart lamp and a framed photo of a woman in last century's clothing. The lamp seemed to drip red light rather than glow, and its coagulated gleam coated the whole room in a sinister, crimson paint.

I couldn't stand it a second longer, and left brusquely without another word. The man didn't even look up.

Outside, I searched around frantically, awakened from my daze by this brief human encounter—I was feeling very *human* again, which meant weak and cowardly and bewildered. My steps became aimless and incoherent—running up to one darkened window after another, trying doors that wouldn't budge, knocking, calling…I felt like a madman broken loose from his cell. I felt like an invalid. I felt alone.

My lungs scratched raw, I brought my thin scarf up around my mouth to breathe, desperately trying to keep the visible breaths inside. I zipped up my coat further, felt the hard throb of my panicking heart from within its padding.

This town was suffering the same curse as I; I would glean from it no momentary comforts—the pursuit seemed childish and futile. I had to get away, get somewhere. I had no idea which direction, or whether to wait the morning. I felt too afraid to wait for a morning that might never come.

With every moment that passed, I felt myself forgetting something; forgetting myself; forgetting her. That must have been what ultimately spurred me on, out of that vacuous illusion of safety, and back into the bogland, into the mist...

*****

I came across another town between cloud and clear, dusk and dawn. This time no windows had been lit, but I could see the street more clearly: it was paved, not just a rocky rut. And there were telephone poles, and the doors had letterboxes, and for a moment it all seemed so real. I couldn't wait for dawn; I knocked on the first door I saw. I didn't care if it was rude. I was coming closer and closer to the precipice of despair, and would clutch at any straw within grasp.

A hollow sound issued from behind the hard blue door: a rustling and click of a lock. My chest tightened with tense hope, but my legs had gone rigid with the cold, and I almost stumbled back over myself when the door finally opened, revealing a toothy middle-aged woman with frazzled hair and a billowing nightie. There was nothing behind her or around her—the hall lay empty, as if someone had just moved in or just moved out. The parquet sat dull and unpolished under the weak hall light.

"Yes? What is it?" Her voice sounded cracked and weary, yet it wasn't the voice of someone who had just awoken, rather the voice of someone who had been trying all night to sleep without avail.

"I'm sorry for disturbing you." I gulped, brushing my tangle of hair back from my brow. "I'm lost. Trying to find my way." My own words sounded pathetic to my ear, yet within them seemed to ring an echo of truth.

"Well, come in, come in." Her response was not at all what I had expected. I don't know what I had really expected. I glanced around, desperately searching for a clock, a calendar, some small connection to the outside world. The bareness, the hollowness, the deadness made my eyes itch.

She began to babble as we walked into the kitchen. "Getting cold lately, isn't it? Good to get out of the cold...hard to walk on the roads..."

In her mouth I found only platitudes; in her eyes only slumber. It was like talking to a somnambulist. And that whining howl seemed to follow me in through the walls, whistling up the chimney, seething through the cracks of the wallpaper and gurgling up from the kitchen sink. It was a shrill shriek like a ghost arguing against its own annihilation—a futile pointless argument with Death.

I sat down at the chintzy kitchen table, a single bulb above boring a white spot in its greasy, glimmering middle like an island of fire. I couldn't feel my hands as I rubbed them together. She had put a tarnished iron kettle on a low blue flame and stood looking down at it, watching it and counting every second until it boiled.

Again came that soundlessness, the muted conversation of the meadow. Last words are always silent. But the woman who stood before me now had nothing in common with *her*—*she* had been youthful, bursting with energy, full of boundless love. The woman in the kitchen was withered, ugly, fixed in place—like a frozen bug stuck to a morning window. It made me violent inside; it made me restive. It made want to destroy. Why was beauty always stolen, and ugliness forever left intact. Why!! Why?

The kettle boiled; she poured me a rusty tea with the scent of rotting wood, and sat there like a little brown cloud; a stinking gas cloud of misery—and I knew we were only halfway to morning.

Before long, the woman seemed to shrink before me, close in on herself between the boundaries of her nightgown. She drained away into a dull grey liquid and dripped into the creases of the filthy tiles.

110

It happened in one great sweeping wave, and before she could cry it was already over.

My heart raced and pelted my chest from within. I swallowed the bitter, cold tea. My bones filled with lime and my shoes with cold stones.

Her thick juices hung in place, slimy like peat. I dared not even call for help; instead I treaded out a trail of muddy blood, fat blurred footprints all over the unpolished floor. The door's sweat of dew still ran freely—the night air burned me on the inside, but it was not enough to freeze.

On the horizon, I caught glimpses of purple, dreary light—sour drips of the moon's cream. In that moment they shone to me as bright as two headlights—as those which had raced towards her, through her, changing everything forever.

*****

I hopped and tripped like a wingless bird along the long, black edges of Tipperary. The cold washed over me like a rash and turned the hair of my flesh to ice. A long procession of ash trees angered me with their fat solid trunks and corpulent bodies, slabs of useless meat shutting out the sky. I wanted to burn them from twig to limb, and bask in the heat of their torture. But I had no lighter or flint, and any sticks around were too damp to rub. So I left the trees behind in my furious wake, cursing under my breath.

Once sparked, that hot fever of disgust did not stop cooking my depths. It came to a simmer, thwacking my leathery insides like the growl of a maddened bear. At first it was enough to make me shake with fear; but I then recognized this rage as my own, and I gave vent to it through clenched red fists, angry sweat trembling along the veins of my body and dripping from the pores of my crooked back. I spat venomous things to the woods; I cursed the road and the rain.

I looked at the sky, still grey, but dawn was finally breaking.

I came upon a silhouette on the hill, a dramatic fortification as grey as old bones. Surrounded by a mossy circular wall were turrets, gables, parapets, battered and crumbling walls. A spattering of graves made up the flowerbed of its garden.

The wind still carried the banshee's wailings, the harsh shrill tone of remorse. I turned a blind ear to that miserable crone, and made my way up the elevation on numbed feet, hoarsely catching a bellyfull of wind when I finally made it to the outcropping.

The chapel was Romanesque and the cathedral Gothic. It seemed like an odd collection of disparate toys shoved into the same playset, a confused tableau.

I stepped inside without a moment's hesitation—the place stood abandoned, forgotten, cloaked in desperation.

Inside the chapel, the chancel ceiling inexplicably glowed with an unknown light—around me I could see no candle, no lantern, no torch. Upon it was painted a fresco of discreet blues and yellows. It stank of the shoddy leftovers of my own soul, which I had so far held onto like loose change in the folds of my pockets, trying not to lose it on the road.

I tried anxiously to work out the confusion of the figures above me—in the corners of the ceiling I saw struggling men and wide-eyed horses, in the center I saw conflict and calamity, and at the end I caught that diluted flavor of hope which peasants call 'faith.'

And all this time, the whistle and groan of the piercing bitch wind ceaselessly hammered at the crumbling corners of the building, ringing against the outside of the roof—but she could not enter, I knew. She would be left out in the cold all night, to howl and screech and squeeze out icy tears in solitude.

Four stone heads peered down at me with mournful gazes of deep and drowsy wisdom, communicating one last prayer for the lost. Their eyes, curious and forlorn, seemed to recognize me.

Suddenly, I heard that haunting gale shriek away and whistle up to the round tower, and I knew no light would ever spark inside its lonely bedroom. But I knew also that in it, that mournful wail would finally find a home.

As I stood there silently conversing with the heads, my rage began to die down into a timid crackle, into a muted rustling in my gut like a field mouse bedding down for winter. At first I was disgusted at my own weakness, but this too gave way to the fatigue, the cold, the misery of existing without her...gradually I found intimacy in the slow and helpless beatings of my tired, broken heart.

I sat on the stone sarcophagus at the head of the room, noticing its ornate engravings: a brambled, tangled pattern which reminded me of the woods that day—her curly hair in my fingers—her love twisting through my veins.

I had intended only to rest just a moment, but I felt the weight of the whole night now, leaning on me heavily. With the shrill voice swept away and snug in its tower, there was peace. No more would I be kept awake. No more would I tirelessly wait for morning. I swung my legs up on the hard, beige stone, and laid my head on the icy slab. I looked up at the curve of the ceiling, its beautiful light from nowhere. My eyes flickered, then sagged, then fell.

I could no longer fight the inevitable. With this realization, I was no longer in Tipperary. I was no longer lost.

I was going home at last.

Would she be there to greet me, with a soft kiss, a bright smile?

I knew that she would be.

About Ed Nobody

Ed Nobody is a writer from Ireland who wants to write daring, engaging stories not restricted by traditional genre conventions. He has published several short stories in magazines such as *Lovecraftiana, Strange Science Fiction Adventures*, and *Tall Tale TV*. He has two novellas under consideration and a novel in the works.

You can find him here: @EdIsNobody on Twitter.

THE LOOMING TUNNEL
by Johanna Carter

The bike path my GPS decided to take me on is deserted for the most part. Looking at my phone, nestled on my windbreaker in the front metal basket, there are still five more kilometers before I reach my destination. Make that four.

As I kept pedaling, following the blue digital trail, people, men and women jogging near their houses, taking their dogs out, fellow bike riders, they all morphed into tall trees and bushes and clusters of greenery. The only constant was the bike path, that smooth pavement in between off-road clearances that never seemed to end. But I really can't remember the last time I saw someone; was it twenty minutes ago? An hour?

Tad-ham.

That dreadful sound coming from my phone halts my advance. "You gotta be kidding me! I have to get there in time." But no matter my lamentations, the screen still blinks *'Recalculating'* at me.

On my phone, Amanda—my only companion on the ride—chimes in robotically, "In 100 meters, take a left and go through the bike tunnel."

Taking a deep breath and wiping my sweaty forehead, I do as instructed and take a left at the next intersection. Back to no man's land.

My playlist blasts cheerful tunes in my headphones, keeping me in the groove for pedaling, the rhythm propelling me forward, even though my novice bike legs feel like they have been severed at the knee a while ago. And the sweat—my shirt is already black instead of navy, glued to my back, my bra, my underarms. A great first impression for any possible employer.

"And go through the bike tunnel," Amanda continues, stopping my music for a couple of seconds.

"I got that, thanks." I reply, although I'm pretty sure she won't answer back and neither will the distant cars swooshing by somewhere past the dense trees. My breath picks up, jolts of electric pain sizzling my thighs, and the bike rolls slower and slower as the level ground turns into a hill. Some concrete walls rise above the hill, only the top of the upcoming tunnel visible. "No, no, I can't... *Agh.* I have to stop for a sec." My brakes screech the silence away.

I get off my bike, my legs uncooked spaghetti. Spaghetti...meatballs...food...I skipped breakfast. Never again will I pull an all-nighter and then sleep through my alarms.

My music stops again and right when I am prepared to let Amanda in on a few nasty comments, I hear the familiar ringtone. I answer the call without a second to spare: "Mom, why are you calling so early? It's a work day."

"Yes, I know, but I wanted to see how you're feeling today. It's your first interview, *ever,* and I...you know me, I couldn't go to work without sending you all the good luck from home."

"I know, I know. I appreciate the thought, really, I do."

"How's the weather there? Is it still chilly?"

"Actually," I begin, one sun ray blinding me in the eye, "it's unusually sunny for fall in Denmark. Global warming will do that, I guess." In other circumstances, like going on a jog Sunday morning, it would've been the perfect weather, but not when I'm struggling to ride my bike up hills and with a time limit. *Tick, tock—*

My mom claps her hands enthusiastically. "That's great, honey. It's a good sign, I'm telling you. Okay, I'm leaving you because you have to be there at 10, right? You still have fifteen minutes, but just... be safe and don't rush. I had a terrible nightmare last night, and you just having learned how to bike—"

116

"I'm paying attention to my surroundings, I swear. No accidents today. And about last night—"

"You don't worry about that," she cuts me off. "Taxes are my worry. You have school filling that slot. Last night I was overwhelmed, yes, but that's all… I'll figure something out." She tried to be reassuring, but I knew my mom, and I knew that this wasn't the first time she had gotten 'overwhelmed'.

"You always do." I say instead. "Talk to you after it's over."

"Remember, good sign. It's a good sign."

I end the call, my playlist coming back to life in full beast mode. With the sun behind me, my legs a little numb but functional again, and with my will resurrected, I straddle my bike ready to speed like crazy through the last kilometers. I am going to get that job and help with the taxes too. This is *my* day.

A shadow running past me scares the living hell out of me. I didn't know I was capable of making that sound. Ok, awkward. But the black, hooded figure—man—doesn't even turn his head to look back at me as he continues his way up the hill, unfazed and undisturbed, until he's only a head and then a figment of the past and my embarrassment.

My heart is still throbbing in my throat when I, too, proceed uphill, giving it my all. "C'mon, Carina—" I can see the top of the hill, inching closer and closer, "—just a little more and then… yes!" I go past the top, the bike rolling downhill effortlessly. Overjoyed, I let my legs relax on the pedals as the bike tunnel, fully erect, comes nearer and nearer, the darkness inside beckoning me to enter.

It's probably the longest bike tunnel I've seen, the end of it but a faint circular dot.
As I relax my grip on the bike, my playlist gurgles in my ears, the music stopping abruptly. I check my phone, making sure not to move too much, and the message *'Recalculating'* glitches, changing

117

its font—from small to big—until it occupies my entire screen…and then the thing turns off completely.

Amanda chimes in from my headphones, "Bluetooth disconnected."

Annoyed, I take my headphones off, letting them cradle my neck. Another problem I have to deal with. "It's fine, after this it was all a straight line anyway. I got this." The looming tunnel is but a few more rolls in front of me, and at its very end I can see the hooded jogger. That was fast, I wonder. Well, I can be fast too.

This time, I pedal like a maniac, my hair catching the wind, floating behind me like a ghostly apparition. In my rush, I pass a rusty, pink bike, nestled in the nearby bushes. Weird, but not uncommon. Maybe if it was bigger I could've taken it and saved some money, but what can you do?

The graffitied tunnel opens its mouth before me, my bike easily rolling over its shadowy threshold, darkness swallowing me whole. "Abandon all hope ye who enter here," I mumble, the echo of my words traveling with me, the sun rays disappearing behind. The cool air within hits me like a brick, small bumps raising on my hot arms and legs.

Muffled sounds from outside the tunnel bounce off the walls and around me, my rattling chain the loudest of them all. Alone, following the straight gray line on the ground, I no longer feel any anxiety, but that same calm I get when meditating. I close my eyes, embracing the peaceful sensations. It feels like I'm in a movie. And is that caramel I smell?

When I open my eyes, although only a few seconds have passed, I'm already at the end of the tunnel, the jogger just slightly ahead of me. I look behind, pride swelling in my chest—I guess I was a faster biker than I thought because that looked like a long tunnel but… What is this? The tunnel… it's gone! I hopelessly look over my shoulder, my bike swerving from side to side and just barely standing upright, but trees and bushes and grass are the only things I can see. How is it possible?

118

The bike keeps rolling forward, but my legs have turned to ice, frozen on the pedals. I shake my head and yet nothing changes in the landscape behind. Maybe I biked too fast and now the tunnel is hidden behind those trees. That's it! That's what happened, of course.

Calming my breath—in, 1 2 3; out, 1 2 3—I focus on the path ahead and another hill is coming up, but this time I'm more than prepared to face it and, in no time, I roll downhill... toward a tunnel. No, it has to be another one. Even though Amanda never mentioned another one nearby, this isn't the same—the kid bike; the pink bike I saw in the bushes close to the first tunnel. There it is. That same rusty bike, in the same position and place!

"This can't be happening." My breath quickens, a lump clogging my throat. Gray stains my surroundings as thick clouds eat the sun. But I keep pedaling, the momentum propelling me forward and into the bowels of the chilling tunnel. The chain echoes in my ears, thumping and scratching at my brain. Spots—blue, green, and red—distort my vision and, at the end of the tunnel, the jogger pushes forward undisturbed, his long, slender legs crushing the gravel underneath.

"Hey!" I scream at him without even thinking. I bike toward him— he jogs away from the tunnel. "Hey, I don't speak Danish, but can you help me? Hello!" My screams do nothing as I, too, leave the abyss behind, my focus solely on the man, seemingly, running away from me. "Please, can you answer me at least?"

Another hill appears and this time, I have a harder time going over it. Not the same can be said of the jogger, who effortlessly runs up the hill and disappears, leaving me all alone, surrounded by more trees blowing their leaves and bugs in my face.

Panic surges my veins as I dare to look behind me and... nothing! A cry escapes me, the high pitched sound mixing with the *woosh* of the picking wind. I try to listen to anything else but my heart and labored breath, and nothing— no cars in the distance, no human speech, nothing else but the wind and my gurgled noises. "A-any—" *gulp*,

"—body? Please?" I look in vain at my black screen, reflecting the clouded sky. My bike slowly mounts the hill, my calves a sorry mass of cramped muscles, and then it picks up speed once over it. I turn my head, not wanting to acknowledge the small, abandoned bike next to me, and I pedal back into the darkness of the tunnel, inside the concrete coffin.

The red, painted line on each side of the walls slithers alongside me, never ending, until it does and I'm out of the hole, breathing in the cold air. My ragged breaths leave marks in the air as the temperature drops further, my skin vaguely remembering the warmth of the sun. I stop outside the tunnel, the jogger disappearing away from my sight, his footsteps getting lighter and lighter as he trails away.

The tunnel is still behind me this time, all looming darkness, all menacing silence. "Screw this," I say as I turn my bike around and go back in, my tired legs straining to obey my desperate commands. All of a sudden, another sound echoes through the tunnel— rapid footsteps. I look behind and I see the jogger, this time, running after me. "Hey!" I scream at him, pushing the words past my sore throat. The brakes screech worse inside the tunnel. Still, the jogger, with his face a mask of shadows, doesn't falter and doesn't stop. "Go away!" But he keeps running, speed increasing.

I start to pedal as fast as I can. Crazy, chaotic, but further away from this weird man. I pedal toward the end of the tunnel, my only escape. The chain of my bike fights for supremacy against the sound of running shoes pushing tiny rocks out of the way. And coming closer... and closer... I'm almost at the end too... I look back. For some reason, I look back and the man is gone! I'm the only living thing inside the tunnel.

I puff out a laugh, my bike rolling away and into the light. Looking ahead, I see the same green, deserted landscape as before, but there's something else too. This time, in the distance, above the line of trees, there's a road. And there are cars on the road! I can't help it and I laugh again. I let out all the strained laughs in the world, tears trailing gently past my cheeks. "What— haha—happened? Ha ha— thank God it's over!" Just to make sure I'm still out of danger, I glance behind and—oh, yes!—the tunnel is getting smaller and smaller, its gaping mouth closing away.

I got out. I don't know how, but I did.

Amanda's neutral voice comes out of the headphones, loud and clear: "Bluetooth connec—"
"I've never been happier to hear you," I sigh, closing my eyes.

"—disconnected," she gurgles as I open them and the tunnel's walls choke me again, the jogger striding toward me, blocking the exit with his huge frame. I turn the handles of my bike so fast that there is no way to avoid the fall. My body flies off the seat, the moving object smashing into the wall nearby and falling—like me— helplessly on the rough ground.

Tiny rocks stab my exposed palms and cheeks, getting inside my mouth, hitting my teeth. I smell rotten eggs as my face kisses the icy ground and those long, naked legs advance… and stop in front of me. The man has his back straight and I try to look for his eyes, but can't find any inside the hood—just a pitless obsidian instead of a face.

"What do you want from me?" I cry, unable to look away from the darkness of his hood. "I just want to go home."

A low gurgle reverberates through the tunnel, pulsating in my chest, my eyes. I see a change in the man—a smile, formed of long, sharp teeth… No, it's writhing maggots that— *smack smack*— fall next to my face! "Carina, you *are* home." The smile says in my mom's distorted voice.

I scream my throat raw as the smile enlarges and the man bends over me.

*****

"Now look at this beautiful weather—no clouds, no wind, and sun. Just amazing."

I bathe in the unexpected sun rays that kiss my face and dry my raincoat. The warm caresses make me think of this morning, when Noah kissed those same exact spots. Oh, that's a nice picture! Better hurry to reenact it.

I guess it's a good thing to go on a different path sometimes, to change the routine. I was getting kind of bored with that same, familiar bike path, from home to the office and back. But this bike path is completely new to me, and it surely doesn't hurt when it's all filled with trees, greenery, and no cars. I hate cars. I got hit by a car this one time—

I almost bump into a jogger as I look around me at the serene landscape. "Watch where you're going, asshole!" I scream at him, knowing full well that he saw me but didn't bother to change lanes. The man—wearing a black hoodie even in this beautiful weather—doesn't even glance back to acknowledge me. He just runs ahead and over the upcoming hill. "Unbelievable."

I pedal harder to get over the hill too and then it's a smooth ride toward the nearing tunnel. As I follow the trail ahead, I pass a small, pink bike caught in the bushes and then another one, red with white swirls, close to the tunnel's entrance. Huh, weird thing to leave behind; the last one seems functional.

"People really are strange sometimes."

I let the image of those bikes disappear as I continue on my way, enjoying the cool air provided by the tunnel. Better not to dwell on insignificant things. I have kids to feed at home and a husband to get back to.

About Johanna Carter

Born and raised in Romania, Johanna Carter is a passionate author and screenwriter, currently earning her BFA in Creative Writing, in a lovely place called Denmark.

Since she can remember, Johanna has always worked on developing new skills and widening her scope: graduated top-of-the-class in a Computer Science and Mathematics profiled high-school, learned to paint and draw, read hieroglyphs (because why not?), video and photo edit, and is now trying to learn a new language while also managing to play the piano after only three days. The only skill that came in a little later was riding a bike, unlocked last year when she turned 20. Today, she is eagerly working on a YA paranormal series with angels and a feature-length screenplay.

FACES IN THE DARK
by Harman Burgess

It is strawberry season in Fenton, a bright spring burning away the remains of winter, little red bulbs dripping from green stems across the town, and I am there to exploit it. A graffiti-coated train spits me out onto a run-down station, and I have until evening to either find work or brave the streets—a return train not due till tomorrow. Naturally, like every prospective employee, I start searching for the bar.

The heat of the afternoon sun envelops me as I step out of the station. The town's dirt-gravel streets are hot coals, the town itself consists of a series of awkwardly placed timber shacks and corrugated iron roofing; people bustling between buildings with their heads down, sticking to the shadows as much as possible.

The strap of my leather overnight bag digs into my shoulder, and I regret wearing a white shirt as rings of sweat form on my back. An old Sergio Leone-style saloon comes into view, with yellow walls and a double door. A chipped sign hanging above the entrance reads: The Oasis.

The heat follows me inside, and I make my way to the bar, pushing past the kind of drunks you can find in any dive-bar across Australia.

A jean-clad, clean-shaven, twenty something watches me find a seat from behind the bar with obvious boredom.

"Just a beer, thanks," I say.

"ID?"

I fish my University card out of my walled and show it to him.

"I need a driver's license. Your library card does nothing," he says, handing it back to me.

"It works in student bars."

"This look like a student bar?" he asks, obviously enjoying himself.

I concede the point. "You don't want me here? That's fine. Just tell me what farms are looking for work and I'll beat it."

He snorts as if the thought of me working on a farm is somehow hilarious. "So you're a farmhand and a student? That's a lot of responsibility."

"Mid-semester break."

"Ah. All the 'student' bars closed, are they?" says the bartender, the other drinkers across the bar start to snigger.

"They are," I reply evenly. "Look, are you going to help me out here or not?"

"I'll help you out, Mr. Student," he says, leaning back and crossing his arms, "for twenty dollars."

"Fuck you," I get up to leave.

"Wait," he says. "I'm just messing with ya. The Adams Estate is always looking for bodies this time of year."

"Where's that?"

"A couple kilometres north of here. Big white building. Can't miss it," then he grins evilly. "And Uni-boy? Watch out for snakes."

I give a mock salute and walk out of the bar without looking back. The sun is a red orb of malice in the cloudless sky, and I regret not pressing him for a drink. I think about turning back, but the longer I wait, the less time I'll have to find a backup if Adams falls through. Pushing down my frustration, I walk on.

*****

The Adams Estate is a largish plantation house that rests on a green hill, surrounded by rolling waves of strawberries. I can see about a dozen hunched over bodies spread out across the grounds, and a fattish gentleman in a plaid shirt watching them work from the shade of the house's veranda, as I make my way up the driveway. I head towards the veranda, the man's beady brown eyes peering out at me from the shadow of his face as I approach.

"Can I help you?" he asks in a slow, accented bass.

"I'm looking for work, if you've got any."

He looks me up and down like a gambler would a debut racehorse. "You ain't look homeless."

"I study law over at Queensland University and I want to make some cash over the semester break."

"You know how to pick?"

"I did some harvesting last season in Marsh County," I lie. "But that was corn, not strawberries."

He sighs, stands up, and stretches. "Right, grab a tray and follow me. You're lucky I need the bodies."

I pick up a rectangular cardboard box from a pile near the veranda and follow him down to the field. I watch as he crouches down and shows how to pick, making a mechanical twisting motion with his hand and dropping a red berry into my tray.

"Got that?" he asks, and I nod. "You get one token for each lot of ten trays that you fill. That token is worth a tenner at the end of the shift. Questions?"

"Is there a dorm or something where I can put my stuff? And maybe stay for a bit?"

"See that building over there?" he gestures to a wood hut hidden behind the house that I hadn't been able to see as I approached. "There're beds in there. And some bottled water by the trays. Anything else you need, Mr.?"

"Dave," I say. "And I think I'm good."

"Nice to meet you Dave, I'm Charles," he dusts his hands on his trousers and wanders back to the shade.

I jog over to the hut. Inside are rows and rows of old-fashioned hospital beds, some claimed with belongings dumped on them, some not. I place my overnight bag on a free bed near the front door and jog back to the field. Snagging a bottle of water on the way, I sit down with the tray and get to work under Charles' watchful eye:

Twisting red orbs off the vine, dropping them into the tray, pausing to take a drink, moving on to the next plant when one runs out, over to Charles for him to record my total, getting a small bronze token every tenth time. Then all over again as the sun pours fire onto my exposed neck and arms. Berries, tray, drink, total, berries, tray, drink, total, token! I become an automaton focused only on collecting tokens and picking berries. The heat slowly cooling as night gathers around the farm.

A sharp whistle calls me back to reality. Charles is standing near the water bottles, his fingers in his mouth. Around me, a symphony of groans and cracked joints breaks out as the workers set down their trays.

"Ok," says Charles. "In a minute we'll take the berries to the warehouse round back, then I'll hand out pay. Then you fellas are free to do whatever you want. Just don't call me to bail you out if the cops bust ya for drunk and disorderly."

Begrudging laughter. I fall into line with the other men as we ferry the trays around to a basement storage room underneath the house. When everything is safely packed away, we line up in front of the veranda for pay. There are about eleven of us in total ranging from local boys to fellow students to wind-beaten homeless; a couple people seem to know each other, and they stick together, but it is mostly silent anticipation. When it's my turn, I climb the steps of the veranda, and hold out a dozen or so tokens. Charles places a bundle of crisp notes in my hand and winks.

I head back to the hut with the people who are staying on the farm, about five sunburnt and dirt covered men. The others stroll off, some walking, some sharing a ride, all tired. I flop down on my bed as showers start up from the other side of the room. I am still too worn out to feel anything, but from the state of my clothes I expect to wake up very sore tomorrow.

The others come marching out of the shower block, trading jokes, and laughing. The leader, a blond who looks only a couple years older than me, pauses. "We're headed to The Oasis," he says. "Wanna come?"

"No thanks," I say. "I'm about ready to die as is."

"Suit yourself," says the blond, and the men exit.

Now alone, I summon the energy to pick a towel out of my overnight bag and head for the showers. There are several cubicles open, and I opt for the cleanest one. Stepping inside, I twist shut the latch and start stripping.

As I turn on the water, there comes over me the most peculiar feeling. It is as if something or someone is watching me. I look around the cubicle, no hidden cameras or anything (Charles didn't look the type anyway). I unlatch the cubicle and look out.

Nothing.

Yet there still seems that there is a presence observing me, measuring me up and judging me. I quickly towel off and get dressed, all the while feeling under a microscope. I can imagine whatever it is making snide comments about the weight I'd put on, about the mole on my thigh, about my budding man tits.

There is no one in the main room either. I reassure myself that this is just a bout of paranoia brought on by being in a new place and slip into bed with a book, the latest Stephen King collection. It occurs to me that horror is not the type of book to induce calm, but it is the only one I brought.

The feeling remains. Little ants of nervousness crawl up and down my back. *This is stupid, I'm an adult, aren't I? I go to University; I'm going to be a lawyer!*

I stay in bed with my book. Waiting…as the crickets sing and the presence watches.

Eventually, the uneasy feeling dissipates as abruptly as it arrived. Nevertheless, I am relieved when the others return. Trusting in the safety of numbers, I close my eyes and try to sleep.
Sleep is not forthcoming.

*****

"Hypothetically," declares Carmichael, pausing to take a sip of rum from an Oasis glass as we wait for him to continue. "There is no actual evidence that the reality we see and experience," he gestures to the interior of the saloon. "Is, in fact, reality."

It is nearing midnight and the pub ramblers are beginning to polish their sophistry. I glance round the circular table at the other workers: Tom, Thomas, Tommy, Thompson (I can never remember their names, but they do all strangely involve the letter 'T'), and when nobody rises to Carmichael's bait, I play along:

"I agree, this thing we call reality doesn't exist. It is a dream in the mind of a distant God; all the objects, all the people, all the everything is only made real because He thinks it is."

Carmichael takes another sip. "I know for a fact you're an atheist."

"But how do you know, you know?" I say. "Epistemology can get real wankey real fast."

"How do you know you don't know what you know?" counters Carmichael.

"I don't," I say, and everyone laughs.

The grumpy bartender who tried to fleece me when I arrived walks past holding a tray of dirty mugs and glasses. I make a face as he goes by.

"Don't you like our Marvin?" asks one of the Toms.

"The bartender? He was a bloody prick to me the other day."

"Tell me a story, Marvin," says Carmichael when the bartender appears.

"Hold on," I say. "Marvin, buddy, I'll give you twenty dollars if you tell us a story!"

I lay a banknote on the table and Marvin eyes it appraisingly. There is even more laughter. He glares at us, reaches down, and snaps it up.

He speaks in a gruff whisper. "Once a year, the devil walks through this town."

I laugh, but the others look grim. The Toms murmur to each other and Carmichael stares at Marvin strangely, as if daring him to go on.

"This is for you," Marvin tells me. "And only once, so listen. You've noticed that there aren't many people in this place, right? For a good reason. Every year, at the end of the picking season, it comes. We don't why it does, we don't know where it goes when it's not here; we don't really know anything. Only that if you see it, you don't come back."

I think of the presence I felt that night in the hut and shudder.

"One other thing," says Marvin, his eyes shining with malicious glee. "If it doesn't get its fill of blood, bad things start happening. Babies die in their cribs, whole neighborhoods burn, the crops stop growing. Now ask yourself this, my friend," his eyes burn into mine. "Why did you find it so easy to get a job here, when you are so clearly inexperienced?"

"That's no story, that's bullshit," snaps Carmichael. "Innit lads? We're leaving. You coming, Dave?"

I don't want to; I want to hear more of the story, but I also don't fancy wandering through the town alone at this time of night... even though Marvin's story is probably a croc of shit, well, the prospect doesn't fill me with confidence. I stand to leave with the others.

We wander out into the night, stumbling into each other and laughing. The moon is a pale scar on the starless sky. Boots crunch on gravel as we head back to the Estate.

"Do you think it's true?" I ask and notice that my speech is slurring.

"No," says Carmichael. "It's just the night talking. All the best horror stories seem real if you hear 'em at night. Even the crap ones take on a new life. Anyway, I wanted to wait, but seeing as everybody's so strung out..." he reaches into his jacket and pulls out a plastic bag with two largish hand-rolled cigarettes in it. "Anyone got a light?"

We cluster together in a small circle, illuminated by the ghostly glow of one of the Toms' cell phones. Carmichael lights up and passes on the joints. They go around the circle like the hands of a clock. The smoke burns a little as it goes down and I cough. My eyes water. I exhale and a giggly sensation comes over me, like I have just finished a darkly absurd French novel and now every drop of sadness in the world is somehow comic.

When the joints are done, we stomp them out and walk on. The Estate comes into view and I head towards the hut as happy as I had left it, laughing about nothing in particular.

"I gotta talk to Charles real quick," says Carmichael.

The Toms and I laugh at him as he stumbles up the veranda's steps and goes inside. Then we walk down to the hut. I fall into bed, fully clothed, feeling like I am made of summer. Slowly, my mind changes gear and I drift into sleep.

A pale thing, humanoid in proportion, is waiting for me in my dream; its eyes are black holes, its white hair is long and unwashed. It vibrates back and forth and it's like looking at a person underwater. It smiles and in its smile I can see pillars of crimson flame, black clouds of writhing sulphur, and an endless undying scream. In its smile, I feel like I am standing before an oncoming, all-consuming tsunami. I run, its laughter echoing behind me. The only thought in my mind is to get away as quickly as possible. I trip and fall into darkness, and there is only the rush of air and the slow timelessness of eternity.

*****

We are almost finished with the strawberries. The once green fields are now devoid of their color, except for sporadic patches near the edges, and soon Charles will call in some actual laborers to tear out the used-up stems and plant new ones for the next harvest.

I've made out pretty well. As soon as the picking is over, I'll return to my studies a few thousand richer. Not bad for a month or so of work. I still drink with the others, work, and try not to be alone, but it is all slowing down. Marvin's story had been spooky—for a time—but I will not be scared out of money this good!

I am onto the tenth tray of the day when Charles motions me up to the veranda. Setting the box down, I wipe away some sweat, and go up to him. He is chewing on a biro like he wishes it were a cigar and staring at a leather-bound lodge book.

"You've been doing some outstanding work, Kid," he drawls.

"Thanks."

"How'd you like to stay on when the machine boys come in for the planting?" he asks. "There's been a scheduling conflict, and there won't be enough of them to get it done in time. What do ya say?"

"I'd love to," I begin. "But Uni starts up again next week. I need to prepare, find textbooks, and all that stuff. I'm sorry bu—"

Charles interrupts me. "Before you say no, think about this: it'll only be for a week, and you'll be paid their rates, five hundred a day. Cash. Plus, you'll have the hut to yourself. I'm a heavy sleep so you could get up to all kinds of mischief in there."

Five hundred a day would be enough to cover my tuition costs for the semester—along with textbooks and a nice bar tab for good measure. But something bothers me about it; childish, yes…but I'll be alone.

"Can I think about it?" I ask.

"No," he says. "I don't want workers who think about things. Now or never, if you don't want it, I'll call Carmichael up and he can do it."

"Okay," I say in a rush. "I'll do it!"

"Good," he drawls. "You get back to picking now. I'll fill you in on the details later."

The rest of the day flies by as usual: picking, packing, tokens, *et cetera*. And all the while, I am thinking of how to spend my sudden windfall. Forget study, I'll have enough for a car. No more trains were people cough on you and bump you while you're trying to read. I could have transport of my own; I should've come out here years ago.

The dream of a car joins my collection of other castles in the sky as I walk into town with the gang, now a couple of Toms short owning to the season tapering down. Carmichael is telling a bawdy story, and we are all laughing along, when I see Marvin waiting outside the station with a bag over his shoulder. He is enjoying a cigarette, tendrils of pale smoke curling around
him like tentacles. I go over to him as the gang heads inside The Oasis.

"What's up, Marv?" I ask. "Where're you going?"

"Outta here, man," he replies.

"Why?"

He sighs and flicks the cigarette butt to the ground. "If you haven't worked it out by now, there's nothing I can say to you. How long are you here for, anyway?"

"Charles asked me to stay on another week."

Marvin laughs at that. It's the first time I've heard his laugh, a high nasally sort of thing. And then, without saying goodbye, he turns and walks into the station, still laughing to himself. Pushing away his reaction, I head into The Oasis where Carmichael is flirting with the new waitress.

He looks over to me. "What happened with the world's worst bartender?"

"He's leaving," I say, sitting down between the two remaining Toms. One of them hands me a beer.

"Good riddance, I say," declares Carmichael, and he returns his attention to the waitress.

*****

I watch with Charles as the last Tom walks down the Estate's long driveway and into the evening. Carmichael and the other Tom have already left, but not before making me promise to call if I am ever in the mood for some extra-legal substances.

I now have the hut all to myself. The grounds of the Estate are covered in wilting strawberry vines, the last plants having been picked clean this morning.

"How long until the new guys get here?" I ask as the Tom recedes from sight.

"Not till Monday," says Charles, sitting on the porch. He stands and cracks his back. "I'm about ready to turn in. I appreciate you staying on for the week. Be up early, though, so I can show you how to use the machinery."

"Will do," I say, also standing.

We say goodnight, and I make my way down to the hut, the night air crawling with bugs and little flying things. I yawn as I enter and start preparing for bed. I feel a bit drowsy. The shower is cold but refreshing, and when I am clean, I push two of the hospital beds together to make a double, before curling up with my book.

A while later, as my eyes are getting blurry, I put down the book and turn off the lights.

Darkness.

I lie spread-eagled across my makeshift bed with my eyes firmly shut, going over what I'll have to do tomorrow. Probably a lot of lifting things and pretending I know what I'm doing and… and my mind starts to go, drifting off into dreams. And right as I'm on the precipice of unconsciousness, I feel it: the burning stare of unseen eyes pressing into my shoulder blades.
I roll over under the covers and try to reassure myself I'm alone, but the feeling persists.

I open my eyes and reach for the light switch. And in the moment between when my eyes adjust to the dark and my mind returns to me, I see a face growing out of the wall.

It is swelling right out of the wood like a water balloon, its features twisting in agony, its eyes black pools of infinity. It is quickly joined by a second face, feminine in structure, and also bent in pain. I stumble out of bed, mute, convinced I am in a nightmare.

The faces begin multiplying, more and more of them popping into existence like raindrops. And moaning. A long continuous groan of suffering that goes on and on, echoed by the thousand faces bursting out of every corner of the room.

Panicked, I run outside, throwing open the hut's doors, to see more faces rising out of the ground, forming a vast spectral funnel into the sky, blue-green light pulsating inside it as screams shatter the night. Planks tear loose from the hut, whipping through the air like darts and exploding into the ground in constellations of dirt.

I run towards the house, wind pulling at me from every direction as the vortex of faces churns with malicious violence. I jump up the veranda steps and grasp onto the door. It is locked. I pull and pull on the handle to no avail.

I sprint away from the house as the faces slam onto the ground, spraying mud and dirt in every direction. I run down the driveway hoping, just hoping. The only thought in my mind a continuous loop of: run, run, run, run…and that's when I see it. The pale thing. It is staring at me from the end of the driveway and when I look into its eyes, my consciousness shatters like so much brittle glass. It reaches for me, and I can feel my body dissolving on the wind like…like…I fall away from myself, a feeling of burning taking root in my soul. There is only the agony of… as…like…

A man continues his stroll through the night. The ground he treads on turning to dead ash beneath him. He is as indifferent to the screaming that surround him as Mt Vesuvius to Pompeii. He is enjoying himself immensely.

136

About Harman Burgess

Harman Burgess studies psychology at the University of Newcastle, Australia. In his spare time he slush-reads for *After Dinner Conversation* and enjoys hanging out with friends. He was nominated for *Spillwords Press'* best November short story, and his short fiction has previously appeared in a number of online journals and anthologies. He likes having an excuse to write a bio about himself, as it is the only way to refer to yourself in the third person without sounding pompous or insane.

THE BAT KEEPER
by John Mara

"It dun happened, Alfred."

"Who the hell is this?"

"Name's Jed. I help'round yer Paw's farm."

"Hello then, Jed. What is it that done happened?"

"Yer Paw, Alfred. He's toes up in that barn out back. The one with all them gol' dang bats."

"Did a bat bite him or something?"

"Hell no! Yer Paw's their keeper. There's got to be a million of them furry devils in that barn. Why, one of 'em—"

"Enough with the bats already!"

"Ya doan sound too broke up none about yer Paw."

"We were estranged, my father and I." College ended for me when Dad fled Boston and bought a lonely farm in northern New Hampshire. Twenty years on, I'm still waiting booths at the Town Diner. I was serving a mountain of greasy bacon when Jed called to sprinkle some green manna from heaven. Finally a break!

"Stranged, was ya?" Jed says."Either way, are ya comin' or ain't ya?"

My grimy apron skids across the counter. "I'm halfway there, Jed."

I'm familiar with bats.

*****

At the end of an abandoned lumber road, my dusty '88 Saab turns right across a wooden bridge spanning a creek, the pine guardrails on one side freshly snapped. In the water below—dark as the river *Styx*—a rusty Ford pickup truck is flipped on its roof. Dried blood cakes the broken windshield, but the cab is empty.

It's twilight, so a dozen sentinel bats—double the size of any native New Englander—land on my car's hood and a row of beady eyes peer through the windshield. It's not too dark yet, so I can see it clearly. With a shudder, I get out of the car and back away with a few bananas for lunch, waiting for the curious bats to leave.

But one monster seems to grin as though marking me forever. Four others land on my shoulders to scent the banana offering. A wriggling bat flutters its wings against my chest, and a dog-nosed fiend nestles its snout in my ear. I make a disgusted sound. The bats snarl when I try to pull away, and to get rid of them, I throw the bananas on the ground.

Smacking lips, the giant bats retreat, but they escort the Saab up to the farmhouse. The darkening sky is silent; no sparrows sing, no mosquitoes buzz. The fields lie fallow, littered with the bleached bones of wild and domestic animals alike. Its clapboards decaying, the farmhouse itself looks dead. A cardboard sign nailed to a porch post is scrawled, *UNH:Don't Feed the Bats!*

The porch light is already on. Jed rocks a rickety chair that creaks in time with his knees. He strokes the gray bristle on an array of chins and spurts tobacco juice onto the rotting floorboards. On the rail facing Jed are four of the beefy bats, flapping vampire-like, membranous wings. The group of five strikes me as a legislative body governing this hidden, desolate realm, Jed presiding. With a vacant look and lolling tongue, Jed waves an arm to end the Congress, and the four bats fly away.

"That you, Jed?"

Shirtless in the humid heat, Jed lumbers down off the porch. He reaches deep into bib overalls to relieve the itch in his crotch and

139

then pumps my hand through the open Saab window. "Hello thar, Alfred!"

Bats circle overhead, first a few and then hundreds as the sky continues to darken, the sentinels having spread the news of a newcomer's arrival. Their droppings smear the Saab's windshield and plop on Jed's overalls. "Dang critters!"

Jed blows a modified bird whistle, and the bats fly back to the barn. "Lots o' bat shit on yer perty red car there, Alfred. Ah he heee!"

"Never mind the car! Where's my father?"

The gnarly hair on Jed's chest gets a raking. "Foller me."

We take the windy path down to the dilapidated barn, where bats fly freely in and out of every crack and crevice in the wall planks, the leaky roof, and the broken windows. The barn and the ground nearby are layered white, like a holiday gingerbread house overdone with frosting.

"Let me turn on the light. Watch yer girly beach thongs, Alfred," Jed sniggers and lays down a few pine planks. We cross the guano moat and Jed opens the barn doors a crack. "Doan wanna disturb the hotel guests."

At the threshold, a bat pup supping Dad's blood-matted gray hair scurries away. Inside, the heat, humidity, and putrid bat shit mix into a miasma that coats my skin and rasps my nostrils. The tee-shirt pulled over my mouth and nose hardly filters the tomb-like stench. But Jed seems immune—no, to thrive—in the dank, dreadful underworld.

The yammering bats withdraw to the white rafters and into every dark, angled corner of the coliseum-sized barn. Rank on rank, thousands of red, vacuous eyes look on.

"Yep, he's dun dead all right," Jed says. "Right where I found 'im."

140

"He's blue. He had a heart attack." Eyes closed, I wish we'd reconciled.

In a moment, the bats begin to stir once again. A few keen and others follow. The bad news is passed down the line: the bat keeper is dead for sure.

"These bats are bigger than any I've seen, Jed."

"They're Bow-livian vampire bats. A loony UNH professor paid yer Paw to put some here fer research. But they bred like rats!"

Around the repurposed barn, pinewood roosts crowd every possible space on the floor and along the walls. Above, the roosts are stacked, layer upon layer, beyond the rafters, so many that they blot out the light.

A new waft of thick air knocks me back. "Aachh, this place reeks!"

Jed swings open the two barn doors. Fresh air rushes in. Jed pulls on a string from the ceiling and another barn light comes in. It casts light on my father's shirtless torso too, dotted with more red bites than a child with chicken pox.

"Why is my father's truck in the creek?"

"Two days ago, yer Paw tried to vamoose. The bats covered the getaway truck three-thick at the bridge. That's when he took a swim."

"How'd get out of the creek?"

"Yer Paw climbed out and tried to run across the bridge. What I saw was a man wearin' a furry bat tuxedo, wings a-flappin' and all. Ah he heee!"

"How'd he get away?"

"That screechin' bat suit calmed itself when yer Paw, lunatic eyes a-bulgin', started crawlin' back towards the farm. Saved hisself, yer Paw did. But he wasn't the same. He wandered 'round here like a mumblin' preacher. Said he didn't keep the bats no more. Said the bats kept him."

"Did you feed the bats, with my father laid up?"

"Huh! Didn't you read yer Paw's warnin' sign? Feed them winged devils a morsel and they *own* you. Won't let you leave here. Jus' ask yer Paw."

"Let's get him back to the farmhouse."

"I'll fetch the wheelbarrow. We'll give 'im a royal procession. Ah he heee!"

Jed plods away and the bats study me with their beady eyes. A host of them scamper aside to reveal, in the deepest cavern of the barn, a puppy-sized, bulbous vampire bat. A few others nearby preen the nappy fur of what is surely the queen of the herd. She gives one of her workers a mango, and the worker presents it at my feet. The queen squeaks a soft salute that cascades from stoop to stoop, louder and louder, signaling my communal acceptance: I'm part of their accursed world now.

The induction ceremony ends when Jed returns. "In ya go, ol' fella," Jed says, and we hoist my father into the wheelbarrow.

The bats begin to squawk, this time in anguish, and the carping reaches a crescendo.

I light a Lucky Strike with trembling hands. "What's the chorus for?"

"Can't ya tell? It's a funeral dirge fer yer Paw."

The send off ends when two vampires alight on my shoulders. This time, their talons take purchase in my skin. They smell fear.

142

Mopping sweat, we coax the wheelbarrow up the path, a two-man chain gang with the bats on patrol. Jed glances at the two guards riding shotgun on my shoulders. "Looks like the inn already hired a new keeper. Ah he heee!"

The farmhouse comes into view and so does the Saab—an escape hatch out of this brooding, mad world. I panic and race to it. The two jumbo guards wail to sound the alarm, and one bites my neck, piercing the skin with its fangs. The other claws through my new Red Sox tee-shirt and gouges the New Hampshire state map into my heart-pounding chest. I beat both bats away with a fist and take refuge in the Saab.

I turn on my headlights and search the glove compartment for my iPhone, a tether line to civilization, to dial 9-1-1 and put an end to this otherworld. But pressed against the windshield are Jed's puffy jowls, grinding the bacon slabs I left on the dashboard. In front of a greasy smile, Jed dangles the iPhone by its lanyard.

"What are you doing!" I scream. "Get out of the way or I'll run you over!"

Jed spins away when I floor the accelerator. In the rear-view mirror—a portal into hell—Jed blows that goddamn bird whistle, this time in a discordant tone. The barn disgorges a phalanx of bats that cast a moving shadow behind me.

They're gaining on me! I reach the bridge, ready to throttle across the boundary of the bat kingdom and to freedom.

Suddenly, the bridge is no longer in sight. An undiluted terror grips me as the shadow descends, and the fastest among the ravening horde blanket the Saab. The bats' noxious body heat fouls the air vents. The interior of my car shrinks into a dismal coffin. I remember the truck in the creek and know there's no way to escape this post-apocalyptic world. Retching at the fetid smell, I summon the courage to shift the Saab. Slowly, very slowly, I back up. I'm familiar with bats and know what they want.

In what seems a lifetime—and in a way it is—the bloodthirsty mass senses surrender and the measured attack subsides. Deathly silent, they dismount the car, two by two, but continue to block the bridge. The little beasts cluster beneath the Saab's front grill to trail the car as it backs up, their yelps trumpeting a prisoner taken and a battle won. Jed, too, registers victory; he blows the bird whistle to call the bats back to the barn. It's feeding time.

Back at the front porch, Jed rocks in his throne. Hotter than the car engine, I flex both fists. But Jed returns my icy glare witha crazed, sideways grin and shows the butt of a .38 revolver in his overalls. "Feed the perty critters for yer Paw there, Alfred. Like a good boy. Ah he heee!"

Behind the barn, I slide open the garage door of a windowless, prefab industrial warehouse. *University of New Hampshire* is printed on its side in green block letters. Inside, crates of imported fruit—mango, guava, and bananas—reach for the ceiling. I haul out the leaky crates and spread the half-rotted feast, keeping ahead of the gorging black tarp that blankets the barren field.

When the buffet ends, a graybeard bat offers a succulent leftover at my feet, and the seething masses pay heed. I am their keeper now, but in reality, they keep me.

"Good job thar, Alfred. 'Bout time for me to skedaddle," Jed says when I return, covered in swill. A full sideways grin frames his glimmering, tobacco-stained teeth.

"What the hell do you mean?"

"I mean yer Paw hijacked my gol dang pickup truck and drove it into the creek!" A spurt of tobacco juice marks his disgust—and my toes. "I never shoulda taken that squirrelly right off that lumber road!" Brandishing the .38 in one meat hook hand, Jed rattles the Saab keys with the other. "Now it's your turn, city boy." A thick tongue mops a thin lick of tobacco juice from his chin.

Jed's blank eyes turn to the sign on the porch post when he climbs into the Saab. "Doan you know how to read? Never shoulda fed them bats! Ah he heee!"As the transmission grinds through its gears, the sky darkens. A legion of bats overtakes Jed and dive-bombs the Saab at the bridge.

I sprint there to watch the heathens blanket the getaway car as they did to Dad and me. But Jed—who knew, at least, not to feed the vampire herd—rambles the Saab across the bridge like a church-goer on Sunday morning.

*****

The next day was calm, but at sunset, a squadron of anxious bats patrols the border against a blood-red sky. A few others watch me tamp the dirt among the marijuana plants in a hippy send off that would make Abbie Hoffman jealous. Then, two guards on my shoulders escort their new caretaker back to the farmhouse. Sliding across the moss-coated porch, I kick aside the remnants of the iPhone that took a beating at the butt end of a .38.

Inside, I settle into my father's bedroom—the bat keeper's room. It's musty, but plenty comfortable. Dad's clothes fit snugly too. Try on those bib overalls and see if there's any bacon to fry, dear reader. We're going to be here awhile.

About John Mara

A 2020 Pushcart Prize nominee, 2020 Best of the Net nominee, and 2020 Best New England Crime Stories finalist, John Mara writes lakeside in New Hampshire with the creative input of his wife Holly. They often attract mortified glances in restaurants, where they too often discuss characters and plots. A multi-genre writer, John tends to converse in the genre he's thinking about and makes better dinner company when it's humor, not horror.

Besides *The Horror Zine*, you can find John's 30-plus short stories published in *Liquid Imagination, J.J. Outre Review, Youth Imagination*, and other venues.

"Spookee" by Adam Plant

146

POETRY

POETRY BY NILOUFAR BEHROOZ

THE HOMELESS BOY

Inside his troubled eyes
He has worlds unknown to man
That colonize my soul.
And his voice
is glazed with tenderness
as he murmurs
melancholic melodies
to fleeting frozen faces
who pass him by
without a thread of
mercy.

FROZEN EMOTIONS (A FAREWELL)

White icicles of hearts hanging
Dark shadows of us impending
Frail frames of happiness shaking
Delicate dreams falling, breaking

Lost in this everlasting fall
Pulled by our pride behind this wall
Too far to hear the distant call
Too cold and numb to move at all

Our eyes, globes of aspiration
Our hands, the sweetest vibration
But words flow with hesitation
We seek the fading sensation

The mist clouds over this damp air
A gentle breeze brushes your hair
In silence we prolong the stare
If only time could stop right there

We share sad farewells as we stand
Burying love in this cold land
I let go of that precious hand
You softly say "Not as we planned... "

INFINITY

Inside this chaos
of living
among the identical faces
I wiggle my way through
the flash forwarding mass.
The hollowness deep in their eyes
relentlessly stares at my soul.
Catching the next bus would be hard
but I store infinity
in my pocket.

FORBIDDEN LOVE (LIKE A SIN)

We steal glances across the room
A secret smile, our souls consume
No one's aware of my chagrin
I hide you within like a sin

A yearning, taboo desire
A love forbidden, a fire
I fight the flame, I hold it in
I must hide my love like a sin

It pains me to feel your presence
To drink the air that's your essence
We're drawn like magnets, yang and yin
But we must hide it like a sin

The heart wants what it cannot own
A truth universally known
When you want something you can't win
You have to hide it like a sin

About Niloufar Behrooz

Niloufar Behrooz holds a PhD in English Literature. She is a musician, night owl, and lecturer at the University of Isfahan, Iran. Her work has appeared in *Raintown Review, Classical Poets Society, Lighten UpOnline, Parody, Literary Hatchet, Litro, Loch Raven Review, World Haiku Review* and elsewhere. Her most recent nonfiction will appear in an upcoming anthology.

You can find her on Instagram @niloufarbehrooz

TIDE LINES

Here where the ocean sees the land,
Where ever-changing, shifting sands
Meet ancient rhythms of the waves,
Rocking the shore, pebbling the beach.
Here solid ends and water worlds
Different, deep and dangerous swirl.
Here's where the world that we now know
Crawled from a slimed, primeval place.
Here is where dreamers stand and gaze
At the horizon's misty edge.

THE LADY BY THE LAKE

A watery, winter sun wept down,
Through a thin, grey veil of cloud,
Over the lake the morning mist,
Hung like a cold, white shroud.
She shivered in the morning chill,
As she waited by the lake,
Shivered from fear as well as cold
Knowing the risks they would take.
For the man she loved was lowly,
A humble, simple squire.
If her father should discover them
His vengeance would be dire
For he was a mighty baron
And she was his only child
She knew that if he discovered their plans
He would rage uncontrollably wild.
He had promised her in wedlock,
He had shown her the golden ring,
That she would wear when married
To the nephew of the king.
So, with her handsome, loving squire,

She planned to elope that day
Regardless of the danger,
They'd be lovers come what may.
Then, riding out of the forest,
The sight that she most feared,
A band of her father's retainers
Suddenly appeared.
They mock her and they taunt her,
Ask, "Is this who you came to meet?"
Then, red with blood, they throw the head
Of her lover down at her feet.
That night, late, after a banquet,
As the baron took the air,
He went to visit his daughter's room
But could not find her there.
They found her in the morning light,
As the dawn began to break.
They found her drowned among the reeds,
In the mist, at the side of the lake.

STRANDS

Snail, sea snail, curled, frozen in stone,
Fossil found on a pebble beach.
How far now from those tropic seas
You lived and died in long ago.
For countless years you slid through time
To meet me in a different world,
To rendezvous here on this strand.
Is that how time will treat us all?
After we've gone to slip through years
And meet again on other shores

About Ed Blundell

Ed Blundell worked as a teacher of English, a school inspector and as Director of Education for the town of Stockport. He has had short stories and poetry published in over thirty magazines in the U.K. and the U.S. including *Popshot, Orbis, Psychopoetica, Carillon* and

Purple Patch and has had a collection of his poems, "Sweet Nothings," published by Atlantean Press. He gave up searching for the meaning of life after discovering there wasn't one.

POETRY BY DONNA DALLAS

NO PLACE LIKE HOME

I miss the vultures
when they pick
and pull
at rotting corpses
along the road

I need to go back
get home bled
we all need
a good bleeding

There's a taint
I need it sucked out
before it spreads

Stare at the lines and
deep crevices in my palms
how long is my life-line?
how long to my end?
I want my mommy
to lull me to sleep
before the vultures arrive…

Bats in the shed
never afraid
they eat all the bugs
there is a purpose for it all
my bleeding heart included

ASTERAL NAVIGATION

Every night I die
fall into my astral self
float out my ass and back in

154

through my eye sockets
to feel connected
fully integrated

While
this yellow
oozy
moon
creeps over my head

I linger in my own scent
bloodhounds sniff a dried turd
there is nothing here but an osprey
she will gouge out your eyes in
protection of her young

Screams push to be released
they lurk in the crevices
between lung and heart
some sound—like a moan
trickles out

It's just my death
over and over
in search of my naked self

DEAD BLUE JAYS

the Garden of Eden
in my backyard
enter if you please
please me if you enter
don't step on the dead blue jays
how lovely they
remained blue
for so long
while their grayed oozy
hearts soak
into my earth

my hearth
my rotting heart

Exit when
I get this way
this awfulness
buried beneath pretty
under blue jays
there's that rot
it's a kind of addiction
this dirt carries me
this overgrowth covers my dead
I am so lonely
I bed the earth

About Donna Dallas

Donna Dallas studied creative writing and philosophy at NYU. She has recently appeared *in Red Fez, Anti-Heroin Chic, The Opiate, Beatnik Cowboy, Burning House Press* and several other publications. Her recent novel, *Death Sisters* (Alien Buddha Press) has just hit the market. Donna serves on the editorial team of *Red Fez*.

You can find her on Twitter at @DonnaDallas15

POETRY BY YUAN HONGRI
(Translated by Yuanbing Zhang)

AN ILLUSION IN THE BRIGHT MIRROR OF ETERNITY

Every day is an illusion in the bright mirror of eternity.
You see yourself from a teenager to an old man with gray hair,
as if you are a role in a play.
And the peace of mind makes you smell the fragrance of flowers
from the Heavens.
You recall yourself in outer space with a smile—
that golden giant and fragrant light;
the huge number of palaces looks lofty, resplendent and majestic,
they rise and fall, like a sea of gold.
Billions of years are like the drops of nectar
crystal clear, sprinkle the music of intoxicated soul.

AS IF THE STARS SMILE AND SHINE TO EACH OTHER

I require new words
Black gem and Sapphire
To decipher the alien password
To open the mystery door of the soul base
Those people who ride the flying saucer
The blue blood runs in their body
On their planet
Every stone has a soul
Even the flowers and trees
like their brothers and sisters
Yet, they have no human emotions
The same as if the stars smile and shine at each other

A REFRESHING BREEZE OF THE DAWN

I came from the outer space,
came from the giant city of the platinum.
My lines, words of the gem
twinkling with the future interstellar smiles,

157

made the wings of your soul to wake up from the dream
made you see yourself in outer space--
time was sweet as wine
the palaces of the heavens were as brilliant as the flowers of gem
the music was a refreshing breeze of dawn that brightened the soul.

STRINGS OF THE LIGHT OF DAWN

When I plucked strings of the light of dawn
A golden lightning burned a huge city
The undulating hills in distance twinkled the ruby smile
Vaguely there came acoustic resonance of the bell
from the center vault of heaven
Who have seen that the palace was towering outside the sky
The gods smiled with stately grace and raised their glass
Female celestials shed datura flowers flying all over the sky.
And a large ship approached from another galaxy
They came from a huge platinum city
Their ships were much faster than the speed of light
Ever visited the earth billions of years ago
They brought new technology
To make the steel have a wonderful spiritualism
Their eyes can prospect the heaven and the world
Heart is as bright as the sun
And body is as transparent as diamonds

About Yuan Hongri

Yuan Hongri (born 1962) is a renowned Chinese mystic, poet, and philosopher. His work has been published in the UK, USA, India, New Zealand, Canada, and Nigeria; his poems have appeared in *Poet's Espresso Review, Orbis, Tipton Poetry Journal, Harbinger Asylum, The Stray Branch, Acumen, Pinyon Review, Taj Mahal Review, Madswirl, Shot Glass Journal, Amethyst Review, The Poetry Village*, and other e-zines, anthologies, and journals. His best known works are "Platinum City" and "Golden Giant." His works explore themes of prehistoric and future civilization.

Yuanbing Zhang (b. 1974), is a Chinese poet and translator, who works in a Middle School, Yanzhou District , Jining City, Shandong Province, China.

A TOUR WITHOUT VIRGIL

a noisy, sweat-beaten tour
of faraway Quiet House,
taken with someone
who's someone else;

we only think words are
what shape our lips
and pictures we see
put a glow in our eyes,

but words here flee fast
like stock quotes on TV,
because the lips you watch
belong to someone else;

the eyes that watch you
are busy painting pictures
for a gallery of private parts,
naked hearts and hair in pain,

and soon the pictures overlap
in waves, the garden hangs on
the wall and the wall walks
behind you, your shadow holds it

for an umbrella, and inside it
locked up is your private 10th
Circle; in the din of brittle ghosts
crashing into solid make-believe

your lips too go crazy and let
the word madhouse slip out,
but the denizens can only hear
themselves, if they listen at all.

And what if your tour guide can't find
the way out and says there's no outside
it had all collapsed into this place
condensed into this black hole universe

NIGHT IN THE OLD TOWN

A night in the old town quickly blooms
into a day-old beard and its mouth
into a chuckle when the night
tries to answer a worried question,

a deep and slow chuckle like an empty
barrel rolling down on the stone steps
of a vaulted cellar where the old
town is hidden from daylight view,

that's why the night is forever here,
in the dim depths night-colored walls
hold sightless windows whose light
was put out by bleeding thumbs;

to get lost here is to become a witch
bereft of magic, because this jilted
bride of the night bears a bastard
child who refuses to be born,

and she wanders forever lost inside
the churning chuckle of the cellar,
it's there that she has to find a word, combing
the beard of the night with her naked fingers.

THE VAMPIRE QUEEN

The darkness is her sultry nightdress,
her crown a glowing scream,
she rules the night with a pale blue fist
embracing your bare throat.

161

With the long sharp nails of her scream
she rips off your mantle and your shirt
and sends lascivious beads of sweat
chasing one another on your chest,

but you don't know you're naked
until she impales your helpless aorta
on her fangs, letting life squirt out of you
in the drunken spasms of immortality.

About Paul Sohar

Paul Sohar has been writing and publishing in every genre, including seventeen volumes of translations. His own poetry: "Homing Poems" (*Iniquity Press*, 2006), "The Wayward Orchard" (*Wordrunner Press* Prize winner, 2011) and now "In Sun's Shadow" (*Ragged Sky Press*, 2020). Prose works: "True Tales of a Fictitious Spy" (*Inequity Press*, 2019) and a collection of one-act plays from *One Act Depot* (Saskatoon, Canada, 2014). Magazine publications: *Agni, The Horror Zine, Rattle, Rhino, Seneca Review*, and others.

DOWNWARD SPIRAL

My world is brilliant, all light kaleidoscopic,
but on a thin ice ledge, fragile, fracturable.
One spot of darkness can ruin my life.
It links to all negative, historical resonance,
snaking through my mind, throughout my time,
dragging the memories of yesterday's slights,
greying the kaleidoscope, hiding my light.
Then anger, hate, sadness, self-loathing,
swallow my personality in gloomy twilight.
Tears rage like a furnace of rain,
burning in uncontrollable floods,
washing me to pitch black,
where I can't think, don't exist.

THUNDERING GIANT

A raised hand
A cacophonous voice bellowing forth
With such furry
The wind from his lungs ruffles my fur
Almost as much as the drunken swing
That barely misses my snout
I yelp
And scurry into my cave
Allowing myself to be corralled
For fear alone
For I have no love of my captor
No Stockholm syndrome
A little urine trickles down my leg
As I cower from the thundering giant

COTTAGE IN THE WOODS
(Inspired by Rober Frost)

We chanced upon it passing through the wood one autumn
afternoon,
hidden among the ancient oak and knotted pine.
It possessed an eerie silhouette against the haunted sky.
With no path of which to speak,
we picked our way through brambles and vines.
The door was locked and boarded tight,
so we found our way to a broken pain,
glass shattered by the swing of knotted pine.
In we looked at the clean-swept floor,
the red-brick hearth with the roaring green fire,
the cat with a pointed hat and mouse skull on a pike.
We knew we trespassed where, perhaps, we should not.
Turning we noted our path home had been blocked.
I am now surprised we were surprised at that turn of event,
knowing how unholy the sights we saw were in retrospect,
and ashamed of the last moments we spent together on earth.
For it was you who stayed and shrunk and scurried about,
until you were caught and mounted on a stick of knotted pine,
and me who fled screaming into the night.

CRIMSON-BUTTERFLY DAY
(inspired by Robert Frost)

It is Crimson-Butterly Day in autumn.
The sky bleeds in perpetual torrent.
Monochrome reds from top to bottom.
The queasy find it quite abhorrent.

But these are flowers that fly,
at least to the well-trained eye.
For those who feed on others' currents,
this day abstains from common deterrents.

The holy hide in their stone enclosure,
protected by cloth of the divine skirt.

But the unblessed lose their composure
when crimson flows from beneath their shirt.

As I and my siblings swoop about,
cutting life strings before they shout,
reaping the wealth of our harvest moon,
feeding fast for it ends too soon.

About Tony Daly

Tony Daly is a poet and short story writer of fantasy, science fiction, horror, and military fiction. His work was recently published in *Illumen, Silver Blade*, and *The Stray Branch*. He is also proud to serve as an Associate Editor with *Military Experience and the Arts*.

Born and raised in Western New York, he currently lives in the Washington DC Metro Area. For a list of his published work, please visit https://aldaly13.wixsite.com/website or follow him on Twitter @aldaly18.

FALL (A Broken Sonnet)

leaves of fire
cold rain
gusts like groans of pain
mire

everything freezes
everything fades
love has withered, hope has greyed
heaven is a maelstrom of diseases

we remember and we cherish
we have danced and we've enjoyed—
evil things and lovely things now perish
flesh and spirit slide into the horrifying void
one last swirl of dead leaves, red and garish,
and then

VERNAL DAMNATION (A Broken Sonnet)

It's March and April when the coffins crack
The tomb-gates creak and quiet corpses wake
Life's only comfort, Death, contorts and breaks
Slime-weeds and moss come slinking, crawling back

The bitter promise of the bygone Fall—
Eternal rest, escape from putrefaction—
Shall face the lying, dying god's redaction:
Unwanted resurrection blights us all

Exiled from ice, life rots and shits and fucks—
The trap of Spring snaps shut upon our necks—
we cannot die—we cannot die—oh equinox—

please

let us
die

NIGHTFALL IN UTQIAGVIK

The polar night has come. Two months of black.
Pale frozen stars long dead. The slopping Sea.
The Borealis, flare of lunacy.
Lean ravens pecking at dead Autumn's back.

The earth is carrion. The sky is ice.
Seagulls like Grendel shrieking from the Pole.
The dark between the stars. The tomb of souls.
Wolves haggard as the birches, grey as Christ.

Cadaverous and gelid universe—
Decomposition—entropy—decay—
Despair and dark and death a world a hearse

. . .the dancing night upon the corpse of day
the fall of all the everlasting curse

About J.B. Toner

J.B. Toner studied Literature at Thomas More College and holds a black belt in Ohana Kilohana Kenpo-Jujitsu. He has published two novels, *Whisper Music* and *The Shoreless Sea*, and many shorter works. Toner lives and works in Massachusetts with his beautiful wife and their beloved daughters. Twitter: jbtonerz

GHOST SHIP

Mizzen mast rimed with salt spray
Tattered sails flap like Death's shroud
As the vessel ploughs midnight seas
A skeleton crew aboard
A horror in the hold
Satan at the wheel
Seeking souls on storm-swept seas
To see it is to die
Turn your face from storm-lashed horizon
To see it is to die

VACANT POSSESSION

Wizard sends soul soaring
Swimming through starry vistas
Far from mortal world
And strange.
Silvery thread guides the way
Homeward-bound through the starry seas
Returning to their mortal shell
Occupied.
Staring at them with distorted features
Demon laughs at their discomfort
Snaps silver string, banishes them, gains
Vacant possession.

LAMIA

As her tail coils about my body
So desire coils about my heart
It may be foolishness to love her
Yet I know we can never part
Perhaps I delude myself
That something such as she can feel

The sensation of selfless love
Yet I am certain our love is real
So, I slip willingly into her arms
Accept her proffered embrace
Whether a moment or a lifetime
It is her that I shall face

THE GHOST AND THE TREASURE

Once a year
A spirit appears above its burial mound
Legend says
The ghost knows the location of a treasure
If only
Someone dares to enquire of it
One day
A warrior boldly approaches the mound
He waits
As darkness falls to blacken the scene
It appears
He steps forward to question it
It speaks
He is found dead the next day

About D. J. Tyrer

D. J. Tyrer is the person behind *Atlantean Publishing*, was placed second in the 2015 Data Dump Award for Genre Poetry, and has been published in *The Rhysling Anthology 2016*, issues of *Cyaegha*, *Frostfire Worlds*, *The Horrorzine*, *Illumen*, *Outposts of Beyond*, *Scifaikuest*, *Sirens Call*, *Star*Line*, *Tigershark* and *The Yellow Zine*, and online at *Grievous Angel*, *Lonesome October*, and *Three Drops from a Cauldron*, as well as releasing several chapbooks, such as *The Tears of Lot-49*. The echapbook *One Vision* is available from Tigershark

You can find D. J. at https://djtyrer.blogspot.co.uk/

EARTH-IN-SPIN

I dozed late into the evening swirl—
The sun a blue-nosed monkey,
Face colors sashayed into yellows and orange/blue bloom,
The colors of somber chagrin...
The glistening rivers ran polluted
Along the steel vectors heading west—
Rivers of dark vast, vapid pulchritude—
Heading west to the sliding of,
Every man's integral health—
As earth's status turns on a dime...
As rivers burn sickly wide and high—
Will things recompense
Beyond the hollow melancholy,
Of a ghostly, strung-out, planet and flaccid mumbling star?

THE DEAF

The *heaviest* darkness,
We can see...
Is that we can't *envision*—
It hides, draws surreptitious kinks
In the breathless, dark air—
That—as in wily night bogs,
Engulfs the turbulence of the unholy,
Seeping world,
The dry *undertow,* severed land regions
Of the deepest *grit,*
Where man thinks of towers of higher narratives—
Sonic *booms* embellishing nightfall—
'Booming pranks' tethered to a timeless moon...
Scattering through a thousand-dark hallways,
'Vacuous,' untethered *darkness*—
Appraised in a mad, horn lock,
Before the creeping shafts of a rising day...

THE KISS

She puffed up, muted, soiled clouds at a sneering, hazardous moon,
Thirsting darkly, huffing the twisting black dirt path—
So deliberately moon-bone-cleaned—
Following the dangerous, ghastly, mournful, exquisite, sweet,
Subtly wafting, eidolon tainted scent,
Of his wicked, phantasmagorical pores—
For she loved him too much to let him go—
Even though she must pass this vast, serpentine, bone-silver quarry
Where the haunted, blackened, morning scorpion winds blow—

She knew she must swiftly arrive at the site of red-halos—
The place where monstrously golden, billowing-nosed, pig-bulls,
Trample all who enter without an empty, shivering-stone mourning
core—

Ahead she found the empyrean rings of wanton glory—
She stood in make shift peace before the
Thousand white colossal pillars, under red-rings, of the night—
And stood in make shift peace before
The titans of the Godless, hideous night—

And made her peace with him—
Her boy who, while in a cycloned dominion of the freest,
Jagged, fiend-like, madfest—
Retired several, grim, rounds at his blackened, bloodied, once
festive,
Restaurant crowd—

He was there, down inside this scoop of hell, this silver
Quarry, she knew—
Eying her upwards, as only a terrible conscience will do—

She kissed the wind-chilled air in a grafted, determined itinerant
moan;
Hoping for the ravenous hour her own impassioned soul would
Deliriously alight at his home—

No reply—only the wintry zenith of hell's black still—

She kissed again, aiming closer to his scoped core—
Dropped to the path, in blanching moans, the urging, throbbing
Muscle, rubbing rabid against the dirt-path floor—

Sitting up, she saw through bleary eyes, everlasting wings,
Darker than the hour of their plotting, sick-bellied sin,
Emptying outward like ghoulish kites—

He dropped from his transient height on the mounds of gravel—
All the while her feeling inside the virile scent,
Of his, too effortless, and empty, redolent kiss—

As he perambulated in orbit about the quarry for a while,
Then dropped swiftly inkwell deep into a blind-spot, now a blatant
hole—
Down, deeper than all the severely cut quarry—
His forlorn spirit, arced, then plunged straight into hell.

*About **Mark Powers***

Mark Powers, 66, has been formerly trained in the art and craft of literature since he was 22, when he took his first class in fiction writing at the University of Illinois at Chicago Circle Campus. The class, taught by author James Park Sloan (National Book Award nominee for his novel The Last Cold War Cowboy), so inspired him to want to become a fiction writer that he enrolled as an English major the following fall quarter at this university, and thereby received his B.A. in English there.

He's worked at various labor jobs, and a circulation and writing position for a trade magazine at Putman Publishing Company; and as a reporter for two local newspapers. At one paper he interviewed master crime writer, Eugene Izzi, who so strongly liked this feature story, that he urged Mark to finish a short story. Mark then submitted it to the horror author Mort Castle (three-time Bram Stoker Award winner) to critique, which led Mr. Castle to become his mentor.

Mark thrived under Mort Castle's tutelage, having poetry accepted in *The Oyez Review, Space and Time*, and the *Riverside Quarterly.* His work has also appeared in anthologies and comic books.

OCEAN

the ocean is a profound mystery
deep and billowing with much history

the dead rise from fathoms—deep, ocean floors
as if a synchronized signal sounded
currents move wildly with extra vigor
as silent seas give up their soaking dead
bobbing with no ability to swim
waiting for the tide to travel to food
with the brine, some make it to the shoreline
oceans yet latch on to the passing boats
some are caught by unsuspecting fishing nets
there are many terrors riding the seas

the ocean is a profound mystery
populated by death and the undead

MOONWALKERS

time for discoveries in space ended
when a discovery found us instead

it was supposed to help us in the move
from terrestrial earth into the stars

that magic little pill, that miracle
how could spacemen even see it coming

pill's effect reached pandemic proportions
infected earth could not reverse its course

contamination, impossible thought
communication, puzzling at best

left on the moon, safest place at the time
until the oxygen and food ran out

the age of all space traveling glimmer
it was glorious for a short moment

SPRING

spring, a time for re-growing and flowers
budding like the blossoms of coming warmth
are the extremities reaching for me
through the four-inch by four-inch wire squares
of the vast fence line of a former farm
stretching as if to touch my inner soul

spring, a time for brand new relationships
to enrapture the next humanity
grabbing as if to grasp understanding
tugging as if to tear away this reality
taking whatever is left fresh in me
gurgling not for air but from eating

spring, a time of continued vigilance
springing into whatever hell this is

QUESTIONS

you probably have a lot of questions
on how I ramble about the undead

well maybe I am one? or maybe not?
does it matter? do I have to be one
in order to write about the zombies?
look here, writers are always at writing
about living in just a certain way
about things we don't really understand
like why zombies are much better lovers
once going, there's no desire to stop
promise them a choice, fresh piece of your ex

and they will have your piece in fresh order
no better way to hide all those bodies
than to eat them in case there are questions

About Juan Perez

Juan Manuel Pérez, a Mexican-American poet of indigenous descent and a Poet Laureate for Corpus Christi, Texas (2019-2020), is the author of several books of poetry including *Screw the Wall! and Other Brown People Poems* (FlowerSong Books, 2020). The award-winning poet, history teacher, and Pushcart Nominee, is also a member of the Horror Writers Association, the Science Fiction Poetry Association, and the Military Writers Society of America. Juan worships his Creator and chases *chupacabras* in the South Texas Coastal Bend Area.

.

POETRY BY NORBERT HIRSCHHORN

TAGINE

Dusty lanes, flies, beggars and touts,
colored costumes, smells of henna and sweat,
mournful sounds of an oud from an upper floor—

our group of friends on holiday
in a postcard North African town,
indulging orientalist reveries.

Everyone off to the souk to shop but me,
to drink over-sweet tea at carpet stalls, breathe
in spices—cumin, cloves, nutmeg, cardamom—

haggle over pennies, though we stay
at a posh hotel. My task: to trek
into Old Town, bring back lunch for all—

my hotel room key on a pewtered
crescent ring firmly in hand
(9-11-something-something).

At a food stall I order couscous,
tajine, salads, fruits—go to the cashier
and pay; yet on reflection, maybe

not enough, so—leaving my package,
I return, but now the stall is far away,
through a maze of alleys; I have to run,

barefoot, over cobble-stones. Too late! Shut tight.
Breathless, back to the till, but what I've bought
is gone, and no one seems to know or care.

I shamble back to the hotel, search for my room,
but the sections all shuffled, 13-somethings

177

next to 5-somethings,9-somethings out of sequence—

a cleaner tries to help—it's just been refurbished, Sidi,
yes, a mess, try the front desk. There, a clutch of *shebabs*
in tight jeans and tees, smoking, grinning,

all pretty funny—hee, silly old tourist,
can't speak the language, lost—send me
to a back office where a kindly man

retrieves floor plans from a stack of dusty folios
and after near-sighted perusal says sadly:
9-11-something-something—despite the key in my hand—

doesn't exist, not since.

FALSE

He came under false pretenses
And left under false colors.

I suspected him to be false
When his pants revealed a false bottom.

He spoke in a falsetto,
Always telling falsehoods.

I tried to keep him with money,
A false economy. Between us, a false start.

When he left at false dawn,
He promised to return. False alarm.

The worst part was when he left
His false teeth behind.

GHOSTORIES

We sat by the fireplace one Halloween

trying to scare ourselves with out-of-body
tales and ghost stories.

My neighbor in the Victorian said its builder
was a retired whaler with a stump for a leg,
and on stormy nights he hears a *thump*,

thump on the back stairs. Another told
how she once felt a tearing, a ripping,
across her belly, like when you peel

an infected scab away from flesh,
that screeching pain; and later the phone
rang, her son, stabbed in a park—

alive! thank God. My turn came around.
I said how dull I felt. I had nothing
of that sort to tell, but I lied....

Two days after my mother died, I saw her
at the foot of my bed in perfect silhouette.
I remember how my voice came out too small,

too high—"Ma? Ma?"—and it said nothing,
nothing. It just stood there. And hated me.

About Norbert Hirschhorn

Norbert Hirschhorn is a public health physician, commended by
President Bill Clinton as an "American Health Hero," and proud to
follow in the tradition of physician-poets. He lives in Minneapolis,
Minnesota. He has published six collections, the most recent a
bilingual Arabic-English co-translation with Syrian physician-poet
Fouad M. Fouad, *Once Upon a Time in Aleppo*, of the latter's poems
(Hippocrates Press).

See his website, www.bertzpoet.com.

POETRY BY JUDSON MICHAEL AGLA

FOOTPRINTS

I've been following the beast for days
Armed with vanishing politics and torn flags
I've got a can of gasoline and my monkey has the matches
Ever since the war ended, I've been delusional; it's the clearest I've
ever felt and aside from walking into random government
buildings…screaming…it's been quite beneficial

The footprints were getting fresher; I was close on its tail, I could
smell it, a stench of death, lavender and gunpowder
They burned the books in the name of god, they burned the witches
because they could, they burned the hopes that the new children
would learn to burn
The castles offered little history and even less poetry, the rivers
shone with glistening rainbows of oil, and garbage filled the banks,
rat heaven. The corpses piled so high children used them as forts
playing war

Me and my monkey found the fresh feces of the beast, it was here, I
could hear the terra crackle under its feet, then its eyes, two bright
yellow glowing eyes and fangs, white, shinning in the moonlight
I won't kill for those greedy bastards anymore, I won't plant the
seeds of ignorance and I won't slaughter for anyone

Death comes as a cool breeze, a friendly tap on the shoulder, a black
raven watching, waiting for its meal.

MY ENEMY IS RESTING

I can hear breathing like calm ocean waves
Claws and teeth in atrophy somewhere close
One day I'll build that Treehouse
A place where our thoughts won't betray us
My enemy is waking
I hear labored breathing and claws digging through dirt and stone

You died before you became famous
Your absence born a silent revolution like those that they make
documentaries about
I'll have to start moving now
I am the hunted and my history will be painted black like coal
My enemy is here

THE VINES HAVE STOPPED CREEPING

The vines have stopped creeping, the walls won't have them, and
they bleed on the dead flowers that have lost their keeper, dust and
rust are all that remains in this garden. I'd give my bones, my flesh
and my crippled mind, just to see a single bud, a sparkle of color, but
the bolt already flew and there are no other offerings because the
vines have stopped creeping.

About Judson Michael Agla

Judson Michael Agla is an artist working in a lot of different
mediums, like painting, drawing, sculpture, and writing in both
poetry and flash fiction. His work has always leaned towards the
macabre, and he's been able to find a place for his voice in the
horror genre.

POETRY BY DAVID M. HOENIG

GRAVEYARD

In still, morbid corners,
cobweb memories cluster thicker than pain;
fragments of yesterday molder,
neglected.

Amidst the clutter,
half-formed, half-mad ideas lie decomposing,
no fit foundation for the morrow.

These are my unshriven dead,
which haunt of a night,
of a day,
never content to rest
in pieces.

REVELATIONS

Lights are kept bright in the house
where that which would kill you is excised,
cauterized,
exorcised.

Horologists cry the hours of lives
down painted halls,
stalking painted walls,
exquisite calculations totaling exactly
the sum of one's scars.

Supplicants come to the house
shrouded in mysteries of esoteric arithmetic,
dreading the moment
when the tallies do, finally, add together,
in case the balance is wanting.

BECAUSE YOUR KISS/HEALS BREAKS

You almost make me want to rethink flaws
because
you glued back the broken pieces for
your
fractured self with gold, as though the remiss
kiss
of self-pitying bristles somehow made precious the fixes.
Is
that your pithy little secret? Conclusion forgone
on
some regrets checklist? The kind of huge lie
my
anxiety would anxiously tell, yet my self-worth resist?
List
for me where you got the metal, the brush, the prophetic vision from
above
of
how pleasing the final form would look, and ensue my own ta-da!
The
conceit has its appeal. Surely I, too, would be blessed
best
seeing scars of my flaws transformed to art, and thus lessen the
stings
things
I wish I'd handled better might leave etched on too-thin skin.
In
sadness, I think I'll not make so pretty a repair as you, of my paring
knife
life.

About David M. Hoenig

David M. Hoenig is a multiclass surgeon/writer with the "time management" feat. He's had stories published with *GrimDark Magazine, Flame Tree Publishing, Cast of Wonders*, and others. He has published a novel-told-through-surreal-verse-and-art with Oscillate Wildly Press, called *Queen to His King*. He is editing his first novel (sci fi), at somewhat slower than the speed of light. He's also a soul-gem carrying member of the HWA.

His website: https://davidmhoenig.wordpress.com/about/

"The Shuar in the World of Arutam" by Bobby Cooper

ABOUT THE ARTISTS

Front cover: Jean Sarnay

Jean Sarnay is also known as PalmerEldritch135 on Deviant Art. He is a French hobbyist/traditional artist living in Nantes.

He is interested in horror/macabre and science fiction topics and he tries to tell a story with each drawing. He mostly uses a black and white inking style.

His favorite artists are H.R. Giger, Gustave Doré and M.C. Esher. His favorite writers are P.K. Dick, H.P. Lovecraft and Georges Orwell.

You can visit Jean's art gallery here:
https://www.deviantart.com/palmereldritch135

Marije Berting

Marije Berting lives in Germany with her partner. She has two daughters, two grandsons and two cats. In the past she worked at Tilburg University, Department of Medical and Clinical Psychology. Since she is now retired, she divides her time between her family, gardening and creating fractals.

She was always interested in fractal images. On Deviantart, she saw the work of other artists, especially fractal art. She started to download software applications for creating fractal images and followed tutorials. The results made her decide to go on with it. She has been a deviant for five years.

Marije is creating fractals and fractal manipulations on a daily basis. Most of the time she uses Mandelbulb 3D (MB3D). Mandelbulb 3D is a free software application created for 3D fractal imaging. MB3D formulates dozens of nonlinear equations into an amazing range of fractal objects. The 3D rendering environment includes lighting,

186

color, specularity, depth-of-field, shadow- and glow-effects; allowing the user fine control over the imaging effects.

With Pixelmator, an image editor for the iMac, she often combines the beauty from MB3D fractal images and the images of natural objects and subjects. Adding a real element to a fractal is a technique that gives the viewer a non-fractal element to visually latch on to. It instantly grounds the fractal image in the familiar and usually gives the viewer a sense of scale. The fractal image isn't just a cool, geometric pattern or abstract, it contains a recognizable element.

You can see more of her Marije's work here:
https://www.deviantart.com/marijeberting

Maksim Alimetov

Maksim Alimetov is an artist, born in Bishkek, Kyrgyzstan in 1991. At age three, he moved to Volgograd in Russia, where he graduated from a vocational school. He has lived and worked in St. Petersburg since 2017.

Maksim is self-taught, and his art is inspired by childhood memories, nature, and subconscious images. The driving force of his art is a feeling of nostalgia, which is achieved by the play of light and shadow, and soft, half-crushed pencil strokes.

To learn more about Maksim, please go here:
https://www.deviantart.com/maxalimetov/gallery

Adam Plant

Adam Plant may seem like yer typical ugly art guy who does typical ugly art but this simply isn't true... he also has a dirty little moustache (so that's gotta mean something, right?)

Since 2015, Adam has worked as a multimedia artist, filmmaker, music composer, discount-author, and founder of the record label EEZY SLEEZ. Adam's work is heavily inspired by a morbid appreciation for his childhood nostalgia, as well as his scathing apathy for the modern digitalized world. Both his art and film has been showcased around the globe where it was described as "a feast for the senses followed by conceptual food poisoning."

All of Adam's indecency can be found here:
https://www.lonelyaroma.com/artwork

Bobby Cooper

Bobby Cooper has had many adventures. He lived in a tribe in the Amazon for 10 years, and walked the Camino de Santiago in Spain. He's lived in caves and other holes in the wall for years. He has walked an innumerable amount of kilometers with a backpack and 50 dollars in his wallet in foreign countries, and almost died twice, contracting hepatitis, dysentery, and some other illnesses along the way. He's been shot and stabbed, and robbed, which is a small part of the adventure, too. He prefers the 4th World (the world where indigenous peoples live) as his home most of the time, either in the jungle with his native kids or, meeting new cultures.

Bobby lives his artwork and never loses contact with it. At age 54, he's tasted the cold sky and the hot stars, and reached inside himself to take lonely walks along the shores of his confusions and pains, delights and loves. That way we unfold, to wake up to being a Human that is recognizing its Being part: that which is covered by too much extreme and imbalance in the world, by an industrial civilization choking on itself.

His work is a huge mix of experiences and struggles, mostly internal, with the loving influence of the struggles and lifeways of indigenous peoples, and that of his children and his father specifically.

He uses black paper with colored pencil. The black paper entertains an opposite to the common white paper. It's like bringing a light into the dark, rather than shadow into the light. The black paper is a mysterious cave, a haunted house, a killer clown under the bed, a flower discovered while walking at night, or a thick arm of stars in the sky.

Bobby sells his artwork on Redbubble as BCooperArt, an online marketplace for print-on-demand products based on user-submitted artwork.

You can see more of his art here:
https://www.redbubble.com/people/bcooperart/shop

MORE FROM
THE HORROR ZINE BOOKS

The Horror Zine Books offers

THE BEST OF THE HORROR ZINE:
The Early Years

Really the best! Available now.

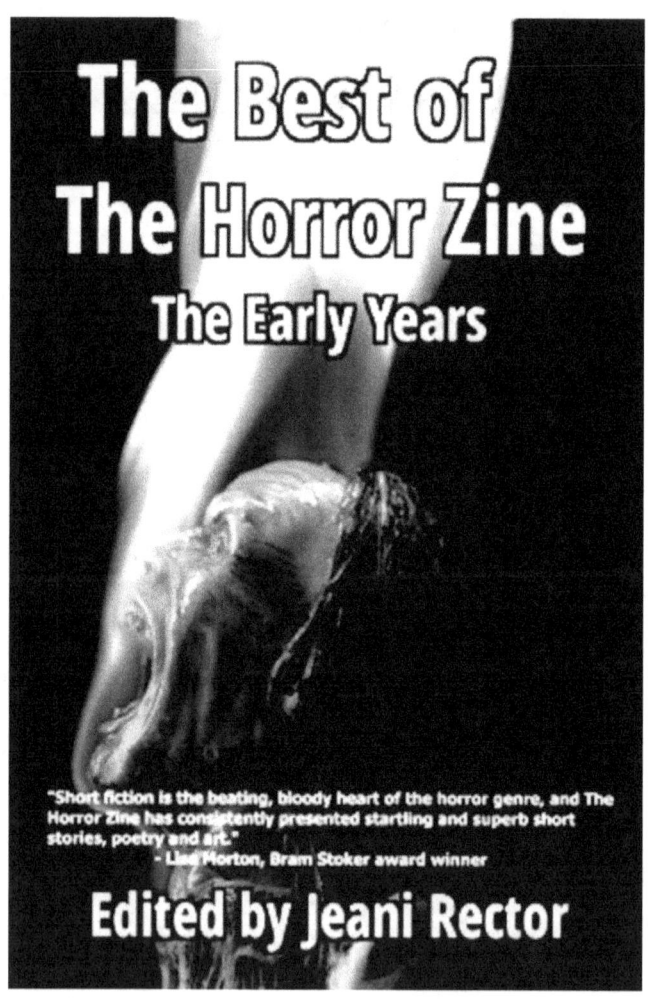

THE BEST OF THE HORROR ZINE: THE EARLY YEARS

Many anthologies have come out of The Horror Zine, but none like this! Here you will find a compilation of the very best from the first four anthologies, hand-chosen by editor Jeani Rector: AND NOW THE NIGHTMARE BEGINS, TWICE THE TERROR, WHAT FEARS BECOME and A FEAST OF FRIGHTS. Some of The Horror Zine's early years have been lost in time...until now. Featuring dark fantasy, mystery, pure suspense and classic horror, THE BEST OF THE HORROR ZINE: THE EARLY YEARS is relentless in its approach to basic fears and has twisted, unexpected endings.

THE BEST OF THE HORROR ZINE: THE EARLY YEARS contains fiction from such renowned masters of the macabre as Bentley Little, Joe R. Lansdale, Elizabeth Massie, Scott Nicholson, Joe McKinney, Susie Moloney, Jeff Strand, Simon Clark, Taylor Grant and Eric J. Guignard. This book also contains the very best of emerging writers, poets, and artists from the award-winning, long-running ezine: The Horror Zine.

"Short fiction is the beating, bloody heart of the horror genre, and The Horror Zine has consistently presented startling and superb short stories, poetry and art. This fine anthology not only collects work from established pros like Joe R. Lansdale, Elizabeth Massie, Scott Nicholson, Bentley Little, Jeff Strand, and Joe McKinney, but it also presents dark visions from the new voices that you'll be talking about in years to come." – Lisa Morton, multiple Bram Stoker Award-winning author and co-editor of HALLOWS' EVE

ALSO FROM THE HORROR ZINE BOOKS
(Published by Hellbound Books)

THE HORROR ZINE'S BOOK OF GHOST STORIES

The Horror Zine's Book of Ghost Stories is delighted to present to you original, never before seen, spine-tingling tales from Bentley Little, Joe R. Lansdale, Elizabeth Massie, Graham Masterton with Dawn G. Harris, Tim Waggoner, and the very best up and coming writers in the genre. Includes a foreword by Lisa Morton.

Only $13.99 paperback and $3.99 Kindle.

See the praise for this exciting book:

"This collection of ghost stories is fresh, varied, and entertaining. Perfect company for long a winter's night." – Owen King, co-author of *Sleeping Beauties*

"An incredibly creepy collection of stories of the recently and not so recently dead, written by some of the finest writers in horror. I suggest that when reading, do so in the daylight, because reading these at night will only make you more aware of your own, unempty house." – Susie Moloney, author of *The Dwelling* and *The Thirteen*

"Gruesome, eerie, horrific, sometimes uplifting; this is a terrific selection of ghost stories that satisfy the soul—they chill the blood, too." – Simon Clark, author of *Whitby Vampyrrhic*

"Looking for a perfect evening? Spend the night hunkered down in your favorite chair with only a reading light on, and dive into *The Horror Zine's Book of Ghost Stories*. Forget sleep, these tales will keep you enthralled till daybreak." – Tony Tremblay, author of *The Moore House*

"Nobody keeps the supernatural alive like The Horror Zine." – Scott Nicholson, author of *The Red Church*

CHAPTER FOUR

A dying town

SHORTCUT, UTAH was a sleepy little resort town a little west of the Wyoming border and only a few miles south of the Idaho line. The small town was tucked into the side of the mountain a few miles below a good-sized lake the town stocked with new fish each year. Fishermen came from as far away as the east coast to fish the lake during the summer, along with hunting deer and elk during the fall and winter months.

Just a short drive east from the lake was a good-sized log-pole lodge resort area, which provided food and rooms for the weary fishermen and hunters who came there year after year to fish and hunt. In the evening they would sit around and drink and tell whoppers about the one that got away, or about being chased by a bear and narrowly escaping with their life.

Because of the popularity of the lake and the lodge, the town of Shortcut thrived and enjoyed prosperity for a great many years.

US Highway 15 was the main highway going north out of Salt Lake City and ran right through the town of Shortcut, bringing both tourists and travelers, which accounted for another part of the town's income. But, when push came to shove, the town of Shortcut thrived mainly on the money brought in by the hunting and fishing business.

Things had gone well for the town until two years ago when everything changed. The manager of the lodge, a man the city council thought was ideal for the job, ran off with that year's income, along with a comely waitress who made the patrons smile at her with lust in their eyes.

Before they disappeared, for some unknown reason, the man had made sure the place was left in less than favorable condition. A lot of the furniture had been dragged out into the yard and burned, along with appliances and other things like pictures and such. Most of the windows were broken and there was structural damage.

It was rumored the comely waitress had a difference of agreement with one of the town councilmen about supposed favors rendered and was about to be let go, but no one was admitting anything for fear of self-incrimination.

The estimate to put the lodge back into useable condition was over one hundred and forty thousand dollars, which included restocking the lake with fish and cleaning up the area. The rickety old bridge leading up to the lake and lodge was also in bad need of repairs, but hadn't been included in the

This is a white man's world! And will be again when the new order is in place!"

His head was beginning to hurt and he was trembling as he went to the bedside table and poured himself a drink of liquor from the jug of moonshine one of his men had given him. Within minutes, the homemade liquor rushed throughout his entire body. His throbbing headache began to dissipate and his nerves began to relax.

He wouldn't have to wait much longer before the world would be clean again, he thought as he poured himself a second glass of the soothing liquid.

CHAPTER TWO
Relax, we have security

ALONG WITH THE PRESIDENT, Vice President, eight hopeful candidates, several governors, including the governor of Utah, senators, congressmen, lobbyists from at least a dozen large corporations, along with any other person who could afford the thousand dollar a plate dinner would be in the Salt Lake City Convention Center to cheer on and vote for his or her candidate; and in some cases, vote for the one he or she was being paid to vote for. No one said the system was perfect.

More than fifteen hundred tickets had been sold so far and the list was growing, which meant the leaders of our nation would be grouped together under a single roof.

Security people were everywhere, checking people's identifications, causing turmoil because the left hand didn't know what the right hand was doing. Men in black suits from the federal government wouldn't lower themselves to work side by side with the local authorities, let alone co-operate with them. The local men were hostile toward the federal agents and the

agents retaliated by letting it be known through the news media and verbally that the locals were not wanted, nor were they needed. They told the press that they found them to be inefficient and in the way most of the time.

It was like a three ring circus with all the acts going on at the same time without a ringleader. Camera crews, lighting and sound crews, electricians, all trying to set up and get ready for this most important event with both local and federal people slowing them down. They were stopped to check their badges and bombarded with questions by both, local and federal people. Even the cleaning people were stopped and harassed - mop buckets were checked, passes were examined, along with being interrogated like criminals.

One local security agent, a young man on his first assignment, was not only checking every bucket, broom and mop, but also patting down every person who came within his reach, searching for hidden weapons that he was sure he would find.

His supervisor, a man who was about to retire from the firm providing security for this event, shook his head from side to side. From a short distance away, he watched as the young security officer patted down a pretty girl of no more than eighteen. She stood ramrod still, gritting her teeth while the young man checked places she'd rather not be checked. This was her first day on the job and she wasn't sure how to react, so she said nothing, hoping it would be over soon.

The supervisor walked over and thumped the young security guard on the back of his head with his middle finger, and when the young man swung around with a scowl on his face, the supervisor curled his finger and said, "Come with me."

To the young lady, the supervisor smiled and said, "You're free to go on with your duties, and I hope you won't be bothered again."

The soon to be retired supervisor turned and walked toward one of the out of the way exits, while the young guard trailed a few feet behind, pleading his case.

"I was just doing my job. The President of the United States will be here plus all those other officials. We can't take any chances."

"First day, is it?" the supervisor asked.

"Yeah, but what's that got to do with it. Look, I've watched enough television to know the score. Anybody could be an assassin. I remember, once on this episode of. . ."

That's as far as the young man got before the supervisor stopped, turned around, and pinched the young man's lips together, making a be-quiet sign with his other hand.

By now, they had reached the lesser-used exit. The supervisor took the young man by the shoulders and stood him next to the entryway. "Now, listen to me and listen to me good, because I'm only going to say this once. You stand right here in this spot and as people come and go, you check badges only. No patting down, no harassing. . . You got that?"

The young man nodded his head yes, and said, "But. . ."

"No buts," the supervisor said and gave the young man a look that told him the discussion was over. "If you think someone looks suspicious, you come and tell me; no acting on your own, you got that? This isn't open for discussion."

Again the young man nodded his head.

The supervisor turned and started to walk away, then stopped and said over his shoulder. "And don't come running to me without positive proof. Your job depends on it. Let the federal people handle it. That's why they get the big bucks. You get my drift?"

"You just want me to just check badges."

The supervisor walked away shaking his head. Retirement couldn't come fast enough. He found a chair and sat down to rest his aching feet. While his eyes wandered around the room, he pulled a large cigar out of his inner jacket pocket and stuck it in his mouth. He'd stopped smoking two years ago, but he still liked to chew on them.

CHAPTER THREE

And so it began

IN THE DIM LIGHT OF DUSK, three men, dressed in black military uniforms covered by camouflage ponchos, left the main lodge house with their heads bent low to keep the rain out of their eyes. The men trudged through the downpour toward a large barn some three hundred feet to the north. They sloshed through what looked to be a shallow lake covering the entire area; their boots sinking into water well over ankle deep until they reached the barn, which sat on a slight rise just above the water line.

As they entered the darkened building, one of the three men stepped to the side and flipped a switch to the 'on' position. A lone bulb illuminated a black van sitting just inside the double doors. One of the men opened the rear doors of the van and climbed inside, leaving the doors open. The third man climbed behind the wheel of the van and started the engine.

The man who had turned on the light walked over to a table and gently lifted a small crate into his hands, then walked

to the open rear doors of the van and handed it to the man inside. The man took the crate and placed it in a sling suspended from the ceiling of the van. NITROGLYCERIN was stenciled on the side of the crate.

After handing over the small crate, the man closed the rear doors then walked to the driver's side of the van and motioned for the driver to roll down his window. By then, the man in the back had climbed into the passenger's seat.

"You drive real careful like," the man standing next to the van said. "We got us some politicians to send to hell and the Captain don't want any slip-ups."

The driver, a man with a chiseled face, a long pointy nose and the unlit stub of a cigar sticking out of the side of his mouth, grinned and said, "Now don't you be worrying none, Bull. By this time tomorrow, this country won't have no president any more, or any of them other big shot politicians." He raised his hands in the air and said, "Ka-boom!"

The man in the passenger seat leaned toward the driver and said, "It'll be just like the Captain said, time to wash this country clean of them heathen sons ah bitches so's we can start over like it shoulda been in the first place; with an all-white race."

The man standing next to the van pointed his thumb in the air as the driver rolled up the window and put the vehicle in reverse and backed out of the barn.

After putting the van in the forward gear, the chiseled faced man eased the van slowly through the water in the direction of where the road should be.

The man left behind closed the barn doors and then turned and sloshed his way back to the lodge to await the news of their victory. For the next several hours, he would relax on his bed with his Penthouse magazine while nursing the jug of rotgut he had hidden in his room.

As the man entered the lodge, lightning struck somewhere nearby. The sky lit up enough to see a lone figure standing at a second story window, the curtain drawn back. The man was dressed in a Nazi officer's uniform. He observed the black van as it turned onto the road and disappeared down the mountain: destination, Salt Lake City, Utah. When the van disappeared, Adolph Hemmlick smiled and released the curtain. "And so it begins," he said to himself as he checked his watch.

Once out into the world, for reasons he didn't understand, Zebedia changed his name to Adolph Hemmlick. The name came to him in a dream, and Zebedia believed in the power of dreams.

Shortly thereafter, he joined the Klu Klux Klan and quickly rose to a somewhat lower level leadership position, but wasn't happy with his rank or the Klan; they were too limited in their thinking – they had no visions of the future on the grand scale like he did.

The leaders of the Klan were not thrilled with him either. Adolph seemed to have a strong affection for young girls and boys of any race. Short, fat, tall, skinny, pretty or ugly, he didn't care. The only thing that mattered was for them to be young, and willing.

It didn't take long for the Klan to realize that, Zebedia or Adolph, or whomever he called himself, was not Klan material.

By the time he was asked to leave, Adolph didn't much care. He was ready to move on and try something new – something more to his way of thinking.

After attending a few meetings with a group who called themselves Skinheads, Adolph was introduced to a book entitled, Mein Kampf. The author was a man by the name of Adolph Hitler. Mein Kampf was their bible and soon became a prized treasure of his.

4

government as the people knew it. For all intense purposes, the United States would no longer exist.

Shortly thereafter, the new order would come into power. The extermination or deportation of all blacks, Jews, American Indians, or any other persons outside their organization would become the law of the land. These non-pure would have a choice, leave the United States and never return; or, face a firing squad or die at the end of a hangman's noose. The choice would be theirs.

The leader of this minuscule guerilla army, a self-proclaimed Captain, was a man who could barely read or write above a sixth grade level, but seemingly had been born with an inbred leadership quality about him that his followers found mesmerizing.

Zebedia Budroe Palasco was born in the vilest part of the Okefoenokee Swamp to a man who made moonshine and hunted alligators for a living.

At the age of thirty, his father forced Zebedia, at gunpoint, to leave his home, such as it was.

Zebedia had been having sex with his twelve-year-old sister, who looked and acted like she was at least eighteen as she came crawling into his bed at night.

For the record, Zebedia's father was also having sex with the young lady and didn't like his son competing for her favors. It was and wasn't a close-knit family.

estimate. The bridge needed to be torn down and a new bridge built. And it would be, all in good time, the newspaper article said.

For the past two years, the people of Shortcut had been putting aside what little money they could each month and what work that had been done was done by doing the labor themselves.

Without the lodge or the lake, the town was slowly dying because of the lack of income. Several months would go by without any work being done out at the lake or the lodge because there was no money to purchase the needed supplies.

In the meantime, with no income and without enough money to make the needed repairs or restock the lake, the lodge sat deserted and was quickly beginning to look like a place inhabited by only ghosts and spiders.

The truth of the matter was, no one had been near the place in several months, which accounted for the fact that they had absolutely no idea of what was going on up there - at least not yet. But that would soon change, and not to their liking.

Several businesses in Shortcut had depended solely on the revenue the hunting and fishing business brought in, but when that income dried up so did their livelihood.

As it turned out, the buildings were owned by the city so all the business owners had to do was cancel their lease and walk away, leaving the town with a lot of vacant buildings and even less income.

Little by little the town was decreasing in population. If something didn't change soon, Shortcut, Utah would become nothing more than a wide spot on the map. The only business that would possibly survive would be the four-pump gas station at the Redwood Restaurant and Bar, which sat alongside the highway.

Truck drivers and tourists had been stopping at the Redwood for years. The food was good and the gas cut rate. The owner of the Redwood had decided years ago that he liked selling his gas at a decent price. Not only did he wind up getting most of the trucking trade that traveled up and down the highway, the locals and tourist travelers also brought in their trade. When travelers stopped for gas, they usually went inside and had something to eat. This was mainly because of a scheme he'd come up with.

After his first year in business the owner of the Redwood came up with a brilliant idea. He installed fans to blow the smell of bacon, hot cinnamon rolls, hamburgers and several other tantalizing smells in the direction of the gas pumps. When the travelers got a whiff of the wonderful aromas emanating from the restaurant, it was like they were hypnotized and followed the tantalizing smells straight to the waiting booths inside.

There was no doubt about it, Blaine Whifflemire just might be the only person in Shortcut who would stay in business and earn a decent living even if the rest of the town faded into the side of the mountain. While he might be able to stay in business, he wouldn't go unscathed. The hunting and fishing section along with the bait shop where he sold bait, hooks, poles, rifles, shotguns, ammunition and other supplies, would take a beating. But, being a man who looked ahead, he was ready. Souvenirs would replace the hunting and fishing equipment, although those things would still be available when needed.

For some time now, Rafe Talltree, a full blooded Shoshone Indian who lived up on the mountain, had been stocking a small area of the station with Indian relics he'd made, along with stuffed animal heads, tanned hides and other things like, bone-handled knives, which were selling almost as fast as Rafe could make them. Rafe did good work and because of that and his reasonable prices, travelers bought his goods, which made Blaine Whifflemill a happy man.

CHAPTER FIVE

The town drunk

THE STORM had not yet reached Shortcut so it was just another cool, balmy night. The sky was full of stars. The town was just about to drift off to sleep as it did most nights about this time – the people never realizing they would soon be waking up again and not due to the upcoming storm.

Shaun Tilford's jeep wrangler sat in the city parking lot across the street from the local liquor store and was the only vehicle in the parking lot at this time of night. Shaun, the town's leading jock and quarterback of the football team was trying to make out with his girlfriend Kristi Lange, the head cheerleader.

He kissed her on the neck and tried to put his hand inside her blouse, but she pushed him away and said, "Did you see that?"

Not relenting, he reached out again. "See what?"

Once again, she pushed his hand away. "The lightning up near the lake."

"No big deal," Shaun said. "A little storm, so what? It'll be cleared up by the time we go up there tomorrow."

Kristi turned and looked in the direction of the lake. "I don't know, it looks pretty bad," she said as Shaun slumped back into the driver's seat, feeling disgusted and dejected. He turned sideways and reached into the cooler sitting on the back floor and pulled out a can of beer – popped the can open and quickly sucked at the foam spilling out through the hole, then chugalugged the rest of the contents.

"Why do you drink so much?" Kristi asked, giving him a frown.

Shaun crushed the empty can and tossed it in the back. "What else is there to do in this graveyard town, except maybe. . ." he said, as he pulled her to him and tried to fondle her, again.

Once more, she pushed him away and said, "Don't, Shaun. Here comes Barney."

Shaun leaned back in his seat and slammed the heel of his hand against the steering wheel. "Prude."

"I am not! I just don't like being pawed at in front of people."

Barney Hopple was the town drunk, and for a gallon of cheap wine he could be talked into buying beer for the local teenagers, which was well known by the owner of the liquor store who turned a blind eye. After all, money was money and times were hard right now.

Sheriff Buford Tucker had warned Barney several times about buying alcohol for the kids, but when it came right down to it, the most he could do was put Barney in the cooler overnight. The city councilmen didn't like having to feed the town drunk. It put a strain on the already skimpy budget and they told the sheriff about their feelings on a regular basis. So, he never kept Barney in jail longer than he had to, to sober him up. Which didn't do any good because as soon as he got out, Barney Hopple would be back in his cups within a matter of a few hours.

Still brooding, Shaun jumped out and ran around to the back and opened the rear door of the jeep. As Barney walked up, Shaun took the case of beer from him and slid it into the back.

It was about this same time that Sheriff Tucker came within sight of the parking lot during his nightly cruise around town and saw Barney walk up to Shaun Tilford's jeep with a case of beer and a jug of wine. He slammed his fist against the dashboard and grumbled, "Dammit, Barney! How many times do I have to warn you about buying beer for these kids! Damn drunks, anyway!"

Sheriff Tucker was still half a block from the parking lot when he flipped the switch that turned on the flashing red lights atop his four-wheel-carryall and then turned on the siren that made loud whooping noises, while at the same time, pushing his foot down on the accelerator.

Both, Barney and Shaun jumped when they heard the whooping noise made by Sheriff Tucker's siren.

"Just what I need, Sheriff Tucker," Shaun said as he slammed the jeep's rear door, jumped back into the driver's seat and fired up the engine. With tires squealing and rubber smoking, he flipped a U-turn and raced out of the far side of the parking lot.

Sheriff Tucker turned into the parking lot in time to see Shaun's jeep roaring out the far exit. "That damn Tilford kid is goin' ta jail this time, father or no father," Tucker mumbled as he sped across the parking lot, siren blasting and lights flashing.

In a panic, Barney ran out in front of Sheriff Tucker's carryall and stopped dead in his tracks and stared directly into the blinding headlights. He stood there, his feet frozen to the pavement; terror in his eyes. What used to be his jug of wine, lay shattered into a hundred pieces at his feet. A large wet spot appeared on the front of Barney's pants. He closed his eyes and clinched his fists as he waited for what he was sure would be his last day on this earth.

Tucker smashed his foot down on the brake pedal. The carryall screeched to a halt just inches from the town drunk's trembling body.

Tucker threw the carryall into reverse and backed up far enough to go around Barney and the broken glass before putting the carryall back into forward gear. As he sped past, Sheriff Tucker yelled, "Go to the station and lock yourself in a cell!"

When Barney was sure the sheriff was gone, he opened his eyes and looked down at his feet. Red wine and tiny pieces of glass covered his feet and the surrounding area. Tears streamed down his cheeks at the sight as he reached into his back pocket and pulled out the small reserve bottle of wine he kept there for emergencies like this. He took a long drink before turning and heading off in the direction of the police station. He would have to finish the bottle before he got to the police station because he knew the sheriff would never let him keep it in his cell. They just didn't understand, he thought to himself as he reached the end of the parking lot and headed down the sidewalk.

Everyone in Shortcut knew the story behind Barney Hopple and felt sorry for him; along with turning a blind eye to his drinking. At one time Barney had been a successful businessman and an important part of the community. Hopples Hardware and Lumber Supply was the only store of its kind for more than forty miles and had been used by everyone in the county at one time or another. He not only gave the city a big discount on any and all materials they purchased, his generosity expanded to the other organizations in the area as well. Barney was a good man to deal with and everyone liked to go to his store.

Barney was always there, speaking to every customer who came through the door, and if you had the time, he always had a tall tale to tell, which drew a laugh or two. And in all the years he owned the store, he'd never told the same story twice – unless he was asked to.

But when his wife Ernestine died, so did Barney Hopple's world. He had been in love with her since they were in the first grade and she with him. They had spent their entire lives together. As far as Barney was concerned they may as well have cut his heart out of his chest and tossed it to a pack of hungry wolves. He felt there was nothing left to live for, but didn't have the courage to commit suicide. So it was not inconceivable that shortly after her passing, Barney sold his business to a company out of Salt Lake, then climbed into a bottle and had been there ever since. That had been nine long years ago and the town still tolerated him, even if he did get into trouble once in a while with the sheriff for buying beer for the kids.

Barney stumbled into a cell, leaving the door wide open and laid down on the bunk and thought about tomorrow. In the morning, he would wake up with a headache, pay the fine and if the sheriff was around, listen to him harp at him for the thousandth time about buying beer for the teenagers.

He would then stop by the restaurant and get one of their huge bacon and egg sandwiches and a large, black coffee, to go. Betsy Ryan always made the sandwich extra-large, just for him. She would give him a wink and tell him if he would stop his drinking; she would like to get to know him better. Barney would smile back at her and say, "Maybe, one of these days, Betsy. Maybe one of these days."

On the way home, he would force himself to eat the sandwich and drink the coffee. Even though he didn't feel hungry, he knew he had to eat something at least once a day. After a hot shower and clean clothes, he would walk over to the liquor store and purchase a bottle of wine and a loaf of day old bread. He liked to sit on the park bench and feed the birds while he sipped on his wine and slipped back to that place where he didn't have to think about his loneliness. He hoped the sheriff didn't catch the Tilford kid - the boy bought a lot of beer.

With the next day planned, Barney Hopple curled up on the cot and fell instantly into a dream where his beloved Ernestine was still alive and they were in a small boat, up at the lake. She was crocheting and singing while he fished.

CHAPTER SIX
The Old Bridge

THE BLACK VAN slowly approached the river bridge leading off the mountain. A short distance beyond the bridge the road would meet Highway 15 which would take them down through Shortcut, then on down to Salt Lake City.

As they crossed the rickety old bridge, both men looked down at the raging water flowing beneath and felt the bridge move. The two men held their breath as the ancient bridge creaked and swayed as the van inched its way across. When they reached the far side and were on solid ground again, they both gave a big sigh of relief.

Because of the storm, US Highway 15 was mostly deserted as the van made a left turn onto the highway and picked up speed. A short distance down the highway the man in the passenger seat pointed at a sign that read,

WELCOME TO SHORTCUT, UTAH –
THREE MILES AHEAD
POPULATION 2010
BEST HUNTING AND FISHING IN NORTHERN UTAH

The man in the passenger seat punched the driver lightly on the shoulder and said, "They should add, 'and the home of The New Beginnings Headquarters."

Both men laughed as the van sped down the highway, the glow of lights rising from the town in the distance. The man in the passenger seat reached down between his feet and retrieved a jug of moonshine.

CHAPTER SEVEN
Miss Amelia Gibbons

At the tender age of sixty-six, Miss Amelia Gibbons was still a strikingly attractive woman. She was a retired history teacher from one of the larger high schools in the Salt Lake City school system. Amelia had never been married, but even so, she had never lacked for male companionship. At one point during her last year as a teacher, Amelia Gibbons was suspected of having an affair on more than one occasion with at least two of her students - both at the same time; but that was never proven. Along with the boys, she denied the whole thing. Several members of the school board gave thanks when they heard she had put in for retirement.

Shortly after leaving the teaching profession, she moved to Shortcut to get away from her sorted past. But she was a woman who had needs and after three months of becoming a resident of Shortcut, it was whispered that men were seen leaving by way of her back door during the wee hours.

When she wasn't entertaining, which was mainly late at night, Amelia gave piano lessons and did a bit of tutoring to make a little extra money. But with all the gossiping lately, that was dropping off.

Amelia preferred to do her shopping during the evening when most people were at home so she didn't have to listen to the snide whispers behind her back, or run into any of the men supposedly seen sneaking out of her back door during the time when everyone else should have been asleep.

On this particular night, Amelia had just exited the all night drugstore with a paper sack in each arm. Strolling across the street to where her Volkswagen bus was parked, she was singing an old love song she liked, when she heard the police siren.

Looking up, she saw a pair of headlights coming toward her at a very high rate of speed. She desperately wanted to run but her legs wouldn't move. 'I've had an exciting life,' she thought as she stood waiting for the inevitable.

Shaun Tilford was looking in the rear view mirror to see if he could tell how close the sheriff was getting when Kristi yelled out, "Shaun! Look out!"

Shaun jerked his eyes away from the mirror and saw Miss Gibbons standing in the middle of the street.

Cranking the steering wheel to the left, he swerved the jeep around her, barely missing her van, then pulled the jeep back into his lane in time to make a high speed left turn at the next intersection.

Sheriff Tucker, in hot pursuit, saw Shaun's jeep swerve left and then saw Miss Gibbons standing in the middle of the street. He yanked his steering wheel to the right and drove up onto the sidewalk to keep from hitting her. As he roared past, he yelled out through the open window, "Get out of the street!"

Miss Gibbons, who by now was recovering from her near heart attack, shifted one of her sacks to her other arm and lifted her fist in the direction of the sheriff, with her middle finger standing straight up in the air.

"Go to hell!" she shouted. "And just for the record, I voted for Sam Pitts, not you, you redneck, son of. . ." She was so flustered she couldn't go on. Besides, his carryall was already turning the corner in pursuit of that young hellion, Shaun Tilford.

Oh, if she was only a few years younger, she thought with a wicked smile as visions of a young stallion paraded through her brain.

She loaded the sacks into her van, then climbed in behind the wheel and took a deep breath to calm her nerves. Right then and there she decided Shortcut was getting a wee bit too rowdy. Maybe she should scout around for a different town to live in - one where her past reputation was unknown. A fresh group of male suitors might be just the thing to lift her spirits;

possibly some younger men this time. Young men were so eager.

Satisfied with her decision, she started the engine and was about to pull away from the curb when a light tapping sounded on the curbside window. Turning her head, she saw the school principal, motioning for her to roll down the window.

A smile crossed her face as she reached over and lowered the window, just a smidgen. "Hello, Jim," she said with a come hither look. "Is there something I can do for you?"

CHAPTER EIGHT
Kristi's problem

"WHOA, AM I GREAT OR WHAT?" Shaun yelled, after he got the jeep under control and was racing down the street at twice the speed limit.

Once Kristi recovered from nearly being in a fatal accident, she reached across and slugged Shaun on the shoulder as hard as she could. "Not funny, Shaun! You almost ran over old lady Gibbons!"

"No way!" Shaun said as he leaned in her direction. "Give this stud-man a kiss!"

Kristi folded her arms across her chest and leaned back in her seat. She was still breathing hard and had a scowl on her face. "Take me home, now!" It was a demand, not a request.

Shaun shrugged his shoulders as he glanced into the rear view mirror and saw the flashing lights of Sheriff Tucker's carryall closing the distance in hot pursuit.

"As me lady wishes," Shaun said, pressing down on the accelerator to put more distance between him and the sheriff.

Shaun didn't care for the sheriff and his highhanded bullying ways and there was no doubt how the sheriff felt about him. But, with Shaun's father being, both, the mayor and the bank president; it put a major crimp in Sheriff Tucker's style.

Shaun knew he got away with a lot more than the ordinary kid in this town and he enjoyed rubbing it into Tucker's sore spots every chance he got.

Being the quarterback and captain of the football team, was also another perk in a hick town that had little to offer a young man. 'He was privileged, so what? He'd earned it,' he thought to himself as his jeep roared down the street.

Even though he had a good idea where Shaun was going, the sheriff wasn't sure he could catch him before he got there, and there were no shortcuts he could take.

At this point, the sheriff began to talk to himself. "Shaun Tilford, you're spoiled and reckless and you take more chances than is good for you," Tucker admitted out loud. "you're one hell'va driver, I'll give you that, but one day your luck is gonna run out and I just hope I'm not there when it happens."

He didn't want to be the one to tell Shaun's parents their son had been killed in a high-speed chase, especially with him being the one doing the chasing.

Rather than having to explain to Shaun's parents how Shaun had wrapped his jeep around some power pole, or ran into somebody's house or car, or possibly ran over someone, he decided to call for backup.

Keeping Shaun's jeep in sight, Sheriff Tucker reached for the radio microphone and pushed the button. "Tucker to car two, Tucker to car two. Come in car two."

After a long silence, Sheriff Tucker pushed the button again and yelled into the microphone, "Dammit, Andy, you better answer me, boy!"

When there was still no reply, the sheriff threw the microphone down on the seat and continued in his fruitless pursuit of Shaun Tilford, gripping the steering wheel even tighter; patience was definitely not one of Sheriff Tucker's strong suits.

Shaun knew he could out run the sheriff because he wasn't afraid to race through intersections at high speed and the sheriff was. So, just for the fun of it, he took the long way taking Kristi home. He turned up and down several streets for no good reason other than staying just far enough in front of the sheriff to drive him up the wall; making him wonder where he was going next.

Kristi did not share his amusement and told him so. "Shaun, I'm not stupid and I see what you're doing. You can continue this insane game of hide and seek if you want to, but take me home first, before you get us both killed."

"What's up with you lately? You're no fun anymore. All of a sudden you're Miss prude of the year! What happened to, Miss I love excitement? Where did she go?"

Kristi started to say something, then clammed up. Through clinched teeth, she said, "Just. . . just take me home! Now!"

Normally, she would have been jumping up and down with excitement and urging him to go faster. She loved excitement almost as much as Shaun did. But a few days ago, all of that changed. Suddenly, she was no longer a carefree teenager, but she wasn't sure who she'd become. Her brain was a whirlwind filled with thoughts - thoughts that changed the way she looked at life and her future. These new thoughts made her nervous to the point of being afraid of things she used to love.

Even though they had always been open about their thoughts and feelings, and as much as she wanted to at this very moment, she just couldn't find the courage to express herself; at least, not right now. Maybe tomorrow she would find the right time.

Shaun turned down yet another street, shaking his head, totally confused. She used to get a rush from doing this kind of stuff, but all of a sudden she had turned into this other person. And he was none too crazy about this, this, new whoever she was. He took a quick look at her as he turned yet another corner. Maybe it was one of those girly things they were always talking about. He sure hoped that was all it was and she would get over it soon. He wanted his old Kristi back.

CHAPTER NINE
Come in, Andy

FRUSTRATED, the sheriff tried once again to reach his deputy on the police radio. "Tucker to car two. Tucker to car two. Come in Andy." After a long, irritating pause, the sheriff yelled into the microphone," Dammit Andy, you better not be down at the donut shop, again!"

When he heard nothing but static, he slammed the microphone down on the seat so hard it bounced onto the floorboard. Driving one handed, the sheriff reached into his shirt pocket and pulled out a long, black, cigar and stuck it in his mouth and began to chew on the end, trying to resist the temptation to light it. He'd stopped smoking three weeks ago but at times like this he was sorely tempted.

The town had only one sheriff and one deputy. Andrew Singer was an ex Viet Nam soldier who had been wounded in action, making him walk with a limp. Andy was well liked by everyone for a couple of reasons. First, Andy had returned from Viet Nam with a purple heart, and a medal for bravery above and beyond the call of duty. Secondly, Andy was what you might call, one of those good ole boys. He could write you a ticket and make you feel happy about receiving it, and then make you feel sorry for having made him issue it.

On the other hand, Buford Tucker was loud, abusive, and a bully; but all in all he had been a competent sheriff for the past seventeen years. The town's only real beef was that they felt that for some unknown reason, the sheriff was a bit too hard on the teenagers.

In the end, the people of Shortcut conceded that when he had been elected sheriff, they gave him full authority to keep the peace in Shortcut. So, when it came right down to it, he was, after all, only doing his job - as he kept reminding them. 'The law is the law and I'm only doin' my job," he would say when something came up.

Although Andy took his job seriously, he didn't let his authority give him the big head. Normally the biggest things he had to deal with would be a few drunken hunters or fishermen, along with the kids speeding through town trying to find some way to quell their restless energy. Otherwise, it was a pretty dull job. But the trouble with dull jobs was they could change at the drop of a hat, as Andrew Singer was about to find out.

Like most other nights, the town had settled down early and all was quiet. During these times you could almost always find Andy sitting at the counter down at the local donut shop, making time with the waitress who seemed to encourage his advances. Andy was the first man she had been able to talk to and not be afraid of in a very long time.

CHAPTER TEN

Skeleton in the closet

TRACY BABCOCK had shown up one day a few months ago, looking for not only a job and a place to live, but also a community to settle down in.

And as fate would have it, the owner of the donut shop was not only in need of a waitress to run the place so he could try to build up his trucking business, but he also had a small studio cottage at the far end of town that he rented to hunters, fishermen or tourists who were just passing through. As part of the deal, she could live in the cottage.

For the owner of the donut shop, Tracy's arrival was a double bonus. She was intelligent, knew the business, could run the place alone, and on top of that, the woman was drop dead gorgeous. So they made a deal and she went to work the following morning. From the first day, the male traffic began to pick up and the donut business was suddenly very good. After the first two weeks, Woods Trucking was back on the road, again.

At first, Tracy wondered if she'd made the right decision, working here where most of the customers were male. But for some reason, she was drawn to Shortcut and didn't feel afraid. Even though almost all of the men flirted with her, she trained herself to tolerate the attention, all the while keeping an isolated distance from them. As time went along, she found she could banter with them without getting involved; that is, until Andrew Singer showed up one evening just as she was about to close the front door. He stood there, sad eyed, pleading for a donut and a cup of coffee.

Not only was he an officer of the law, but also he looked adorable standing there with his hands folded beneath his chin, his eyes, sad and his lips drawn up in a pucker.

She let him in and within minutes they were sitting in a booth, where they talked until almost midnight.

For some unexplained reason, from the time he walked in the door with his limp and boyish charm, she felt relaxed. And for reasons she couldn't explain to herself, she felt attracted to him and decided to tell him about her past and let the pieces fall where they may.

But each time she tried, Andy would insist that he didn't care about her past unless she was a homicidal killer with an obsessive urge to cut him up into small pieces or planning to burn down the town.

She had found that funny and laughed for the first time in a long while.

He went on to explain to her that everyone had a skeleton or two in their closet, but the only thing that really and truly mattered was the here and now – and hopefully, the future.

Andy's eyes told Tracy Babcock that he wasn't lying. He honestly didn't care about her past. The deputy of Shortcut, Utah, was smitten, and Tracy could sense it.

It wasn't one of those quick roll in the hay kind of romances. It was as though Andy really and truly liked her as a person, and enjoyed spending time with her, which went a long way helping Tracy change her attitude toward men – at least this man.

So, as it turned out, Tracy Babcock never revealed that a man back in Charlotte, North Carolina had attacked her one night and dragged her, screaming and kicking into an alley, where he attempted to rape her. During their struggle, Tracy's hand found a short piece of pipe lying in the alley and smashed it against the man's head with all her might. When his body went limp, Tracy rolled him off of her and slowly got to her feet.

While she stood looking down at her attacker with the piece of pipe still in her hand, a police cruiser drove by slowly, shining a spotlight down the alley. The cruiser stopped and with a gun in his hand, the policeman got out and surveyed the scene.

He approached her cautiously, instructing her to put the piece of pipe down and keep her hands where he could see them.

Stunned and shaken, she looked up at the officer and then down at the piece of pipe in her hand. After a moment, she dropped it to the ground and held her hands out in front of her.

Fortunately, another woman on her way to her own car had seen the man drag Tracy into the alley and heard their scuffle. She ran to the opening of the alley just in time to see Tracy wrestling with the man on top of her. She wanted to help, but she was paralyzed. She saw Tracy find the piece of pipe and hit the man in the head with it and was still standing there when the policeman arrested Tracy. She introduced herself and told the policeman what she'd seen.

Because of the woman's testimony, Tracy was not charged with murder. The judge explained that based on the eyewitness testimony, Tracy had acted totally in self-defense and the man's death was deemed, involuntary manslaughter.

That had been a little over two years ago. Tracy had not been able to let go of her fear and she found herself jumping at shadows every time she passed a dark alley. She even began to shy away from any man that looked at her suspiciously, crossing the street to avoid them.

After two years of jumping at shadows and driving herself crazy; because every man she met she viewed as a potential rapist, she knew she had to find a way to get over her fears. She tried repeatedly to convince herself that all men weren't like that, but it didn't seem to make much difference. She remained afraid of all males, young, old, and in between.

One Saturday evening, Tracy was sitting in her apartment all by herself, eating a TV dinner while reading a book about two people desperately in love and the life they planned to build for themselves. When at last, she finally laid the book on the coffee table, something came over her. It was time she faced the truth. She wanted a normal life and the only way she was going to accomplish that was to get out of Charlotte; get out of the state of North Carolina. There were too many memories here.

The next morning, Tracy quit her job as cashier of one of the leading restaurants in Charlotte, packed her car and headed west. Six weeks later, she pulled into Shortcut, Utah and immediately felt a calmness wash over her. It was like she'd come home even though she was in a town she knew she'd never heard of until today. It seemed crazy, but that's how she felt.

She'd been at the donut shop barely a month when Andy Singer walked into her life and she knew this is where she wanted to spend the rest of her days and was pretty sure Andy would like that idea, too.

That night, her dream shifted from a nightmare of being dragged into a dark alley and raped, to one of her and Andy twirling around a large dance floor to the sound of The Blue Danube waltz.

CHAPTER ELEVEN
The fickle finger of fate

ANDY AND TRACY were sitting in a booth, enjoying each other's company when the raindrops began to spatter on Andy's police car windshield and Sheriff Tucker's voice came roaring from the speaker inside the car and out through the open window.

Unfortunately, the man he was yelling at was not within the sound of his voice.

"Andy, this is Sheriff Tucker!" he yelled, as if there could be someone else calling him in this two-man police department. "Dammit, Andy, you better answer me! For your sake you'd better not be down at that donut shop, again!"

At that moment, the black van from the lodge with the two supremacists inside, came slowly down the street - passing by the donut shop as it continued on into town. Both men from the van saw the police car, but since they weren't breaking any laws, they paid it scant attention. They were just two travelers passing through town.

Andy and Tracy were too caught up with each other to notice the black van going down the street with strangers inside, which was nothing new. Strangers came through town on a constant basis. Besides, nothing exciting ever happened in Shortcut, Utah.

By the time the black van approached an intersection with a stoplight, the rain was beginning to fall much harder.

As fate would have it, Shaun's jeep was approaching the same intersection from a different direction at a high rate of speed. In his rearview mirror, Shaun could see that Sheriff Tucker was still in hot pursuit. As Shaun approached the intersection, the light turned yellow and Kristi screamed, "Shaun! The light!"

Shaun looked back and yelled, "Okay! Okay! I see it! Hang on!"

Shaun pushed the accelerator to the floor and the jeep leaped forward, racing through the intersection at the same time the black van was beginning to enter from Shaun's left. The driver of the van saw the jeep and reacted instantly, making a hard right turn to avoid ramming into the speeding jeep.

"Look out!" the man in the van's passenger seat yelled when he saw the sheriff's carryall, also bearing down on them.

Cranking hard on the steering wheel to keep from colliding with the jeep or the carryall, the van rolled up on two wheels. The two vehicles barely missed each other as the sheriff's carryall with its lights blinking and siren blasting went roaring through the red light.

Both supremacists saw the sheriff staring at them with eyes as big as saucers and his mouth hanging open.

From that point on, everything seemed to happen in slow motion. Shaun's jeep disappeared down the street; Tucker's carryall barely missed ramming into a black van that was turning the corner. The van was up on two wheels like the ones he'd seen at the car races.

The whole thing seemed to happen in no more than the blink of an eye. Tucker's carryall roared through the intersection in pursuit of Shaun Tilford - the sheriff amazed that he hadn't collided with the oncoming van and the driver of the van reacting in the only way he knew how.

What happened next could only be explained by realizing that sometimes the fickle finger of fate just shows up when we least expect it.

The van proceeded down the street on two wheels for only a short distance before it slowed to a stop and hovered for just a moment, then dropped down hard on its right side.

While all of this was happening, the man in the passenger seat of the van was trying to get his seat belt undone and get out of his seat so he could grab the crate containing the nitroglycerine before it came out of the sling and slammed against the side of the van.

He made it out of his seat and was stretching out his hands, but the crate was just inches beyond his fingertips. The man's eyes grew wide as he watched the crate containing the nitroglycerine roll out of the sling and fall three feet before slamming into the side of the van. The scream that was lodged in the man's throat was never heard.

The van split open like a watermelon being struck with a machete. A large ball of fire rose more than a hundred feet into the night sky above Shortcut, Utah, then coiled itself into a large, black cloud of swirling smoke. Neither the driver nor the passenger felt any pain. Their deaths were instantaneous.

Tucker slammed on his brakes and before the carryall came to a complete stop, jumped out and looked behind him. He could feel the heat from the blast. Looking up at the sky, which by now was lit up like high noon, he saw the gigantic ball of black cloud swirling in the night sky as the rain grew in its intensity.

"What the hell?" he yelled. After climbing back into the carryall, he did a U-turn and drove the short distance back to the intersection, stopping far enough away from the burning pieces of van so as to not be in harm's way, yet close enough to block traffic, should there happen to be any. The overhead signal light was no longer there.

Shaun and Kristi had just turned the corner onto the street where Kristi lived when they heard the explosion.

"Holly crap. What was that?" Shaun yelled.

"I don't know and I don't care. Just get me home, Shaun!"

By now Kristi was a nervous wreck and just wanted to be in the safety of her parent's home. The way Shaun was drinking and driving, speeding, almost hitting Miss Gibbons, running the light; it was a mystery they hadn't gotten themselves killed! They were all good reasons for keeping her secret to herself, Kristi's mind reasoned as she tried to calm her ragged breathing.

Andy and Tracy both jumped when they heard the explosion and saw the night light up. They ran out the door of the donut shop and stood in the rain, looking around to where a large plume of swirling, black smoke filled the sky.

With a noticeable limp, Andy ran to his squad car and jumped in, burning rubber as he left the parking lot with his siren blaring and red lights flashing.

All Tracy Babcock could do was stand there and watch Andy speed away, hoping he would be all right. After a moment, she realized it was raining and hurried back into the donut shop where she began cleaning and getting ready to close. Suddenly, Tracy placed her hand on her chest when she realized she was falling in love with this small town deputy sheriff who made her laugh.

The van, or what was left of it, lay smoldering on the street with pieces scattered in all directions. Large chunks of the van, along with other debris was scattered for a half a block in all directions; some of it was still burning.

People came running out of their houses; some with umbrellas, some with rain coats and hats, while others had no protection at all.

The sheriff was kept busy motioning for them to stay back in case there were any more explosions. "All right, all right, the excitements over, nothing more to see. Go on back home and go to bed. You can read all about it in the paper, tomorrow," he yelled.

Of course, no one paid any attention to him as they gawked at the smoldering wreckage scattered all over the street and nearby lawns, wondering how such a thing could happen here in Shortcut. Several of the elderly women, dressed in night gowns and house coats, with toilet paper wrapped around their heads to keep their hair in place, hovered beneath umbrellas and gave Sheriff Tucker looks that were downcast and sneering. One of them, a woman of nearly eighty, whispered to the others. "He was probably chasing some poor, innocent child on their way home from church and caused that van to turn over – killing the poor, poor occupants." The other women nodded their heads in agreement, making, tsk, tsk, tsk noises.

Sheriff Tucker was not liked by as many of the womenfolk as he would like to be. They were voters and he would need as many as he could get come the next election.

Andy cut the lights and siren as he pulled his vehicle up next to Sheriff Tucker's carryall. Andy climbed out of his police car with his jaw hanging open. He'd seen things like this in Nam, but not here in Shortcut, Utah.

As he walked up, Andy noticed the scowl on the sheriff's face and held back a grin. For some reason, the sheriff seemed to always be in a bad mood these past few months, especially if he thought Andy was seeing the pretty waitress down at the donut shop.

"What happened?" Andy asked, as he got close.

"Glad you could make it, deputy," Tucker said with a sneer. "What happened here? I'm so glad you asked. We're having a wiener roast and I thought you might want to attend. Would you like onions on your hot dog, or would that upset your girlfriend down at the donut shop?"

Andy ignored Tucker's remark and looked around. "Did you call an ambulance?"

Sheriff Tucker got a disgusted look on his face and shook his head. "Why the hell bother?" he said as he picked up the blackened license plate lying just in front of his vehicle. "Whoever was in there won't be needin' no ambulance. Take a look for yourself and if you find anything left, call the coroner. He can bring one of his little bags."

The town folks stood on the grass between the sidewalk and the curb, watching and waiting to see if anything else was going to happen, knowing no one could have survived the explosion.

Andy made his way over to what was left of the front part of the van, stepping over smoldering pieces of metal. When he looked inside the front part of the van, his stomach began to turn. He wanted to go somewhere and throw up, but there was no place to go. Besides, he was an officer of the law and was supposed to be above such things as burned chunks of meat. In less than five seconds, he'd seen enough and had taken a step backwards when he noticed a charred hand lying outside the van close to where he was standing. On one of the fingers was a large blackened ring showing a German Swastika on the face of it. Even though it was tarnished, it had somehow survived the explosion intact.

Andy retrieved a medium sized, plastic evidence bag from his police car and had just finished bagging the hand and ring when the volunteer fire department arrived.

Andy took the evidence bag to his car and stored it without anyone noticing. This wasn't something to be showing around just now. You didn't see this kind of thing every day, at least not around here. He would show it to the sheriff, later at the station. Next, he called the coroner from his car radio.

The fire chief and two volunteer firemen began applying water to what was left of the wreckage and surrounding area, using water pressure to push the spilled gasoline toward the gutter, away from the heat and fire before it sparked another explosion.

Once the chief saw his two men had things under control, he turned and headed toward the Sheriff and Ben Callaway, owner and editor of the local newspaper. Ben had arrived about the same time the fire department had and after a quick look, had headed straight for the sheriff, pencil and notebook in hand.

Ben had been working late at the Crier, putting together tomorrows front page when he'd heard the explosion. By the time he got to his car he could see the plum of fiery smoke rising into the air. Like any good newsman, Ben sped off down the street - knowing he would have a new front-page article to put together before this night was over.

"Any idea what caused the explosion?" the newsman asked the sheriff.

"Not a clue, Ben," he said, with a nonchalant attitude, "but we'll be looking into it. Maybe I'll have a story, later."

With that, the sheriff dismissed the newsman and turned to the fire chief. "I think my deputy called the coroner, so wait till all this cools down and the coroner can bag up whatever's left in there, then get this mess cleaned up. Call Bill Nichols and have him haul all this junk out to his place. Maybe he can get a few scraps of metal to sell after we're finished with our investigation. And tell him to keep it separated from the other junk."

The fire chief gave the sheriff a two-finger salute, then turned his head to see how his men were doing. When he saw they had things under control, he turned his attention on Ben. "You make sure you spell our names right this time, Ben."

Ben grinned from ear to ear. "Who said I was going to use your names in my article?" then added, "Maybe I better write the names down anyway; just in case."

The sheriff walked away in the direction of his carryall, leaving the fire chief and the newsman speculating on what had happened.

As he reached his carryall, the sheriff glanced down the street and realized that Shaun Tilford's jeep was long gone. He knew where the Tilford boy lived, but decided not to pursue that avenue right now. First, the boy's father was an important man in town. Second, the kid was the high school's top sports jock and important to the school. And third, he'd probably already ditched the beer somewhere, so there wouldn't be any evidence. At the very best he could give him a ticket for speeding and driving with wild abandonment. Suddenly, his head began to hurt. "I'm getting too old for this," he said as he reached for the door handle on his carryall.

Before getting into his vehicle, sheriff Tucker yelled out to his deputy. "If you think you can stay away from the donut shop, I'll be going home."

The bystanders all looked at Andy with grins on their faces, waiting to see what he would say.

Andy turned red and waved his hand and nodded his head in the affirmative, then pulled a pad and a pen from his shirt pocket and began asking if anyone had seen anything? No one had seen a thing. The first they knew anything was when they heard the explosion. No one knew any more than that, although the elderly ladies secretly had speculations.

Andy gave a sigh of relief when the carryall's tires squealed as the sheriff drove away. Sometimes the sheriff's sarcasm was just plain hard to deal with.

The color of the sky had gone back to dark gray clouds, with only the rain coming down by the time Shaun pulled his jeep to a stop in the driveway of Kristi's house.

As the jeep came to a stop, Shaun reached over and turned off the engine and headlights; but before he could try any of his shenanigans, Kristi jumped out of the jeep and ran for the front porch. With a disgusted look on his face, Shaun was only a couple of steps behind her.

When she turned toward him, Shaun kissed her passionately before she had a chance to object. He knew she was mad at him for drinking a few beers and the game he'd played with sheriff Tucker, again. But, with a little loving, she would warm up. She always did. When the kiss ended, instead of snuggling into him, Kristi stepped back and reached for the doorknob. "I have to go in now."

Shaun knew the look and decided not to make things worse, hoping she would forgive him by morning. "I'll come by early. Okay?"

"Not too early. Call first."

Before Shaun could protest, the porch light came on. Kristi gave him a quick kiss on the cheek. "Gotta go," she said as she disappeared behind the front door. From his peripheral vision, Shaun could see Kristi's father peeking out from behind the front room curtains.

"Sure," Shaun said to the tightly closed front door.

As the porch light went out, Shaun leaped off the porch and ran for his jeep. This sure wasn't the way he saw the evening going. Shaun backed out of the driveway and headed down the street, quietly. Kristi's father didn't care for tires squealing or any kind of reckless driving.

Less than five minutes later, Shaun stopped his jeep under the overhang of a large tree half a block down the street from where the van had exploded. He didn't want to get too close in case Tucker might still be there. The beer was still in the back of his jeep. When he saw Andy giving orders to the cleanup crew and the sheriff's carryall nowhere in sight, Shaun gave a sigh and eased the jeep forward and pulled up a short distance behind Andy's patrol car and got out.

"Hey Andy, what the heck happened here?" he asked as he climbed out of the jeep, slamming the door.

Andy looked up and saw Shaun walking toward him. With a wide grin, he said, "Haven't got a clue other than a van must have come around the corner too fast and rolled over and blew up."

"It must have been carrying explosives because it sure blew up with a big bang," Shaun said, pointing at all the wreckage. "Heard it and saw the smoke clear over at Kristi's folk's house."

"By the intensity of the explosion," Andy said, "I'm guessin' nitro, but we don't know for sure, yet. And that's another question. Who would be stupid enough to be drivin' around with nitroglycerine in their van?"

"Beats me," Shaun said, shrugging his shoulders.

Andy stopped his explanation there. He wasn't about to say anything about the hand with the ring, or any of the questions the ring might bring to mind.

When Andy didn't offer any more information, Shaun began to shake his head. "Nitro? Whoa, that's heavy, dude. Nitro? Really? And you don't have any idea why the guy was drivin' so erratic? I mean, how fast do you have to be goin' to make a van turn over, just by turning a corner? Was he tryin' to avoid hittin' somebody or something?"

Andy looked up from his pad and stared at Shaun. Something in Shaun's eyes caused Andy to wonder why the boy was asking so many questions? Placing that bit of information in the back of his mind, he said, "No, we have no idea what happened. You know anything?" Andy asked off-handed.

"Me? No! How would I know why some nut would be drivin' around like ah wild man with nitroglycerine in his van?"

"No reason. Just askin'," Andy said. "Part of my job, to ask questions."

Shaun stood quietly looking sheepishly down at his feet and the puddle of water he was standing in.

'Shaun Tilford, me young bucko, I'm thinkin' you know something that you're not telling me,' Andy thought to himself. Near panic had registered in Shaun's eyes. Maybe the sheriff knew something about it and would fill him in tomorrow morning. In the meantime, he had work here that he needed to finish up.

"Well, I see you're busy and I should be getting on home, big day tomorrow, our annual picnic up at the lake," Shaun said as he backed away toward his jeep.

"Drive safely. And don't drink and drive!" Andy called after him.

The fire chief approached and said they were almost finished; and also informed him that Bill Nichols was on his way. Andy nodded as he watched the jeep drive away and wondered how the Tilford boy was involved in all of this.

"Sure, Tom," Andy said, "Just make sure it's clean enough for people to drive on before you leave."

When Shaun's jeep disappeared around the corner, Andy looked back over his shoulder and watched as the fire chief gave orders to his men and then walked over to greet Bill Nichols, who had just driven up in one of those heavy-duty trucks you could tow a semi up a mountain with. He was pulling a high-sided trailer to haul the pieces of wreckage away.

Tom Bailey had been with the volunteer fire department for eighteen years and chief for the past eleven. He knew his job and was good at it; had even gone down to Salt Lake and taken some training. Andy felt safe in leaving him in charge, which would allow him some extra time to go back to the police station and fill out his report. It was going to be a long night.

The ring with the swastika brought up a lot of red flags, Andy thought as he got into his cruiser and put it into reverse and turned on the windshield wipers. The wind had picked up and the rain was beginning to come down harder.

Through the windshield, Andy watched as the gawkers scurried for the shelter of their homes.

"At least they get to go back to bed," Andy said as he backed up a short distance before making a U-turn and heading for the donut shop. He would make a quick stop to see if Tracy might still be there waiting for him. If not, he would give her a call from the station, just to let her know things were all right.

As he turned into the parking lot, he saw her standing inside the front door. She had her hand up to her forehead and was peering out. When she saw the cruiser, she rushed out to meet him. She had a sack in her hand.

"Are you all right?" she asked, anxiously, as Andy climbed out of the police car.

Andy grinned. "Fine as frog hair," he said, grinning and showing a lot of teeth.

"Good," she said, reaching out and punching him on the shoulder. "I was getting worried."

"What's in the bag?" Andy asked, trying to act innocent.

"I figured you might need something to munch on while you're making out your report," she said, handing him the bag, then reaching up she gave him a quick kiss and backed away before he could react.

He watched her sashay back toward the donut shop instead of running to get in out of the rain. She knew he would watch her until she was inside and she wanted to give him something to remember.

Grinning, Andy got back into his cruiser and headed for the police station. As he drove down the street with his windshield wipers working hard, Andy looked through his windshield and said, "Lord, I don't know why you gave this ole country boy one of your angels, but I want ta thank you kindly."

CHAPTER TWELVE

The Sheriff's parking place

BY THE TIME the sun came creeping over the horizon the storm had moved on and the sun was trying to fight its way through the lingering clouds.

Shortly thereafter, Rafe Talltree came driving down the main street of Shortcut in his battered up, mud spattered, nineteen fifty Chevy pickup. He turned the pickup into the parking space marked, "Sheriff Only," and killed the engine. After getting out and stretching, he sauntered toward the sheriff's office. He was tall and lanky, with a bit of a swagger, dressed in clean but well-worn button down blue jeans, a red shirt that had seen better days, a weathered Levi jacket, cowboy boots and a beat up old cowboy hat.

Practically every female in Shortcut considered Rafe Talltree, a hunk – even if they wouldn't admit it in public. After all, he was a full-blooded Shoshone Indian and they were good Christian women – most of who were Mormon and not allowed to have such lusty thoughts.

He walked into the sheriff's office and directly over to the coffee pot, where he poured himself a cup like it was something he did every morning. He then walked over and sat down in a chair in front of the deputy's desk and waited for Andy to finish his telephone conversation.

"Yeah, you too – and thanks for the information," Andy said before placing the receiver back on the old style, black desktop telephone. He gave Rafe a nod and said, "Mornin' Rafe. What brings you into town today?"

Before Rafe could answer, Andy picked up his coffee cup and headed for the small table that held the coffee pot. As Andy was adding cream and sugar to his cup, Rafe stood up and followed the deputy. "You know I run traps up on the mountain."

"Yeah, and I know you've got permits to do it, I signed them myself. What's the problem?"

"It's not that," Rafe said. "Well the thing is, I've been hearing a lot of gun fire lately, up near the lodge and the surrounding area."

"So," Andy said, grinning as he walked back toward his desk. "Maybe things are looking up. Maybe we're getting some hunters up there, again."

"No, it wasn't that kind of gun fire. It sounded like a damn war was goin' on; like people firin' automatic weapons and settin' off explosives. Like the kind you'd remember from Nam."

Before Andy could respond, the door opened and Sheriff Tucker stormed in. "What the hell do you know about war or automatic weapons, Talltree? I'll tell you what, nuthin! You think that little skirmish in Viet Nam was war? You talk to those boys who were in the big one. They'll tell you what war is all about."

The sheriff wrote out a ticket and shoved it in Rafe's direction. "Here's a little present for ya."

Rafe looked down at the ticket, and then took a step back. "What's this for?"

The sheriff grinned. "You're parked in my space, that's what for. Injuns ain't allowed to park in my spot," he said as he took a step forward and stuffed the ticket into Rafe's shirt pocket.

Andy wanted to say something, but knew when to keep his mouth shut.

Rafe gave the sheriff a hard look, then reached into the front pocket of his jeans and pulled out a wad of bills. He counted some out and tossed them onto the sheriff's desk, along with the ticket, then stormed out of the sheriff's office, slamming the door as he left.

In less than ten heartbeats, the sound of tires squealing could be heard as Rafe's old bucket of bolts roared off down the street.

The sheriff grinned and walked over to the coffee table expecting to get him a cup, but the pot was nearly empty, which irritated the sheriff to no end. "What the hell? Did Talltree do this?"

Without answering him, Andy took the pot from Sheriff Tucker and began making a fresh pot. "You think maybe you could cut him a little slack, Sheriff? He's not a bad guy. If you'd just give him half a chance. . ." Andy began to say, but the sheriff cut him off.

"You just worry about making another pot of coffee, deputy, and let me worry about Talltree."

Ignoring the sheriff, Andy went on. "About those gun shots he said he heard, maybe I should. . ." Once again, Andy's words were cut off.

"Maybe you should follow up on that license plate, like I told you to do."

"I did. . . Sheriff," Andy said with a bit of temper in his voice.

"And?"

Andy shook his head as he finished making a new pot of coffee. He hit the on switch and headed for his desk, picking up a piece of paper as he sat down. "The Idaho State Police said the plates are a probable match with one seen at the site of a robbery three weeks ago."

This got the sheriff's attention. "A robbery, huh? Where?"

Andy glanced down at the paper. "A mining store in Idaho Falls. Whoever did it got away with a fair amount of explosives, including some nitroglycerine." Turning the page, he said, "On the same night, a black van was stolen from a used car lot a few miles away. Sounds like a match to me; dark van, nitroglycerine. . ."

Even though the coffee wasn't ready yet, the sheriff poured himself a cup, letting coffee drip onto the hot plate of the coffee maker as he poured. There was a sizzling sound when he put the pot back in place but he seemed not to notice. "I reckon that would explain that van exploding like it did."

"It sure would. Anyway, they'd like us to send them a copy of the coroner's report as soon as we can."

The sheriff almost spit up his coffee. "What the hell was the coroner supposed ta find in that mess?"

Andy looked at the sheriff, shrugged his shoulders as he raised his hands in the air, palms up. "Oh, I don't know, maybe a finger print or two; maybe some dental work? They seem to think the information might tie in with one of their other cases; something about a group of skinheads in the area up there."

Sheriff Tucker didn't seem to take note of the information, or Andy's sarcasm, as he swallowed down the last of his coffee. "Yeah, right, whatever. He picked up the money Rafe left and stuck it in his pocket. I'll be goin' over to the Redwood for some breakfast, then up to the lake. I have a hunch that Tilford kid and some of his buddies might be havin' a beer party up there today."

Andy looked at the sheriff and shook his head. "Why are you so down on those kids? They're just teenagers, being teenagers."

By now, the sheriff had gotten to the door. He stopped and turned back slowly. He looked at Andy and said, "Because they're trouble and I don't like trouble in my town. Who knows? One of 'em might get drunk and fall in the lake and drown, and then what would I tell their parents? I'm sorry but I wasn't doin' my job. I was down at the donut shop starin' at the waitress's big tits." With that, Sheriff Tucker turned and walked out the door, slamming it behind him.

The anger on Andy's face caused the blood vessels to stand out on his forehead. He sat down at his desk, trembling with rage. He picked up a wooden pencil and broke it into several small pieces.

The sheriff sauntered down the sidewalk, talking to himself. "Plus, mister smart ass deputy, as a reward for doing my duty, I get to keep all the beer."

The sheriff began to whistle the tune, Camp Town Races, as he climbed into his carryall and drove off down the street in the direction of the Redwood Café.

CHAPTER THIRTEEN
Rafe Talltree

IT WAS AROUND TEN in the morning when Shaun's jeep turned off the main highway and headed for the lake. The radio was blaring rock and roll music. Both Kristi and Shaun were singing along. Kristi's mood was happy and easy going, like she was her old self again which made Shaun extremely happy. Neither of them paid any attention to the swollen river that was raising havoc to the pillars of the old wooden bridge they had to cross to get to the road leading up to the lake and resort area.

The muddy water was still flowing strong, carrying small logs and other debris along its path. The logs and large chunks of debris smashed against the rotting poles used as bridge supports. Even a person with an untrained eye could see that this was a catastrophe in the making.

For several hours before Shaun's jeep came roaring across and added extra weight and strain on its weakening supports, the bridge had already been weaving back and forth precariously in its effort to keep from being torn apart and dragged down the raging river. After the jeep had passed, the bridge continued to hang on, but just barely.

Oblivious to the faltering bridge or the world around him, Shaun took the turnoff that led up to the lake, never realizing this day was going to be something far different from the one he had planned.

Fate can have a way of sneaking up on people and taking them by surprise, and today was going to be one of those days.

Without anyone realizing it, it had already begun with the van exploding the night before. The explosion became the new front-page cover story in the newspaper, over shadowing the upcoming church bizarre, which had been moved to the back page. The newspaper was only four pages long and most of it was spent on the exploding van, with pictures for added effect.

Everyone had their own ideas as to why the van exploded, but not a one of them understood the enormous impact the accident would have on their lives and the lives of the entire nation, once the whole story played itself out.

This quiet little resort town was about to be turned upside down without anyone having a single clue yet as to what was happening or why; not until they came face to face with reality and the seriousness of the situation.

It should have been just another spring break beer party at the lake, with Sheriff Tucker breaking it up and giving them all a lecture on the use of alcohol; but not even the sheriff could see what the future held. If he had, he most assuredly would have done things differently.

Rafe Talltree had been out since early morning, checking his traps. The day had been good to him so far. He'd captured two rabbits, two forest grouse and one, fat, wild turkey - enough meat for a week. His last trap was near an overhang that looked out across the beach and the lake. Before Rafe got close to his trap, which turned out to be empty, he could hear rock and roll music coming from down on the beach area along the east side of the lake. With all that noise it was no wonder the trap was empty, he thought as he approached.

Rafe had a good idea of what was going on as he eased up to the edge of the overhang and looked down.

A large bonfire was blazing. The huge boom box sitting on the picnic table was blaring its tunes loud enough for the whole world to hear. Several half naked teenagers were dancing on the beach, while a group of boys were chasing each other around the beach, all with cans of beer in their hands, chasing a girl with a football in hers.

"Ah, the annual beer bash," Rafe said, remembering his high school days. Back then the people of Shortcut accepted him as one of them. He was an 'A' student and a top jock in every sport he'd entered. He'd lettered in football, baseball, basketball, wrestling and track. The girls had chased after him like he was wearing a chick magnet.

That was before Viet Nam; before his world had been turned upside down.

Shaking his head, Rafe turned and was about to leave when he heard Shaun Tilford's jeep come roaring up to the beach with its horn honking as the jeep slid to a stop not far from the other vehicles.

Rafe watched as Shaun climbed out of his jeep and saw his best friend Trace Bozeman running toward him, whooping like a wild Indian. When Trace got near, he began to dance all around Shaun like an Indian dancing around a fire. Then, all of a sudden, Trace stopped and poured a can of beer over Shaun's head, making whoop, whoop, whoop, sounds. When the can was empty, Trace took off running, with Shaun right on his heels. Near the edge of the lake, Shaun tackled Trace and they rolled into the water, laughing and splashing water at each other as they got to their feet. Rafe shook his head at the memories that he had of the beer bash.

Tackling someone wasn't what a quarterback would normally do, but this was not a football game; it was a beer bust at the lake; far away from teachers and parents, a time when anything goes and usually did.

Trace Bozeman, on the other hand, as the team's wide receiver, and only black player on the squad, was used to getting tackled.

The Bozeman family was one of only three black families living in the community of Shortcut, Utah. Big Mike as he was called, had his auto mechanic shop down at the southern edge of town and got almost all of the town's business, including the school, the police and fire department, because he was a good mechanic and his prices were reasonable.

One of the other two black families was Melissa Walker's family. Alderman James Thomas Walker, Melissa's father, had recently risen to the position of assistant of the Mormon Church in Shortcut. He was the first black man to attain such a high position within the Mormon Church and he let everyone know it.

The newest black family to move to Shortcut was Lance Adams and his pretty wife, Barbara. Lance had recently been hired as the new athletics director at the high school. He had once played pro football in Canada, until he broke his back and had to walk with a cane. He and his wife, Barbara, had no children, but were hoping that would change in the near future. Barbara was an assistant teacher at the grade school.

There were no longer any American Indians living in Shortcut - not since Rafe's mother and father were killed in a car wreck a week after Rafe left for Viet Nam. They were coming home from a visit to relatives on the reservation when a drunken hunter lost control of his truck and hit them head on.

Nearly the whole town had turned out for their funeral. They were well liked. Marshal 'Walking Bear' Talltree had been one of the most respected hunting and fishing guides that could be found anywhere in North America. Rafe was the fourth generation to be born in Shortcut and planned to make it his home, but three months after Rafe came home from his tour of duty, he sold his parent's house and land to an oriental man by the name of Chi Cheng Chong who wanted to move into the area.

Rafe bought a small pull trailer and hauled it high up on the mountain to a piece of land well above the lake.

A month after moving to Shortcut, Mister Chong opened the first and only oriental restaurant in Shortcut. Because of his pleasant smile, hospitality, reasonable prices and excellent food, the China Palace did a thriving business from the first day.

The people of Shortcut honestly believed they were nothing, if not open minded about restrictions because of race, color or creed, except for the reappearance of Rafe Talltree after his tour of duty in Viet Nam. Of the three boys from Shortcut who went to Viet Nam, Rafe was the only one to return walking upright, while the other two came home two months ahead of Rafe, laid out in caskets.

The two dead boys had been god fearing white boys and Rafe was a full-blooded Shoshone Indian and not even Mormon. It just didn't seem right to them. What made Rafe so special that he was kept alive? Of the three, why was he the only one to come back?

Hostilities began to fester and soon grew into the shunning of someone who had done nothing to deserve their anger.

While they were in Viet Nam, both of the boys, like many others, got themselves hooked on dope. Then one evening, high as a kite, and tanked up on local booze, they wandered into a minefield, laughing about how funny the moon looked.

The reason behind the two young men's deaths seemed to make no difference to the people; they were dead and Rafe Talltree was alive.

Rafe felt the shunning the first day after he got back, and wasn't sure how he was supposed to react. He at least expected some of his old buddies and maybe a few of his old girlfriends to be excited to see him again. Instead of embracing him, they hung their heads and averted their eyes, barely mumbling, hello. Some of them crossed the street to keep from having to talk to him.

No one said anything to Rafe about Viet Nam or questioned him about what had happened. And even if they had, Rafe wouldn't have been able to tell them anything. They hadn't been in the same outfit and were miles apart when it happened.

Rafe had been part of a small Special Forces group, who tracked the enemy through the jungle and sent back information about their whereabouts, their size and other pertinent information he found. Rafe was also a crack shot and had been sent out on several special assignments that were kept on the hush-hush.

In fact, he hadn't known the boys other than by name. They hadn't been in the same grade or classes in school. As a matter of fact, Rafe didn't know anything about their deaths until he came home.

The people of Shortcut had made up their minds about him and Rafe wasn't sure the people would try to understand, even if he tried to explain it to them.

Rafe felt hurt. He loved this part of the country and used to think he had friends here. He didn't want to live anywhere else, but he couldn't see himself living in Shortcut; not like this.

One of the only people in town who had anything to do with him was Blaine Whifflemire and it was strictly business. Blaine and Rafe had an agreement. In a small corner of his store, he agreed to sell Rafe's tanned hides, handmade knives and other Indian artifacts Rafe made. The tourists who stopped by gobbled them up, and from the first day, it had been a profitable venture.

Some of the locals gave him a bad time about doing business with Rafe, but he didn't care; not as long as the money kept rolling in.

Except for the deputy sheriff, Andy Singer, who was also a Viet Nam veteran, Rafe had no one he could just talk to. The two had become friends because Andy paid no attention to the town or what they thought. He liked Rafe and was his friend and that was that. He didn't care who knew it. He also knew what it had been like in Nam.

Andy was not one of their homeboys. He had come to Shortcut from Montana in response to an ad in his hometown paper stating the police department in Shortcut, Utah was looking for a deputy sheriff.

After returning home, Andy too, found things different. The day he got back he found out his girlfriend had just married his younger brother and they were on their honeymoon in California. The next day, Andy started searching for jobs in other states when he found the ad. He'd had police training in the army and had been a brig chaser.   He wrote them a letter, stating his qualifications and they wrote back, asking for a face-to-face interview.

The city council liked Andy immediately and hired him on the spot, much to the complaints of Sheriff Tucker, who had another candidate in mind.

Approximately four months after coming home, while Rafe was sitting near the edge of the lake fishing, an idea came to him. The city owned the mountain where the lake and lodge were, and neither was doing very well right now. Because of that, they were in dire need of money. The next day Rafe went to the city council and made them an offer, which they accepted. For a pittance of money each year for the next five years, Rafe bought a small, unused piece of land near the top of the mountain, with the proviso that he make at least one improvement every year. If he met the requirements, the land would be his. It was similar to a homestead deal, except it was with the city of Shortcut and a small amount of money each year was involved.

While still living in his small trailer, the first thing Rafe did was drill a well so he would have water. Next, he cut down timber, cleared a small piece of land and built himself a cabin around the well, with the pump in the kitchen. Next he made himself some furniture. After six months of hard work, he moved in. He figured with the well and the cabin he'd made two years worth of improvements.

He put his trailer up for sale down at the Redwood and sold it within three days to a man from southern Utah. The sale gave him enough money to live on until he could get a small business started as a hunting and fishing guide, along with capturing game, tanning hides and stuffing birds and small animals. He also made knives and Indian artifacts that Blaine sold to the tourists who stopped at the Redwood. Plus, he'd made deals with several hunting and fishing stores throughout the state that would also carry his wares on consignment.

Because of his new business, he kept busy and didn't have time to worry about going to town and facing people. Sometimes Andy would come up and they would go hunting or fishing, together. Andy would keep him apprised of the goings on in town.

Rafe watched from the top of the cliff as the partying continued. Once in a while someone would break out laughing. And of course, there were already a few who had retired to their blankets for some heavy petting.

Before heading back into the woods, Rafe reset his empty trap, then gathered up his bounty and headed for his pickup. He had rabbits to skin and birds to pluck, along with some bones to set out to cure for knife handles and trinkets. Nothing went to waste.

CHAPTER FOURTEEN
Breakfast at the Redwood

AN OLD, EDDIE ARNOLD SONG, 'Any time you're feeling lonely,' was blaring loudly from the juke box when Sheriff Tucker entered the Redwood Restaurant and headed for the empty stool located at the end of the counter. As the waitress sat a coffee cup in front of him and began pouring, Sheriff Tucker yelled his order to her over the noise. She nodded and then headed for the kitchen, writing his order on her small pad as she went. She hadn't needed to hear the order - he always ordered the same thing.

While the sheriff sat on the stool, sipping his coffee and waiting for his breakfast of ham and eggs to arrive, he glanced around and saw that it was mostly full of regulars from town. Here and there people who were passing through had also stopped. They were like him when he was traveling. If he saw a restaurant that had its parking lot filled with cars and trucks, a person could bet this was the best place around to get a bite to eat, not realizing it had been the delicious smell being blown toward the gas pumps that helped entice them to come in.

When his breakfast came, the sheriff forgot about the music or the loud talk. He took his time, enjoying his morning meal while he thought about the party the kids would be having up at the lake, and breaking it up. Confiscating their precious beer would be the highlight of the trip. He grinned as he shoveled in a mouthful of ham, egg, biscuit and gravy into his mouth and began chewing. Life was good.

The waitress freshened up his coffee and gave him a wink as she turned with a flip of her hips and sashayed toward a table filled with men.

The sheriff took notice of her flirting and figured one of two things; either she wanted a nice tip, or a roll in the hay, or both.

Even though neither of them considered the other as marriage material, they had shared several cold winter nights together. Maybe he'd invite her over to his place this evening. He would have plenty of beer.

When he finished his breakfast, he did in fact leave her a nice tip and one of his cards with a note on the back.

"My place, 8 o'clock?

At the door, he turned back and watched as she read the note, then looked at him. With a big smile, she gave him two thumbs up.

Sheriff Tucker headed toward his carryall, singing "and there'll be a hot-time in the old town, tonight."

This was turning out to be a good day after all. He climbed into the carryall and backed out of the parking space, shifted into drive, and headed toward the lake without giving the van explosion another thought.

CHAPTER FIFTEEN

The truth doesn't always set you free

JUST BEYOND the clearing from the old lodge, two men dressed like hunters were crouched behind some shoulder high brush. Had anyone looked in their direction, the surrounding forest would hide them from view. Both men were observing the lodge and surrounding area through high-powered binoculars.

"I don't see any activity. Maybe they've pulled out," the man on the left said as he lowered his glasses.

The other man nodded as he slipped his binoculars back into their case. "You may be right, but we'd better check to make sure before we call in."

With great stealth, the two men circled around and came up next to the barn from the side that couldn't be seen from the lodge. After trying the side door and finding it locked, they moved on, heading for the front of the barn. Halfway to the front, the man in front leaped backward and yelled, "Look out!" Both men jumped back and reached for their pistols as a Ruffed

Grouse hen squawked and leaped from her nest next to the side of the barn, and took flight. The two men looked at each other with grins on their faces for being so jumpy. They took a long moment to allow their hearts to quiet down before continuing on.

Once they rounded the corner of the barn, both men searched the area with their eyes, and when they didn't see anyone they hurriedly entered the front door as quickly and quietly as they could. Both men were still somewhat gun-shy and a bit keyed up by the ordeal with the grouse.

From a second story window, the only thing visible was a hand holding back the edge of a curtain. On one of the fingers was a large ring with a swastika on the face of it, but neither of the men sneaking into the barn looked toward the upper window so there was no way they could have seen the hand with the ring on it.

The first man inside the barn found the light switch and turned it on as soon as the door was closed. A lone bulb illuminated the interior. The men looked around and both gave a low whistle. The walls were covered with Nazi flags and other banners that declared white power. A huge blow up of Adolph Hitler hung on the wall at the far end of the barn, behind a makeshift stage with thirty chairs sitting in front of it. A table on the near side of the barn was filled with small crates that had the name of an Idaho mining company stenciled on their sides.

The first man took a look around and said, "Bingo!" after which he looked around some more and then asked, "Where's the black van?"

The second man was studying a newspaper he found lying on one of the tables and motioned his partner to come over. "You need to come take a look at this. I think it will explain where the black van is."

The first man hurried over and read the headline on the front page of the Salt Lake City Daily Journal newspaper. SALT LAKE CITY HOSTS NATIONS LEADERS AND NEW PRESIDENTIAL HOPEFULS.

Who will be the next president of the United States? The first line of the article asked.

While the two men were reading the headline, shadows of men silently moved in

behind them. Suddenly, the air was filled with the sound of bolts on weapons being cocked.

The two agents spun around and faced a dozen men in camouflage uniforms, pointing automatic weapons, rifles and shotguns in their direction.

One of the gunmen walked up and motioned with the end of his double-barreled shotgun for them to raise their hands. One of the other men handed his weapon to the man standing next to him, then strutted over and searched the two men from head to foot, and found their weapons and credentials.

"FBI," he said to the others.

"This is not your lucky day," the man who had searched them said with a chuckle.

From the back of the crowd, a large man with the look and swagger of a leader, dressed in black military fatigues stepped forward and stared at the two FBI men. When he raised his hand to remove the cigar from his mouth, the two FBI men saw the large ring with the swastika on it.

"You won't get away with any of this," the agent on the left said, waving his arms in a wide circle.

"They're expecting trouble down in Salt Lake and have security everywhere," the second FBI man lied. In reality, they did have a lot of security, but knew nothing of the Supremacists plans.

Even so, because the president and vice president would both be there, the FBI was taking extra precautions and had in fact put on extra security by hiring a local civilian security company who was used to covering high profile events.

Adolph Hemmlick, self-appointed leader of the White Supremacists group smiled broadly, then turned to look at the men standing silently, waiting to see what he was going to do. "They think they're smart, but in truth, they know nothing of our plans and by the time they figure it out," he said, raising his hands over his shoulders, "it will be too late for anyone to stop us. The new beginning will have begun."

Walking toward the barn doors, he waved his arm and said, casually, "Tie them up securely. After breakfast will be soon enough for what everyone knows has to be done."

Before leaving the barn, he called over his shoulder, "Bear, come with me. I'm giving you the honor of getting rid of these two pieces of white trash."

Bear grinned and followed after his leader. As he walked toward the front doors of the barn, his comrades gave him pats on the back, while several of them raised two thumbs in the air. It was a sign that he was being accepted as a minor leader.

The two FBI men looked at the group of armed men, trying desperately to think of some way to escape their fate and realized as their hands were being tied behind their backs; there wasn't any. Even though they hadn't called in, they knew someone would eventually come to check, but probably not soon enough to save their lives.

CHAPTER SIXTEEN
Another brew, wench

KRISTI, MELISSA AND TRACE were all roasting wieners on sticks over the fire when Shaun came running up and flopped down next to Kristi. He popped open a can of beer and took a long pull, then belched. "Ah, now this is the life, no school, no teachers, no parents, and best of all, no Sheriff Tucker climbin' all over our backs."

Trace picked up his can of beer and he and Shaun clashed cans. "Right on, man, right on," Trace shouted as he took a long pull, and then he too belched, long and loud, and when he finished, they both rolled on the sand, laughing like he and Trace had just pulled off some hilarious joke.

Melissa had a frown on her face. "Don't you guys think you should slow down at least a little bit? Isn't it a little early, even for you two?"

Trace sat up and got an indignant look on his face as though he'd been mortally wounded. He raised his hands in a defensive position. "Whoa, whoa, whoa; lighten up, Melissa. We're here to have a party, remember?"

Shaun and Trace finished draining their cans and tossed them into the fire. "More brew, wench," Shaun yelled at Kristi, as he took a swipe at her rear end.

Kristi scooted away from him and swatted at his hand. "I'm nobody's wench! If you want more, go get it yourself."

Trace scooted away from Melissa and Kristi and held up his fingers like a cross and said, "My, my, but don't the fairer sex seem a bit testy this morning."

Melissa shot him a look that made him back away even further. "Lay off, Trace," she said, "and don't expect us to help you two get ripped."

By now, Shaun was getting bored and thirsty. He stood up and headed for the jeep. "Just forget it, ladies. I gotta go water the wild flowers," he said as he sauntered away with a look of indifference on his face.

By now, Trace was on his feet, a bit tipsy, but steady enough to follow Shaun. "Me too, Kemo-sabe, me too. Time ta empty da ole water pouch."

As the girls watched them head for the jeep, Kristi called out, "And not in the lake this time, please."

Kristi and Melissa exchanged looks, and then broke out into laughter. When the laughter quieted down, Melissa gave Kristi a serious look and asked, "Have you told him yet?"

A despairing look came across Kristi's face as she looked out across the lake and shook her head, no.

Melissa laid her hand on Kristi's shoulder. "Kristi, you've got to tell him."

Even though Trace couldn't understand what the girls were saying, he could tell by their expressions they were discussing something serious, and mistakenly was sure it was about him. He threw them a frown, and then hurried to catch up with Shaun, who by now had reached the back of the jeep and was already relieving himself.

Trace went around to the other end of the jeep and also rid himself of his excess beer.

As Trace walked to the back of the jeep, Shaun was retrieving two beers from the cooler. Shaun tossed one of the cans of beer to him in the form of a hook shot. Trace caught it with one hand and turned it away from him to open it. The can made a loud whooshing sound as the foam erupted.

After taking a sip, Trace became serious. "Hey man, what's up with Kristi? She seem up tight to you lately?"

Shaun opened his can and took a long pull before answering. "Yeah, she's been on my case all week. I haven't got a clue what's wrong. I'm hoping it's just her girl thing, but the truth is, I don't know. So, how about Melissa, you score with her, yet?"

Trace kicked the ground with the bottom of his foot and looked at the sky. "Not even a hand inside her blouse. She's as cold as that water out there," he said pointing at the lake. "I thought Kristi said she was hot for me."

Shaun turned and looked at the girls. "She, ah, she did. . . You just wait until tonight. She'll warm up. You just wait and see."

Trace gave Shaun a look that said he wasn't sure he was convinced, and then turned his attention toward the sky. "May not be a tonight, or at least not here. Looks like another storm comin' our way."

Shaun didn't bother checking the sky. Instead he nudged his friend in the ribs and said, "Think positive ole buddy, think positive."

After knocking back their beer, they tossed the cans into the back of Shaun's jeep and grabbed two more before heading back to the girls. By the time they got there, black clouds were rolling in and the wind had kicked up, Flames from the bonfire were leaping in all directions as the other kids began to grab their blankets, coolers and what other things they had brought with them, and headed for their cars and trucks.

Shaun, seemingly oblivious to the coming storm, yelled at them, "Hey where you whimps goin'? The party's just gettin' started."

Kristi and Melissa were also beginning to gather up their things. "They're worried about this new storm, and so are we!" she yelled in answer to Shaun's question.

"Com'on, you're not gonna be like those spineless cowards, are ya?" Shaun said as he pointed at the departing vehicles.

Melissa sheltered her face from the rain that was beginning to fall and said, "I think maybe they've got the right idea, Shaun. I think we should go!"

"I agree with Melissa,' Kristi said with pleading eyes.

Shaun, not wanting to spoil his plans, finally looked at the sky and then back at Kristi and Melissa. "Hey, what's a little rain? Besides, it's gonna blow over our heads and be gone in no time." Stretching his arms wide, he smiled and said, "Then we'll have the lake all to ourselves."

Trace wasn't so sure about Shaun's theory and said so. "I don't know, man. Ah storm up here can get pretty gnarly, real quick like."

The wind was beginning to blow Melissa's hair around and into her face and she was getting nervous. "I vote we go home, now!" she pleaded.

"Me to," Kristi said, stepping over next to her friend.

Not to be thwarted, Shaun yelled above the wind, "Com'on, you guys! Don't turn chicken on me now. Where's your spirit of adventure?"

Trace chuckled and shook his head. "Don't mind him, ladies. As you know, sometimes he thinks he's Superman."

Kristi put one hand on her hip and wiped the hair out of her face with the other. "Tell me about it," she said with a frown.

The whole thing went right over Shaun's head and he looked at them with a question on his face. "What?"

Trace slapped Shaun on the back and said, "Nuthin', buddy. Just forget about it."

"Okay, here's what we'll do, we'll move up to higher ground til it blows over," he said pointing to a spot sheltered by the trees. "Okay? Trust me, it's gonna blow over in a few minutes and everything's gonna be all right."

Trace, Melissa and Kristi exchanged looks, but in the end they gave in, and like always, allowed Shaun to have his way.

If there had been some way for them to know what the future held, they would have definitely gone back to town with the others, but since they weren't soothsayers, they were left to the mercy of the storm and the fickle finger of fate.

CHAPTER SEVENTEEN

And he laughed in the face of death

SOMETIMES things can happen so unexpectedly that we are caught unaware. With the consequences being fatal, or at the very least, devastating, they wind up affecting not only a single life, but a multitude of other lives as well.

To get out of the now full blown storm, the kids moved all of their belongings to an area away from the lake, up among the trees and under a wide overhang protruding out from the mountain. It was not a cave, but a deep enough indention in the side of the mountain that would shelter them somewhat from the wind and rain, at least for now.

Rafe Talltree had just put his catch of the day into the back of his pickup and had opened the door of his pickup and was about to climb inside when he heard the sound of automatic weapons being fired a short distance down the road, mixed in with a loud clap of rolling thunder. When the thunder ended, the short bursts of gunfire could still be heard. Rafe eased the truck door closed as quietly as he could and then slipped into the forest, making his way in the direction of the gunfire.

At the same time Rafe was inching his way through the forest, Sheriff Tucker was turning off the main highway onto the lake road. Country music was blaring from a small portable radio propped up on the dash of his carryall. Sheriff Tucker was feeling good and was thinking about the beer he would soon have for his date later this evening. As he drove along, he was singing, off key, along with his favorite singer, Hank Williams, to one of his favorite songs, 'Your Cheating Heart.'

Engrossed in his singing, the sheriff didn't notice that the river had risen to less than two feet from the bottom of the bridge, and was about to flood over the banks on both sides. The windows of the carryall were rolled up because of the rain. The wipers were trying in vain to keep up with the water beating against the windshield.

Between the sheriff's loud singing and the radio blaring away, the noise of the rushing river had been drowned out.

On separate blankets, under the overhang, and shaded by the trees, the kids were doing what most teenagers do; making out. At least, Shaun and Kristi were.

Kristi seemed to be her old self again, much to Shaun's liking and relief. 'It was just one of those girl things,' he thought to himself.

Melissa, on the other hand was doing everything she could to keep Trace at bay. When she heard the gunfire she reacted by sitting up and pushing Trace away. "What was that?" she asked.

Trying to be funny, Trace answered by placing his hand on his chest. "The sound of my heart," he said with a smile, and then pulled Melissa back down onto the blanket.

At first Melissa resisted, wondering why she was the only one concerned about hearing gunfire.

Now that she thought about it, she wasn't really all that sure what gunfire was supposed to sound like, other than what she'd heard in the movies. Suddenly it stopped as quickly as it began, and after a few minutes the only thing she could hear was the wind and thunder and rain.

She willed herself to relax and after a moment, allowed Trace to kiss her. He was very good looking and a better than average kisser, she thought, trying to forget about the gunfire. Probably just hunters, she surmised as she pushed Trace's hand off of her breast.

But, like any girl her age, with all the hugging and kissing and Trace's hard body pushing up against her, feelings and desires were beginning to rise up inside her.

Even though she may have wanted to go further, she had decided when she let Kristi talk her into coming along on this blind date that she would not give in to her female yearnings. She had plans for college after high school and getting pregnant was not a part of those plans. Going to classes with a child in her backpack instead of books and jumping up and running to change a diaper right in the middle of a class, was in no way her idea of getting an education.

She'd learned about that problem by watching her two sisters go through it. The would be fathers had disappeared as soon as they learned what they had done, leaving both her sisters alone and having to find jobs to support themselves and their babies – which left no time or money for either one of them to further their education.

They had opened a house cleaning business in a small town south of Shortcut, which just barely made enough money to get by on. One week, one of them cleaned houses, while the other watched the babies; then the next week they would switch, allowing each one short bits of time to be with their child. There wasn't enough work for both of them to work at the same time.

She was brought back to reality when she felt Trace's hand on her leg. Before things went any further, Melissa got to her feet and suggested they take a walk.

Misunderstanding Melissa's meaning, Trace jumped up and looked for a place that was dry where they could go; a place that was out of sight from Kristi and Shaun.

Melissa had two reasons for wanting to take a walk - first, to take a break from Trace's roving hands, and second, to allow Kristi and Shaun some privacy so Kristi could discuss something with him – something important that Melissa knew Kristi would not talk about as long as she and Trace were nearby.

When Trace found out why Melissa wanted to take a walk, he was livid with rage. By now, his hormones were almost out of control. With a scowl on his face, Trace left Melissa standing under the shade of a large pine tree and hurried off in the direction of Shaun's jeep, then angled off into the woods.

When Melissa saw Trace disappear into the trees, she chuckled even though she knew Trace's problem wasn't funny. "I guess boys have their problems, too," she said to the howling wind, while at the same time, trying to calm her own desires. It would have been very easy to let him have his way if not for the possible consequences. Look what had happened to her sisters, and to Kristi, she reminded herself. Besides, the first time should be special; with someone she loved, and someone who loved her back.

By now, Sheriff Tucker had crossed the bridge and was coming up to the split in the road. The road to the left would take him up to the lake, while the road to the right led up to the lodge. He was about to take the turn leading up to the lake, when off to his right, almost out of sight, he spotted a pickup with two men standing at the back of it.

Both men were dressed in camouflage clothing and both had automatic weapons slung over their shoulders. They were laughing and staring at something on the ground that looked like two bodies.

"Now what the hell is this all about?" Tucker said to himself as he slowed down and put the carryall into reverse and slowly backed down the road until he was out of sight.

Sheriff Tucker checked his pistol - a western style forty-four caliber, to make sure all six cylinders were loaded, and then eased out of the carryall just as another roll of thunder sounded. He took a deep breath as a knot in his stomach began to grow.

With his pistol gripped tightly in his right hand, and his western style hat pulled tight onto his head to keep the rain out of his face, Sheriff Tucker made his way into the woods just far enough to not be seen. Tucker moved silently until he was close enough to see what was going on.

He watched in shock as the two men picked up one of the men lying on the road, by his hands and feet. The body was riddled with bullet holes and blood was dripping onto the muddy road as they tossed the corpse into the ravine, where it landed in the muddy water at the bottom with a splash.

As the two supremacists reached for the second body, Sheriff Tucker stepped onto the road less than twenty feet from where they stood. "Hold it right there! Put that body down, now!" he yelled with as much authority as he could muster. His nerves were jumping around inside him like Mexican jumping beans. In all his years as a peace officer, he'd never had to deal with anything like this. He felt stupid. He hadn't followed procedure and called Andy to come out as a backup. Too late now, he thought as he swallowed down his fear and forged ahead.

The two men looked up and saw the sheriff standing a few feet away, pointing a large pistol in their direction. The rain was beginning to get heavier. They dropped the second body unceremoniously back down onto the road, and then turned to face the lawman.

"Get those hands in the air where I can see 'em!" Tucker yelled.

Smiling, the two supremacists slowly raised their hands into the air.

"Now, why don't one of you tell me who these two men are, what's goin' on, and why you're tossin' these bodies into the ravine?" Sheriff Tucker was suddenly aware that he needed to urinate. "Not now, not now," he said to himself.

"What was that, Sheriff?" the tall, skinny man in bib overalls, asked.

"Nuthin'," Tucker said, embarrassed that he had spoken out loud.

The two men stared at the sheriff for a moment, then burst out laughing.

"You think this is funny, do ya? Well, we'll see how funny you think it is when you're sittin' in a jail cell waitin' to be tried for murder. Now load that body back into the truck and fetch the one from the ravine, or do you need a little pursuadin'? Tucker said, pulling the hammer back on his pistol." He swallowed as he tried to calm the Mexican jumping beans raising havoc in his gut along with his urge to pee.

The two men were laughing because a third supremacist had stepped out of the woods from where he'd been relieving himself and was standing less than two feet behind the sheriff.

Bear stuck the business end of a shotgun against the back of Sheriff Tucker's head, and said in a voice just loud enough to be heard over the storm. "Easy Sheriff, this here shotgun of mine has ah hair trigger, so real careful like, un-cock that hog leg of your'n and hand it by the barrel, over to Vernon. He's the tall, skinny one."

Vernon, walked over and took the sheriff's weapon, then stepped back a couple of paces and pointed the big pistol at the sheriff as a wide grin spread across his face.

"Now that's ah good feller," Bear said. "Next, I want you ta walk over and stand next to that dead FBI agent."

FBI agent? What were two FBI agents doin' up here? Sheriff Tucker wondered.

"Now!" Bear yelled.

The sheriff did as he was instructed and when he reached the spot where the dead man was lying in the mud, still acting like he was in charge, he said, "I don't know what the three of you are up to but you ain't gonna get away with it, and that's ah fact. You can't go around killin' FBI agents without somebody comin' to look for 'em. Why don't you give yourselves up and I'll see what I can do?"

The three men laughed like the sheriff had just told a joke.

Bear poked the sheriff with the end of the shotgun and said, "Oh, we'll get away with it alright; this here and ah whole lot more. You have no idea of our strength or what is about ta happen, real soon. This here country is about ta get reborn," he said, waving his free arm in a circle. "Ah new day is ah comin'!"

"Should I shoot him?" Vernon asked, pointing the barrel of the sheriff's pistol at Tuckers forehead.

Tucker turned his head and looked Bear in the eyes. "Oh yeah? Well why don't you tell me all about this here, rebirthin'," he said in a snide, offhand manner, trying to buy some time.

Bear looked at the sheriff with disdain and eyes filled with hatred. His grin turned ugly and for the first time in his life, Buford Tucker knew what real fear felt like.

From a spot behind a tree, some forty feet above what was taking place on the road, Rafe Talltree watched the scene unfold from just after the two supremacists shot the two FBI agents and dumped one of the dead men into the ravine. He was numbed by what he saw, but when Tucker stepped out of the woods with his pistol drawn. Rafe felt like he should go down and offer his help, but a third supremacist came out of the woods and sneaked up behind Tucker with a shotgun.

He'd wanted to yell out to warn the sheriff, but realized that wouldn't have helped the situation. The man with the shotgun would have killed Tucker from reaction and then turn his shotgun on him.

Rafe hoped that if he waited, something would present itself so he could help the sheriff out of this mess and capture these lunatics at the same time.

Even though he and the sheriff had never seen eye to eye, he didn't want to see the man get himself killed. But the truth was, Sheriff Tucker wasn't helping himself. He was letting his bravado and big mouth dig himself deeper into the hole he was already in and Rafe wasn't sure what he could do about it, if anything. He was in no position to tell the sheriff to shut his big mouth.

Bear looked over at Vernon and said, "Vern, get rid of the sheriff's vehicle."

Vernon nodded, un-cocked the sheriff's pistol and trotted off down the road, stuffing the sheriff's pistol into the right pocket of his pants.

The sheriff turned and watched Vernon go, wondering if he could make a run for it into the woods before this Bear guy shot him in the back?

"Turn around and face me sheriff, or would you prefer the coward's way, with a blindfold so you won't see it comin', or maybe in the back of the head?" Bear asked.

Sheriff Tucker took a deep breath and made his decision. The Mexican jumping beans disappeared and calmness took their place. He didn't want to die, but he was no longer afraid. His mind was whirling, searching for his chance to escape or at least take the shotgun away from this lunatic before he did something stupid.

Tucker took a step closer to the man called Bear and asked, "What's the matter, sheep-dip, you ain't got the cahonies to look me in the eyes when you do it?"

Rafe listened to what the sheriff said and couldn't believe what he was hearing. "Ahhh crap. He's gonna talk himself into getting' blown away by those crazy rednecks. Com'on Tucker, you're smarter than that," he whispered.

Rafe was trying hard to think of some way to distract them other than leaping into their midst and probably getting himself shot in the process. Even if he didn't get shot, forty feet was a long way to jump and the fall would probably kill him, so that was out.

Nothing came to mind that would allow the sheriff a chance to get away, or take the shotgun away from the man pointing it at him, and before his mind could find a way to help the sheriff, things went from bad to worse.

The sheriff's words sent Bear into a rage and he swung the barrel of the shotgun, hitting Sheriff Tucker alongside the head. The sheriff dropped to his knees, groaning. It took all his strength to keep from being knocked unconscious.

When the sheriff looked up at Bear and spit a glob of something putrid at him, Bear lost control and shoved the end of the shotgun barrel against the sheriff's forehead and pulled the trigger.

Rafe watched in horror as a whole lot of what used to be sheriff Tucker's head disappeared; bits and pieces flying in all directions. Tucker's body was thrown backward onto the road. It made a couple of convulsive jerks, and then went rigid. Raindrops beat against Tucker's dead body, washing away the blood.

Even though the military had trained Rafe not to react in this kind of situation, he   didn't seem to be able to control himself and heard himself yelling, "Noooo!"

Rafe knew the sheriff was dead and there was nothing he could do about it, so rather than getting himself killed he jumped to his feet and disappeared into the forest before anyone had a chance to react.

Akers, who had been the quiet one during this whole affair, turned as the sound of Rafe's, "Nooooo," echoed throughout the woods and looked up in time to see a man disappear into the woods. Without being told, Akers ran in pursuit of the man, firing his weapon in the hope of making a lucky shot.

Quickly, Bear took the toe of his boot and rolled Sheriff Tucker into the ravine, and then did the same with the second FBI man. He reloaded his shotgun, and then headed in the direction Akers had gone.

Vernon came running up just as Bear headed into the woods. "I heard somebody yellin' and shootin'. I left the sheriff's carryall in the ditch and come ah runnin'. What happened?"

"Somebody saw us!" Bear yelled over his shoulder.

Without asking any more questions, Vernon followed Bear into the woods in pursuit of the mysterious man who had witnessed the killings. The man could go to the authorities and tell them what he saw. He had to be found and killed.

Rafe knew the woods in this area far better than the supremacists and in a short time had out distanced them by quite a ways. Even so, he knew that in his haste to get away, he was leaving a clear trail for them to follow and now he needed to think about his options.

CHAPTER EIGHTTEEN
The Bridge

BY NOW THE STORM had gotten much worse and the trees and overhang no longer protected the young people from the wind and rain. This time, Shaun had been outvoted three to one. They were going home, with him or without him.

Melissa and Kristi picked up their wet blankets and other belongings and headed for the two jeeps parked a short distance away. Shaun ran up next to Kristi, relieving her of part of her load.

"I knew we should have left when the others did. What's gonna happen if we get stuck up here?" Melissa yelled as she and Trace ran toward his jeep.

"You bunch of wimps, we're not gonna get stuck up here," Shaun yelled, over the wind and thunder. "We got four-wheel drive, jeeps. They can go anywhere!"

Kristi hit him on the shoulder with her fist. "You don't know that for sure!"

Trace, who was also convinced they should have left with the others, yelled through the howling wind, "What about those gunshots we heard?"

"Hunters, no big deal," Shaun yelled back, giving Trace a look that meant, 'duh, you should have figured that one out by yourself.'

"I don't think so. That didn't sound like hunters to me. And let me ask you, who would go huntin' in a storm like this? Doesn't make sense, does it? And what if those guys have been drinkin'? You know what happens then, they start shootin' at anything that moves. Sweet Jesus, they might shoot one of us!" Trace was genuinely worried as he looked behind them, just as a precaution.

"Please, Shaun," Kristi said, tugging on his arm. "Get me off this mountain and take me home!"

By now, they had reached the two jeeps and Shaun threw up his hands. "Alright already, we'll go. My folks are out of town, so we can finish the party at my house where it will be safe and dry for you tender little children." If he was being honest, he too would be glad to get out of this storm and somewhere dry and warm, but he didn't want to look weak, so he kept up his bravado. It was his way.

At this point, they weren't in the mood to argue with Shaun anymore and began loading their things into the two jeeps. They wanted to get off the mountain as soon as they could, and if agreeing to go to Shaun's house would do it, then so be it.

"Make sure your jeep is in four-wheel drive," Shaun yelled at Trace just before he climbed into his own jeep.

Grinning, Trace gave Shaun the finger, then jumped into his own jeep.

Shaun led the way down the mountain with Trace following a short distance behind, far enough so he didn't get any splatter from Shaun's rear tires. It was hard enough to see as it was.

At the same time the kids headed down the muddy road, Rafe stopped to catch his breath and decide what to do next. In the near distance, he heard Bear's gruff voice call out to the others. "Don't spread out too far. Keep each other in sight. We don't want him sneakin' between us. And be careful, he might be armed."

Bear didn't like any of this, especially trying to run up the side of a mountain in the rain, chasing an unknown man who could put him in jail. "Dammed redneck sheriff, why couldn't he have stayed back down in town where he belonged," Bear uttered to himself in between gulps of air. "No sir, running up the side of a mountain in the rain was not what I'd intended to do, today."

Bear was further plagued with other thoughts. The captain wasn't gonna like this. He wondered what he was going to tell him if they didn't catch this guy. And who the hell was this guy anyway, and what was he doin' up here sneakin' around, spyin' on people in the first place? Could he be another FBI man? And what was the sheriff from town doin' up here? The beginning of a headache started to throb in the front part of his head.

Just then he heard the caw of a crow and looked up and saw the large black bird staring down at him. Crows were bad luck and Bear wondered if the crow was an omen of things to come. He shook off the shiver that ran up his back, and then moved on.

Rafe had an inspiration and grinned, then set off at an easy pace, leaving a clear trail that a boy scout could follow.

After a short distance further up the mountain, Rafe stopped at a place he knew would leave them scratching their heads. He was standing at the edge of a rocky cliff overlooking the lake.

Rafe doubled back by climbing up onto a large boulder where he would leave no tracks. Stepping lightly, Rafe jumped from boulder to boulder taking him away from the easy to follow trail he'd left as he went higher up the mountain.

Rafe had gone nearly a quarter of a mile before heading back down the mountain in the direction of his truck, still being cautious and leaving hardly any trail to follow. The situation being what it was, he was happy he'd paid attention to his father's teachings about how to travel without leaving a trail. Even so, Rafe wasted no time. He needed to let Andy know what he'd seen so he could get some state troopers up here, along with maybe the army reserve. These guys were crazy and dangerous. Plus, he didn't know how many of them there might be.

After a half a mile, Rafe began to jog to make extra time. He figured he was far enough away so that leaving tracks wouldn't make any difference. His pickup was just a short distance down the road. He would be there in a few minutes and hopefully headed for town before they caught up to him.

The road was muddy and getting worse by the minute. The rain continued to fall like the sky was emptying large buckets of water on it. Outside, the howling wind was threatening to push both jeeps into the ditch. As hard as they tried, neither of the jeep's windshield wipers could do the job they were designed to do, which didn't help Shaun or Trace see where they were going.

Both Shaun and Trace had to slow down to keep their vehicles on the road, and even then, each one had almost gone into the ditch on several occasions.

"I'm so glad you have four-wheel drive," Melissa said, trying hard not to show her fear.

"Me too," Trace said, gripping the steering wheel with both hands and straining to keep Shaun's tail lights in sight, while keeping his jeep between the ditches.

It was obvious that Kristi was nervous as she chewed on her fingernails. "Can't you go any faster?" she asked with a nervous squeak to her voice.

"No," Shaun said without taking his eyes off the road, or what of it he could see. "Is Trace still behind us?" he asked as he fought to stay where he thought the road was supposed to be. Everywhere he looked, all he could see was a river of muddy water.

Kristi turned and strained to see through the Plexiglas window on the rear of the jeeps canvas top and siding. After a minute she turned back and said, "It's raining too hard and I can't see through the back window. Do you think we should stop and check?"

Shaun was gripping the wheel tightly to keep the vehicle under control. "No," he said. "We can't stop. We have to get across the bridge and out onto the highway. Trace is a good driver. I'm sure he's right behind us."

Kristi turned and climbed into the back of the jeep and put her face up next to the Plexiglas window and stared hard. Finally, she saw what she thought were headlights in the near distance behind them. "I think I see them!" she yelled, excitedly. "You're right, they're right behind us!"

After climbing back into the passenger's seat, Kristi was able to relax, at least a little bit. She had been worried about them getting stuck in a ditch and not being able to get out. Once they got off this mountain and onto the paved highway, she hoped they would all be able to breathe easier. She bit off another piece of fingernail and spit it onto the floorboard.

Shaun knew he had to get them off this mountain and back to town. Kristi's dad would kill him if anything happened to her.

The three supremacists followed Rafe's footprints right up to the edge of a cliff and stopped. They stood looking over the edge, then all around them and saw nothing but empty forest. The footprints just disappeared! There was no way he could have gone over the side of the cliff and lived to tell about it; it was at least a hundred feet straight down to the first place where he could have dropped. And in this rain it would have been suicide to attempt it.

"Damn!" Bear roared, as he peeked over the edge, just in case the man had accidentally gone over the edge - and sighed when he saw no dead body.

"He must have circled around us somehow," Vernon announced as though the information had cleared up a big mystery.

Bear shook his head and yelled, as he started at a dogtrot back down, "Com'on, we've got to find him before he gets off this mountain!"

As they ran, Vernon offered up information that was long overdue. "After we took off chasin' this feller, I saw an old pickup sittin' alongside the road not far from where we was ah disposin' the bodies. S'pose it coulda' been his? Ya think maybe that's where he's headed?"

"Thanks for sayin' somethin' when you saw it," Bear yelled, as he picked his way down the mountain as fast as he could without slipping and falling. "Let's get ah move on. Come on, let's go, let's go."

Rafe came running out of the woods and leaped onto the road close to where his pickup was sitting. He jumped into the pickup and shoved the key into the ignition and turned the key. Nothing happened! "Not now!" he screamed and tried again, but still nothing happened. Rafe climbed out of the pickup and raised the hood. Holding the hood with one hand, he wiggled the battery connector with his other hand then dropped the hood back down and climbed back into the old pickup and turned the key. "Com'on ole girl, don't fail me now. If those idiots catch me I'm ah dead man."

This time the old six cylinder Chevy engine caught hold and roared to life. Sweat was running down Rafe's face and body, mixing with the rainwater that already had him soaked from head to foot. When the engine came to life, Rafe gave a sigh of relief.

At that moment, the windshield of Rafe's pickup shattered, the bullet lodging itself in the back of the seat on the passenger's side, as the sound of the shot echoed through the forest. Rafe jerked the old truck into gear and shoved down on the accelerator as he let out the clutch. Mud flew out from behind the rear tires in a high arc as Rafe cranked the steering wheel around hard to his left and the pickup made a fast, sliding from one side of the road to the other, U-turn, and then sped off down the mountain. Another shot blew the side view mirror off of the passenger side of the truck just before the pickup disappeared around a curve, throwing up a wall of mud in its wake.

The three supremacists ran out onto the road and fired several more shots at the pickup, but to no avail. By now, there weren't even any taillights to shoot at.

Bear looked at the other two men and shook his head, "Let's get back down to the truck. We've got to catch him before he gets back to town! And no screw-ups this time!"

At the same time Rafe was having his troubles Shaun's jeep came to where the fork in the road should be. Shaun angled his jeep to the right and headed for the bridge, with Trace and Melissa not far behind.

A hundred feet or so from the bridge, Kristi and Shaun saw a wall of water come cascading down the river, tearing up everything in its path, including the bridge.

Kristi screamed, "Shaun, the bridge!"

Flabbergasted, Shaun watched as the huge wall of water ripped the bridge loose from its pilings and dragged it down the river like it was nothing. Never in his wildest dreams did Shaun ever think something like this could happen. His adrenalin kicked into gear and he yelled, "Hang on Kristi!" He sucked in a large breath of air and held it as he downshifted into a lower gear and cranked the steering wheel to the right as he applied the brakes. The jeep was sliding through the mud sideways, throwing up a wall of floodwater nearly as high as the jeep. Shaun prayed his jeep would stop before it went sliding into the raging floodwater.

Right behind Shaun and Kristi, Trace was fighting his own battle. He downshifted and applied the brakes, trying to angle his jeep away from hitting Shaun's jeep or sliding off into the flood enraged river.

Trace turned the steering wheel to the left just enough for him to see that he wouldn't hit Shaun's jeep, but not hard enough that his jeep would get itself in a position to be turned over on its side by the water coming down the mountain, and maybe even pushed into the flooded river.

Through all of this, Melissa uttered not a word but her hand was holding tightly to the door handle. She was prepared to jump if it became necessary, hoping Trace was prepared to do the same. Losing your car was a whole lot better than losing your life.

When both jeeps finally came to a halt, they were sitting close to each other, just short of going into the river. After a few moments, when their nerves had finally calmed down, they climbed out of the jeeps and found themselves standing in knee-deep water that was coming down the mountain and running almost strong enough to knock them over.

Kristi and Melissa made their way over to each other and hugged, tears mixing with the rain running down their faces.

Shaun and Trace walked over close to the river and stared in wide-eyed awe at the destruction the flooded river was causing.

Shaking his head from side to side, Shaun yelled over the wind and the roar of the rushing water, "Can you believe this?"

By now Trace's heart had had time to get back to beating its normal rhythm and he was more than a little upset. "Dammit, Shaun, we're in a world of hurt here. What're we gonna do now?"

After a few moments, when Shaun hadn't said anything, Trace poked Shaun on the shoulder and yelled, "Com'on man, what are we gonna do?"

Shaun shoved Trace's hand away and yelled back at him, "Just. . . just shut-up for a minute and let me think."

Trace looked at his friend and realized Shaun was also feeling the effects of what almost happened. He hadn't meant to yell at him, but dammit if they had gone back when the others did they would be at Shaun's house, downing some brews and maybe getting lucky instead of being stuck up here with no food and no place to sleep except in the jeeps and he didn't have enough gas to run the jeep all night to keep the heater going. Even at this time of year it got cold up here at night.

The two girls came up and stood next to Trace, rain soaking them from head to foot as Shaun paced back and forth in front of them in the rushing, knee-deep water. Finally, he turned and looked at them with a blank look on his face.

Kristi moved a step closer to him and said, "Well?"

Shaun looked at the three of them and began to laugh.

"What's so funny?" Kristi asked, putting her hands on her hips.

"You all look like a bunch of drowned rats," Shaun said, still laughing.

They looked at each other but none of them laughed.

Finally, Shaun squared his shoulders and got a stern look on his face. In his best commanding voice, said, "Let's get these jeeps turned around. We're going back."

Incensed that Shaun would make such a statement, Trace asked, "With all this flooding and those guys shootin' off their guns, you want to go back to the lake?"

"Not the lake, the old lodge," Shaun said as he headed for his jeep.

Melissa stood her ground and folded her arms across her chest. "I don't think that's a good idea," she said, trying to sound like she knew something the rest of them didn't.

Kristi shook her head from side to side, rainwater flying in all directions. "I agree with Melissa; the old lodge is miles from here. Plus, there are some pretty deep ravines that we couldn't get out of if you misjudged the road. And they're probably flooded to the top. No, I don't like it Shaun. This is a bad idea."

"And what about those hunters?" Trace asked.

Shaun stopped just short of his jeep and turned around. "It's the only thing that makes sense," he said. "In case we have to be up here for a couple of days just what do you think we should do, sit cooped up in the jeeps, cold and hungry. Maybe there are still some cans of food up there. We can light a big fire in the fireplace and be warm and dry while we wait. And when we don't show up by tonight, you can bet somebody will come looking for us."

Even though what Shaun said made sense, they still hesitated.

Shaun raised his hands; palms forward and said, "Since the lodge is closed, if there are hunters up there," he said pointing toward the mountain, "they probably have campers they're staying in."

"How are the people who come to rescue us going to get across the river?" Melissa asked.

Exhausted, Shaun hung his head and said, "I don't know, Melissa. They're adults and I'm sure they'll figure it out. Now come on, we're wastin' time."

After a moment, each one of them realized this was their only real option. They looked at each other, shrugged their shoulders, then headed for the jeeps as the rain continued to pound down on them.

Inside Trace's jeep, Melissa wiped the water from her face and tried to dry her water soaked hair with a towel she found in the back seat. As Trace started the engine, Melissa voiced her opinion. "A voice inside me is telling me this is wrong, even though in theory it makes sense," she said as she patted her hair with the towel.

Her brain told her going back up to the lodge was the logical thing to do, but the growling in her stomach was convincing her that going to the lodge was a bad idea and she couldn't understand why her brain and her stomach had such conflicting thoughts. It was driving her, nuts. What could be up at the abandoned lodge that would make her feel this way? Nothing that she could think of. She finished drying her hair as best she could and dropped the towel on her lap.

Trace didn't want to argue with her right now, the friction between them was bad enough as it was; besides, he had his hands full trying to keep his jeep between the ditches, but after several minutes of silence, he could stand it no longer; fight or no fight he wanted to set the record straight. "Look, Melissa, don't give me no looks or go tryin' to lay the blame on me for going up to the lodge. This is Shaun's idea, remember?"

Melissa picked up the towel and wiped her face and arms. Then through gritted teeth she said, "Oh yes, the great and powerful, Shaun Tilford, king of Shortcut, Utah! Whom I believe is also the one who got us stranded up here in the first place. So, tell me Trace, why do you follow him around like a puppy dog and jump when he tells you to?"

Trace frowned and clamped his jaw shut as he fought the wheel. 'She's definitely spoiling for a fight but I'm not about to get sucked in,' he thought to himself. Besides, he wasn't Shaun's puppet. "I'm the star running back and Shaun is our quarterback. And he is not just the quarterback but he's also the captain of the team, which means we all take orders from him," he mumbled under his breath. He guessed he'd just gotten used to Shaun being the leader; but the biggest reason he hung around with Shaun was, he just happened to be the coolest guy in town. The dude was definitely a chick magnet - and the overflow wasn't too shabby; except maybe for Melissa. He couldn't figure her out. One minute she was like a hot tamale and the next, she was giving him the brush-off.

The sound of a horn honking loudly interrupted his thoughts. He saw Shaun's jeep swerve to the left and then go out into the field. When he turned his eyes back to the road, there was an old Chevy pickup, heading straight for him at high speed.

Trace jerked the steering wheel to the right and drove off into the ditch, then up the other side and off the road just as the pickup roared past.

Trace wanted to yell at the driver and tell him the bridge was gone; that it had been washed down the river by the flood, but there wasn't time. The pickup roared past at breakneck speed.

Trace and Melissa both jumped out of the jeep and watched as best they could. The rain was still making it hard to see. Both of them were holding their breath as they watched the pickup head straight toward the raging river, praying that somehow the driver would see that the bridge was gone and stop in time.

Just before the pickup went head first into the river, the door on the driver's side opened and a man jumped clear of the truck, landing head first in the mud, rolling over twice, then coming to his feet.

The pickup nose-dived over the bank and drove itself front end first into the mud, leaving the bed and rear tires sticking up in the air. The rear wheels continued to spin for only a moment before they stopped. The truck was struggling to stay where it was lodged, but the force of the river was moving it back and forth, trying to rip it free from where it stood, nose down in the mud.

Trace and Melissa were the closest to the man, which meant they were the first ones to reach him. When they got close, Trace came to a sliding halt. "Rafe Talltree, is that you?' he called out to the tall hunk of mud standing in front of him.

Melissa rushed up next to him and asked, "Are you alright? My god, you almost got yourself killed!"

Without saying whether he had injuries or not, and without explanation, he yelled over the storm, "We've got to get out of here!"

"Yes, we know, we were. . ." Melissa said. But before she could say anything else, Shaun came running up, yelling like a wild man.

"Talltree! You crazy bastard! You almost got us killed!"

"And you're gonna get killed for real if we don't get outta here, right now!"

Kristi was confused by his statement and said so. "I don't understand. Is there a giant flood coming down the mountain, too?"

Rafe Talltree shook his head and said as a quick explanation, "In a sense, yeah. There's some crazy bastard's up here with guns. They've already killed Sheriff Tucker and two other men. They were dumpin' the two dead men's bodies in the ravine when the sheriff showed up. I was checkin' my traps when I happened onto the scene and I saw them kill Sheriff Tucker. I yelled and when they saw me, they started shootin' at me and I lit out. They're not far behind me and I'm pretty sure they won't hesitate to kill me and anybody who is with me and they won't ask any questions! So, if you don't mind, since we can't get across the river and you have four wheelers, let's get outta here, right now!"

Shaun shook his head in disbelief. "Tucker, dead? I don't believe it. You sure you ain't been drinkin' or takin' dope or something?"

Rafe looked up the road before he turned back to Shaun. "Well you better believe it, hotshot! Tucker and I never got along, but I'll give the man his due; he looked them straight in the eyes and spit at the guy right before he went down like the man he was, headstrong and defiant right down to the last when that crazy redneck stuck the end of his shotgun barrel against Tucker's forehead and pulled the trigger. Now, no more talk! If we don't get a move on muy pronto . . ."

"That sounds like a load of crap to me," Shaun cut in, not wanting to believe him.

"Why do you think I was driving like a crazy man in this weather, just for kicks? I'm telling you, we have to get out of here now, or we're all going to die. So here it is, I'm leaving with you, or without you. Whether you come along or not is totally up to you, but I'm not ready to die just yet."

Melissa stepped up close to Rafe and asked, "What do you want us to do?"

"Get in the jeeps and head into the woods," he said. "We'll decide where, later."

Kristi, Melissa and Trace all headed for the jeeps as Shaun yelled out, "Hey, wait a minute. Who put him in charge?"

Trace had had enough and turned on his friend. "Shaun, for once, just shut up and get in your jeep and let's get outta here!"

Before Shaun could respond, water splashed up in front of them just before the sound of a shotgun rumbled across the rain filled sky. Fortunately, no one was hit.

Without another word, they all ran for the jeeps. Rafe followed Shaun and Kristi. Shaun was in the lead, running like his life depended on it, which in this case, it did.

Kristi was trying hard to keep up, but just as she reached the back of Shaun's jeep another shot rang out and Kristi fell to the ground, grabbing her right leg. "Oh my God! I've been shot! I've been shot!"

Shaun started to turn around, but Rafe lifted Kristi into his arms and yelled, "Keep going, I've got her!"

As Shaun fired up the engine, Rafe placed Kristi in the passenger seat, and then climbed into the back. "Let's go! Let's go!" he yelled as he pointed to an opening in the woods.

With tires spinning, throwing up a wall of mud and water, Shaun raced off toward the direction Rafe was pointing. Trace was not far behind and off to the side so his jeep wouldn't be covered with flying mud and water.

The two-wheeled drive pickup came down the road slipping and sliding back and forth across the muddy road. Bear was driving and having a difficult time. Vernon and Akers were standing in the back, trying to keep from being thrown out.

Vernon pointed his shotgun over the roof of the pickup in the general direction of the retreating jeeps, while Akers tried to aim his rifle. With all the swerving and bouncing around, their chances of hitting anything was small, but they both hoped maybe one, or both of them would get lucky.

Akers fired just as the pickup swerved and to his amazement, he saw the girl go down.

"Yee, haw! I got one of 'em!" he yelled.

"Where did those kids come from?" Vernon yelled.

"Don't know. But they're with the one we're ah chasin', so that means they're the enemy, too!"

The pickup hit a bump and momentarily went air borne, throwing Vernon to the bed of the truck. Grabbing the side of the pickup, he stood up and regained his balance. "If anybody is askin', this here is get 'in way too complicated fer me. We only had one ta get, and now we got five. I don't like this. I don't like it a'tall."

The look on Akers face showed that he was giving Vernon's words a lot of thought but wasn't about to voice his opinion out loud.

CHAPTER NINETEEN
Vernon learns to fly

SHERIFF TUCKER'S CARRYALL had been driven off into the ditch next to the road with the driver's side window still rolled down. Fortunately, the carryall was faced with the window away from the direction the storm was coming from and therefore not much rain was getting inside.

Andy's voice came tumbling through the open window, "Base to car one, base to car one. Come in Sheriff."

Not far away, at the bottom of the ravine, Sheriff Buford Tucker lay bobbing up and down in the runoff. He was on his back, staring skyward with dead eyes, as blood from what remained of his head mixed with the rainwater and flowed down the mountain in the direction of the river. A protruding tree root was the only thing keeping the sheriff from following his blood.

Andy stood next to the police radio with the microphone in his hand, frustration scrawled across his face as he waited to hear the sheriff's voice. After a minute passed without any response from the sheriff, he tried again. "Base to

128

car one. Base to car one come in. Sheriff, I sure do need you to talk to me."

When he still got no response, he whispered, "You hard headed, cantankerous bastard, talk to me!"

After another minute, Andy set the microphone back in its cradle and walked over to the coffee pot and poured himself a cup. "He's probably givin' them kids what-for," he mumbled, trying to convince his grumbling stomach that that was what was happening and nothing was wrong.

As he walked past the sheriff's desk, he noticed the walkie-talkie was still sitting in its charge cradle. "No wonder he isn't answering the radio," he said to the empty office.

Andy walked over and sat down at his own desk. Sipping on his coffee, he lifted the plastic evidence bag with the ring in it and studied the Nazi emblem. "Something weird is going on; I can feel it in my gut; I just wished I knew what it is. A van blowing up, right here on the streets of Shortcut; a charred hand with a Nazi ring on one of the fingers. This definitely is not what I'd call a good sign," he said, not realizing the full impact the exploding van would have on this quiet little community.

Andy tossed the plastic sack with the charred hand and ring back into the desk drawer. He sat there, sipping his coffee; pondering all the possibilities that could be associated with the ring and the van, and the explosion. The beginnings of a severe headache caused his temples to throb.

The two jeeps, aided by their four-wheel drive had an easier time driving through the raging storm and weaving back and forth between the trees than did Bear's pickup.

The pickup Bear was driving was sliding every which way, it's back tires throwing mud high into the air as it sashayed back and forth, trying to find traction. In the back, Vernon and Akers, when they could, kept up a steady barrage of bullets and shot gun pellets aimed toward the two jeeps. But most of their time was spent just trying to stay upright and in the back of the truck.

Fortunately for Rafe and the kids, the shots were killing nothing but a lot of tree branches, while the rest flew off into the forest, who knew where?

Being young and full of bravado, along with being scared out of their wits, Shaun and Trace slowly but surely began to put distance between them and the men shooting at them. The further the distance got, the harder it was for Vernon or Akers, to get a clear shot. There were times when the trees and brush allowed the jeeps to disappear completely.

Being shot is an experience most people are fortunate to never have, so it wasn't unusual that Kristi, a young, teenage girl who had been mostly pampered all of her life, wasn't handling being gunshot too well. "Oh God, Shaun, I'm bleeding bad! I don't want to die! I don't want to bleed to death! Can't somebody do something? Don't let me die. Shaun, please take me to the hospital, now! And then call my parents!"

As much as Shaun wanted to do something to help her, Kristi's problem was not his number one priority right now. "I'm sorry babe, but I can't do anything about it right now! Just hang in there," he pleaded. "I'll get you to a doctor as soon as I can get these crazy guys off our tail. Just hang on, babe."

Kristi seemed to be out of control and was babbling on like a hysterical child. "I can't feel my leg or foot! What's happening? Am I dying? Please Shaun, don't let me bleed to death!"

Rafe leaned forward between the two front seats and spoke to Kristi in a stern but calm voice, "Just quiet down and try to relax. You're not going to die."

As far as Shaun was concerned, no matter what Rafe said, or the tone he said it in, would cause Shaun to take umbrage. "Hey man, just shut up and don't talk to her like that," he yelled as he turned the wheel just in time to miss yet another tree.

Rafe knew that Kristi was scared and hurting and he felt for her, but she was in no imminent danger at this point, and putting distance between them and their pursuers came first. So at this particular time he was in no mood to listen to her complaining or Shaun's big mouth. To Shaun, he said with gritted teeth, "Just drive, hot shot!" And to Kristi he said in a softer voice. "You're gonna be alright; I promise; you're not going to bleed to death. Put your hand over the wound and press down. That will slow down the bleeding. We'll take care of your leg as soon as we can."

For some reason, Kristi felt she could trust Rafe and immediately began to calm down as she reached down and pressed against the hole where the bullet had gone in. By now Kristi's leg had gone numb, so there was no pain when she pressed down on the wound.

As the jeep entered a small clearing, Shaun turned and looked at Rafe. "Who are those guys back there? And why are they runnin' around killin' people they don't even know?"

Rafe shook his head from side to side. "I don't know. Maybe you'd like to go back there and ask them!" Rafe yelled. This whole thing was making him short tempered and he was ready to take it out on anyone who looked at him wrong.

After a moment, Rafe realized he was acting just like Shaun, which was the last thing he wanted to do. He had to stay calm and think things through. If he was still in Nam and trying to get some guys to safety and they had no weapons to fight back with, what would he do?

Shaun's face got red with anger. He didn't like Talltree and he for sure didn't like taking orders from him. "Look dude, we didn't ask to be chased by a bunch of lunatics with guns, and for dammed sure we don't like bein' shot at. We wouldn't be in this kind of predicament if it weren't for you. You're the one who brought them down on us, so just lighten up with your superior attitude!"

"Superior attitude?" Rafe said, trying to hold his tongue, but couldn't. "If you had even as much sense as a retard, you would have left when you saw the storm coming, like the others did!"

Shaun gave him a look of pure hatred. "What do you know about it?"

"I was checking a trap at the top of the ledge overlooking the beach. And if you had left when everybody asked you to," Rafe continued, ignoring Shaun's angry look, "then you wouldn't have been down by the river when I came down the road, so don't go blaming me for your stupidity!"

If the men in the pickup weren't still chasing them, Shaun knew he would have stopped the jeep right then and had it out with Rafe. Instead, he said, "Look Chief, I'm givin' you fair warning, when we get outta this mess, I'm gonna take you apart!"

"Your call big mouth, you name the time and place, but right now save all that macho crap and get us the hell outta here!"

Rafe was beginning to feel like an idiot for letting Shaun goad him into lowering himself down to his level. There was just something about this kid that got under his skin.

Shaun's jeep had just crossed an open space and was now back into the woods, swerving this way and that to miss trees and large boulders, with Trace still following in the near distance behind.

Trace was trying to keep Shaun's jeep in sight, along with keeping his vehicle under control. The last thing he wanted to do was to run into something and get left behind. He was also trying to keep a safe distance between his jeep and the screwballs shooting at them - and if that wasn't enough to occupy his mind, Melissa was beginning to ask questions that he didn't have answers for.

"Where are we going?" she asked as though it was a simple, easy question to answer.

Keeping his eyes on Shaun's jeep, Trace said, "I don't know."

"Why do you suppose those men are shooting at us?" she asked, looking out the back window of Trace's jeep, even though she couldn't really see much.

"I don't know that, either," Trace replied.

Melissa let out a sigh. "Why would they want to kill us? We didn't do anything to them. We don't even know them. Maybe if. . ."

By now Trace was about to blow his top. "Melissa, please! Just shut up and let me concentrate! Can't you see I'm busy? I can't drive and talk at the same time! So just chill out, okay?"

Melissa swallowed her pride and tried to hold back the retort that was about to choke her. She was hurt by Trace's reply. She was only trying to relieve some of the tension she was feeling. She felt that talking would help calm her nerves. She hadn't meant to upset him. She was probably more scared of those men behind them than he was. "Of course, I'll be quiet. I didn't realize you were so sensitive," she replied as she slumped against the passenger door, gripping tightly to the handle, immediately regretting her snippy comeback. None of this was Trace's fault, except for the fact that he allowed Shaun to do his thinking for him. She wondered if she should apologize? No, she realized, that would be talking and Trace had made it very clear that he didn't want her to talk, so she just sat there with her jaws clamped tightly together, determined to hold her tongue.

Trace felt bad that he had yelled at her, but right now he had a lot on his mind. One of the main things was not getting him or Melissa killed. Maybe, after they got away he would get the chance to explain. He seriously hoped Talltree knew where they were going because Trace knew that neither he nor Shaun knew their way around up here. He'd heard that Talltree lived up here alone, somewhere high up in a log cabin, but he didn't know for sure or where, exactly. He wondered if maybe that was where Rafe was taking them. Although in reality, wherever it was didn't matter to him, just so long as it was far, far away from those crazy men chasing them, and their desire to kill everybody in sight.

With the continued downpour and muddy ground, Bear's pickup was difficult to control. Sweat was running into his eyes and he was having trouble seeing. He swerved to miss a tree, only to find a large boulder right in front of him. He slammed on the brakes but the pickup slid head on into the large rock with a loud crashing sound, buckling the bumper and caving in the grille. The headlights were in a hundred pieces and the hood had a large hump in it. Steam hissed from the radiator and the engine died. Bear was thrown forward and banged his forehead on the windshield, but was not seriously injured.

Vernon was not in a good position and went flying over the cab of the pickup and smashed headfirst into the boulder. His skull split open like a melon being cut with a large knife, and his neck snapped, leaving his head hanging over at a funny angle. His body bounced backward and landed on the hood of the pickup. Vernon's nerves gave one final jerk as his body flipped over and went rigid. He was lying face up with his eyes wide open. Due to his head being split apart and his broken neck, he had a grotesque look about him. One eye was looking in one direction and the other eye was looking in the opposite direction as if he were trying to figure what had happened. His brain was exposed and blood ran down over the hood, mixing with the rain.

Like a flash, Akers came flying out of the pickup and ran to where Vernon's body lay. Bear was only a step behind him. Akers looked at the mess and almost vomited. He looked at Bear and tried to speak, but no sound would come, He shook his head back and forth. "He was my friend," Akers finally said with tears running down his cheeks.

Bear looked down at Vernon and felt his stomach turn. Anger began to rise inside him and his chest hurt like he was about to have a heart attack. Bear slammed his fist into the palm of his other hand. "Damn that intruder all to hell! When I get my hands on him. . ." He couldn't finish the sentence. The knot on his head began to throb and he felt like he was going to pass out. Pain radiated throughout his brain and down into his eyes. He put his hand against the fender of the pickup to keep from falling.

A few minutes later, when Bear calmed down and the dizziness had gone away, he cradled Vernon in his arms and said, "Akers, stretch the tarp out in the back of the pickup so we can wrap him in it."

Akers rushed to do as Bear told him, and when they were finished, Bear said, "I'll call the captain. We're gonna need some more guns up here."

Akers could only nod his head as he searched for a cigarette and his lighter. He needed a smoke to help calm his nerves.

CHAPTER TWENTY
Weeu, Weeu, Weeu

MEANWHILE, with Shaun still in the lead, he and Trace continued trying to put as much distance as they could between them and the men who were trying to kill them. But with the windshield a blur and him trying not to run into any trees or boulders, the strain was eating at his nerves. So, between Kristi's wailing and the rate of speed they were going, Shaun didn't see the ditch until it was too late and the jeep went flying into the air.

"Holy crap! Hang on, Kristi!" he yelled, just before the jeep nose-dived into the far bank of the ditch, just below the top, then came down hard on four wheels, and slid to the bottom with the horn blaring at the top of its range – Weeu, Weeu, Weeu.

Trace came close to following Shaun into the ditch, but was able to turn his jeep sideways and slide to a stop just a few feet from the edge. Both he and Melissa jumped out and stared down at Shaun's jeep, its horn bellowing loud enough to wake the dead.

Shortly after getting his jeep, as another way to bug sheriff Tucker, Shaun had installed one of those horns that sounded like a European police car with that irritating *weeu, weeu, weeu,* sound. This would have been a good time for the horn not to work. The loud, irritating sound was echoing throughout the forest, and had by now alerted everyone within a three-mile radius that something was wrong.

Melissa was standing at the edge of the ditch with her hands over her ears and staring down at Shaun's jeep. She was in shock and screaming, "Oh my God! Oh my God, Oh my God!"

Realizing the situation could be serious; Trace grabbed Melissa by the arm and yelled, "Com'on! We've got to get them outta that jeep!"

At the sound of Trace's voice, something inside Melissa brought her back to her senses and she scooted down into the ditch, passing Trace on the way. At the bottom, she raced through almost knee-deep water trying to get to the passenger's side of Shaun's jeep as fast as she could.

As Trace and Melissa were hurrying to the aid of their friends, the weeu, weeu, weeu sound from the blaring horn made its way through the forest and caused Bear to turn his head in the direction it was coming from. "Somethin' must'a happened - and it's not far off!"

"Maybe they ran into a tree or somethin'," Akers said with a grin.

Bear handed the radio's microphone to Akers and said, "You wait here. I'll go on ahead and see if I can locate 'em."

Akers reached into his inner coat pocket and pulled out a walkie-talkie. "Take this," he said, "I'm purdy sure the Captain will have one with him. That way you can give us directions when you find 'em."

Bear took the walkie-talkie, nodded his head and then headed into the forest. "Why would anybody have ah horn like that?" he mumbled to himself. "Must be ah damn foreigner."

As Melissa rushed up to the passenger side of the jeep, the door swung open and Rafe climbed out, and then turned and lifted Kristi out of her seat. Without thinking about it, she put her arms around his neck for support and held on tight.

Kristi grimaced with the pain of being moved when Rafe lifted her from the jeep and handed her to Trace. "Here, take her, but be careful. She's been shot in the leg."

Melissa's hand flew to her mouth. "Shot! Oh my God! Kristi, is it serious? I can't believe they shot you! Are you in much pain?"

Melissa held Kristi's hand as Trace sloshed through the water and sat Kristi on a large rock protruding out of the side of the ditch.

Kristi nodded her head, "Yes, it hurts something awful," then began to explain the entire experience to Melissa, who was by now, patting her hand and crying.

Melissa raised her hands, palms up, and shrugged her shoulders, indicating she couldn't hear what Kristi was saying over the blaring of the horn.

"Will someone please turn off that horn? I can't hear what Kristi is saying!" Melissa yelled at the top of her lungs.

Rafe lifted the already damaged hood and propped it open, then headed for the driver's side of the jeep, yelling over his shoulder, "Trace, kill that horn!"

While Rafe lifted an unconscious Shaun from the driver's side, Trace began pulling wires until the horn went silent.

Rafe layed Shaun stretched out on his back, on another large rock protruding out from the ditch.

Rafe then went to the back of Shaun's jeep and pulled out a good-sized piece of canvas and spread it on the boulder next to where Kristi was laying. Melissa helped him move Kristi onto the tarp, and then he covered her with the unused portion.

When he finished, he felt a hand on his shoulder and turned his head. Melissa was smiling at him, and for a moment Rafe forgot where he was or what he was doing. There was something in her eyes and smile that made his insides do flip-flops. It was like a huge magnet had grabbed him and was drawing him to her and wouldn't let go.

Shaun made a loud groaning noise that brought Rafe back to reality. He gave Melissa a sheepish grin, then hurried over to where Shaun was trying to sit up.

Trace also rushed over when he heard Shaun moan. As soon as he got there, he asked, "Hey, man, you okay?" Which was sort of a dumb question since the goose egg on Shaun's forehead was as big as a golf ball; the color somewhere between red, black and a dull purple. Another clue was the fact that Shaun's eyes had a wild, glazed look to them and he was having trouble keeping his balance.

Shaun touched the goose egg on his forehead, gingerly, and winced, "Not sure. Must' a hit my head on somethin'."

Rafe grinned. "Yeah, the steering wheel, but I think the steering wheel got the worst of it," he said, hoping Shaun didn't have a serious concussion.

"Very funny," Shaun snarled as he looked over and saw Melissa holding Kristi's hand.

Kristi was talking a mile a minute and waving her other hand as she explained what it felt like to get shot.

"Kristi, how you doin', babe?" he called out.

Both Melissa and Kristi turned their heads at the same time and cast questioning looks in his direction.

"Other than being shot in the leg, losing a lot of blood and being traumatized by this whole ordeal, I think she'll be all right, but we need to get her to a doctor, ASAP," Melissa said with a matter a fact tone that sounded a whole lot like an order.

Melissa looked at Rafe, her eyes sparkling, giving him a smile that would have melted a giant ice glacier.

Rafe felt a flush come to his face and a tingling feeling suddenly running rampant throughout his entire body. He turned away before anyone noticed. After getting his breathing and heart rate back to normal rhythm, he looked at the four of them and said, "We'll be going on foot now, so let's get a move on."

"Are you crazy?" Shaun yelled. "What about that bullet in Kristi's leg?"

Rafe shook his head; not understanding the level of stupidity Shaun was showing even in the face of danger. "There isn't time for a debate or to do surgery. We'll remove the bullet later. With the message that horn sent, it's not gonna take those lunatics long to figure out something is wrong and the sound it was making will make it easy for them to find us. Now, tough guy, when they get here, what're you gonna do then, throw rocks at 'em?"

Rafe was letting his temper take control of his mouth again. For some reason he had a hard time keeping his cool around this jerk.

Trace jumped in before Shaun's thick head and big mouth got them into more trouble than they already were. "He's right, man. We need to get outta here, fast."

"What about Kristi? She can't walk with a bullet in her leg," Melissa inquired.

"Yes I can," Kristi said, trying to sound brave, but when she tried to stand up, she fell back down on the tarp, groaning from the pain.

"No, you can't!" Melissa screamed at Kristi. Next, she turned her attention to the others. "Jesus, you guys, her leg is bleeding! Don't you realize she's been shot! People die from gun wounds!"

"We'll carry her on the tarp," Rafe said.

"To where?" Shaun asked.

It was just about then Trace realized they wouldn't be taking his jeep and he felt a panic spread over him. "What about my jeep? I can't just go off and leave it for those lunatics to chase us with. It's a four wheeler."

"Leave it here is exactly what you will do," Rafe said. "Pull some wires to disable it so it can't be driven, and then take only what you can carry. We'll make a litter out of the piece of canvas Kristi is laying on. Now, go! We need to move out, muy pronto."

Shaun climbed to his feet a bit wobbly and dusted himself off as he shook his head to clear the cobwebs. If he had a concussion, it was a minor one. He looked at Rafe and said, "You still haven't said, where."

Rafe pointed toward the top of the mountain. "Up there. Now get whatever you want to take with you and don't waste a lot of time doing it. Do either of you have any rope?"

Trace raised his hand as the rain dripped from his face. "I have a hundred foot coil I use for climbing, or towing, or whatever."

"Good. I'll carry it. We may need it."

After grabbing what little they needed to take with them, Rafe took the lead and carried the front end of the tarp. Trace carried the other end as they climbed out of the ditch and disappeared into the woods.

Shaun walked along next to Kristi, holding her hand while Melissa brought up the rear. She was nervous and constantly turning to see if the men chasing them had found their trail, yet.

Climbing up a mountainside was frustrating. Between the rain, the muddy slope and trying to carry a makeshift litter with dead weight on it made their progress painfully slow.

Rafe was like one of those plow horses you see in the movies, never wavering or stumbling. He just kept moving forward. But Shaun and Trace were not used to being in the mountains and had a hard time keeping up. Approximately every ten minutes or so, they would be winded and had to take turns. Even though they were both jocks and in good shape for participating in school events, climbing up a steep mountain, slipping and sliding in the mud, along with carrying dead weight, was a whole different ball game.

From time to time, Rafe would glance over his shoulder and smile when he saw Shaun's red face and hear his labored breathing. He didn't actually dislike the kid, only his attitude, which was like most of the people of Shortcut. He felt sorry for them, being thrown into a situation like this, but what could he do except try to help them get away; even the big mouthed Tilford kid.

Rafe glanced over his shoulder, his thoughts on the men who had killed the sheriff and the other two men and were now planning to kill him and these four kids. He didn't know why they'd done what they did, but enough was enough. There would be no more killing if he had any say about it. "Not on my mountain," he said aloud.

"What was that?" Trace asked.

Embarrassed that he'd spoken out loud, he mumbled, "Nothing. It didn't mean anything. Forget about it."

Trace gave him a shrug, wondering what was going through his mind.

CHAPTER TWENTY-ONE

Unplug the phone, please!

WITH THE SHERIFF GONE, Andy had to carry the entire load. Which, in a small town like Shortcut, wasn't much during normal times. But this was anything but normal times.

Added to the mystery of the ring with a swastika on it, the exploding van and the disappearance of the sheriff; suddenly the entire population of Shortcut was calling to tell him about their problems.

At that particular moment, Andy was on the phone with Prudence Ditwiller, one of the town's foremost fuss buckets.

"No ma'am, I can't drop everything and come over right now. You see, the sheriff is gone. . . and. . . and, I'm here alone, and. . ."

The woman's loud talking caused Andy to move the earpiece away from his head until he could finally jump into the conversation, again. "Yes ma'am, how many did you say were on the porch as we speak?"

After a pause, Andy said, "Just one. Well, to be honest with you, I don't think you need to worry yourself too much. I'll bet as soon as the rain lets up that ole skunk will skedaddle on back into the woods."

Andy pulled the phone away from his ear again as she gave him an ear-full, and when he was finally able to get a word in, he said, "Well, ma'am, I'm real sorry you feel that way. . . Hello? Hello?"

Grinning from ear to ear Andy dropped the phone back into its cradle, leaned back in his chair, propped his feet on the desk, and took a sip of coffee. "A skunk on Miss Prudence's front porch just trying to get out of the rain, which doesn't look to be letting up any time soon. Now that's funny," he said to the empty room. "I'll bet she's having a hissy fit and already on the phone to her cronies, using the party line to enlighten them about her skunk problem and what an inept deputy sheriff Shortcut has."

Just then, the phone rang again and Andy leaned over and picked it up, prepared to hear more about his stinky-ness, Mister Skunk. "Sheriff's office," Andy said in a jovial tone into the phone. After only a couple of seconds Andy sat upright, placing his coffee cup on the coaster. "Yes, Mister Walker, I know the phone has been busy for the past twenty minutes. Yes sir, it most certainly was police business," he said, almost bursting into laughter. Then getting serious, Andy said, "No sir, I haven't heard of any problems up at the lake. Sheriff Tucker is up in the lake area as we speak, and I think the sheriff would have notified me if there were any problems. In fact, I'm sure of it."

He listened while Mister Walker explained why he was calling. Andy said, "Yes, we heard the kids were having a party up there. They do it every year. It's become sort of a tradition."

By now Mister Walker was almost yelling into the phone. Andy pulled the phone away from his ear and could still hear him, loud and clear. "Look deputy, when I saw those storm clouds, I started calling around and from what I could gather, all of the kids came home, except for Kristi Lange, that Tilford kid, his friend Trace and of course, my daughter Melissa! Why didn't they come home, too?"

Andy gave the question a moment's thought as he tried to come up with a plausible answer. "Well, they probably did and I'm sure they'll be along pretty soon. You know how kids are. They may have stopped at the Redwood for a burger, or maybe they're over at the donut shop. Have you called down there?"

After another tirade from Melissa's father, Thomas Walker, Andy said, "Look, if they're still not home in say, two hours, you call me back, okay?" He was trying to keep a calmness in his voice that he really didn't feel, and wasn't sure he was pulling off. The hairs on the back of his neck were standing on end. Something strange was going on; only he didn't know what it was or what to do about it.

"Two hours, deputy, then I'm going to go up there myself!" Thomas Walker yelled into the phone.

"Now don't go. . ." was all Andy got in before he heard the phone slam down in his ear. "off halfcocked. I'll call you if I hear anything," Andy said to the buzzing sound of a broken connection.

After a moment, Andy stood up and stretched - walked over to the window and looked out at the empty street. He stood there for several minutes, staring at the parking space where the sheriff parked, as if he expected the sheriff to pull in at any time. After a bit, he turned and walked over to the two-way radio and stared at it - making sure it was on and the frequency was correct, Andy reached for the microphone. "Base to car one, base to car one. Come in, Sheriff."

Nothing but static hissed through the receiver, and after another long moment, Andy put the microphone back on its cradle. "What's goin' on? Why don't you answer me?" he said, running his fingers through his hair.

At this point, Andy was beginning to understand the frustration the sheriff must feel when he would get no response when he tried to call him on the radio. From now on, he wouldn't leave his walkie-talkie in the squad car when he went to the donut shop.

Three, four-wheel drive Jeep Cherokees sat in front of the old lodge house; their engines idling quietly as their windshield wipers moved back and forth trying their best to win a losing battle with the pounding rain.

Twelve heavily armed men, dressed in fatigues, rain jackets and rubber combat style boots, stood on the front porch of the lodge waiting for orders. A few of them were talking and cracking jokes, while the others were smoking and drinking from small flasks they kept hidden under their rain jackets.

The front door opened with a loud bang and their leader stormed out of the lodge without a word. Straight and tall, he marched across the porch and down the steps, and without any hesitation, he waded through ankle deep water and mud before he was able to climb into the passenger's seat of the lead jeep. He closed the door and waited.

Lit cigarettes hissed as they hit the water and whiskey flasks disappeared as all twelve men raced out to the vehicles. Just as the men were scrambling to get into the jeeps, lightning lit up the sky like high noon.

A chill ran through the soldiers as each one of them was reminded of the monster movie they'd recently seen, where there was a raging storm with lightning just like this just before the monster appeared. They all looked around apprehensively.

The driver of the lead vehicle listened as his leader gave him instructions. He nodded his head and put the jeep in gear, and the small convoy headed out.

CHAPTER TWENTY-TWO

Finding a place to hide

RAFE TALLTREE was in the lead as the group made their way up the steep incline in the rain and mud. Their progression was going slower than before due to the fact that it was Shaun and Trace who were now carrying Kristi in the makeshift litter, allowing Rafe to scout ahead. To relieve them of some of their burden, both Shaun and Trace's packs were slung over Rafe's shoulders, along with the coil of rope. Melissa carried two packs with both her and Kristi's gear and continued to bring up the rear; peering behind her from time to time to make sure their back trail was still clear.

When they reached a small clearing in the forest, Rafe held up his hand bringing the group to a stop. "We'll take a short break here before we climb up there," he said, pointing to a large boulder jutting out from the mountain, rising to approximately thirty feet above their heads. "I'll go up first, then toss the end of the rope down."

Turning to Trace and Melissa, he said, "You two will come up next, first Melissa, and then Trace. If either of you needs help, don't yell out, just wave your arm and I'll help all I can.

"Shaun, I want you to put Kristi over your shoulder and come up last. The three of us," he said, pointing at Trace, Melissa and himself, "will basically haul the two of you up."

"Why do I......?"

Shaun's words were cut short by a hard look from Rafe who turned and began to climb up the side of the boulder.

"She's your girlfriend, dude," Trace said with a grin and a shrug of his shoulders. "With all three of us at the top it will be easier to haul you two children up."

Shaun's body tensed and he felt the anger rise within him, until he realized Trace was just making a joke. "Okay, okay, I guess I see what you mean," he said reluctantly. "Just hurry, I don't want me and Kristi trapped down here if any of those lunatics come charging out of the woods with their guns blazing."

Trace chuckled as he took Melissa's packs and slung them over his shoulder. "You got it man," he said, giving Shaun a thumbs-up.

Melissa was in good shape and went up the side of the boulder without any help from Rafe.

As she climbed up the boulder, he thought she looked like an experienced rock climber. "This girl just keeps getting better and better," Rafe mumbled to himself as she climbed up and stood next to him, smiling brightly; very pleased with herself.

Melissa noticed the way Rafe watched her, which caused her to get a funny feeling in her stomach. She thought she heard him say something, but it seemed to be almost a whisper. "Did you say something?" she asked when she was standing next to him.

"Uhhh, no, just. . . just thinking out loud," he stammered.

Melissa thought it was funny to see Rafe blush, but held her laughter inside.

Trace tied the rolled up piece of canvas they'd used as a litter, to the end of the rope. Rafe pulled it up, and with Melissa's help, spread it out on the flat surface of the boulder. With that finished, he and Melissa watched as Trace helped put Kristi, belly first over Shaun's shoulder so he would be ready when it was his turn. When that was done, Trace also climbed to the top without any help.

Kristi was trying her best not to cry out when she was moved, but couldn't help a small groan from escaping.

Shaun patted her back and said, "Hang in there, babe."

Holding Kristi with one arm and the rope wrapped around his other arm several times, and gripped tightly in his hand, Shaun gave the rope a tug.

Rafe and Trace began to haul on the rope. Shaun helped with his legs as much as he could, while still trying balance the heavy burden on his shoulder.

Shaun and Kristi made it to the top with only one small mishap. Halfway up the boulder, Shaun slipped on the wet rock, causing him and Kristi to slide sideways. The combined weight of Shaun and Kristi, along with the surprise jerk on the rope, came close to pulling both Rafe and Trace over the edge of the boulder. If Melissa hadn't rushed over and helped by lending her small amount of weight and pulling on the rope, Rafe, Trace, Shaun and Kristi just may have wound up back at the bottom where they started. A fall from that height might have caused serious damage to all of them.

By the time they finally pulled Shaun and Kristi to the top, they were all breathing heavily. Melissa looked at Rafe and said, "We need to rest. We can't go on like this. We don't live in these mountains like you do. Plus, Kristi needs tending to, she's still losing blood."

Trace stepped up next to Melissa and said, "I ain't one to complain, and I'll go along with the majority, but just for the record, I second the motion to take a break."

Rafe gave a rare grin and said, "We don't have to go any farther. This is it. This is where we wait until they give up hunting for us."

Shaun, Trace and Melissa all got confused looks on their faces as they looked at the area where they were standing and saw only a small flat space that, except for its height, wouldn't hide a rabbit, let alone four people.

The closest thing that could be considered shelter was a large piece of scrub brush at the backside of the boulder where the rock protruded from the mountain.

Giving Rafe a disbelieving look, Shaun shook his head. "What are we supposed to do, hide in that bush over there?"

Rafe nodded his head in the affirmative, "Something like that."

"You're not serious? Did you get hit in the head by one of those bullets those lunatics were shootin'?" Shaun asked,

"I'm just jerking your chain hot shot. We don't hide in the bush; we hide behind it." And with that Rafe pulled the large clump of brush to the side, revealing the entrance to a cave.

"That isn't a bear cave, is it?" Trace asked with a lot of trepidation.

"At one time maybe," Rafe said, "but not now. Believe me, it's safe. I found it a couple of years ago. It was empty then and it's empty now. If any critters had gone in, the brush would be dragged aside, and as you can see, it hasn't been. Now, com'on, get in there and out of this weather. It's both dry and safe," he said as he started over the side of the boulder.

"Says you," Shaun said with a snarl.

"Where are you going?" Melissa asked with a hint of fear in her voice.

"Don't worry," Rafe said, "I'll be right back. I'm going to lay down a false trail that will lead them away from here and drive those hillbillies nuts. Make Kristi as comfortable as you can. We'll take care of her wound when I get back."

Rafe had climbed about half way down the side of the boulder when Melissa called out, "What about snakes? They could go in there without messing up the brush."

As his feet touched the muddy ground, he called back up to her, "There's no snakes in there, we're too high up. But I will tell you what is in there; a hiding place that is dry and out of sight from those idiots chasin' us."

Melissa smiled down at him and said, "That's good enough for me." She turned and said, "Com'on, what are we waiting for? Let's get Kristi out of this rain."

Shaun and Trace placed Kristi onto the makeshift litter as Melissa held the brush back far enough to allow them to carry her inside.

CHAPTER TWENTY-THREE

And you were chasin' them, why?

WHILE THE KIDS were taking shelter in the cave, Bear had returned with the news about the jeep going into a ditch. He climbed inside the pickup to try and dry out some before the others arrived. He wasn't looking forward to seeing the captain. "The captain is not gonna like what happened," Bear said as he lit a cigarette.

Akers stood next to the rear of the pickup trying to keep his cigarette dry enough to smoke, wondering when the others would show up. He had just dropped his cigarette butt into a puddle of water when he heard loud engine noises. He looked up and saw several vehicles coming his way. A smile spread across his face as he watched four Jeep Cherokees pull up behind the pickup and stop. The captain would know how to catch them, he thought to himself. "Bear, they're here," he called out.

Bear climbed out of the pickup at the same time the captain climbed out of the lead jeep. Both, Bear and Akers came to attention and saluted their leader and received a salute in return.

Adolph had ice in his voice when he asked, "What happened? You said you were chasing several people? Why?"

When Akers saw the look in his captain's eyes, he stepped back, leaving Bear to face the captain's anger all by himself.

Bear started to say something to Akers, but thought better of it.

Adolph watched the bi-play between the two, but said nothing.

Bear had braced himself for this confrontation. "Yes sir, I think there are five of them. The guy we was chasin' jumped out of his pickup just before it went into the river. Four people was standin' by the river. I'm not sure where they come from but they had two jeeps and the guy we was chasin' jumped into the lead jeep and headed off into the forest, with the second jeep right on his tail."

"And you were chasing this man, why?" Adolph asked with a confused look on his face.

"Besides them two FBI men, we had to kill the hick sheriff from town. Out of the blue, he came out of the woods while we was dumpin' them two FBI guys in the ravine. He was holdin' a weapon on Vernon and Akers. I had stepped into the woods to take a leak just before the sheriff showed up. I came up behind him and got the drop on him, but he got real belligerent like and I had to shoot him. And this other guy, the one we been chasin', for some reason we don't know about, was hidin' behind ah tree just up the hill from us, and saw the whole thing. We don't know why he was there, but when he took off runnin', we went after him," Bear said, matter of factly.

"And you say you were shooting at them?"

"Yes sir."

"Did you by chance, happen to hit any of them?"

Bear swallowed hard. "I'm pretty sure we wounded one of 'em sir, but it was mighty difficult shootin' from the back of the pickup with it ziggin' and zaggin' all over the place."

"And did they return fire?" Adolph asked, almost out of patience.

"No sir. They just drove off into the woods like a bat out of hell."

Adolph nodded his head and said, "Well, that rules out more law enforcement or hunters. Did you get a good look at any of them? Would you recognize them if you saw them again?"

Akers answered. "Not really, sir. Me and Vernon was in the back of the pickup and with the pickup swayin' this way and that," he said, waving his arms all around, "and us tryin' ta keep our balance while at the same time shootin' through all that heavy rain, and them ah zig zaggin' all over the place too, well sir. . ."

Adolph waved his hand and shook his head from side to side. "Well, at this point I guess it really doesn't matter. We've too much at stake to leave any witnesses running around. Where are they, now?" he asked.

"One of the jeeps drove off into a ravine up ahead and crashed nose first into the opposite bank. The other jeep is sitting on this side of the ravine, but it's been disabled. There are four sets of footprints on the far side of the ditch that head off into the woods. Two sets of those footprints are deep, and one trailin' directly behind the other, like they are carrying a heavy load; which leads me ta believe that maybe we hit one of them. I figure they're carrying the one that got shot," Bear reported, proud of himself at being so thorough.

"Very good, sergeant," Adolph said, somewhat appeased. He turned to the other men who were standing nearby. "They won't be able to travel fast or far in this weather, especially carrying a heavy load up a mountainside. It should make them easy to track."

CHAPTER TWENTY-FOUR

A case of the nerves

WHILE ALL OF THIS was taking place, Andy was beside himself. He paced the floor until he felt like he was wearing the soles off of his boots. He wondered what was going on with the missing kids, and where the sheriff was, and why didn't he answer his radio. The questions never seemed to stop. It was hard to believe the sheriff could be in trouble and in need of backup. Everyone in and around Shortcut believed that Buford Tucker was indestructible, even though some prayed for it to be otherwise.

It was always possible the rain was blocking the signal, or maybe the thunder and lightning had knocked out his radio. It could also be that he and the kids had taken shelter someplace to get out of the storm and they were high and dry, just waiting it out.

His mind was swirling. There were way too many possibilities to narrow it down to one.

Suddenly, ugly thoughts rushed into his head; the kind he didn't want to consider, but he couldn't help himself. Could the disappearance of both, the sheriff and the kids, have something to do with those men in the van? And why did some of the kids make it home and not the four who hadn't come back, yet? Did those dead men from the van have friends up on the mountain? Was that where they'd come from - the abandoned lodge, maybe? Should he and the kid's fathers go up there and investigate or should he go alone, or should he wait for a call from the sheriff?

The more he thought about it, the more confused he became.

Suddenly, Andy stopped his pacing and looked at his desk, then up at the clock on the wall and saw it was close to midnight. The phone hadn't made a sound in the last thirty minutes. He walked over and cautiously lifted the receiver and listened. A dial tone buzzed loudly in his ear. After a moment, he sat the receiver back in its resting place.

Andy turned and hurriedly walked over to the two-way radio, but didn't pick up the microphone right away. Instead, he stared at it for a long moment before slowly lifting the microphone from its cradle and saying, "Base to car one - base to car one, come in sheriff."

After what seemed to be an eternity, Andy set the microphone back in its cradle and went back to his desk and dropped into his chair. Even as exhausted as he was he knew he couldn't sleep. With all the worry and the gut feeling that something was very wrong, his stomach began to growl. "Too much coffee and no food," he said out loud.

Andy stood up, stretched, and made a decision. He grabbed his hat and headed for the door before any more worried fathers called and yelled at him because he had nothing new to tell them. He'd go over to the Redwood and get a bite to eat, and at the same time, ask around about the sheriff. In a small town like this, there was always gossip and somebody who would know all the answers to all the questions; and that someone just might have some information about the kids and the sheriff.

If he didn't learn anything or hadn't heard from the sheriff by the time he got back, he would seriously consider going up there and checking things out for himself, without any overwrought fathers tagging along. If there was trouble, he didn't want to put the kid's fathers in harm's way. The city councilmen would raise three kinds of holy-hell if he did. They might even ask for his badge.

CHAPTER TWENTY-FIVE
Adolph speaks

RAIN CONTINUED to fall as the men mulled around the back of Bear's pickup, glancing now and then at the covered body of Vernon. Each one of them was eager to go after the ones who'd caused the death of their friend and comrade, never concerning themselves with the fact that they were the ones who created this mess in the first place.

After stepping out of the jeep where he'd been looking at a map, Adolph walked over and climbed into the back of Bear's pickup truck and stood up. He stared out over his men for a moment before speaking. In a commanding voice, he said, "Men, this is rough country we're going into, and in this kind of weather it will be tough going. There will be a great many places where the people we seek can hide, so don't spread out too far. Stay within eyesight of each other. Stay alert; check out any and all places where it looks like they could hide or find shelter."

Waving the map in the air, he said, "They have to be close by. They're on foot, and they haven't had time to go very far."

He let this information sink in, then continued. "Bear seems to think they've got a wounded person with them that he believes they are forced to carry; if that is so, it is to our advantage because they will need to stop and rest, often. Plus, they will need to find a place that is sheltered so they can treat the person's wound."

Adolph looked out over his small army and saw them nodding their heads in agreement.

"So," he continued, "whoever finds them, don't try and be a hero; yell out and the rest of us will come ah running."

Once again, Adolph saw heads nodding up and down. He raised his hands in the air until they got quiet.

"Let me say this again, stay alert! We don't know if they're armed or not, so don't take any unnecessary chances. We don't want more fatalities, at least not on our side."

The men raised their weapons in the air and cheered, and when they quieted down, Adolph made his final statement.

"In the end, armed or not, they are unpures! There will be no survivors! Is that clear?"

To the man, they pumped their weapons in the air and shook their heads, as they called out, "Seig Heil! Seig Heil!

Adolph jumped down from the back of Bear's pickup and walked to the jeep and climbed inside, lit a cigar, turned on the dome light and studied the map with greater detail.

CHAPTER TWENTY-SIX
The Cave

THE CAVE was not huge, but large enough for their purpose. It was maybe thirty feet deep and twenty feet wide, with close to seven feet of headroom.

When Melissa entered, she looked around and said, "Spooky, but dry."

Trace stared hard toward the rear of the cave looking for critters, but didn't see any. He sighed and said, "Beats bein' out there," pointing his thumb towards the outside to which Melissa nodded her agreement.

When Rafe returned, he pulled the pile of brush back in front of the entrance and then looked the situation over in the dim light that filtered in from outside, which wasn't much. Rafe flicked on a flashlight he'd taken from Shaun's pickup, shining it over the walls and then toward the back.

Kristi was lying on the canvas litter, near the middle of the cave. Her face looked pale in the beam of the flashlight.

Rafe handed Melissa the flashlight and said, "I'll get a fire started from the wood I stored here last summer. It's against the back wall where it will stay dry."

As Rafe headed for the small woodpile, Kristi opened her eyes ever so slowly and looked around. She felt feverish and in the dim light she could see no one. Fear reared its ugly head and she was about to scream when she saw Shaun in the shadows a short distance away. "Shaun! I thought I had died and was all alone! Oh Shaun, please help me. My leg hurts! I feel like I'm on fire!"

Shaun rushed over and knelt down next to her. "You're okay, babe. I'm right here and everything is gonna be alright," he said, taking her hand but looking up at Melissa with pleading eyes. He had absolutely no idea what he was supposed to say or do in a situation like this.

Kristi tried to sit up but fell back down and cried out, "I don't feel good, Shaun. I'm so hot! Please don't let me die!"

At that point, Trace dropped down on one knee. "Hey, Kristi, it's me, Trace. Just try to relax. You're gonna be okay. Really," he said in his most reassuring voice, trying to calm her down. The last thing they needed was for Kristi to cry out at the same time those guys looking for them were going by down below. Sound carried a long way in the woods. The last thing they needed was to turn their safe haven into a deadly trap they couldn't get out of. Those guys would pick them off like targets at the carnival.

Kristi tried looking around, but it was hard to see in the semi-darkness of the cave. "Why is it so dark? Where are we?"

"We're in a cave, where hopefully those lunatics can't find us. We're safe and dry," Shaun said, trying to make her feel comfortable even though he wasn't all that sure himself.

Suddenly her eyes went wide and she began to yell, "I'm afraid, Shaun! I want to go home, now! Please Shaun, take me home! I want my mother!"

Melissa took Kristi's other hand and patted it as she leaned close and said, "Hi Kristi, it's me, Melissa. Lay back and relax and be very, very quiet. You need lots of rest and I'm going to be right here with you. Take a nap if you can, and try not to worry, we'll all be going home very soon."

At the sound of Melissa's voice, Kristi fell silent. She looked up at Melissa, who had tears in her eyes while smiling down at her, and nodding her head.

Melissa put her hand on Kristi's forehead, then looked at Shaun and Trace and mouthed, "She's got a fever and I think she's delirious, sometimes. Doesn't realize what she's saying."

Kristi turned to Shaun again, and whispered, "Please don't let me die, there's something very important I need to tell you."

Shaun knew he was out of his element and not sure how to deal with it. And what in blazes did she want to tell him that was so important at a time like this? Frustration and confusion, mixed with a short fuse, sent his temper sky high, "Dammit,

Kristi, you're not gonna die!" he said, louder than he should have.

His voice carried throughout the interior of the cave and probably beyond as he slumped back on his rear end, knowing he'd gone too far.

Rafe was kneeling next to a small round depression in the rock floor where he'd placed some pebble-sized rocks on the bottom and some medium sized rocks around the top, making a workable fire pit. The pebbles on the bottom would heat up and help keep the wood burning.

Rafe placed a clump of dry grass on top of the pebbles, and then placed small, dry sticks over the clump of grass, which would be the beginnings of the fire.

He had heard everything and turned his face toward Shaun. "Not so sure about that, hot shot. If we don't get the bullet out and stop the bleeding, it's very possible she could," he said in a whisper. "And keep your voices down. Those people chasing us are out there and with all the yelling you've been doing, you could be heard clear down into Shortcut. That is, unless you want to lead them straight to us?"

Shaun's eyes spit fire as he turned and looked at Rafe. "Shut your damn mouth, Talltree! She ain't gonna die," he yelled, ignoring everything Rafe had just said.

Shaking his head at Shaun's ignorance, Rafe tried to ignore him and looked up at Trace and said in a low voice,

"Trace, will you check and make sure the brush covers the front of the cave and looks like it did when we got here?"

Trace looked from the fire to the entrance and back. "What about the smoke? We could suffocate – you know, choke to death from all the smoke."

Rafe smiled. "Not from this fire, my friend. This fire will not only be warm, but will be virtually smokeless. What little smoke there is will filter itself through a small air hole near the back of the cave, and cause no problem."

Shaun, angry at being ignored, was spoiling for a fight. "Talltree, you are so full of crap. You want us to believe you're gonna build a fire inside this cave and there will be no smoke? What do you take us for, some kind of country bumpkins?"

"You don't know much about fire building, do you city boy? It's an old Indian method, something you wouldn't know anything about." He looked up at Trace and said, "It's okay Trace. Make sure the brush hides the entrance like it did when we got here."

Trace went to the front of the cave and began wiping away what evidence there was with his foot, then pulled the brush back into place, hoping the rain would wipe out anything he might have missed.

Melissa was holding Kristi's hand and patting it while Kristi stared at the roof of the cave, tears seeping from the corner of her eyes. By now, the area around the wound had turned reddish, purple.

Shaun was not used to being put down in front of his friends, or anyone else for that matter. He got to his feet and stood, glaring, wanting to punch Rafe's face in, but knew this was not the time, nor the place.

By now, Rafe had a good fire going from the dry wood, and it was throwing off a lot of heat, but like he'd said, there was hardly any smoke.

Trace grinned and nodded, giving Rafe a thumbs-up as Rafe put a larger chunk of very dry wood on the fire.

All this friendly interaction between Trace and Talltree caused Shaun to be even further enraged. He clenched his fists and put them on his hips and then stepped closer to Rafe and declared, "I'm getting damn tired of you actin' so high and mighty. Who put you in charge, anyway?"

Rafe shook his head and let out a sigh as he glanced up and noticed the scowl on Shaun's face and fire in his eyes. "I never asked for the job, but somebody has to be. And since I'm the oldest and the most experienced, along with the fact that none of you knows this mountain like I do, I guess it just makes sense that I be the one."

The information hung in the air for no more than a moment before Rafe asked, "So who would you suggest we put in charge, hot shot? You?" Rafe's patience with this young hothead was nearing the breaking point.

Shaun's eyes were shooting daggers and his breathing was getting ragged.

Rafe knew he should just shut his mouth and forget about it. The kid was angry about his brother and wasn't thinking straight. That's what he should do, but for the life of him, he couldn't. "For a bigmouth, you're awful quiet," Rafe said, feeling the anger boiling inside his own brain.

This last verbal assault by Rafe proved too much for Shaun to hold in. Right or wrong, Shaun launched himself at his enemy. He was going to beat Talltree to within an inch of his life.

Shaun hauled up short when he realized Rafe had somehow gotten to his feet without him noticing, and was crouched in a fighting stance, dancing lightly on the balls of his feet.

Shaun swallowed and began having second thoughts. He was more than a little relieved when Melissa stepped between them and said, "Stop it you two! Shaun, you don't want to do this. Rafe, please back off and think about what you're doing!"

Rafe looked at Shaun and said in a low, growl, "That's right city boy, you don't want to do this. Listen to the lady."

Trace knew Shaun was about to bite off more than he could chew. Talltree was an ex-veteran and knew a lot more about fighting than Shaun did. Even back in high school there were stories about Talltree.

Before things went any further, Trace joined Melissa and raised his arms in each one's direction. "Stop it, both of you!

Don't we have enough problems without you two goin' at each other's throats? You want ta fight somebody? Go fight those guys who are trying to kill us."

Shaun realized his friends were giving him a way to back off without losing face.

It was Kristi who brought the would be fight to an end when she cried out, "I'm freezing and my leg is hurting really bad! Please can't somebody help me?"

Rafe drew a military K-bar hunting knife from its sheath hanging at his waist and placed the tip of the knife in the fire.

"We need to move her over here close to the fire so she can get warm while we take care of that wound. And then we need to get out of these wet clothes and get dry and warm ourselves, before we catch pneumonia."

Trace turned and would have gone to Kristi, but Rafe grabbed him by the arm. "Let Melissa and Shaun bring her over by the fire. I need you to go to the back of the cave and get more firewood."

Trace nodded and headed for the back of the cave while Melissa stripped Kristi out of her outer clothes, leaving her in only her panties and bra, then folded the canvas over her nakedness.

When Melissa looked up, Shaun was staring at Kristi. She shook her head and said, "Shaun, help me carry Kristi over next to the fire, now."

His hands were shaking as he knelt down and picked up the end of the tarp.

After laying Kristi down next to the fire, he went over to his pack and poked his hand inside, rummaging around.

Melissa saw him and asked, "Any food or medicine in there?"

Without answering her, Shaun pulled a can of beer from the pack and chugged it, which irritated Melissa to no end. "Way to go, Shaun! As always, you think of nobody but yourself."

Shaun glared at Melissa for a moment before throwing the empty beer can against the wall of the cave.

Melissa saw the terror in Shaun's eyes and realized that he must be dealing with some heavy fears of his own. "I'm sorry Shaun, really I am, but you're not the only one who has problems," she said in a harsher voice than she'd meant to.

Rafe's voice carried through the cave as though he was speaking to everyone or no one. "The wound is going to have to be cauterized."

Trace sat an armload of dry wood next to the fire and looked at Rafe. "What 'a you mean, cauterized?"

"I mean, once we get the bullet out we're going to have to seal the wound to stop the bleeding and prevent infection."

"Shouldn't that be done in the hospital, by a doctor?" Melissa asked.

"Damn straight! And it will be just as soon as we get outta here and down off this mountain!" Shaun proclaimed.

Before standing up to face the others, Rafe checked the tip of his knife. It glowed red, which sent a chill down each one of their spines and caused their hearts to beat a little faster.

"She can't wait that long. We don't know how long those lunatics will keep up their search. We have to get that bullet out of her leg and stop the bleeding, now, or two things will happen. The bullet will cause lead poisoning, and if we don't seal the wound, she will bleed to death. We have to stop both of those possibilities, right now!"

Rafe placed the tip of his knife back in the fire and took a smaller knife out of his pocket and layed it close to the fire, but not close enough to get red.

Shaun, Melissa and Trace stood there, staring at Rafe, trying to comprehend his words.

Melissa's mind was forming pictures that made her breathing quicken. After digging into Kristi's leg to remove the bullet, which would be bad enough, Rafe was talking about pressing that hot knife blade against Kristi's bare leg.

Rafe was about to do what he knew needed to be done and was thinking about what else he would need in the way of medicine and bandages, when he heard men's voices coming from outside.

Rafe brought his finger to his lips in the sign of silence, then moved to the front of the cave. Doctoring Kristi would have to wait until he could find out what was going on.

With the silence of a snake, Rafe belly-crawled out of the cave and close to the edge of the boulder.

CHAPTER TWENTY-SEVEN
Orders

DARK STORM CLOUDS covered the sun causing night to come early to the mountain area north of Shortcut, Utah. In the fading light, the Supremacists stood around looking at each other. They were, to the man, soaked from the rain and cold to the bone. A few were trying to keep their cigarettes lit so they could smoke. One of the men filled his jaw with Red Man chewing tobacco, took a few chews and began to spit.

"There ain't no way they could' a doubled back thout one of us seein'em," Bear said to several of the men standing close to him. "Jest ain't no way. We covered all the land from here to the road and a fair piece in the other direction."

"I agree, Sergeant," Adolph said as he scanned the forest, trying to see deep into the woods that were getting darker by the moment. "They're here; close by. I know it in my bones. I can feel it."

The men looked at each other and several of them nudged Bear in the shoulder, nodding in the leader's direction.

Knowing what they wanted him to do, Bear tried his best to pay them no attention but when they kept it up, he let out a long breath and hesitantly walked up to Adolph. "Sir," he said, and took a large step backward when the man turned his menacing eyes in his direction.

"Yes, Sergeant?"

Bear swallowed and then ran his tongue around the inside of his mouth in hopes of creating some moisture. Even with all the rain, the inside of his mouth felt like the Sahara Desert and his throat felt constricted. "Well sir, it's ah, it's like this, it's late and the men are tired. Sir, they're soaked to the bone and powerful hungry. The troops have been ah wonderin'," he said, pointing at the men, "if'n maybe we could head on back to the lodge and take this up again in the mornin'. The rain will have probably stopped by then and.. ."

Adolph Hemmlick was the kind of man who didn't appreciate being questioned, especially by underlings. Very slowly he pulled a cigarillo from the inside pocket of his coat and lit it before saying anything. He needed time to let his temper subside. Surely they knew what was at stake? His eyes slowly scanned the faces of his small army as they stood in the rain, shifting from one foot to the other, waiting patiently.

When he finally spoke, it was like Bear had never said anything about anyone being cold or hungry or wanting to return to the lodge. In a loud, commanding voice, he said, "We'll set up a perimeter line along here," waving his arm in the direction he was indicating, covering a wide area. "We'll conceal ourselves wherever we can find cover, and wait for them to try to sneak back down the mountain."

An audible groan resonated throughout the men.

Bear spoke up. "All night, Sir? In this storm with no coffee or anything to eat?"

Adolph looked around, then stepped onto a log and with cold, menacing eyes, stared at the men. What would it take to impress the seriousness of the situation on them, he wondered? He took a puff from his cigarillo and held it in for some time as he made up his mind what to say. For effect, he let the smoke out in a long stream.

"Need I remind you, this is a war and we are soldiers; soldiers in a dire struggle against the mongrels infesting the shores of our forefathers. Like our comrades spread across this great land, we must persevere in our cause to rid our land of unpures. We have been appointed the guardians of white power - given the monumental task of building a strong, racially pure world!" His voice reverberated throughout the forest like an evangelist casting out demons. "These scum we're searching for tonight are in part the very ones who would destroy everything we've been struggling to accomplish!"

From somewhere in the back, one of the men said to the man standing next to him, "Don't he ever let up?"

Adolph went deadly silent, took another puff from his cigarillo, then blew smoke into the rain filled air as he let his eyes search for the man who had made the comment. And when he did not see the culprit, he called out, "Who said that?"

The men all looked down at their feet and went deadly silent. Not one of them wanted to cross this man they followed. For the most part, it was because each one of them was deathly afraid of the man's wrath. One look and you would be ostracized, and then in his kangaroo court, you would be sentenced to die, either by your own hand or the firing squad; the choice would be yours, but in the end it meant the same thing – you were going to die.

Adolph's face turned red and his breathing became ragged. After a moment, he yelled, "I want an answer! Who said that?"

Every man there, including Bear, kept his eyes lowered and said nothing.

When Adolph realized he would not be getting an answer, he decided to answer the question. "Will I ever let up? Is that what you want to know? Well, let me make it very clear. The answer is, never! Not while there is even one breath left in my body! Nor will I allow any of you! Don't you understand? We can never let up! Do you hear what I'm telling you? We can never let up, nor can we give up. We have a mission and I mean to see it to the end. Now, set up the perimeter like I told you, and be quick about it!"

Without another word, Bear began giving the men orders, and with grumbling stomachs and chattering teeth, the men began moving into the woods in pairs to find a place to spend the night, hopefully out of the rain.

From his position on the flat surface in front of the cave, Rafe heard everything Adolph had to say. He watched flashlights glowing as the men set up their positions for the night. He could hear the men grumbling to themselves and realized they were afraid to stand up for themselves, or say anything.

As he watched, he thought to himself, 'that guy is one crazy dude. Why do men follow somebody like that?' Then he thought of Adolph Hitler, and several others, which answered his own question. When he figured he'd seen and heard enough, he snaked his way back into the cave just before a bolt of lightning lit up the sky. Thunder rolled and the ground shook, then it was quiet again except for the wind and rain.

Rafe adjusted the brush so the glow of the small fire could not be seen. When he was finished, he turned and saw Shaun, Trace and Melissa staring at him.

"Are they still out there?" Melissa asked in a very quiet voice.

"Yes, and it looks like they're sitting up a line of defense. So, we'll be here a while longer than I'd hoped."

CHAPTER TWENTY-EIGHT
Andy's frustration

WHEN ANDY RETURNED from the restaurant and still hadn't found out anything, he paced the floor, trying to decide what to do. After only a short deliberation, he talked himself out of going up to the lake and checking things out until daylight.

As Andy walked toward the coffee machine, his stomach growled and he hurried off to the men's room at the back of the office; too much hot sauce, he thought as he ran for the john.

When he was feeling human again, and washing his hands, he heard the front door open and close. Thinking Sheriff Tucker had returned he rushed into the office. "Well, it's about time you. . . "he started to say, but stopped short when he saw it wasn't the sheriff, but three of the town's leading citizens, Trace's father, Big Mike Bozeman; Melissa's father, James Thomas Walker; and Bill Lange, Kristi's father – fathers of three of the missing teenagers. And none of them looked happy.

As soon as they saw him walk into the room, they all began talking at the same time, besieging him with questions. Andy's only recourse was to hold up his hands and yell, "Quiet! All of you! Just calm down, one question at a time, please."

When they quieted down, Andy said, "I know you're all worried and believe me, I understand. I still haven't heard from the sheriff, and I admit, I'm becoming concerned. But there is no way we can mount a search party tonight. Not in the dark, and in the middle of this storm. I admit to having thoughts about going up there tonight, just before you men arrived, in fact; but now I realize how stupid that would have been."

Melissa's father was the first one to speak up. "What do you expect us to do, sit around here all night and do nothing when our kids might be in trouble up there?"

Once again, Andy held up his hands. "Mister Walker, please believe me, I do understand. You're worried about Melissa; the same as Bill and Mike here, are worried about Trace and Kristi, but give those kids a little credit. If this storm has caused any trouble up there, it wouldn't surprise me if all of them, including the sheriff, are holed up at the old lodge, high and dry - just waitin' for the storm to run its course."

There is a long silence while the three men pondered Andy's words.

After a moment, it was Andy's turn to ask a question as he looked around. "I see Mister Tilford isn't with you, is he not worried?"

Trace's father spoke up. "Ain't nobody home over there. I tried callin', but got no answer. Then I stopped by their place on the way over here but the house was dark and locked up tight. Their car and the boy's jeep are both gone."

"Mister and Missus Tilford went down to Salt Lake for the weekend," Melissa's father said in an embarrassed voice. "Sorry, I forgot to mention that."

They all nodded their heads. Bill Lange turned to Andy. "What you just said about them being high and dry with the sheriff, you don't know that for sure, do you?"

Bill jumped in before Andy could say anything. "That's right, you don't know. You even said you hadn't heard from the sheriff since he went up there. Isn't that right?"

The room went quiet as the three fathers waited patiently for Andy's answer.

"That's right," Andy said with a sigh. "But there could be a lot of reasons why we haven't heard anything. In this weather, the radio could have gone out or maybe a bolt of lightning struck the tower and burned up some wires so the radio won't work."

"What about a backup? Don't you guys carry ah hand held?"

"He forgot to take it with him," Andy said, weakly. "It's still plugged in the charger over by his desk. But that don't mean anything. It would be out of range, anyway."

"But. . ." Melissa's father started to say before Andy interrupted him.

"Besides, you have to admit, it makes more sense to wait until daylight so we can see what we're doing. We're only talking a few more hours. I promise, if we don't hear something by then, we'll go have a look-see. We can leave at first light."

The three fathers looked at each other for a moment and reached a mutual decision. Trace's father looked directly at Andy and said, "Alright, Andy, we'll wait for first light. But we won't wait any longer."

Andy felt himself relax just a little. "Thanks, guys. Heck, if the storm is over like I think it will be, I'll bet we meet them comin' home before we even get up there."

"I hope you're right, Andy. You'll call us if you hear anything between now and then?" Bill asked.

"You know I will. The weatherman is talkin' clear skies for tomorrow and maybe I'll have a chopper from the ranger station do a fly over, might be faster."

Before they left, each man shook Andy's hand and thanked him for his help as he walked them to the door.

When they were gone, Andy rubbed his face and ran his hand through his hair as he walked over and poured himself another cup of coffee. The hot bitterness burned its way down his throat. He was far more worried than he'd let on. After all, he was the law and supposed to be above that sort of thing. Besides, they were troubled enough as it was.

He walked over and stared out the front window, his mind clinging to a nagging thought. There was something about that ring he found on the charred hand that was driving him nuts. He knew in his gut that it was important to this whole situation, but for the life of him he couldn't figure out why.

Andy checked the radio to make sure it was turned on and working properly. For what seemed to be the hundredth time, he picked up the microphone, "Base to car one, base to car one, come in Sheriff."

CHAPTER TWENTY-NINE
New Information

TWO OF THE SUPREMACISTS were assigned the job of patrolling the road and just happened to be passing by the sheriff's vehicle when they heard a man's voice coming through the open window. They hurried over and climbed down into the ditch and stood as close to the sheriff's carryall as they could without standing in the running water.

Andy's voice came through the open window loud and clear. "Sheriff, maybe you can hear me and maybe you can't; but on the chance you can receive but not transmit, I'll pass on some information. First, I hope you're with the kids, cause we got some anxious parents down here. The good news is we're comin' up first thing in the mornin' with ah search party. So you just try to hang in there awhile longer. And last, but not least, I'm still trackin' down the leads we have on that van that blew up last night here in town, along with that Nazi ring one of 'em was wearin'. Anyway, like I said, hang in there and we'll see you in the mornin'. Try to stay dry. Base, over and out."

The two supremacists looked at each other, and then as if they had the same thought at the same time, climbed out of the ditch and hurried up the muddy road in the direction of their comrades.

Andy hung up the microphone, then yawned and stretched; satisfied he done all he could do for now. He wasn't used to such long days; especially ones with so many problems that still needed solving. He walked over and dropped into his chair, leaned back and propped his feet up, hoping to get at least a little rest before the sun came up.

Before he closed his eyes, Andy took one last look at the door and said, "Sheriff Tucker, there's no doubt about it, you're a cantankerous, stubborn, bigoted S.O.B., but it sure would make me happy to see you walk through that door about now."

Andy watched for a moment, but when nothing happened, he leaned his head back and closed his eyes. He was in dire need of some rest.

CHAPTER THIRTY

The scream

NOT FAR FROM THE ENTRANCE to the cave, two of the supremacists were slowly patrolling the woods. One of them thought he'd heard something and held up his hand. They were nervous and keyed up, looking for the slightest movement, but only the rain continued to pound the forest and everything in it.

"Awww, you didn't hear nuthin' but the rain," his partner said. "Com'on, let's get back to our hidin' place.

"I sure could use some coffee with ah mite of whiskey in it, bout now. And maybe ah big ole steak with french-fries and some hot buttered rolls," the other man said.

"Be quiet! Don't let the Captain hear you talk like that! He'll skin you alive!"

"Well, I don't care. I'm hungry and I'm cold and I don't think sloshin' around out here in the woods is gonna accomplish anything. Them kids is long gone and that's all there is to it."

His friend nodded his head in agreement, but instead of saying anything he lit a cigarette to curb his growling stomach and climbed back into their hiding spot beneath a small overhang, that was at least, dry, if not warm.

The other man climbed in next to him and hunkered down. Once they were settled in, he reached inside his coat and pulled out a small flask and held it up.

"How about a small nip to keep away the cold?"

His friend grinned. "You been hold'in out, you son of ah gun."

By now, the cave was warm enough to be comfortable, and like Rafe had said, there was hardly any smoke. Kristi was lying near the fire, looking scared.

Rafe nodded his head. Shaun and Trace took ahold of Kristi's arms and Melissa held tightly to Kristi's injured leg.

When Rafe knelt down next to Kristi, she took one look at the knife in Rafe's hand and her eyes went wide and she began to struggle as he unwrapped her wound. He studied it for a moment, and then put the knife back next to the fire.

"Apparently, the bullet went all the way through," he said to everyone. That's a lot better than having to dig lead out of her leg. But we still need to cauterize the holes to stop the bleeding." Looking down at Kristi, he whispered, "Sorry, but it has to be done."

Kristi stared at her friends with terror in her eyes.

Rafe took a rag and washed the wound as best as he could with some water from one of the canteens, then placed a stick sideways in Kristi's mouth for her to bite down on.

"I won't lie to you Kristi, it's going to hurt a lot," Rafe said, trying to be as honest with her as he could. He figured she was a tough girl and could handle the truth.

"Worse than it does now?" Kristi asked, slurring her words because of the stick in her mouth.

Rafe sighed and said, "Yes. It's going to hurt worse, but just for a little bit. And since the bullet went all the way through, we're going to have to do it, twice, but trust me, the second time will be easier, and before you know it, it will be over."

"Jeeze, don't tell her that," Shaun hissed.

Rafe looked around at all of them. "I'm not going to lie to her." Then he looked down at Kristi. "Kristi, we don't have a choice, we have to do this to try and save your life. You're going to need to be very brave."

Melissa looked at Kristi, then over to Rafe, tears welling up in her eyes. "Please, can't we just get this over with so she can start feeling better?" she pleaded.

"You'd better know what you're doin', Redman," Shaun hissed.

Rafe looked down at Kristi and said, "When the pain comes, bite down on the stick, it will help. And try not to yell," he said, knowing it was an impossible request.

To the others he said, "Make sure you hold onto her tight."

Kristi's breathing began to get heavier and ragged from looking at the red tip of Rafe's knife. She had to avert her eyes and looked up at Shaun, who wasn't looking so hot, himself. She couldn't stand to see what was coming and figured he was having trouble with it too. Suddenly, his eyes turned and looked down at her and she tensed.

Trace closed his eyes and gripped down on Kristi's arm with all her might. Only Melissa kept her eyes on each move Rafe made. She was mesmerized. She hoped she would never have to do anything like this, but just in case she wanted to know exactly what to do and how to do it.

First, there was a sizzling noise and then the pain hit her brain and every muscle in her body stiffened. She bit down on the stick, trying as hard as she could not to cry out, but it was no use. Without realizing it, she spit out the stick and unleashed a blood curdling scream that erupted from deep inside her. The scream exceeded anything she could control. It filled the cave for what seemed an eternity, and then it became quiet.

For Kristi, there was nothing but blackness. Her brain had taken her away to that place where there is no pain.

Shaun glanced at Rafe and the others with a concerned look on his face.

Rafe assured them all that she had only passed out temporarily. "It's the body's safety mechanism. When the pain gets too intense, we black out for a while," Rafe said as he reheated the tip of his knife so he could seal the second hole before she woke up.

Kristi's scream had not been contained to just the cave. It reverberated off the trees throughout the forest; sounding like some wild animal in its last throws of death. The sound seemed to be coming from all around them. Each one of the supremacists gripped his weapon a little tighter and waited to see what was going to happen.

The scream stopped as quickly as it started and all was quiet again, except for the sound of the rain and a slow roll of thunder.

Rafe gently pried Melissa's hands from Kristi's leg and allowed her to sit back on her rump. She began to shake all over. "I'm so sorry, Kristi. I'm so sorry," she sobbed as she stared longingly down at her friend.

Rafe pulled her close to him and held her as she sobbed on his shoulder. "It's gonna be alright," he said as gently as he could. "At least now she'll have a chance."

Melissa sat up, wiped her eyes and took a deep breath. "I'll be ok, now. Thank you Rafe," she said, putting on her best smile for his benefit.

Rafe nodded and turned to Trace. "Trace, get the first aid kit from whichever pack it's in and see if there is any bandage material. We need to get this leg bandaged before she wakes up.

As Trace rummaged through the packs, Rafe sealed the second hole in Kristi's leg; but this time she only flinched and groaned as he pressed the hot knife blade against her skin.

Shaun crawled up close to Kristi and stared at her for what seemed to be an eternity, but in reality it was only a few moments. It was obvious to everyone that the mighty Shaun was shaken by what had taken place and Kristi's soul retching scream had not helped his nerves.

"She's just passed out, right? I mean, she's not gonna die or anything. I mean, she's gonna get well now, right?"

Rafe looked down at Kristi and then back to Shaun. "Yes, she just passed out, which is common in a situation like this. As far as surviving, I honestly don't know. She lost a lot of blood. We can only hope she didn't lose too much. She's young and strong, so she has a good chance. But we'll need to keep a close eye on her for a while and get some blood building food in her as soon as we can."

Trace handed Rafe a roll of gauze, then walked over and put a few sticks on the fire, like he'd seen Rafe do. He wanted to make sure the cave stayed warm, for Kristi's sake.

The day had been exhausting to say the least, and by midnight, it was all any of them could do to keep their eyes open. Rafe volunteered to take the first watch as the others crawled away to places near the fire and went instantly to sleep.

Once he was sure everyone was asleep, Rafe mixed some herbs he'd picked along the way into a cup of water, and heated it over the fire. After a few minutes, he carried the cup with smoke rising from it, over to where Kristi lay. After checking once again to make sure the others were asleep, he kneeled next to Kristi and softly began to chant an old Indian healing song, while at the same time, allowing the smoke to drift across Kristi's face.

As she inhaled the smoke, she began to relax and her breathing evened out as peacefulness washed over her.

While keeping an eye on the others to make sure they were still sleeping, Rafe kept up his chant until the cup stopped smoking. Before getting to his feet, Rafe passed his hands back and forth about a foot over Kristi's body, while finishing his chant.

After cleaning the cup, Rafe squatted down next to Kristi and kept watch on her until it was time for Melissa to relieve him.

By the time Melissa took over, Kristi was somewhere in dreamland, dressed in a white, sleeveless, transparent gown, running barefoot through a field filled with daises and clover. The sun was shining brightly and a cool breeze cascaded over the land. She leaped high into the air, maybe ten or fifteen feet off the ground as though she could fly. Kristi threw her arms wide as she twirled in the air, then landed gracefully, ran a short distance and leaped into the air again, like a ballerina. Her soft laughter echoed across the land, and was carried away on the wind.

In the real world, Melissa got a puzzled look on her face as Kristi began to smile, and then laughed.

When Melissa realized Kristi was just having a good dream, she relaxed.

Rafe heard Kristi's laughter and opened one eye. He watched Melissa's reaction and grinned. She had no idea why Kristi was laughing, but he knew it was her reaction to the smoke. It was doing its job. He couldn't tell the others, they would think he was a pagan or nuts, but he knew and believed in what his grandfather had taught him, and that was enough.

CHAPTER THIRTY-ONE
The G Men

DURING THE WEE HOURS of the morning, a little before sunrise, a dark gray sedan with the words, U.S. Government stenciled on both front doors entered the city limits of Shortcut, Utah. There were two men in the car. The man behind the wheel drove slowly through town until he spotted the lighted sign in front of the Sheriff's office. He pulled into the curb and turned off the engine. The two men got out of the car and stretched. Other than being Caucasian, and African/American, there wasn't any difference. Both were six feet tall and both weighed in at one hundred ninety pounds. Both were dressed in gray suits and wearing gray felt dress hats. If it wasn't for the color of their skin, they might be mistaken for twins.

As the two men entered the front door, the minute hand on the wall clock clicked and the clock read, 4:20 am. Deputy Sheriff, Andrew Singer was leaned back in his chair with his feet on the desk. His head was tilted back, causing his breathing to sound like a buzz saw hard at work in a lumber mill.

The driver headed for the sign that read, MEN, while the other one headed for the coffee pot.

When both men were back and standing in front of Andy's desk, the Caucasian man made a loud sound in his throat, "Ahem, excuse me Sheriff?" Nothing happened. The two men looked at each other, then the black man said in a loud voice, "Sheriff!"

Andy opened one eye and yawned as he surveyed the two men standing in front of his desk. Andy slowly swung his feet down off the desk and stood up, stretching out the kinks.

"Name's Andy Singer and I'm not the sheriff, just the deputy," Andy said as he surveyed the two men a bit closer, wondering why two men dressed exactly alike in gray suits, would be in Shortcut and standing in front of his desk at this ungodly hour. "It's a bit early for business, but if you have a problem I'm all ears."

The black man stepped forward and held out his hand. "I'm Burns and this ugly white boy next to me is my partner, special agent Jacobs. We're with the FBI."

As the three men shook hands, Burns and Jacobs presented their credentials.

Andy felt the hair on the back of his neck stand on end, but tried to stay calm. "So what is the FBI doin' in this neck of the woods, and how can I be of assistance?"

Without waiting for an answer, he went over to make a fresh pot of coffee and found that it was already brewing. He turned around and faced the two men, realizing he hadn't heard them come in. "I'm sorry but I've already forgotten who is who."

"That's not something we hear very often," Burns chuckled. "I'm Special Agent, Ralph Burns," he said, pointing to himself. "And this fella here," he said pointing at Jacobs, "is my partner, Special Agent Billy Jacobs."

"I promise; I won't forget again. My thanks to whichever one of you made the coffee."

Burns grinned as he picked up a cup and began to pour. "The white boy made it, but even so, I'll risk a cup."

"If you be afraid o bein' pizened, boy, da masser will drink da first cup," Jacobs replied in his best southern slave voice.

Burns and Jacobs grinned at each other and Andy realized ribbing one another was something these two did on a regular basis. They were different than the few FBI men he'd met a few years ago. He liked both of them immediately but wasn't sure how the sheriff would react to their banter.

Andy took a sip from the cup Burns handed him and said, "Hey, this ain't half bad." Andy took another sip as he sat down at his desk. "So, as I asked ah moment ago, what brings the FBI out to our neck of the woods?"

Without any dallying around, Jacobs got right to it. "Have you seen or had any reports of any strange goings on around here, lately, especially things like gunfire coming from up on the mountain?"

CHAPTER THIRTY-TWO

Not all decisions are the right ones

BY MORNING the storm had moved on, leaving the lake and mountain an incredibly beautiful scene to behold. The morning air was cool and refreshing. Birds were singing and the creatures of the forest were jumping around and playing as though they had been reborn. A huge buck deer raced down the mountain right in front of the cave and leaped over a fallen tree so high that he could almost see the entrance to the cave.

Inside the cave, Rafe was already up and dressed. The fire had been put out and he was shaking each of the kids awake.

Trace jumped to his feet, and looked around, "What's wrong?"

Rafe patted him on the shoulder. "Relax, it's morning, the storm has passed, the sun's up and shining bright. The men chasing us are gone, and its time to move out."

Shaun woke up at the sound of Rafe and Trace talking. He moved over next to Kristi and gave her shoulder a shake.

"Kristi, time to wake up. Wake up sweetheart, it's time to take you home."

Kristi's eyes fluttered open and she looked at Shaun through bewildered eyes. "Shaun?"

He shook his head and gave her a wide grin. "In the flesh."

Kristi looked around, trying to get her bearings. She had been deep in a dream where she was dressed in an all-white, full flowing skirt, and had on a white blouse with short, puffy sleeves. Both the blouse and skirt were made of soft cotton and felt good against her skin. She was wearing a crown made of daisies that had been woven into her hair, and on her feet were silver ballet shoes. The sky was bright blue with soft white clouds floating across no more than ten feet above her head. She was dancing across a field of forget-me-nots and daisies that swayed back and forth in the light breeze as she leaped high into the air, twirling around and around, feeling light as a feather. The sound of birds singing filled the air. She was happy and pain-free.

Then suddenly, without warning, she was thrust back into reality. Her beautiful dream disappeared and she was now lying in what appeared to be a dark cave. Her body felt like it was on fire and her leg was screaming with pain as though someone was poking her leg with giant needles.

"I don't feel good. I feel like I'm on fire and my leg hurts really, really, bad," she heard herself saying, with a confused tone to her voice.

Shaun patted her arm. "You were injured, but you're gonna be okay, now."

"What happened to the beautiful field Shaun, and all the flowers?" she asked.

Discombobulated, Shaun asked, "Beautiful field? What beautiful field? I don't know what you're talking about, Kristi? We're in a cave." He was rambling on and he knew it, but he didn't know what else to say or do, he was out of his element. All he could do was to stare down at the confused look on her face. He looked around for Melissa. Maybe she would know what Kristi was talking about.

At Rafe's touch, Melissa opened her eyes, smiled up at him and then crawled over next to Shaun and Kristi. "How's our patient doing this fine morning?" she asked, glancing over her shoulder to see Rafe staring after her and for just a moment her heart seemed to beat a little faster before she turned her attention back to her friend.

Shaun looked forlorn. "Not too good. She's talking weird."

"What do you mean, talking weird?" Melissa asked as she reached out and felt Kristi's forehead. "She's burning up with fever. She's delirious. That's why she's talking weird." She looked at Shaun and said, "Get me the canteen. I need to sponge her head, maybe that will help bring the fever down."

Shaun jumped up and bumped into Trace. "Help me find a canteen, Kristi needs some water. She's got a fever."

Trace reached over next to his bedroll and picked up a canteen and handed it to Shaun, who rushed back over, and after giving Kristi a drink, handed it to Melissa.

Melissa poured water onto a small towel she had in her pack and wiped Kristi's forehead and neck. She wanted to pour water over Kristi's head but was reluctant until Rafe laid his hand on her shoulder.

"It's okay, use it all. We'll get more, not far from here."

Melissa looked up at Rafe and smiled, and for some unknown reason he felt a weird fluttering in his stomach. Before he could figure it out, Shaun spoke up. "Kristi is burning up with a fever. We've got to quit this messin' around and get her back to town. She needs to go to the hospital and see a doctor."

"I agree, she does need to see a doctor, but aren't you forgetting something?"

Shaun looked around the cave. "What are you talkin' about, mountain man?"

Rafe pointed toward the entrance to the cave. "Those crazy guys with the guns. Even though they're not still right outside, my guess is, they're still out there roaming around, trying to find us."

Shaun scoffed. "Your nuts. They aren't still out there. They're not stupid enough to stay out there all night in that storm. No way, dude. They're long gone."

"They murdered three men that I know of, including Sheriff Tucker, and I have no clue as to how many others they may have executed. But, they do know I saw them kill the sheriff, plus, I saw those other two dead men. Oh they're still out there all right. And there is no way in hell they're gonna let any of us off this mountain to blab about it to the authorities.

"Then there's the issue of the bridge being washed out. They know it's no longer there and we have no way to get off this mountain. Add all these little facts together and the answer is, they're still out there because they can't afford to leave any of us alive to testify against them. They're just waiting for us to make a mistake and let them know where we are."

"I don't know, man," Trace said, scratching his head. "You're probably right about some of that stuff; like they'd kill us all cause they're nuts, but it's really hard to believe they'd stay out there all night in that storm with no shelter or food. And even if, by some miracle they did, how do we know they're still anywhere close?"

"I agree with Trace," Shaun interjected. "Look, they're probably ah hundred miles away by now. They know it's only a matter of time before somebody comes looking for us because we're kids, right? So, my guess is they hightailed it outta here. I vote we get Kristi back to town, now!"

"A hundred miles from here, you say? Are they magical? Can they fly? Oh yeah, now that I think about it, that's probably what happened, they just flapped their arms and flew away."

Shaun glared at Rafe with hate in his eyes. "Don't play cute, Talltree. I never said they could fly, but maybe they left by goin' over the other side of the mountain. That's a possibility, right?"

"No, it's not, because there is only one road, the one that comes across the bridge that no longer exists. And that road dead-ends at the lake and the lodge. As a matter of fact, there aren't any logging roads either because this mountain has never been logged. This mountain is owned by the town and is actually inside the city limits and they have a clause in the original charter that the mountain is to never be logged."

Melissa looked up at Rafe and asked, "Are you saying we should stay cooped up in this cave? We're out of food and water and Kristi needs medical attention."

"No, I'm not saying that at all. My cabin isn't far from here; a little higher up. And I'm pretty sure they don't know about it, so they won't expect us to keep going higher. As far as they know, the lake and the lodge is it. There's no regular road up to my place because I take a different route each time and cover my tracks. So I'm pretty sure they'll be watching the road and the place where we left Trace's jeep sitting next to the ravine."

Shaun stood looking at Rafe, his fists on his hips and fire in his eyes.

Rafe looked at him briefly, and then looked at the others and said, "I have food and medicine at my cabin, plus a two-way radio. I can call Andy and let him know where we are. He's been up to my place a few times, so he'll know how to get there. He can bring help. It just makes sense that we go on up to my cabin. Besides, in case they happen to find us, I have a few weapons we can fight back with."

"Let me give you a news flash, mister high and mighty mountain man, Kristi is my girlfriend and I make the decision where she goes or doesn't go. And first of all, I think you're full of crap about them still being out there waitin' for us. And second, takin' her up to your cabin is just a waste of time. So, like I said, I'm takin' her back to town where she can see ah real doctor and get some real help, not some mumbo jumbo Indian ritual, like waving your hands back and forth and blowin' smoke at her in some heathen ritual. . . End of discussion."

Rafe realized Shaun had seen him last night, but for some reason hadn't said anything. He looked at Melissa and Trace, who had confused looks on their faces, but hung their heads and kept their mouths shut.

Even though he knew Shaun wasn't thinking straight because of some lame idea he had about Viet Nam and his brother getting killed. He also knew Shaun was angry because

Talltree had come back alive and his brother hadn't, and closed his mind to the truth about what had happened.

The kid was nuts, Rafe thought. He'd explained the situation in plain terms, which seemed to have gone in one ear and out the other. With the bridge gone, there was no way they could get Kristi into town – except maybe by helicopter, and without a radio to call for help that probably wasn't gonna happen.

Even though he knew it would be a fruitless attempt, he had to give it one more try. "If we take her to my cabin, I could radio Andy and ask him to send a helicopter."

"We don't need you, your radio or a helicopter, Talltree," Shaun said, stubbornly.

Rafe had had enough of Shaun and said, "Okay, hotshot, have it your own way. But remember, when you've got a boat load of gun barrels starin' you in the face, don't say I didn't warn you."

Melissa's head came up and she stared at Rafe. "That sounds like you're not coming with us."

"That's right. I'm not," Rafe said, nodding his head.

"Well now, that's just great," Melissa, said, her mouth turning into a pout. "How are we supposed to. . ."

Shaun interrupted her. "Hey, Melissa, no big deal, me and Trace can handle it. We don't need mister know-it-all Indian guide to get off this mountain."

Before he could stop himself, Rafe blurted out, "Don't be stupid, Shaun. Open that thick skull of yours and listen to reason. There is no bridge and no way any of us can get off this mountain without a helicopter. Plus, this is not just about you; it's about getting your friends killed right along with you. Those men out there won't hesitate to kill the lot of you and will probably laugh all the while they're doing it."

"Maybe they want to kill you, but not us," Shaun yelled. "We don't know anything and we didn't see anything. It's not us they're after, so just step aside Red Man and let us be on our way."

Shaun nodded his head at Trace. "Let's go."

As Shaun and Trace picked up the litter with Kristi on it, Rafe turned to Melissa and said, "You don't have to go with them."

Melissa felt a tug at her heart and for just a moment she was tempted to stay with him. He was so handsome and seemed to always know the right thing to do. From the first, she'd felt safe with him and wanted to stay, but in the end, she heard herself say, "Yes I do – for Kristi's sake. I'm her best friend and she needs me, no matter what."

"You may be risking your life," Rafe said.

Melissa laid her hand on his arm. "I know, but. . . she's my friend and she's hurting, and she needs me."

Even though Melissa's eyes belied the words coming from her mouth, Rafe had to admire her loyalty. He felt the chemistry between them and wanted to keep her safe and protected, but he wouldn't force her; that would only put a wedge between them – and for some unknown reason, he didn't want that. Rafe nodded, then turned without a word and pushed the brush aside to make way for Shaun and Trace to carry Kristi out onto the ledge.

By now, Trace was having mixed emotions. One part of him wanted them to go up to Rafe's cabin where they could get something to eat; he was ravenous. Kristi could get some medical attention. Rafe could call Andy for help and a helicopter, along with a doctor. That sounded to him like the thing to do, but on the other side of the coin, Shaun was his best friend and he had to live with him every day – so to speak. He was sorely tempted, but what if Shaun got mad at him and never threw another pass to him, how would he get a scholarship to go to college? His folks didn't have that kind of money.

As they carried Kristi toward the entrance to the cave, Trace bit down on his bottom lip, praying silently that the bad guys were long gone and that Shaun knew what he was doing.

Earlier, before the others were awake, Rafe had heard the men outside talking as they headed back down the mountain. He'd heard their leader tell them to watch the road and the area around Trace's jeep. That was how he knew it was safe to leave; but not down the mountain, to higher ground and his cabin. Down the mountain there was a chance they would be captured and executed.

CHAPTER THIRTY-THREE

Something in common

Andy and the two agents had been talking for some time and Andy was more than a bit over whelmed by their news.

"It's hard to imagine that what you're saying is true," he said, shaking his head.

"Well believe it, deputy," Burns said with a bit of an attitude.

Jacobs saw Andy bristle up and jumped into the conversation before things got out of hand. "C'mon deputy, you talk like a good ole boy but you're not foolin' me, you know the score. These supremacist groups have been around since the civil war, callin' themselves by one name or another, but other than that, they're all pretty much the same."

"Hey, lighten up," Andy said. "I didn't say I've never heard of them or don't know anything about them. I can read, you know, and I watch the news."

"I'm sorry," Burns said. "I get steamed up just thinking about them and what they stand for."

"Yeah, I can understand that," Andy said. "But here's the deal. First, it was hard for me to believe they could be hanging around a dull little town like Shortcut, Utah. But then, when I thought about it some more, this would be the perfect place. Plus, it just might explain something I've been puzzled about."

This got Burn's attention. "And just what might that be?" he asked.

Andy opened his desk drawer and pulled out the small plastic bag with the ring with the swastika on it and tossed it onto his desk.

"A van rolled over and exploded last night, right here in town, and because of the magnitude of the explosion, we're guessing they were carrying nitroglycerine. Luckily, the streets were empty, so none of the town folk were hurt, but of course, the two men inside were killed; blown to pieces is more like it. In what little was left, I found this ring on a burned hand that was lying next to the van."

Burns picked up the ring and examined it carefully, then tossed it to Jacobs who inspected it. "That's his signature, alright. His real name is Zebedia Budroe Palasco but when the Klu Klux Klan threw him out, he changed his name to Adolph Hemmlick and attached himself to a group of skinheads. After a few months, he took over and became the chief nut case of a group that now calls themselves, The New World Order, or some such."

After examining the ring for himself, Jacobs nodded and said, "I agree. This is their signature; plus, this confirms our thinking and the reason we sent two other agents up a few days ago to investigate."

Andy nodded. "And you say you haven't heard from them since early yesterday morning? And I haven't heard from the sheriff since yesterday morning. Doesn't sound good. You think they may have run into these guys up there on the mountain?"

Burns gave Andy a stern look. "Guys?"

"All right, all right, White Supremacists," Andy said, throwing up his hands.

"How about Neo-Nazi scum," Burns countered.

Once again, Jacobs jumped into the conversation. "Back off, Burns. The deputy is on our side, remember?"

Agent Jacobs turned to Andy and said, "Nothin' personal deputy, but one of the men who went up there was a friend of his," nodding toward agent Burns. "They were in Nam together."

Andy smiled and nodded his head. "I understand. I was in Nam, too. Lost some good friends. Worst three years of my life."

Jacob's eyes squinted and he got wrinkles on his forehead. "You spent three years in Nam?"

Andy patted his bum leg and said, "Didn't seem right to leave without givin' Charlie some payback. Besides, it wasn't like I had anybody back here waitin' for me."

Burns smiled and extended his hand. "You're okay. I'm sorry."

Andy grinned and returned the agent's handshake.

Jacobs placed a hand on each man's shoulder and said, "Okay, now that we're all on the same side, what are we gonna do about it?"

CHAPTER THIRTY-FOUR

Words mean nothing to deft ears

USING THE ROPE, Trace and Shaun climbed down first to receive Kristi when Rafe and Melissa lowered her. Next came Melissa, followed by Rafe after he pulled the brush back over the entrance to the cave.

Once he was down, Rafe pointed to a trail leading downward and said, "Don't go down the road or they'll spot you for sure. If you're bound and determined to do this, go down through the woods along that trail for about a mile or so. You'll run onto a wider path that will lead you back to the bridge area. It will be a little harder going than the road, but I have a hunch it will be a whole lot safer."

"Sounds good to me," Trace said, grinning at Rafe and shaking his hand. He then turned to Shaun and asked, "You okay with that?"

Shaun was staring into the woods and just shook his head and said, "Yeah, sure, whatever."

Shaun and Trace lifted the makeshift litter with Kristi on it and started down the trail. Rafe watched them, knowing in his gut that Shaun was going to reject the advice he had given them. He thought about trying one more time, but then realized it would only make Shaun more determined to do the opposite, even if he knew he was wrong. When it came to trying to talk to Shaun, it was just words falling on deaf ears.

Melissa held back and when the boys were a short distance down the trail, she walked over to Rafe and said, "If Kristi could, I know she would say thank you for all you have done. And... I want to thank you, too." With that said, she reached up and gave him a quick kiss on the lips, then turned and ran after Shaun and Trace.

A wide grin broke out on Rafe's face as he watched her disappear down the trail.

By now, the group of men who had been searching the woods and road all night were almost to the point of rebelling. They were tired, hungry and soaked to the skin. One of them said to the man he had been teamed with, "For a decent breakfast and some hot coffee, I'd quit this outfit."

"Don't say that! Don't even think it!" the other man said. "You could wind up in a ditch somewhere, like them others."

"Yeah, you're right, I reckon," the disgruntled man replied. "I ain't thinkin' straight. But dammit, I'm hungry and I can hardly keep my eyes open. Besides that, the big toe on my left foot is hurtin' me somethin' awful from wearin' these military boots."

A short distance from where they started down the trail, Shaun made a decision and veered off to his left, weaving through the trees.

"Hey man, where you goin'?" Trace asked

"This stupid deer trail ain't nuthin' but up and down and my back and legs are starting to hurt. The road is just a short ways ahead in this direction and that's where I'm headed. Those clowns with the guns weren't dumb enough to stay out here all night. I'll bet they're long gone or still snoozing away back at the lodge. We can be down next to the river when Andy and the others come to get us. We'll be home before they even get up, if they're still up here, which I doubt. Trust me, this is the best way.

"I don't know, man. You heard what Rafe said," Trace said, weakly.

Shaun stopped and turned to look back over his shoulder at Trace and Melissa. "I am sick and tired of hearing what Rafe Talltree said! Mister Blanket-ass ain't here and I'm making the calls. Now com'on, let's get off this mountain and get Kristi to a hospital!"

With that, the three of them continued on toward the road, with Melissa bringing up the rear, glancing over her shoulder every ten steps or so. Something inside her told her they should have stayed on the trail, but what could she do but follow along? She knew that Shaun was aware that she sided with Rafe and had only come along because of Kristi. She also knew he needed her to help with Kristi because he had no clue as to what to do when Kristi was hurting.

Once on the road, they stopped to take a break and Melissa poured some water onto a rag and mopped Kristi's feverish face and neck. Even though she didn't see any men with guns, she said to no one in particular, "I still think we should have stayed on the trail. At least we wouldn't be out here in the open."

Shaun may not be the smartest guy she knew but he must have ears like a cat, she realized, as he stepped over next to her and looked down at her and said, "This is the fastest way. How's she doing?"

"How do you think she's doing? Look at her!" Melissa couldn't help herself. She was not only worried about Kristi, but right now, she was also very upset and scared.

"Hey, lighten up!" Shaun said, backing up a step and holding his hands up, palms forward. "You've been moody ever since we left the cave. What's bothering you?"

Melissa wiped Kristi's face before looking up at Shaun. She stared at him with fire in her eyes. "If you really want to know; there's several things bothering me and one of them is your attitude."

Shaun got a surprised look on his face and said, "Well now, miss prissy pants, what's wrong with my attitude?"

"For one thing, you didn't have the courtesy to even say thank you to Rafe for what he did for us," Melissa said as she poured a little more water onto the rag.

"Oh. . . you mean because he almost got us killed? And for getting Kristi shot? As far as I'm concerned, he's the reason we're in this mess in the first place."

Melissa bristled up. "Damn you Shaun. You know that's not true." Hearing Shaun downgrade Rafe seemed to get under her skin for some reason that she couldn't quite explain.

"Oh really? Well, for your information, in case you forgot, they weren't chasin' us until he showed up. Mister mountain man led those crazy guys straight to us!" By now, Shaun was yelling and his face was red. Melissa defending Rafe Talltree was more than he could tolerate. Hell, the whole town was glad he'd moved up on the mountain so they wouldn't have to look at him every day and be reminded.

"Com'on, Shaun, he didn't know we were stranded next to the river or that the bridge had been washed away. His pickup ended up in the river and him almost with it, remember?" Trace said, trying to break up the argument.

Shaun stared at Trace for a moment with a look of contempt on his face and then turned back to Melissa. "Sounds to me like you got the hots for Talltree. You turnin' into a squaw-woman all of a sudden?"

Melissa jumped to her feet and before Shaun could duck, she slapped him hard across his face.

Shaun staggered back a couple of steps, in surprise and pain. His eyes turned from surprise to a mean, angry scowl. Both of his hands balled into hard fists and he looked like he was about to attack Melissa when Trace jumped in between them.

"That's enough! You two forgettin' what we're supposed to be doing here?"

Shaun took a deep breath to let his temper subside. After a few deep breaths, he unclenched his fists.

"Let's just get outta here," Shaun said as he reached down for the front end of the litter.

"Right," Trace said as he picked up the back end. When he stood up, he looked at Melissa and asked, "You gonna be alright?"

"Yes, I'm fine," she said as she picked up her and Kristi's packs and slipped them over her shoulders.

"Good! Everybody's fine, except Kristi! Can we get a move on?" Shaun shouted in a disgusted voice.

By the time they'd gone a short distance down the road, the sun had climbed over the tops of the trees and was trying in vain to dry up all the havoc the storm had caused.

CHAPTER THIRTY-FIVE

Where is help when you need it?

RAFE APPROACHED his cabin with care. From a place of concealment near the front, he studied the ground for any signs of tracks, man or beast. The front door was closed, but that wasn't good enough. Someone could have closed it when they went inside. He circled around and came up from the backside, then eased his way along the side until he came to the side window.

First, he listened for any sound coming from inside, and then using caution, he peered inside. Once he was sure the cabin was empty, he went to the front door and checked the strand of hair on the lower part of the door. It was still in place. Rafe gave a slight sigh of relief before he opened the door and went inside.

Immediately, his nose was assaulted by the smells of gun oil, wood smoke and cooked meat. The cooked meat caused his stomach to growl.

Without a doubt, this was a man's place. There was only one large room, which served as a kitchen, dining room, living room and bedroom. The giant room had three large wooden columns with heavy beams spread out down the length of the room to support the roof. There was a half loft that served as a storage and work area. On one side of the loft was a long worktable where he loaded his own ammunition, tanned hides and did the taxidermy work, or other work that needed to be done.

Down below, there was a homemade bed that was more than large enough for two. The bed sat in a twelve by twelve-foot area of one corner of the cabin. It held one of the few things he'd brought from town - a very comfortable, king-sized mattress. The bed was covered with a blanket made from bearskins. In the corner, was a homemade desk and chair. The desk was littered with papers and a ledger book.

The center part of the cabin contained a couch that had belonged to his parents. The couch sat in front of a large fireplace set into the front wall. There was no television, but tall bookshelves adorned each side of the fireplace and were filled from top to bottom with novels and how-to books. A long mantle made from a piece of left over wood from a tree he'd cut down while building the cabin stretched from one side of the fireplace to the other.

The rest of the cabin took up the kitchen and dining room. The kitchen held the other thing he'd purchased and hauled out from town, a wood-burning cook stove that had a large oven. Next to the stove, was a container filled with wood for the stove. Along the far wall, was a long counter with a sink next to the water pump; below were three shelves where cleaning supplies were held. Above the counter and sink, were three long shelves that held cooking utensils and food.

The dining room was sparse, just a homemade square table and four homemade chairs. The table was clean with a lantern sitting in the middle, along with the salt and pepper shakers.

A two-way radio sat on a small table in the far corner of the cabin, not far from the dining room table. At this moment, the radio was silent, waiting to be turned on and used. There was no electricity. The only light came from three windows, a couple of lanterns and three coal oil lamps. A heavy-duty battery sat on a small bench directly below the table that held the two-way radio. Connectors dangled from the radio, waiting to be connected. The battery was traded back and forth with the one in the pickup so that it was always charged.

Even though it was a man's digs, the cabin was clean and neat and everything in its place. There were no signs of frilly things a woman might want, which made him think of Melissa. He wondered what she would do to make the place more, homey.

Sitting on the fireplace mantle was an eight by ten-inch picture of Rafe and several soldiers who were standing in front of a tent in Viet Nam. Above the picture, hanging on pegs, were several rifles of various caliber along with a compound bow with a quiver of arrows. Two nine-millimeter pistols hanging in holsters and next to that were knives of various size and type hanging in their sheaths.

Sitting on a table in the work area up above, were several projects waiting to be finished. Down below, close to the kitchen stove, a large hunk of cooked deer meat hung from a piece of rawhide. After slicing off a good-sized chunk, Rafe headed straight for the radio.

After connecting it to the battery, he turned it on and while he waited for the radio to warm up, he ate the piece of dried venison with great relish and wanted more.

The green eye on the face of the radio lit up and he picked up the microphone and pressed the call button. "This is Wolf Scout calling Cub Master. Wolf Scout, calling Cub Master. Come in, patrol leader."

This was a code he and Andy had worked out so Andy would know who was calling without mentioning any names, just in case any of the town folks or the sheriff might be in the office. If the sheriff would happen to be in the office, he would pick up the microphone and yell, "Stay off this radio!" and hang up.

"Wolf Scout calling Cub Master, come in patrol leader," Rafe repeated, and then stood back and waited. Rafe waited for more than enough time for Andy to answer, but there was nothing but static. After a few minutes, Rafe tried again, and when no one answered, he left a message.

While Rafe was leaving his message, Andy was standing on the sidewalk in front of the sheriff's office with the two FBI agents, along with approximately twenty of the local townsmen. Big Mike Bozeman, Bill Lange and James Thomas Walker were all standing at the front of the group not more than three feet from the curb.

Being outside the sheriff's office, Andy never heard Rafe's call for help, or the information Rafe left for him, which would have changed things dramatically.

There was a lot of muttering going on and out-right stares at the two men in suits who stood quietly a couple of steps behind Andy.

The two FBI men gave Andy a nod and he stepped up next to the edge of the curb and raised his hands in the air, indicating he had something to say.

The men stopped talking and turned their attention to the deputy.

"Thank you all for coming out this morning to help. As some of you already know, Sheriff Tucker and four of our kids are missing and presumed to be stranded up in the lake area because of the storm that came through. I also know that you're all anxious to go up there and bring 'em home."

A round of cheers went up from the crowd until Andy raised his hands, again, waving at them to quiet down.

"And I agree with you, but. . . well. . . I've just received some news that changes things."

"What news?" Bill Lange asked with a bit of trepidation in his voice.

Big Mike Bozeman stepped closer to Andy and asked, "You been holdin' out on us, deputy? What's wrong?"

With this, everyone commenced talking again, which caused Andy to wave his hands in the air. "Hold on, hold on. No, I haven't been holding out on any information. I just got this news myself a few minutes ago. We don't know that anything has happened to them, but there are some new wrinkles." Pointing toward the two FBI men, Andy said, "These two men are from the FBI, and I think they should be the ones to explain." With that said, Andy took a step backward, allowing the two FBI men to step forward.

The small crowd got so quiet you could hear grass grow. Jacobs nodded toward Burns, who looked out over the crowd and cleared his throat before speaking. "Good morning gentlemen. I'm special agent Ralph Burns and this is my partner, special agent Billy Jacobs," he said, pointing in Jacobs's direction.

"We don't give a damn if you're on the president's staff. We want to know what the hell is goin' on and if our kids are in trouble? You just tell us the situation, then stay out of our way when we go up there and bring 'em home," Big Mike Bozeman shouted.

A round of encouragement from the other men filled the air.

Andy could understand their concern, but it also made his temper flare up. They were ready to take action before they even knew what they were up against.

"Nobody's goin' anywhere! Now just shut up and quit bein' so quick to jump into action until you have all the facts!" Andy shouted.

The men all looked at each other. They were stunned by Andy's outburst. None of them had ever seen Andy lose his temper before.

From somewhere in the crowd, Bert Henderson, said, "Sorry about that, Andy. We're just concerned, that's all." Then he said, "You go ahead mister government man, give us the facts and please don't leave anything out."

The rest of the crowd nodded their agreement as Big Mike Bozeman turned to look at Bert and give him a nod and said, "thanks,"

After a moment, his face sobered and he said, "Believe me, I understand your concern. I would probably feel the same as you do if I were in your shoes, but this has now become a matter for law enforcement, and I'm truly sorry, but none of you will be allowed in the vicinity until we find out for sure what is going on and get the situation under control."

Big Mike Bozeman was a hard man to keep silent when his back was up and he butted in again. "You tellin' us the FBI has an operation goin' on, up to the lake? Since when? And why all the hush, hush?"

Andy gave him a stare that made Big Mike take a step backward and shut his mouth.

"We understand your concern, truly we do." Burns said, and then took a moment to compose his next statement. "I know you men are level headed and won't go off halfcocked, so here are the facts as I know them. The FBI has good reason to believe there are men up at the lodge that are wanted by the US government on suspicion of treason. These men are heavily armed and trained in warfare, which makes them dangerous. Two of our agents who were sent up there to take a look around, are also missing. Since talking to the deputy here, I called for backup and more agents are on the way as I speak. Hopefully, with their help, if these people are up there as we suspect, we can apprehend them without any gunplay, but, as I'm sure you can understand, we can't endanger the lives of any civilians by allowing you to go up there with us."

What sounded like pandemonium erupted as everyone began talking all at once.

Burns held up his hands, and after a moment they began to quiet down. "I know it's hard for you men to stay down here, especially you fathers, but the bottom line is, you're just going to have to trust us. Please, be patient and let us do our job."

Bill Lange, who was by now so enraged he couldn't contain himself, yelled at the top of his voice, "Be patient, my ass! My little girl is up there and you tell me she might get killed by a bunch of lunatics who want to overthrow the government, and you want me to be patient? There ain't no way in hell!"

A loud roar of agreement went up from the other men, until Bill Lange held up his hands for them to quiet down; and when they did, he looked at Burns and said, "Mister, I don't give a damn what you say, or how many lunatics are up there, I'm goin' up there and get my daughter and the rest of them kids and bring 'em home - and the only way you or anybody else is gonna stop me, is to shoot me in the back!"

Before Andy could react, Melissa's father yelled out, "And that goes for me, too!"

By now, the group of men had all turned and were heading toward their cars and pickups.

In vain, Burns yelled after them, "Hold on a minute!"

Only one man, who was at the rear, even bothered to react, and turned back to face Burns.

He was a wiry little man with a scraggly red beard and mustache, whose name was Rufus McKay but everyone in Shortcut called him, 'Red.' "We know that mountain better than any of you, ceptin' maybe that Indian that lives up there. So, understand what I'm tellin' ya, and understand it good. We're goin' up there, and like Bill said, the only way to stop us, is ta shoot all of us."

As Andy watched them go, he turned to the two agents and said, "Looks like your people better get here muy pronto, cause those men are serious. And I've got no grounds to arrest them. Besides, my jail ain't big enough."

Jacobs looked down the street and pointed, as three black, government vans came down the street toward them.

CHAPTER THIRTY-SIX

Shaun Tilford comes face to face with reality

MELISSA WAS LEADING THE WAY down the road, her eyes darting from side to side. She had a worried look on her face even though the storm had passed and the sun was shining brightly. They were on their way home and she knew she should be happy, but she wasn't. She couldn't get Rafe's warning out of her head. But on the other hand, she had to admit; Shaun's decision was gaining them valuable time. The river wasn't far now and they hadn't seen any of those men who had been shooting at them last night.

She hoped, like Shaun had said, they were long gone.

If that was true, then why was she keyed up like a wire stretched too tight? Her eyes searched the forest on either side of them. She glanced over her shoulder and all she saw was Trace and Shaun carrying Kristi on the litter, but when she turned back to the road, her breath caught in her throat.

Two men in camouflage clothing stepped out from the trees and were grinning at her. They were carrying guns, which they were pointing directly at her. She came to a sudden stop and wondered if they were about to die?

Looking at them, standing there, brazenly pointing guns at them, she realized why she had been so nervous. Rafe had been right when he said staying inside the woods would give them a better chance of reaching the river.

"Well lookey what we found," the man on the right said to his partner, who was already pulling a walkie-talkie radio out of his jacket pocket and putting it to his ear.

Pressing the talk button, he said, "C patrol to headquarters. Come in. Over," And when he lifted his thumb off the talk button, a voice came out of the speaker almost immediately.

"C Patrol, this is headquarters. Have you found them? Over."

The man with the walkie-talkie was grinning like a Cheshire cat as he spoke into the speaker of his unit. "Not only have we found them, Captain, we captured them! They come ah walkin' down the road, pretty as you please, like they didn't have ah care in the world. And like you said, one of 'em is bein' carried on ah stretcher. Over"

The voice of the captain came back to them, asking, "How many are there?"

This made the man stop and count. "Four," he said into the walkie-talkie, "two teenage boys and two teenage girls. One of the girls is the one bein' carried on the stretcher. Over."

The pause that followed caused the two supremacists to look at each other with confused looks on their faces. Then, the captain's voice came over the speaker, again.

"You're sure there are only four? Over."

Both supremacists looked at the teenagers again and counted by pointing their fingers before the man with the walkie-talkie responded. "Yes sir. We both counted and there are four - two boys and two girls. And like I said, one of the girls is bein' toted on the stretcher by the two boys. Over."

After another long pause, the voice of the captain came over the speaker again. "I'm sending help. I want them brought back to the base camp immediately, and be careful in case this is a trap. There might be another one nearby, and he could be armed and dangerous. Over and out."

Both the men of patrol C raised their weapons, scanning the forest, but saw no one, and after a few anxious moments, they decided this wasn't a trap and relaxed their guard.

Shaun spoke for the first time. "We don't want any trouble. My girlfriend has been shot and needs a doctor, real bad. If you'll let us go, I promise we won't say anything."

Melissa shook her head, not believing Shaun could be that naive.

"You hear that Slim?" one of the supremacist said, "They won't say anything if we let 'em go. Like we're stupid or somethin'. Do you believe that load of crap?"

Slim grinned and said, "Don't reckon I do. No sir, don't reckon I do."

While the two men were making merriment about the situation, Melissa came to a decision and slid the coil of rope off her shoulder and drew back her arm, then hurled it at the two men, catching both of them in the face.

By the time they reacted, Melissa was already heading into the forest, hoping to make an escape and somehow find Rafe.

She had gone only a short distance before she heard the gunfire and saw where bullets were peppering the tree limbs above her head. She heard one of the men yell, "Next bullets goes in yer back, little lady."

Melissa hated giving up, but what could she do at this point. She didn't want to be shot in the back, or anywhere else for that matter. She came to an abrupt halt, took a deep breath, exhaling slowly to compose herself before she turned and walked back. She took her time, walking slowly, hoping maybe she would get another chance. She observed their every move, hoping her next chance would come soon. She wondered what Rafe was doing right now?

Melissa would have been very pleased had she known that at that very moment, Rafe was coming down through the forest in search of them and had heard the burst of gunfire. He had stopped only long enough to get a fix on the location, then headed in their direction, never realizing it had been Melissa's action that had caused the man to fire his weapon.

Rafe only knew that somehow, he had to find the teenagers and help them if he could. They had no experience with people like this. And neither did he for that matter, but war was war and these lunatics were soldiers, led by a maniac, just like the ones he'd faced in Viet Nam. Add to the fact that Shaun was heading up their little group with his stubborn, bullheaded ways and there could only be one conclusion - disaster. The sound of gunfire confirmed his suspicions. He just hoped none of them had been killed.

When Melissa stepped onto the road again, she gave the two men a defiant stare that caused them both to realize she was going to be a handful. Both men wanted to get her back to the lodge and into somebody else's care as soon as they could.

But for now, Slim knew it was up to him to deal with the situation. Filling himself with bravado, he stepped up to Melissa and said, "Try that again girlie and I won't be shootin' over yer head."

He turned and stared at Shaun and Trace, letting them know he had the upper hand and hoped they believed him.

As if it could be predicted, Shaun's ego got the best of him and he said, "Real tough guys. Picking on an unarmed woman makes you feel big does it?"

Slim walked over and slammed Shaun in the kidney with the butt of his rifle, which caused Shaun to drop to his knees, sucking for air.

In all fairness, Shaun didn't make a sound, nor did he release his hold on the litter; he just went to his knees with a grimace on his face, which changed to an angry glare once he was able to breathe again.

Melissa grabbed Slim's arm and yelled, "Leave him alone!"

Slim shook Melissa's hand away and was turning to take a swat at her.

Trace lowered his end of the litter and said, "So, I guess you're gonna kill us just like you killed the sheriff and those two men. Is that what we have to look forward to, dying out here on this mountain where our folks will probably never find us?"

This stopped Slim in his tracks and he turned his head, looking directly at Trace, as his partner stated as a matter of fact, "I didn't kill nobody. Did you kill anybody, Slim?"

Slim got a sly grin on his face and said in mock innocence, "No.. . at least not today."

Both supremacist burst out laughing until they heard Kristi, call out, "Shaun, are we home, yet? I want my mother! Please, Shaun, I want my mother!"

At her outburst, Slim looked down at Kristi, then raised his head and asked the other three captives, "Just what was it you said was wrong with this girl?"

Melissa stepped up and looked Slim in the eyes and said, in a defiant tone, "One of your big brave men, shot her in the leg."

Before Slim or his partner got a chance to challenge her statement, more of the supremacists came charging up the road in their vehicles, sliding to a stop just a few yards from where they were standing. They jumped out with their weapons ready to fire, and to the man, stopped and stared when they saw that the captives really were just teenagers.

"Hell, these are just kids," a short, rotund man with a scraggly beard stated. And after looking around, he asked, "Where's the other one; the tall one that looks like an Injun?"

Melissa's mind was working at lightning speed and the words came tumbling out of her mouth before she could stop herself. "He's dead. We were trying to make sure you didn't catch up with us and weren't paying as close attention as we should have and he slipped in the mud - fell down into a ditch, hit his head on a rock and broke his neck. We didn't have a shovel or time to bury him for that matter, so we just left him where he landed." She said with as much conviction as she could muster while pointing at Shaun and Trace.

Both, Shaun and Trace shook their heads in agreement, secretly marveling at the ease with which Melissa came up with that story.

"Maybe that's true and maybe it ain't," Slim said. "But that there story don't mean a hill of beans til we've seen the body for ourselves. Now where do we find him?"

The three teenagers looked at each other, shrugging their shoulders, with blank looks on their faces.

Finally, Trace broke the silence. "How the heck would we know that? It was dark and the rain was pouring down like it was coming out of a faucet. We were soaked clear down to the bone, worn down from running, and hungry, along with being scared out of our wits. He's dead and lying face down in a ditch somewhere up there, he said, his arm pointing up the mountain. That's the best we can do."

Shaun and Melissa both shook their heads in the affirmative.

After pondering that information for a moment, Slim looked at his men and took a deep breath before he spoke. He pointed at the four teenagers and said, "Any one of these kids can send us to the gas chamber, or the electric chair, or whatever they do in this state. And you can bet your last dollar that's just what they'll do if they get loose ta go blabbin ta the authorities. So here's what we'll do. We'll take them back to the lodge and let the captain decide what to do with 'em. And in the meantime, we don't let 'em out of our sight." Slim turned to one of the men and said, "Bones, I want you to pick two other men and go up the mountain and search the ravines and ditches. We need to find that other body."

The rest stood glaring at the kids and raising their rifles like they would rather shoot them than take them back.

Slim shook his head in wonderment at the depths of their stupidity. Oh well, they were the captain's worry, not his. "Okay, the rest of you, let's get these kids back to the lodge. Load 'em, separate - one to ah vehicle. They might be just kids, but we ain't gonna take any chances. My younger brother had already killed two men and a woman by the time he was their age."

Melissa eased herself forward until she was standing right next to Slim. When he noticed her, she looked up at him with pleading eyes. "Please let me ride with Kristi in case she wakes up and needs attention. She's in a bad way. . . Please?"

Slim looked at Melissa and wondered how much trouble she would give him if he said, no? To keep the peace, at least until they got back to the lodge, he nodded his okay and watched as Melissa climbed into the back of the pickup and sat down next to the girl who had been shot.

"Tell her I'll see her soon," Shaun called out as he and Trace were herded into the other vehicles.

Hidden behind a tree, just off the road, Rafe had seen and heard most of what had gone on, except for the part where she tried to escape. He was especially pleased with Melissa's spunk and the quick way she came up with that story about him breaking his neck, and then staying with Kristi. He wished he could do something right now to help them get away, but there were too many of them to take on alone. For now, all he could do was watch as the kids were driven away. He knew where they would be taking them, so he turned and headed back into the forest.

After a short distance, Rafe came to a large outcrop. He climbed to the top and took a deep whiff of the forest. Turning his face upward, he stared at the clear blue sky, but not really seeing it. His mind was working overtime on how to go about rescuing the kids and at the same time, raise havoc with the supremacists. These were some really bad people and he would need to be careful not to endanger the kids any more than he had to. He wondered how much help he could expect from them if he wound up needing help? He wouldn't bother with the three idiots searching for his body - at least not right now. With them out in the forest stumbling around, it would be three less to deal with.

Lowering his head, he climbed down off the huge boulder and re-crossed the road, then disappeared back into the woods, heading in the direction of his cabin.

Back at the cabin he immediately began putting his plan into action. The first thing he did was try to contact Andy, but it turned out to be a one sided conversation. Next, he put a chunk of roasted deer meat and some bread into a knapsack; then filled a canteen with water and set it on the table, near the knapsack. Earlier, he had acted foolishly and rushed off in search of the kids without taking any weapons with him; a mistake he wouldn't make again. This was going to be a lot like Viet Nam - him against the enemy with innocent civilians to bring home.

CHAPTER THIRTY-SEVEN

A new plan

Activity at the lodge was quiet except for two men down by the entrance to the barn. They were loading cardboard boxes from the barn to the inside of a ton and a half moving van.

The vehicles with the kids and the returning supremacists made their way down the muddy driveway trying to stay in the ruts they had made earlier.

The two men loading the large truck, stopped and watched with interest until the convoy of pickups and four-wheel drive jeeps came to a halt in front of the lodge.

The kids were ushered out of the vehicles and lined up in front of the lodge, with Kristi's litter placed in front of them on the muddy ground.

Hearing the engine noise, four other men came out of the barn and walked over to where the captives were standing. One of the four men sauntered over to Slim and asked, "Give ya much trouble?"

"Nothin' we couldn't handle," the sergeant said as he headed for the front of the lodge.

Adolph Hemmlick was in the common room on the first floor. He was standing in front of the fireplace, tossing non-essential papers into the flames when he heard the engines of the returning vehicles. He smiled for the first time since this whole thing began.

Since he'd already gotten a call on the two-way radio, he was in no hurry to go outside. It was especially good for prisoners to await their fate. It let them suffer longer.

He picked up the last box and began tossing handfuls of paper into the fire, watching as the flames turned the paper to ashes. He wanted no evidence left behind. When the box was empty, he turned and walked out the front door, stopping on the wide front porch, where he took his time lighting a cigarillo before descending the steps. At the bottom of the stairs, Adolph glanced at the teenagers who stared back at him with fear in their eyes. He gave them a smile, then turned to Slim and said, "Take them to the barn, we'll deal with them there."

Slim gave the Nazi raised hand salute. Adolph returned the salute, and then walked off toward the barn, leaving the captives to wonder about what was going to happen next.

Adolph smiled for the second time that morning as he walked toward the barn, blowing smoke rings into the air.

Even the men were afraid of him. He could see it in their faces and that's the way he liked it. To a man, they'd all heard the story of how he had once been an eliminator for the Klu-Klux Klan, but not one of them had the *cajones* to ask him about it or what it felt like to be a hired killer - to kill someone you'd never even met - or knew anything about.

He stopped and glanced over his shoulder, surveying his men one by one with envy for the feeling they would get when they eliminated their first non-pure. It was like no other feeling he'd ever experienced before.

Shortly after organizing this group of White Supremacists, he typed a letter to the head of the Klan, reminding them of how they would miss him and his abilities as an eliminator of unpures. Then he had purposely left it lying on his desk where it was sure to be found. From that day on, he'd had no trouble controlling them. They might grumble a little from time to time, but they did as they were told because they were afraid not to. It made no difference whether the letter was ever mailed or not. To the last man, the men had all heard about the contents of the letter from their sergeant, and that was all that mattered.

Melissa, Shaun and Trace looked at each other with worried looks. The only one who didn't was Kristi. She was lying on the litter, staring straight up at the sky as though she was in a world all her own, which at that point, she was.

When they had been captured on the road and she thought she was going to die, something snapped in her head and her brain had taken her to a place far away from any danger, and had not yet released her back into the real world.

Melissa looked at Shaun and whispered, "What are you going to do to get us out of this mess you got us into?"

"Me?"

"If we had stayed in the woods like Rafe told us to. . ." she said, allowing the statement to hang in the air.

Shaun stared at Melissa as though she'd lost her mind. "Look around, Melissa. What can I do? Have you noticed they have guns and would like nothing better than to fill us with lead and dump us in some ravine? And if you want to lay blame, lay it where it belongs, on Talltree, he's the one who got us in trouble in the first place!"

"Don't give me that! If we had left when the other kids did, we would be at home right now and not. . ."

Their argument was interrupted by Trace, who noticed the supremacists were all staring at them. In a loud whisper, he said, "Hey, you guys calm down. Just stay cool. Somehow, some way, we're gonna figure out how to get out of this mess, but standing around blaming each other ain't gonna help. Besides, they're all staring at us."

Just then, Slim walked over and said, "Shut yer traps and head for the barn."

He stepped back and pointed in the direction of the barn with the barrel of his rifle.

As Trace started to pick up one end of the litter, he noticed his shoelace had come untied and he stooped down to re-tie it, saying, "Hang on a minute dude, I need to re-tie my shoe."

While Trace was bent over re-tying his shoestring, Slim booted him on the hip, causing Trace to fall over on his back, into a puddle of muddy water.

When Trace rolled over onto his side to get to his feet, Slim smashed him in the kidneys with the butt of his weapon. "Keep your hands where I can see 'em."

Melissa's temper got the best of her and she ran over and grabbed Slim by the arm. "Stop that! He was only going to tie his shoe!"

Slim jerked his arm away and yelled, "Shut up you piece of black trash, or you'll get the same!"

When Adolph heard the commotion, he turned and walked back to see what was going on, not liking what he was seeing and hearing.

As he walked up and saw one of the boys lying on the ground, groaning and holding his side, a grin spread across his face. Patting Slim on the shoulder, he said, loud enough for everyone to hear, "That's enough for now, Slim, I believe they get the point."

Adolph looked around at his small, ragtag group of men who were standing next to the vehicles, waiting for orders.

What he did next surprised them when he turned to them and said, "You've done well today, all of you. But let us not forget, we still have one more to capture and deal with. We cannot let even one of them get off this mountain, especially the Indian."

They all looked at each other and nodded their heads, but said nothing. It was unlike the Captain to give compliments and they weren't sure how to react. On one side, he'd just given them a compliment, and on the other he'd just told them they hadn't completed the mission he'd sent them on. The man was a puzzlement, for sure.

Slim moved over next to Adolph and asked, "You still want me ta tak'em to the barn?"

Adolph blew cigar smoke into the air as he gave the question a bit of thought. Finally, after some deliberation he said, "No, lock them in the shed for now. We'll deal with them later, after we've captured the Indian - the one who actually saw what the disposal unit did."

Slim snapped to attention and saluted. "Yes sir."

Adolph returned the salute with a halfhearted gesture, and then headed back to the lodge. He had things to think about - like how to find and dispose of that trouble making Indian who had done so much already to upset his plans. The man could send them all to prison, or worse.

After Trace tied his shoe and stood up, he whispered to Melissa, "Thanks, you saved my bacon."

Before Melissa could respond, Slim turned back to them and yelled, "You heard the man. Pick up the girl and move out! Now!"

The shed was located between the lodge and the barn, but beyond and back of both structures. It was about ten by twelve feet and had seen better days. Slim removed the lock that was hanging loosely in the hasp and motioned them inside.

Melissa entered first, followed immediately by Shaun and Trace carrying Kristi on the litter.

As soon as the kids were inside, Slim closed the door and hung the lock back in the hasp. They heard the loud click as Slim snapped the lock closed.

There was no electricity inside the shed, not even a lantern, but there was light coming through the cracks in the walls so that they could see well enough for now. Although when it got dark, that would be a different story.

Shaun and Trace set the litter down on the dirt floor and looked around. Except for the four of them, the shed was empty. There were no tools or anything stored inside the shed.

Melissa knelt next to Kristi and gave her a sip of water from the canteen she was carrying. Trace heard voices and went to the door and looked out through a wide crack.

Not far from the shed, Trace saw the supremacists gathering around the man he had seen come out of the lodge.

Adolph had come back outside because he had things he wanted to say; things that he felt the men needed to hear, things that would put them in the right frame of mind.

Someone brought a wooden crate and placed it on the ground. After a moment Adolph stepped onto the crate and looked around at the men who were staring back at him, wondering what he was up to now.

When they had all gathered around him he raised his hands for quiet, and then said, "Listen up. I have news and it's not good. I have reason to believe that Miller and Post are dead, and the mission has been aborted."

A murmur fanned out through the men until Adolph raised his hands again.

"Something went wrong. I don't know what, and it's my guess we'll never know. Billy heard the information coming from the sheriff's car radio as he was passing by where it had been pushed into the ditch. It seems the van rolled over and exploded down in the town of Shortcut. The van was destroyed and both men were killed."

"You ah sayin' they didn't get no further than Shortcut?" one of the men asked.

"That's right," Adolph responded. "The mission terminated itself before it began and I'm not sure there is still time to rectify the situation, but I'm going to try. The first thing I need to know is how much explosives we still have and what kind? Do we still have both dynamite and nitro?"

251

Two men hurried off in the direction of the barn.

By now, both Trace and Shaun were listening with their ears pressed against the cracks in the door. Melissa touched Trace on the arm and asked, "Trace, what are they talking about? Are they talking about us?"

"Shhhh, listen," he said, pointing at the other cracks.

Melissa found a wide crack in the front wall that would allow her to see through and listen from.

Adolph was considering what more he could say to keep their mission alive and also keep them under his command. They were all volunteers; civilians who could leave any time they chose. But he could not allow that to happen. They had a mission and by God if there was any way possible they were going to see it through. Besides, he didn't know when they would get another opportunity like this.

After a moment, he raised his hands and waited for them to quiet down, then said in the best commanding voice he could muster, "Even though your comrades failed to complete their mission, this is not the time to fall apart. This is the time to take up the challenge and move on! If the president and the others down in Salt Lake are to be destroyed in order to start our new order, we must act now, and act swiftly! To do that, we must leave here before the authorities find our location, which may already be too late.

Adolph took a pause to let the information sink in. After lighting a cigarillo, he continued. "We know the two men we found in the barn were in fact, FBI agents, and when they do not report in, well. . . you all know what that means. There will be others who come to investigate and we cannot afford to have them find us. Our victory is too close at hand!"

A cheer went up from the men and Adolph smiled as he stared down at his followers. He still held the command.

"If we have enough explosives, I believe we still have enough time to do what we came here to do!"

His voice rose to a high pitch as another round of cheers filled the air and the two men who had gone to the barn returned and handed him a sheet of paper.

After he'd read the information, he nodded his head and spoke to the men. "We have enough! Now get it loaded as quickly as you can. We need to be on the road as quickly as possible! Seig Heil!" he said as he raised his arm, palm down.

After the men returned his salute, the two men who'd brought him the information about the explosives hurried off toward one of the vans sitting near the barn.

After they'd gone, he looked at the rest of the men and said, "When we leave here, we must leave nothing behind to give them a trail to follow or a hint as to our mission. There must be no trace that we've ever been here. If it's not absolutely vital to our mission, burn it. . . or kill it."

He let his last words hang in the air, knowing they were all wondering what to do about the captives and the Indian who was still running free. And now they knew.

"Now, who's with me?" he shouted.

To the man, they all raised their arms in the Nazi salute. Seig Heil! Seig Heil! After a moment, he reached into his shirt pocket and withdrew a piece of paper and waved it in the air. "Assignments will be made from this sheet of paper," he said, holding it for them to see. "As your name is called, come inside the lodge. For reasons of security, so that no one can disclose the whereabouts of any of the others, there will be two man teams and your assignments will be given to one team at a time. No team will disclose their assignment to anyone else! There can be no exceptions! None! Is that clear?"

To the man, they all shook their heads in the affirmative.

When no hands were raised, or questions asked, Adolph handed the sheet of paper to Slim, and then turned and walked back into the lodge where he would hand out the assignments he'd just finished putting together before he came out to rally his army.

As he climbed the steps leading to the porch, he heard Slim's voice and he smiled. If there was one man he could count on to do his bidding, it was Slim. Slim was an ideal sergeant at arms; he was as faithful as a good dog.

"Alright, you men listen up," Slim called out. "When I call your names, line up at the bottom of the steps by teams - first team, Pilfer and Langley.

CHAPTER THIRTY-EIGHT

Accidental hero

WHOA, SHAUN, DID YOU HEAR what he said about a van exploding right there in town?" Trace asked in an excited whisper.

Shaun's mind was running a hundred miles a second as he remembered running the red light and almost hitting that van, and then the explosion. "Yeah, I know all about it, and would you believe it, I think I was the one who caused it to turn over."

"No way," Trace said.

Shaun shook his head. "Tucker was chasin' Kristi and me last night and I ran a red light, right in front of a black van. The van did a hard right to keep from runnin' into my jeep and rolled over and exploded. We didn't stop cause Tucker was still chasin' us, and Kristi was yelling for me to take her home, but I'm sure that had to be the one they were talkin' about. I mean, how many black vans roll over and explode in Shortcut?"

Trace lifted his fist into the air and shouted in a loud whisper, "Way to go, Shaun! Score one for our side!"

All though Shaun had inadvertently saved the life of the President of the United States of America, along with the Vice President and a whole group of very important people; at least for the moment, Melissa wondered why they were both so happy? After all, Shaun running that red light was purely accidental. And she was sure he had no idea that he was doing something useful or he would have been bragging about it to anyone who would listen.

At that moment, Kristi began shouting, "Mommy, I'm hot! Do something! Please, mommy, I'm so hot!"

Melissa was the first one to reach Kristi and put her hand on Kristi's forehead. "She's burning up with fever and I don't have any water left in my canteen."

"Don't be mad at me momma. I love him and, well, things just happened," Kristi said in a pleading voice.

After a moment, Kristi opened her eyes and said, "Shaun? Shaun, where are you?"

Shaun knelt down next to Kristi and took her hand. "I'm right here."

Kristi turned her head so she could see him better. "Don't you be mad at me too," she said in a pleading voice.

Shaun was totally confused and looked over at Melissa, who averted his stare, not wanting to reveal Kristi's secret. Shaun looked back down at Kristi and said, "I'm not mad at you, sweetheart. Why would I be mad at you? I love you, don't you know that?"

For the first time since being shot, Kristi smiled. "Then you're happy about the baby?" she asked.

The expression on Shaun's face was that of someone totally in shock. Shaun looked up at Melissa who smiled and nodded her head in the affirmative.

By now, Trace was standing next to Shaun and had heard everything Kristi had said. He broke in to a wide grin and said, in an excited whisper, "Kristi's gonna have ah baby? Does that mean I'm gonna be an uncle, or somethin' like that?"

Kristi smiled and had tears in her eyes as she nodded her head, yes, then looked up at Melissa, who was also crying.

Shaun broke the mood as he stood up and dragged Trace with him to the far end of the shed. Shaun's eyes were wide and he was breathing hard as he looked at Trace and whispered, "We're gonna be nuthin' but four corpses if you don't help me figure a way outta this mess, and quick, man. Those lunatics out there don't plan on leaving us alive when they pull out of here."

Suddenly, the shed got deathly quiet. Trace began to pace back and forth inside the small enclosure that was for the time being, their prison cell. Close to the door, he turned back and stared at Shaun and shrugged his shoulders. "Man, I got nothin'. We can't just wave a magic wand and make ourselves disappear."

"Don't go stupid on me, man," Shaun said, running his hand over the top of his head. "We gotta think straight. "We need a plan and we need it now."

If only Rafe was here, Melissa thought to herself, he'd know what to do.

CHAPTER THIRTY-NINE
An unexpected foe

THE SUN WAS sending shafts of rays through the openings between the trees as Rafe made his way down through the forest, heading toward the lodge. He had just stopped to adjust his ammo belt that was pinching his shoulder when seemingly from nowhere a large bear came rambling out of the brush and stopped, not ten feet in front of him. For a long moment, the two stared at each other; then very slowly, Rafe began to back up. He couldn't shoot the bear without the supremacists hearing the sound and giving away his location. He was relatively sure they were still out looking for him and could be only a short distance away at this very moment. Getting shot or captured would not help the kids.

Rafe had gone barely three steps backward when the bear began following him, step for step. They continued on this way for another few steps, and then apparently the bear got tired of just following Rafe and rushed toward him, growling noisily.

Rafe turned and began running, but he hadn't gone more than fifty feet when he saw the edge of the cliff; and when he tried to turn to his right, his feet hit a muddy spot and he flew into the air and bounced off a tree and then over the side of the cliff.

As he went airborne, instinct kicked in and he grabbed for something to stop his fall and felt his hand brush against a tree root. He clamped his hand onto the root and almost jerked his arm out of its socket when his body came to a sudden stop and was slammed against the side of the mountain, knocking the wind out of him.

During his acrobatic, tumbling act, his rifle had somehow slipped off his shoulder and went end over end down to the bottom of the deep ravine.

Rafe heard the bear growl again and looked up. The bear was leaning over the edge of the cliff, trying to strike Rafe with his claws which passed only a few inches above his head.

Rafe pulled his head down into his shoulders as far as he could and reached for his pistol. The palms of his hands were wet and slippery and when he pulled the pistol from its holster, he was not able to get a firm grip on it. The pistol slid through his fingers like they were covered with butter. The nine-millimeter Beretta flew into the air and dropped like a rock, finally landing at the bottom of the ravine with a big splash, not two feet from the rifle.

The bear leaned even further over the cliff to strike at his victim and almost slipped over the side. Rafe tried to get his body as close as he could against the side of the mountain so that hopefully the bear wouldn't take him with it if it fell into the ravine.

Not wanting to go over the edge, caused the bear to back off and take stock of the situation. After a minute or so of staring over the edge at his prey, he decided Rafe wasn't worth the effort and ambled back into the brush, sniffing the air, heading in the direction of some fresh berries his senses had just picked up.

Rafe looked over his shoulder and could barely see his rifle and pistol, which by now were sinking into the mud. He made a mental note as to the location so he could remember where to come and get them when this was all over. He could clean and oil them and they would be good as new, that is, if he was still alive to come back.

Secure in the knowledge that the bear had departed, Rafe slowly made his way back up to solid ground and when he was on his feet, he bent over, panting. That had been too close. He checked to make sure nothing was broken or bleeding. When he was satisfied that he was okay, he checked to see what he had left to go to war with. He had his bow and quiver of arrows, his k-bar military knife and his ammo belt. Of course, the ammo would do him no good unless he found a weapon of the same caliber, which might be a good possibility. He also knew he had the one thing no one could take from him; his brain and his knowledge of warfare.

CHAPTER FORTY
The missing bridge

ON THE ROAD, next to where the bridge should have been, a group of frustrated men stood staring at the flooded river. Andy looked at the FBI men and said, "Believe it or not, up until this recent storm, there used to be a bridge, here."

All the men from town nodded their heads in agreement, but it was Big Mike who broke the silence. "I knew that ole bridge was gonna go someday. I just didn't realize it would be when we need it so much."

Thomas Walker turned his head and looked down the river a short distance to his right and saw something moving on the far bank. Detaching himself from the group, he trotted down to where he could get a better look; and after studying the object no more than just a moment, he yelled at Andy. "Hey, Andy, come and take a look at this."

The entire group hurried down to where Melissa's father is standing and looked across the river to where he is pointing.

Rafe's pickup was nose down in the river not far from the opposite shore and all that could be seen of it was the bed.

Burns turned his head and asked, "Andy, you recognize it?"

Andy nodded his head and said, "Yeah, I'm pretty sure it belongs to a fella by the name of Rafe Talltree; ex-Viet Nam vet. He lives up here; has a cabin up near the top of the mountain."

"You suppose he's still in there? In the truck, I mean," Jacobs queried.

Andy shook his head, shrugged his shoulders and said, "I sure hope not, he's ah friend of mine. But I don't know. I can't see inside."

Immediately,

Thomas Walker jumped into the conversation. "There's one way to know for sure." Turning to Big Mike, he asked, "You still got that rope and grappling hook we use for dragging the river, in your pick up?"

After a moment, Big Mike realized why he was asking. He grinned and replied, "Sure do." And with that he turned and trotted off in the direction of the vehicles. "Be right back," he yelled over his shoulder.

Andy looked at Thomas Walker and asked, "What are you up to?"

Melissa's father turned back to Andy and said, "Not only am I going to check the inside of Talltree's pickup to see if he's in there, but I'm also going get us across this river," he said matter of factly. "We came up here to get the kids and take 'em home, and that's just what I plan on doing. My gut tells me if Rafe Talltree ran his truck into the river there's got to be ah darn good reason, and I want to know what that reason was."

Andy thought for a moment and then said, "The river is still runnin' pretty swift. But let's say we do get everybody across, it's still a long walk up to the lake."

"The map in your office shows two roads; one to the lake and one to the lodge, right?" Jacobs asked.

"That's right," Andy said. "What's on your mind?"

"Once we get across the river, we could split up. Half of us could go to the lake and the other half to the lodge. We can radio each other about what we find. Save some time."

Andy shook his head in agreement, but his mind was thinking of a different plan.

"Not a bad idea, but the lodge is a longer distance than to the lake - but if we had us ah helicopter to check things out for us, we'd know for sure which direction to go."

One of the men from town said, "That's all well and good, Andy, but we ain't got no helicopter."

"That's right." he answered, "But they have one up at the ranger station and it's not too far from here. I could contact them and request they send their bird over our way," Andy said with a big grin.

Burns patted Andy on the shoulder. "Sounds like a plan. While you're on the radio, we'll help Melissa's father get everyone across the river." Pointing at Jacobs, he said, "He can go with the ground troops, but I want to be with you in the chopper. I don't swim so good."

"Okay," Andy said with a chuckle, as he headed for his patrol car and the radio, just as Big Mike came running back with the rope and grappling hook.

CHAPTER FORTY-ONE
The trench

MELISSA WATCHED OVER KRISTI while Shaun and Trace began trying to dig a trench under the back wall deep enough for them to crawl under, figuring this might be the only way to escape. Unfortunately, they had nothing to dig with but their hands, and progress was slow and painful.

Trace leaned back on his knees and let out a whoosh of air. Two of his fingers were bleeding at the tips because the fingernails had been pulled loose. Shaking his head, he looked down at the shallow, would-be trench. "We're not getting anywhere and my fingers are beginning to bleed. Even with all that rain, the ground is still hard as a rock."

"Maybe that's because it didn't get wet inside the shed," Melissa said with a bit of sarcasm in her voice, not giving much credence to their escape plan.

Trace gave her a look and she realized he was only trying to help.

"Someone has got to be out looking for us; my dad, Kristi's dad, or even yours. Someone will come for us, you'll see," she said, hoping she sounded more convinced than she felt.

Somewhere, Shaun had found a small rock with a sharp edge on it and had been using that to dig with. He held it up and said, "Com'on man, look around; find yourself something to dig with instead of your fingers. We only need to dig down deep enough to belly crawl under the wall and pull Kristi through."

After inspecting his bleeding fingers, Trace said, "Maybe Talltree has gotten word to somebody. I don't know, like, maybe, Andy, at the sheriff's office?"

Shaun went back to digging. "Yeah, right. Forget about him. He's probably up in his cabin, hidin' out and glad he's rid of us."

"Shaun!" Melissa yelled in a reprimanding voice. "I can't, and won't believe that!"

Shaun shrugged his shoulders and acted innocent. "Whatever."

Sometimes Shaun pushed things too far and Melissa wasn't going to let him get away with it this time. "What have you got against Rafe Talltree? You can't blame Rafe because your brother got killed."

Shaun leaned back, knotted up his fists, and got a mean look on his face. "Just drop it, Melissa!" he hissed through gritted teeth.

Trace knew he should keep his mouth shut, but something inside wouldn't let him. "It's because Talltree didn't die in Nam instead of Danny, isn't it?"

Like a rattlesnake strike, Shaun's fist shot out and landed on Trace's chin, knocking him over backward. "Shut up!" Shaun yelled, drawing his fist back again for another punch.

Melissa jumped in between them and yelled, "Stop it Shaun! Stop it!"

Trace raised himself up and gently pushed Melissa aside, then turned to Shaun, pushing his chin out in Shaun's direction. "Go ahead, hit me again if you think it will make you feel better."

Trace knew Shaun had a lot of bitter resentment about Rafe Talltree inside him that needed to come out. He felt sorry for both, Shaun and Rafe, but it wasn't Rafe's fault that Shaun's brother, Danny, had been killed in Viet Nam. The way he'd heard it, Talltree had been miles away on some kind of special mission and didn't know about it until he came back.

Shaun was breathing hard as mixed emotions hammered around inside his head. He felt bad about hitting his best friend, but in his rage he hadn't been able to stop himself. Just thinking about Rafe Talltree made him angry and he didn't understand why. He knew Talltree had nothing to do with his brother's death, but Rafe came back, walking upright, and his brother came home in a casket. Shaun looked at his friend and was about to apologize when Kristi asked, "What's wrong? Why is everybody shouting?"

Melissa turned and wiped Kristi's forehead with the rag she was holding. "It's nothing, sweetie. You just rest."

Shaun said in a soft voice, "That's right, it's nothing," then turned toward Trace, sticking out his hand. "I'm. . . I'm sorry, dude."

"Forget it," Trace said. "It was my fault for opening my big mouth."

As they were shaking hands, Trace began to chuckle. Shaun got a confused look on his face and asked, "What's so funny?"

Trace thought for a moment, and then said, "I was just thinking about those papers we used to have to write about how we spent our summer vacation."

Shaun grinned and pointed at the back wall. "Dig, and maybe you'll get a chance to write another one. And this one could be a Pulitzer Prize winner."

Trace looked around and found a small piece of wood lying in the far corner of the shed. It was large enough to hold in his hand and thick enough to dig with without breaking. At first, he only used it to scrape with, and then he experimented a bit more and dug the piece of wood into the ground. On the first try, he found it worked much better than his fingers.

With both of them having something to dig with, the job went much faster and less painful to the fingers.

CHAPTER FORTY-TWO

A miffed escape

Inside the lodge, the self-proclaimed leader of the white supremacist group was burning the last of the paperwork when Slim came in and walked up close to him. "Sir."

Adolph didn't turn around. Instead, he continued to stare into the flames in the fireplace, watching the papers turn into ashes; and after a short silence, he heard Slim's voice, again. "The teams have their assignments and the vehicles have been loaded and I have men out looking for the Indian. What do you want done with those kids?"

"Ahhh, yes, the kids. . ." After a moment he said, "Do we have any shovels?"

"Yes sir."

"Good, good," Adolph said. "Right now, I want you to make sure the barn has been cleared of all evidence, then meet me at the shed, in say, ten minutes, with two shovels."

"Yes sir," Slim said. When Adolph didn't turn around, Slim saw no reason to salute, so he turned and left the lodge.

Because of the piece of wood Trace had found to dig with, and the rock Shaun was using, there was now a trench wide enough and deep enough for a person to crawl through. Shaun dropped down on his belly, ready to crawl out of the shed then looked up at Trace. "As soon as I'm outside I'll pull Kristi through, then you and Melissa come through and we'll head into the forest."

Trace raised the thumb on his left hand. "Got it."

As Shaun began to belly crawl under the back wall, Melissa said, "Hey, hot-shot, you be careful."

Shaun grinned, and then continued to crawl under the bottom edge of the shed. He was halfway out when he saw a pair of boots blocking his path. Shaun slowly looked upward and saw a man in camouflage clothing, pointing a shotgun at his head.

"Goin' someplace, pretty boy?"

Shaun froze and didn't know what to do. He couldn't go forward or backward fast enough to keep from getting his head blown to bits by that shotgun, so he just stared at the man who was looking down at him, grinning from ear to ear.

Inside the shed, Trace peeked through a crack in the wall and saw the man pointing the shotgun at Shaun and cursed himself for not checking to make sure the coast was clear before Shaun tried to escape.

Melissa had also heard the man at the back of the shed and immediately pressed both of her hands against her chest, praying the man wouldn't shoot Shaun. She felt a large sigh of relief escape her mouth when she heard him say, "Well, yer halfway out, you might as well come on the rest of the way."

A wave of relief spread over Shaun when he realized the man wasn't going to shoot him. He finished climbing out of the trench and stood up, but didn't see the barrel of the shotgun until it was too late.

Pain radiated throughout his neck and right shoulder from being struck by the barrel of the shotgun, almost causing him to pass out.

"Back inside pretty boy. Move it!" he said, pointing the shotgun at Shaun's head. "I ain't been told ta shoot you, yet. But, on the other hand, I ain't been told not to, either."

Shaun didn't wait for another order and moved toward the front of the shed as quickly as his weak legs would take him.

CHAPTER FORTY-THREE

The plan is revealed

ADOLPH WAS COMING DOWN the steps of the lodge when he saw one of his men poking a teenage boy in the back with his shotgun, ushering him towards the front of the shed.

'He must have been trying to escape,' he thought to himself as he headed off in that direction. He would have to learn the man's name. He was doing a good job and should be congratulated. Off to his left, he saw Slim leave the barn and head toward the shed, a shovel in each hand.

Slim and Adolph both reached the shed just as their comrade poked Shaun in the back once again with the barrel of his shotgun; this time, hard enough to cause him to stumble through the door of the shed and fall on his stomach in front of the others. With a guttural laugh, he kicked Shaun in the side, just as Slim and Adolph entered the shed.

Walt was distracted by the entrance of his leader and his sergeant and didn't see the black teenager swinging his fist until it landed squarely on his jaw, knocking him backward into the arms of his leader, Adolph Hemmlick.

Adolph stood the man upright and patted him on the back. "You are doing a good job, soldier. What's your name?"

Walt stood up straight and said, "Walt, sir."

"Yes. . . Walt," Adolph said. "But you might need to learn to duck a bit faster."

Walt was not only embarrassed, but also furious and wanted to go after Trace, but Slim stopped him.

"You'll have plenty of time later."

Walt just nodded and stood to the side, gritting his teeth.

Melissa walked up to Adolph and looked him in the face and said, "Why are you doing this to us? We've never done anything to you. Who are you people, anyway?"

Adolph looked down at the young black woman whose eyes told him she was not afraid of him and would stand her ground no matter what. He liked her spirit. She was full of spunk. What a shame she would have to die. He would have had fun playing mind games and other things with her, but all blacks were sub-standard creatures and all blacks were to be exterminated. So, instead of bantering with her, he just said, "The future. We are the future."

By now, Shaun was on his feet and looking defiant. "You and your comrades are sick, dude. All of you need to be deported and left on a deserted island somewhere with no food or water," he snarled, spitting in the direction of Adolph's feet.

Adolph gave Shaun an amused look, wishing he had the time to work with him and change his way of thinking and make him realize how wrong he was. The boy had backbone and would make a good soldier. Unfortunately, because of the circumstances there would be no time, which saddened him. He sighed and said, "No. No my young friend, it is this country that is sick. My comrades and I are the cure."

"I'm not your friend," Shaun hissed back at him.

"That is most unfortunate. We can always use more young people to help in the fight for the rights of white Christians, especially those who have as much zeal as you do. But, I can see that you don't understand this, as is evidence by the company you keep," Adolph said, pointing at Trace and Melissa. "But, in the end, the choice is yours, which is indeed most unfortunate for you."

Trace knew he was probably going to die today, and if that was so, before they killed him, he at least wanted to know what these people were doing up here that was so secret that people had to die. "Mind telling us what you people are doing up here and why your hell bent on killing everbody? You're not on vacation, and you're not doin' all of this just for kicks, I'm pretty sure of that."

Adolph looked down at his feet for a moment, then said with a sigh, "No, no, we haven't been up here on vacation or just for kicks, as you put it. . . We've been up here preparing for the future of this country. While we've had a bit of a setback, in the end it will not matter. A few days after we leave this place," he said, waving his arms around, "this country will encounter a brief period of chaos, then, when the dust settles, we will bring in the New Order to cleanse this country of all the unpures and restore the white, Christian way of life and set up the new government."

"Chaos? New Order? Where? Here in Shortcut?" Melissa asked.

Adolph chuckled and said, "No. The chaos I speak of will be for a short period of time and will spread across the entire nation. We will wait until a national panic takes control of this country before we step in and set up our headquarters somewhere near the center; maybe somewhere in Kansas.

"You need to also understand this; while we will be the cause of the disruption, no one will be pointing an accusing finger at us. Oh no. On the contrary, everything will be blamed on the vermin that have been poisoning the very life's blood of this land. We have our propaganda set up and ready to be spread across the entire world."

By now, Adolph was excited and his voice had gone up several octaves. "Politicians, Jews, Blacks, Mexicans, Iranians, nigger lovers and any others with non-pure blood will take the blame for the nation falling apart. And when it looks like all is lost, the New World Order will arise to take control and make this country clean and righteous once again – as was ordained many years ago."

Shaun looked at Trace and Melissa and asked, "Do you guys know what he's talkin' about?"

Trace laid his hand on his friend's shoulder. Shaun might be a big hero on the football field, but his mind was small town all the way. "He's talkin' about racism, Shaun. These people are against the Jews, Blacks, Hispanics and anybody else who ain't white and thinks like they do. Since you is ah friend of this here darkie, you is on their hit list, cause you is associatin' wit darkies and dat makes your blood unpure."

Trace turned toward Adolph and said, "Is that about it?"

The leader of the Supremacists nodded his head and said, "Close enough. . . Now, it's time for me to go. I have a new a plan to put into motion."

The sun was pushing its rays through the cracks in the walls of the front part of the shed, leaving weird looking streaks across the floor as the four teenagers stared at Adolph as he turned to leave.

"This is crazy. You can't go around killin' people just because we don't think like you do. You'll never get away with it!" Shaun shouted as Adolph reached the door.

Adolph turned back and faced the teenagers. "Of course we can, and will. We will finish what we started and when out of the ashes, the new America emerges, it will be the young people, guided by us, who will restore this great land to a racially white America, with its borders closed to anyone not pure."

278

With that said he stepped outside, nodding at the sergeant. "Slim, a word."

Slim followed Adolph a short distance away from the shed in the direction of the lodge.

When they were out of hearing distance of the others, Adolph stopped and struck a match, taking his time lighting a cigarillo. When he had it going sufficiently, he said in a low voice, "I'll be leaving with all but a few men." He then angled his head toward the shed. "Find the Indian and then make sure they're all taken care of, permanently, and before you and your people leave, burn this place to the ground. I want no traces left. No traces. Is that understood?"

Slim nodded, then stood up straight and saluted with his right arm and hand pointed in the air.

Adolph came to attention and returned the salute. After the formalities had been addressed, he reached out and shook Slim's hand. "Well then, if there's nothing else, I'm off. Remember, I'm counting on you."

Slim nodded his head and took his leader's hand, feeling very privileged that his commander had enough confidence in him to leave him in charge of such an important mission. He would not fail. After all, he had been promised a high position in the New World Order as soon as this country was pure again. Slim wondered what it would be like to allow only the superior race inside its borders, with him as a part of that leadership.

Adolph nodded his head slightly, then turned and headed for the jeeps.

CHAPTER FORTY-FOUR
Digging their own graves

BACK IN THE SHED, Walt was standing guard at the door when Slim approached from his talk with their leader and entered the shed. Walt grinned and followed him.

As the two men entered the shed, both, Shaun and Trace stood up and moved in front of the girls, not sure what they could do against full grown men with guns, but they felt they had to at least make an effort.

Slim smiled at their efforts, but for only a moment, then said, "Since you boys are so fond of diggin', Walt here, is gonna give you two a couple of nice, shiny shovels. I've got ah bit of diggin' that needs ta be done and you two have been elected."

He turned to Walt and said, "You know where the holes are to be dug?"

Walt nodded and came to attention and saluted Nazi style.

"The shovels are just outside the shed," Slim said as he returned the salute and then left the shed.

When Slim was gone, Walt stepped forward and pointed his shotgun at Shaun and Trace, motioning them toward the door. "You heard what the sergeant said, now move out."

As they did, he spit a long stream of tobacco juice right in front of Shaun, but

Shaun stopped just before the juice landed on his foot, which disappointed Walt. "Keep movin', city boy!" Walt yelled as he stepped aside to let them pass.

Melissa, realized by the salute the two men did, that these were not ordinary demonstrators, but a form of white supremacists, like the Klu Klux Klan, who believed certain white people should rule the world. Even though she believed she already knew the answer to the question she was about to ask, she bristled up her courage, took a step forward and asked, "Where are you taking them and why do they have to do your digging for you?"

Walt looked down at Melissa and said, "Don't you worry none about these two, little Missy, nor what they're gonna be doin'; you just think about the good time we're gonna have when I get back." And with that he threw his head back and laughed as he herded Shaun and Trace out of the shed.

"I hope you rot in hell!" she called after him.

"I'm sure I will, darlin', I'm sure I will, but not before I enjoy your sweetness," he said as he dropped the lock in the hasp and pushed it closed.

Shafts of light shown through the cracks in the wall of the shed, giving the illusion of being in prison; which was just how Melissa was feeling.

As his laughter slowly faded away, Melissa began to tremble. Her teeth began to chatter and she sank down onto the dirt floor, gasping for breath. The man had actually indicated he was going to rape her when he got back from wherever he was taking Trace and Shaun and there was nothing she could do about it. Her mind began to race. How much time did she have? Could she crawl under the back wall and escape before he came back? Maybe she could get away and go find Rafe. It was a good idea, except that she couldn't leave Kristi here alone – he would probably do wicked things to her if she weren't here to protect her and Kristi would be helpless to stop him. She began to search the interior of the shed for a weapon, anything, a rock, a sharp piece of wood to stab him with or even a hand full of dirt to throw into his eyes. Her breathing became ragged and she felt dizzy. "Get a hold of yourself," she whispered as she willed her breathing to calm down.

In her delirium, Kristi began to moan and thrash about, breaking Melissa's mood. Melissa moved over next to her friend and reached out and laid a comforting hand on Kristi's forehead and said in a soft voice, "It's going to be okay, Kristi. It really is. We'll all be going home very soon, you just wait and see."

Kristi opened her eyes, slightly and the hint of a smile formed on her lips.

Melissa could no longer control her own emotions and turned away. Tears began to stream down her face and her body began to tremble with fear. The truth was, they weren't going home, except maybe to heaven, because they were all going to die and there was nothing she could do about it. She wondered where Rafe was at this very moment? Had he deserted them like Shaun had said? "No!" she whispered. She would never allow herself to believe that. There was something between them; she had seen it in his eyes. And hadn't he asked them to go with him up to his cabin. And didn't he warn them about the dangers of going down the mountain? He'd even told them to stay off the road, which Shaun had completely ignored. No, Rafe would not abandon them. He would come for them; she knew it in her heart. He had to. He was her last hope. Kristi groaned and Melissa turned her attention back to her friend.

CHAPTER FORTY-FIVE

And suddenly, out of the forest

SHAUN AND TRACE found the shovels leaning against the wall of the shed just as Slim had said.

After picking up a shovel apiece, they were taken to a spot approximately thirty feet behind the barn where the dirt hand been turned for a garden. "This is it. Nobody will think ta look here." Motioning with the barrel of the shotgun, Walt said, "Alright ladies, get to it. I want you to remove three rows of them beans real gentle like, and then dig two holes; each one six feet long, four feet wide and six feet deep."

Shaun and Trace stared at each other as they realized what they were being told to do and what the holes would be used for. When they didn't begin digging right away, Walt grinned and said, "What's the matter tough guys, diggin' don't appeal to you anymore?"

Shaun gave him a hard stare. "And what if we refuse to dig?"

Walt spit a long, brown stream of tobacco juice in Shaun's direction while he pondered Shaun's question. After a moment, he scratched the back of his neck and said, "Well, I reckon we could shoot ya in several places without killin' ya, which would be mighty painful. And while you was ah cryin' about how much it hurt, we jest might toss the two of ya in the ravine with the sheriff and the two of ya could watch each other bleed ta death. We'd probably stand on the bank and make bets on which one of ya would last the longest?"

With that he threw his head back and began to laugh just as another one of his comrades who went by the name of Rooster, came walking up. "What's so funny, Walt?"

Melissa was both physically and emotionally worn down as she paced back and forth inside the small shed, stopping only occasionally to peek through the cracks in the wall, dreading the sight of Walt returning. What would she do when he returned, she wondered? She was still a virgin and had no intention of Walt being her first. She knew he wouldn't be gentle; and what if she got pregnant? A shiver went through her that caused her to wrap her arms around herself.

In her hysterical state she began to laugh, wondering what was she so worried about? When he finished with her, he was going to kill her and throw her body in a hole or a ravine; getting pregnant should be the least of her concerns.

Tears began to run down her cheeks as pictures of Rafe Talltree flooded her mind. If it were Rafe who wanted to take her virginity, she would probably go willingly.

Realization forced its way back into her brain. It wouldn't be Rafe; it would be that animal called, Walt. Somehow she had to prevent that from happening. She was not a person of violence but if she had a weapon she was sure she would use it on him.

Sweat was pouring off of both, Shaun and Trace as they pushed their shovels into the hard ground. Even with all the rain, at three feet down, the ground became hard and the digging slowed to a snail's pace, which pleased the boys, anything to slow down the inevitable. They still had at least three feet to go and as hard as the ground was, it would take some time.

Walt noticed the shovel loads were less than half full. He walked over and kicked Trace in the shoulder. "Faster! We ain't got all day! "

"We're going as fast as we can," Trace snarled. "You think you can do better, hop down here and show me."

Rooster poked Walt in the ribs with his elbow and said, "I say the hole is deep enough. Looks close ta four feet ta me. All we need is for it to be deep enough ta cover the bodies and from here, it looks deep enough."

Walt shook his head, "I was told to make the holes deep and to disguise both holes by putting the bean plants back in place, in rows, with sticks with vegetable signs on 'em after we bury the bodies. You know, make it look like ah garden again. That way it should make it tough for anybody ta find 'em."

At the back corner of the shed, Melissa found a spot where she was able to see a small area behind the barn. The boys seemed to be digging what looked like two graves, which caused a shiver to run through her. After a moment, the reality hit her like a sledgehammer in the gut. She pulled her face away from the crack, then buried her face deep into her hands and began to sob - uncontrollably this time. It was true, they were all going to die and there was nothing any of them could do about it.

Melissa's loud sobbing found its way into Kristi's conscious mind and caused her eyes to open. She was confused and not sure where she was or what was going on and in this clouded state of mind she wondered if something terrible had happened? "Melissa, why are you crying and where are the boys?" she asked, looking around.

Melissa fought back her tears and rushed to Kristi's side. "The boys are gone for the moment, but they should be back soon," she lied, trying to keep the truth from Kristi as long as she could. "What is more important," she asked, "is how you are feeling?"

Kristi put her hand to her forehead. "Oh Melissa, I'm so hot. And my leg hurts real bad. Where are we? Did Rafe get the bullet out of my leg?" Her mind was beginning to drift in and out of reality. Looking down at her leg she asked, Oh my God, what's wrong with my leg? It's all bandaged up and it hurts something awful." She tried to lift it.

Before Melissa could answer her, Kristi felt a sharp pain and slipped once again into that world where there was no hurting, or any idea of what was going on around her. Melissa leaned back, finally out of tears. She'd never cried so much, not ever.

Outside the shed, Melissa heard a noise and saw a shadow pass the cracks in the wall. Her heart began to pound and her breathing became ragged, again. Walt was coming for her and she was not prepared! In her near panic, she dropped to her knees and folded her hands against her chest.

"The Lord is my Shepard. I shall not want. He maketh me to lie down in green pastures. He leadeth me beside still waters." The shadow stopped next to the door. "He restoreth my soul. He. . . he leadeth me in the path of righteousness." She sucked in a huge gulp of air and glanced at Kristi, who was still unconscious.

"Yea, though I walk through the valley of the shadow of death, I will fear no evil, for thou art with me. Thy rod and thy staff, they comfort me. Surely, goodness and mercy shall follow me all the days of my life."

The door made a creaking sound as it opened, slowly. Without conscious thought Melissa moved protectively in front of Kristi as she continued her death prayer.

"And I shall dwell in the house of the Lord, forever. And please, look after Kristi and Shaun and Trace. Amen."

She was determined not to go without a fight as she clinched her fist into tight balls and stared defiantly at the silhouette of the man standing in the open doorway.

The bright sun made it difficult to see; but she assumed it had to be, Walt. He had promised to come back and rape her. She scooped up a handful of dirt, ready to throw it into his eyes when he got close enough. What she would do after that she wasn't sure, but it would be a place to start.

"Melissa, don't be afraid. It's me, Rafe Talltree."

Suddenly everything changed. She let the dirt fall from her hand as her breath quickened and her heart began to pound. "Rafe, is it really you?"

The next thing she knew, he was kneeling next to her and she saw his face and the broad grin spread across his mouth. She felt overwhelmed and grabbed him and pulled him to her, hugging him tightly. "Oh Rafe, oh Rafe, I'm so glad to see you."

Rafe enjoyed the closeness of her, but knew this was not the time. Gently, he pushed her away and looked her in the eyes. "I've come to take you out of here."

Tears of joy were streaming down Melissa's face. Her heart was pounding and she was breathing so hard she could hardly speak. "They took Shaun and Trace away. I. . ."

"I know, I saw them," Rafe whispered. "We don't have much time."

As he spoke, another shadow made its way along the side of the shed and stopped at the doorway.

Walt had left Rooster to watch over the boys. He was eagerly looking forward to what he was sure would be an interesting next few minutes. She was young and well built. And she was black! It would be just like in the olden days when a master took a young slave girl against her will, except when he finished with this one, he would kill her and throw her body into the hole along with the others. He began to get excited as visions ran through his mind - her fighting him as he ripped her clothes off and her screaming as he took her and finally the look in her eyes when he slit her throat.

Propping his weapon against the side of the shed, he smoothed back his long shaggy hair and took a deep breath, preparing himself for the battle he was sure would come. Grinning broadly, he opened the door and entered the shed. He was too excited to notice the lock was missing.

As Walt closed the door behind him, he leered at the young black girl staring back at him. Taking his time, he unbuckled his web belt and dropped it and his pistol to the floor. "It's time for us to have some fun. You ready for a real man, Missy?"

Rafe stepped from the shadow where he'd been standing and said, "Too late, she's already got one."

Walt spun around and stared in confusion at the tall Indian's face but never saw the k-bar knife in Rafe's hand. He only felt the pain as the knife was driven between his ribs and into his heart. He was dead before he had a chance to yell and alert anyone.

As Walt sunk to the dirt floor, Rafe put his hand over the man's mouth to cover any sound that might escape, but there was none.

Melissa stood frozen, making no sound. Rafe had just killed the man who came to rape her, and he did it with no more emotion than squashing a bug. She wasn't sure what to think until Rafe took her in his arms and kissed her, and then held her closely for a moment allowing her trembling to subside. He'd done what he had to, to protect her. When he felt her relax, he whispered into her ear. "I need you to be strong. I want you to go to the back door of the lodge, quickly and silently. I'll be right behind you with Kristi. I need the two of you in a safe place before I go after Shaun and Trace. Are you with me?"

Recovered from her shock and feeling pleasantly warm from Rafe's kiss, along with feeling safe in his embrace, she nodded her head in the affirmative.

He released her and reached for Kristi, who was still in her unconscious state. Kristi felt hot to his touch, which troubled him greatly. She needed medical attention, and soon, but right now he needed to get her and Melissa hidden someplace while he went to see what he could do about rescuing Shaun and Trace.

Before opening the door, Melissa looked through the crack and saw two men next to the jeeps, talking. Both had their backs to the shed. She crossed her fingers for luck and as quiet as she could, she opened the door and stepped out into the sunshine, looking in all directions before hurrying across the open ground between the shed and the back of the lodge building.

She went around the back edge of the lodge and stopped at the bottom of the back steps and waited until Rafe ran up behind her, carrying Kristi in his arms.

"Just in case someone is inside, open the door as quietly as you can."

Melissa did as he requested and stepped aside, holding the door to allow Rafe to carry Kristi inside. Their luck held as they found themselves in an empty kitchen.

Melissa hurried over to the window and peered out, checking to make sure they weren't spotted and followed. Once she decided they were safe for the moment, she smiled at Rafe. "I think we made it."

"Upstairs," Rafe said, nodding in the direction of the back stairway.

Melissa hurried past him and ascended the stairs quickly and quietly, keeping a sharp lookout for anyone who might still be in the lodge. At the top of the landing, she motioned for Rafe to come up.

"The bedroom down at the front should do fine. You will have a wide view from there and can keep a lookout," Rafe whispered.

The door to the front bedroom was closed and before entering, Melissa put her ear to the door and listened. All was quiet. She opened the door.

Rafe slipped past her and layed Kristi on the bed as gently as he could, then turned and went to the French doors that lead to a balcony overlooking the entire front area. When he saw that all was quiet, he turned back into the room and approached Melissa. Without a word, she walked up next to him and put her arms around him as though it was the natural thing to do.

Rafe smiled and pulled her close. They stood that way for several moments. Reluctantly, Rafe held her at arm's length and stared at her smiling face before dropping his hands. He pulled Walt's pistol from the back of his waistband, and after making sure it was loaded, he handed it to Melissa. "Here, take this. Have you ever fired one of these before?" he asked.

Melissa shook her head. "No. Actually, I've never fired a gun of any kind."

"Not a problem. It's very simple. I've made it ready to fire, so, all you have to do is point it at what you want to shoot and squeeze the trigger. It will kick when it's fired so you might want to hold it in both hands, like this," he said, demonstrating how to hold and fire the pistol.

Both, her hands and voice began to tremble. "I. . . I don't know if I can actually shoot anyone," Melissa said, her heart pounding so hard she was sure Rafe could hear it.

"Let's hope you never have to find out. But remember, it's them or us, and they won't hesitate to rape you and then kill you. You're a liability and they don't plan on leaving any of us alive, myself included."

Melissa took a deep breath. "I'll try my best, I promise," she said, not wanting to look weak in Rafe's eyes.

Rafe smiled and then turned to go, but Melissa caught his arm, "Rafe, I. . ."

Rafe turned back to her and looked deep into her eyes. "I understand. I'll be back shortly. Until then, keep this door locked."

Melissa reached up and kissed him lightly on the mouth, then stepped back and watched him leave. When he was gone she went to the door and locked it and propped a chair under the doorknob. When this was done, she walked back over and sat down on the bed, next to Kristi. With doubts about her courage, she stared at the pistol lying next to her.

Using great stealth, Rafe left by the back door of the lodge. Like a large cat on the prowl, he made his way into the woods.

Even though he was outnumbered, Rafe Talltree was about to go to war with the supremacists still at the lodge. And in his mind, they didn't stand a chance. One of them had already been eliminated.

While the war at the lodge was about to begin, a second war would soon be waged not far from the flooded river.

CHAPTER FORTY-SIX

Face to face with the enemy

THE LEADER OF THE SUPREMACISTS was riding shotgun in the lead vehicle as the small convoy made its way down the muddy road, heading toward the bridge that would put them on the highway and the road to freedom. He was relaxed, glad to be leaving. The lodge was beginning to feel cramped. He wanted, no, needed action and he wanted it now. The events that had led up to this point had been a challenge, but that would be over soon and he was looking forward to his new plan. In his mind he envisioned the United States being under his command and the new order would be the law of the land. He leaned back against the seat and lit a cigarillo, blowing the smoke out of the open window.

Big Mike swung the end of the rope with the grappling hook around and around over his head, letting out a little more rope with each rotation until he had the length he wanted. Casting his arm forward, he let the weight of the grappling hook carry the rope across the river. The hook landed on the far bank and partially buried itself in the mud. Big Mike pulled on the rope and set it tightly in the mud on the opposite shore.

Thomas Walker crossed the river by pulling himself hand over hand, while Big Mike controlled the loose end. Once Thomas Walker climbed onto the far shore, he secured the end of the rope with the grappling hook to a nearby tree, then Big Mike pulled his end of the rope taut and secured it to a tree on his side of the river so the others could pull themselves across hand over hand.

While the FBI man, Billy Jacob and the others were making their way across the river, Melissa's father checked Rafe's pickup and found it empty. He let his eyes roam the shore of the river as far as he could see, but saw no body, nothing but debris. He stepped back and looked around the area as he scratched his head. Had the man been swept down the river or had he jumped before the truck took its nosedive?

Even though they were soaked from head to foot, everyone made their way across the river, except for Andy and Ralph Burns. They stayed behind to wait on the helicopter coming in from the Ranger station.

Once everyone was across the river, Jacobs took command and said, "Okay, men, check your weapons and ammo make sure they're usable. Anyone with a problem let me know," and then turned to Thomas Walker. "Any luck?"

Melissa's father shrugged his shoulders. "He isn't in the pickup, nor is his body anywhere along the bank that I can see;

nothing but debris. I don't know if he drowned and his body was swept away, or whether he jumped and headed off somewhere."

Jacobs nodded his head. "Keep an eye out, he may show up yet," he said as he began to check his own weapon and ammo that had been wrapped in a large piece of plastic, sealed with tape and pushed into the waist of his pants. Once this was done, he looked at the others and asked, "Everyone's weapons okay?"

When everyone gave him the okay sign, he said, "All right, stay close together and keep quiet. We don't want to take a chance on anybody hearing us coming. And if we do happen to run onto somebody, don't nobody start shooting; hold your fire and wait for my signal. There could be a hostage situation; and if there is, let me handle it." There was a bit of grumbling. Jacobs raised his hands. "Right now, you men are running on emotions which might cause you to do something you'd regret later. We need to stay calm and hope for the best. Once we ascertain the situation, then and only then will we take action. Do I make myself clear?" he asked, staring hard at the men from town.

The men from town grumbled among themselves, but in the end, nodded their heads in the affirmative. The FBI men were in charge and they would do as they were told.

Jacobs turned and motioned for Thomas Walker to come forward and walk next to him as he started up the muddy, rain soaked road.

"How far is it to the fork going to the lake and the lodge?" Jacobs asked.

"Not far," Thomas said, pointing. "The fork is just up ahead a ways. It's just a short way around that curve. We're supposed to take the road to the left. That's the one that goes up to the lake, which is less than a mile from the fork."

Jacobs nodded. "Let's hope we find the kids are just stranded up there and waiting for someone to come and get them."

"Yes, let's hope," Melissa's father said, then took a pause. His mind was in a whirl. "Talltree's pickup still puzzles me, and from what I know about him, he isn't the type to lose control of his truck like that. From what I've heard, the man knows this mountain better than any of us. So where is he? Was he still inside when his pickup went into the river? If so, did he somehow get out and then get washed down the river, or, did he jump out before the truck went into the water? And, if that's what he did, where is he now?"

Jacobs just shook his head. "I guess we'll just have to wait to find out the answer to that one until we find him, one way or another. Let's hope he jumped and he's with the sheriff and the kids."

Big Mike was walking directly behind them and had been listening. Stepping up a little closer, he interjected the question that was probing his and everyone else's mind. ""What about the sheriff? Where is he and why hasn't he answered his radio or called in? This whole thing has a rotten smell to it, if you ask me."

The tow truck driver, Bill Nichols, closed the gap between him and the three men ahead of him and put in his two cents worth. "I say we keep our heads about us until we find out what's what. The last thing we need to do is go off the deep end and start jumping at shadows. I don't think we want to make a whole bunch of hunches and then do something based on those hunches that we'll regret."

Several of the others within hearing distance nodded their heads in agreement. What Bill had said made sense. It would be better to be sure. Otherwise, they'd maybe get somebody hurt, or, killed.

The washed out bridge and Rafe Talltree's truck, stuck nose down in the river had already had a dampening effect on everyone's spirit and none of them was eager to put their children in harm's way, let alone, themselves.

Whispered mumblings were passed around among the group as they tromped through the ankle deep mud; nerves keyed to a fine point.

Appearing seemingly out of nowhere, Rafe slowly raised himself from the floor of the forest and squatted behind a thick bush so he could scan the area behind the barn.

He now had stripes and dark markings on his face and the backs of his hands that allowed him to blend in with his surroundings. With great patience, he took in not only the area where the boys were digging, but to the sides and beyond to make sure of who and what he would be dealing with. Somewhere in the far distance, a wolf sent a long soulful warning of things to come, which made Rafe smile. The wolf was his totem.

Rooster gripped his rifle a little tighter and looked in the direction of the forest. He was from deep in the hills of Kentucky and had a fear of who-do's and other evil spirits. When the wolf's mournful cry echoed throughout the forest, he began to shiver and had to swallow to keep his nerves in check. "Damn wolves, nuff ta give ah man the heebie-jeebies."

The boys also looked up at the sound of the wolf's sorrowful howl. Trace grinned and wondered if by some chance it might be Talltree giving them a heads up; a signal that he was nearby.

When Shaun and Trace saw Rooster getting all nervous and fidgety, they both grinned. "Wonder if that was a real wolf, or Talltree just trying to scare these guys?" Trace whispered.

Shaun stopped grinning and drove his shovel into the dirt at the bottom of the hole. "You make too much of Talltree," Shaun said with a disgusted tone. "He's up in his cabin, safe and sound. Probably filling his belly with the deer meat and other food he's got stored up there. I guarantee you, he's not within a mile of here."

"I don't believe that, and neither would you if you'd just get over your hurt," Trace whispered. "Talltree is not the bad guy you make him out to be."

"Dig!" Rooster yelled when he saw them just standing there, talking.

After they went back to work, Rooster inched himself back a little deeper into the shadow until his back was touching the barn.

Shaun was not the only one who heard what Trace had said. Rafe allowed himself a closed mouth grin before he silently inched his way a few feet closer and stood up in the shadow of a large tree.

Burns stood on the bank of the river watching Jacobs and the men from town trudge through the mud. He muttered to himself, "Where the hell is that chopper?"

Andy was also watching the sky to the north and heard what Burns had said.

"I expect to see it coming over the ridge any minute now," Andy said, pointing to the place he was talking about.

Burns turned toward Andy, embarrassed that Andy had heard him talking to himself. "Sorry, just keyed up, I guess."

Andy smiled. "Don't worry about it. I'm as anxious as you are for it to show up," Andy looked at his watch, then back to the empty north sky.

The sun had been shining brightly for several hours, but even so the road leading up to the lake and lodge was still very muddy. The men struggled to make their way up the road. Unconsciously, Jacobs took his pistol from its holster and checked to make sure it was loaded.

"You think there might be shootin'?" Thomas Walker asked as his eyes danced back and forth to each side of the road. "Did you see something?"

"No, I didn't see anything," Jacobs said. "And I sure hope there isn't a need to fire my weapon. Checking it has been a long time habit of mine; which has saved my bacon on more than one occasion."

Thomas Walker gave Jacobs a knowing grin, and then he checked his own weapon. He deplored violence, but when Big Mike offered him the use of the thirty-eight-caliber pistol, for reasons he didn't quite understand, he took it.

The mud was thick and clung to their boots making it hard to walk. Sucking noises could be heard each time they pulled their foot out of the mud to take the next step, which didn't help everyone's keyed up nerves that were already strung tight.

Just beyond the townsmen's sight, the small convoy of jeeps and other vehicles were making their way down the mountain road, never expecting to run into a group of armed men.

By now, Adolph was sitting upright and rigid in the passenger seat of the lead jeep, staring through the windshield as the driver fought to keep control of his vehicle and not go plunging into the ditch on either side. At one point, the left front wheel of the jeep hit a rock and sent the jeep skidding toward the ravine on the opposite side of the road.

"Watch the road!" Adolph yelled as he peered out his window at the deep ditch they nearly missed plunging into.

"Yes sir," the driver said, pulling hard on the steering wheel as he slowly brought the jeep back to the center of where he thought the road should be, never suspecting he was about to come face to face with a small army approaching on foot.

A short distance ahead of him, Jacobs saw the fork in the road, one side leading to the lake and the other to the lodge. The hint of a grin was forming on his face until he saw the first in a line of vehicles that came slipping and sliding around the curve.

Jacobs was not the only one to see the vehicles. "Look," Melissa's father yelled, pointing his finger at the convoy.

At the same time, the driver of the lead vehicle saw the group of men walking in their direction, carrying guns. He slammed on the brakes, hoping the vehicles behind him wouldn't ram into him.

Luck was with him because each vehicle had been staying a safe distance behind the man in front of him, so even with the sliding, they had time to stop before running into the vehicle in front of him.

Adolph saw the group of men and to his surprise; the one in the lead spread his legs and pointed a pistol at them as he yelled, "FBI! Hold it right there! Everybody out of your vehicles with your hands empty and high in the air where I can see them!"

When the men from town saw Jacobs pull his pistol, the rest spread out to the side and each man raised his weapon, pointing it at the vehicles, as though they had been trained for just such a confrontation.

Trying to think of a way out of this situation, Adolph climbed out of the vehicle slowly with his hands in the air and motioned for the others to do the same. The tension was as thick as sap oozing from a tree - each side staring at the other, each man ready to start the dance. Even the slightest twitch from either side would be enough to set it off.

Jacobs looked back and forth from side to side and said in what he hoped was a calm voice, "Everybody just stay calm."

On the other side, one of the supremacist inched his way behind the open door of the truck he was standing next to. None of the men from town could see him as he drew his pistol and cocked it. Before anyone realized what the young hot head was up to, he stepped from behind the door of the pickup, raised his pistol, and fired.

As the sound of the pistol shot echoed through the trees, one of the townsmen let out a yell and grabbed his shoulder as he was knocked to the ground.

Jacobs yelled, "Take cover!"

War had just been declared and men from both sides took Jacob's advice and looked for a place to hide and shoot from. Within seconds the road was clear. Silence hovered over the area like the silence before a storm.

Adolph whispered to one of the men behind him, "Who fired that shot?"

The man behind Adolph swallowed and said, "I don't know, sir."

"Well find out!" Adolph replied in a loud hiss.

The man said, "Yes sir," but knew no one would admit to being the guilty party.

After what seemed an eternity, Jacobs called out, "There doesn't have to be any more shooting. Send the kids down and then we'll talk."

"What kids?" Adolph responded. "I don't know what you're talking about."

"Maybe you should check the ravines for dead bodies," came a voice from near the back of the line of vehicles.

Adolph swore as several chuckles were heard from behind him.

There was dead silence from the side of the townsmen as they digested this and the unwanted pictures that filled their minds.

From a place behind a tree, Big Mike Bozeman's voice roared loud and clear through the forest, "You dirty, low down sons of bitches!" He stepped from behind the tree and cocked and fired his pump shotgun four times at the group.

Several yells were heard as the pellets ripped holes into several of the closest supremacists, along with breaking headlights and making holes in the sides of three of their vehicles. One of the men screamed as some of the pellets struck him in the face.

Immediately, other guns on both sides began to bark, sending lead back and forth between the two groups.

Jacobs realized his worst fears. They were now in a full-scale war and there was nothing he could do to stop it. And he still hadn't seen hide nor hair of the kids. From his hiding place behind a fallen log, he took aim and slowly squeezed the trigger. The man he was aiming at reared up and fell backward as a red blot formed in the center of his forehead.

In fact, several of the supremacists found out that even though they had superior firearms, these men from town were hunters and hit what they aimed at. Little by little, the supremacists inched their way back, trying to get better protection and yet still be able to fire at the men from town, or, hide like the cowards they really were. Many of them were only tough when they outnumbered their prey and the prey was unarmed and shaking in their boots. But these townsmen were not afraid and were shooting back with eyes filled with hatred. The New World Order takeover was not going to be as easy as they were led to believe.

Back on the other side of the river, Burns and Andy heard the gunfire. "Sounds like they found the people you boys are lookin' for," Andy said with trepidation in his voice.

"Damn it! Where is that chopper?" Burns yelled, as Andy limped at a fast pace to his police vehicle and grabbed the small microphone lying on the seat.

"Shortcut police department to High Mountain Ranger Station. Come in ranger station. Over."

The microphone crackled and a voice come over, loud and clear. "I hear you Andy. Sorry we're taking so long. We have a slight problem with the chopper. The mechanic is working on it now. Over."

Andy shook his head from side to side. Finally, he pressed the button on the side of the microphone and said, "Hope he gets it fixed, ASAP. We've come face to face with that group I told you about and it sounds like a war goin' on over on the other side of the river. We need you to get us over there muy pronto. Over."

"Hang in there my friend. We'll be there as soon as we can and we'll bring along a few weapons of our own. Over"

Andy dropped the microphone on the seat and rubbed the back of his neck, then turned and stared across the river. It had suddenly gone quiet.

Burns walked up and looked at him. "You suppose it's over?"

Andy lifted up his hat and wiped his brow with the backside of his arm. "I don't know, maybe they all ran out of ammunition, or maybe they gave up."

Burns stared at the young deputy and realized he was as upset about being stuck over on this side of the river as he was. "Or maybe they're just taking a break to reload," he said.

Andy looked at agent Burns for a moment, then began to laugh. In a few seconds, Burns also began to laugh, each one of them feeling the tension subside.

CHAPTER FORTY-SEVEN

An Indian on the warpath

ROOSTER JUMPED when he heard the gunfire. It sounded like world war three was going on and he wasn't sure what to do. Thoughts raced through his brain like a scared deer on the run. Should he shoot the two boys and leave 'em in the shallow hole? But, when he looked at the hole, it didn't look deep enough to even hold the two boys, let alone the two girls, too. Next, he wondered if maybe he should just tak'em out in the woods and shoot'em and leave their bodies for the critters ta feed on?

Then another thought burst into the conscious part of his gray matter. What if his comrades was ah winnin' the shoot out?

Next, he looked around and wondered where Slim and Walt was? They should be the ones makin' the decisions. Yeah, they should be makin' the decisions. Satisfied, he leaned back against the barn. He didn't have ta decide nuthin'. He would wait for Slim or Walt ta tell him what he should do.

He relaxed and stood his rifle against the side of the barn, then reached into his pocket for his sack of Bull Durum smoking tobacco, papers and a stick match. What he needed right now was ah good smoke ta calm his shattered nerves. After making and lighting his cigarette, he blew smoke rings while listening to the sound of gunfire.

Shaun and Trace also heard the gunfire and stopped digging. Trace grinned and said in a low voice, "I'll bet that's Andy, along with our dads and some of the men from town."

Shaun shook his head. "Yeah. And it sounds like they're givin' them what for."

Trace thought for a moment, then said, "I sure hope so, but they don't have the firepower these lunatics do, plus who knows what else they've got. Man, I hope they don't have any more nitroglycerine."

"No offense," Shaun said, "but I'm glad my mom and dad are out of town. He's not real handy with a gun, but I know he'd want to be right there with them, tryin' and I'd hate to see him get shot."

Trace gave Shaun a look, but didn't reply about the thoughts running through his mind. He figured that at this point, it would be better to just keep his mouth shut. He was worried about his father and the other men who were down there risking their lives to save his dumb ass and all he could think about was how glad he was his father wasn't with them.

Feeling feisty, Shaun leaned on his shovel and yelled, "Hey, Rooster, that'll be the deputy sheriff and the men from town. Maybe you boys had better high-tail it up over the mountain while you've still got the chance."

At first, Rooster was a bit shaken by Shaun's words, but then his brain told him that his comrades were trained warriors, with some pretty heavy weapons. At that point, he grinned and said, "Big talk for somebody who'll be layin' in his grave, waitin' fer the worms ta start eat'en him by the time they get here – if'n they get here at all. Them kinfolk of yer'in is just ah bunch of hicks against our trained soldiers. And did you fergit that our boys are carryin' automatic weapons? Fergit that little point, did ya, city boy?"

Shaun and Trace looked at each other, not sure how to respond, since they had both had those same fears.

"Now, you jest keep ah diggin', unless you want me ta leave yer bodies layin' out in ah ditch fer the critters ta get at."

Thinking about wolves and other animals feasting on Kristi's body caused Shaun to begin to dig with wild abandon.

"Hey, I thought we were gonna take our time," Trace whispered.

"I know," Shaun said, "but what about the girls? I can't deal with what the animals would do to Melissa and Kristi's bodies if they were laying in some ravine."

Trace began to dig faster. "I hadn't thought about that."

Rafe also heard the shooting and hoped Andy and whoever he had with him were holding up their end of the battle. He notched an arrow onto his bowstring in case Rooster decided to do something stupid, like trying to shoot the boys. Fortunately for Rooster, he had not done anything stupid except lean his weapon against the side of barn. Unconsciously he had saved his own life, at least for the moment.

Melissa was sitting on the edge of the bed, wiping Kristi's forehead with a barely damp rag when she heard shooting in the far distance. Without realizing what she was doing, she reached over and laid her hand on the pistol, alert for any noise out in the hallway. There was none and after a while she relaxed her grip on the pistol and went back to trying to make Kristi comfortable.

CHAPTER FORTY-EIGHT

Adolph and the better part of valor

ALONG WITH THE OTHERS, Jacobs took cover when the shooting started and within minutes there were wounded on both sides and at least three dead on the supremacist's side. During a momentary lull in the shooting, Jacobs pressed the walkie-talkie close to his mouth, pushed down on the button and said in a low voice, "Burns, Andy. This is Jacobs, come in. Over"

Almost immediately, he heard a crackling sound, then recognized Burns voice. "This is Burns. What's your situation? Over."

Jacobs thought for a moment, and then replied, "They've got several wounded and I think, three dead. On our side we have two FBI personnel and one of the men from town with minor wounds. These men are doing a hell'va job, a lot better than I expected. Most of them are ex-vets. But we're out numbered and they have automatic weapons. Over"

"What about the Indian fella or the kids? Over"

There was a moment of silence before Jacobs answered. "I haven't seen hide nor hair of the Indian, but one of them indicated that the kids might be dead, but I don't know that as a fact. The man may have been lying to rile us. I can only hope they're somewhere safe. Over."

There was a long silence before Burns answered. "They had some trouble with the chopper, but it's on its way now so we should be there soon. Do what you can to keep them pinned down. Maybe we can set down behind them and box them in. Over."

Before Jacobs could respond - directly in front of him, on the far side of the road and closer to the supremacists, one of the men from town stepped out from behind a tree with a stick of dynamite in his hand. The fuse was burned down to almost nothing when he heaved it toward the lead vehicle and then stepped back behind the tree. Jacob watched in amazement at how quickly and efficiently the man had acted.

Not wanting to believe his bad luck, Adolph saw the stick of dynamite come flying through the air and reacted by diving for the ravine.

The dynamite hit the ground and rolled under the front of the jeep Adolph had been standing behind and exploded.

The jeep was lifted up at least two feet off the road before the gas tank exploded, sending pieces of metal and glass flying through the air in all directions like soldiers of death. One of the supremacist had only time enough to get a wide eyed expression on his face before a piece of window glass cut off his head and sent it rolling into the ditch. Another of the supremacist, who was in the act of running for cover, felt a sharp piece of metal being driven through his body from back to front. He was dead before he hit the ground.

Adolph escaped death by the barest of margins. As he went head first into the ravine, a piece of white hot metal singed his back, leaving a burn mark that hurt like hell.

He rolled over and let the water in the ravine sooth the burn, somewhat, then yelled at the top of his lungs, "Retreat!"

A loud roar went up on the townsmen's side. Even some of the FBI men were giving the old man a thumbs up.

The walkie-talkie almost jumped out of Jacob's hand when Burn's voice came blasting out of the small speaker on the front of the walkie-talkie.

"Jacobs! Jacobs! What happened? Are you alright?"

Jacobs chuckled as he answered. "You forgot to say, over. Yeah, we're okay. I think we just scored a big one for our side. One of the men from town blew up their lead vehicle with a stick of dynamite. I saw two of their men go down; both dead and the rest of 'em headed for cover back up the road. Don't know if they have any more wounded or not. And, no, I don't know where he got the dynamite. Over."

After rolling around on his back in the water at the bottom of the ravine, hoping to take away some of the searing pain, Adolph retreated back up the ravine a safe distance before he climbed back onto the road.

Crouched behind one of the rear vehicles, he raised his arm and moved it in a circular motion, signaling his men to gather around him. "Four of you men lay down some cover fire while the rest of you get these vehicles turned around. We're going back to the lodge! Harris, take charge and get us out of here."

Harris called four men by name and assigned them the job of keeping the men from town penned down while the rest of them turned the vehicles around.

At that point, the four shooters began to lay down a barrage of gunfire while their comrades got the vehicles turned around and began to retreat back up the road. The four men gave a final burst from their weapons, and then ran for the open doors of the retreating vehicles.

As the jeeps and trucks headed away from the scene near the junction in the road, the men from town, together with the men from the FBI ran out onto the road and laid down a barrage of their own. One of the men from town had a rifle with a scope and he took his time before squeezing the trigger. The bullet slammed into the gas tank on the rear vehicle. The vehicle was thrown into the air and a ball of fire rose into the air, then crashed back down to the road and rolled over into the ravine. The smell of burning gas and death screams rose above the top of the ravine.

A howl of victory rose up from the small group of men from the town of Shortcut; the same ones the FBI wanted to leave at home, for their safety.

"Hold your fire! Hold your fire!" Jacobs yelled as he pushed the talk button on the walkie-talkie. "Burns, this is Jacobs. A second man from town blew up another jeep with at least six men in it; and the rest of them are hi-tailing it back up the road - probably headed back to the lodge to make a stand. Over"

Burns was overjoyed and said so. "That's a big ten-four. And, well done! Stay after 'em if you can. We'll follow as soon as the chopper gets here. And Jacobs, don't do anything heroic, I don't want to break in a new partner. Over."

"Can't say I'd like that, either. Over and out," Jacobs said, then released the talk button and turned to Melissa's father.

"Do you think they're headed back to the lodge?"

"That would be my guess. It's either the lodge or the lake and the lake offers no place to stand and make a fight of it. The lodge has buildings and possibly more guns and ammunition," Melissa's father stated.

"What about the road? Does it lead over the mountain, or back to the highway?"

Big Mike grinned. "Neither, it's either the lake or the lodge. That's where the road ends. People have tried to get us to do logging up there, but so far the councilmen have said no."

"Okay, okay; one last question. Time-wise, how much of a walk is it up to the lodge?" Jacobs asked.

Thomas Walker scratched his neck and behind his ear and said, "On a good day, which this isn't, I could walk it in about thirty minutes without too much trouble, but in this mud it's gonna take longer. If we stay in their tire tracks, I'd say, at least forty-five minutes, maybe an hour."

Melissa's father turned toward Big Mike and asked, "That about right, Mike?"

Big Mike nodded his head in agreement. "Yeah. Sounds about right."

"Alright men, we're going to the lodge," Jacobs said. "Two single files and stay in the tracks as best you can. Let's move out."

Without a word of argument, the men headed up the road in two lines. This time Jacobs didn't mind pulling rear guard. Good ole boys or not, these men were seasoned warriors. Plus, they knew where they were headed and what to expect.

As they trudged up the mountain road, it came to Jacobs that just possibly, the sheriff had had a run-in with these guys and had lost the battle, which would make a lot of sense. No one had seen or heard for him since he came up here. He just hoped for the sake of the townspeople's that the kids hadn't been killed. If they had, there would be no way to control them and their desire for revenge. Good church goers or not, you could push a person only so far.

CHAPTER FORTY-NINE
Rooster & Joe-Bob

ROOSTER WAS JUST stamping out the butt of his third cigarette when the sound of a second explosion broke the silence, sending his mind into a merry-go-round filled with questions. Did his comrades have explosives with'um, he wondered? It had to be his comrades he concluded, because the hicks from town wouldn't have explosives, would they? The questions and uncertainty was driving him up the wall.

What if they hadn't won? What if the captain and the rest had been killed or captured? And if any of his comrades were still alive, would they be able to come back? Would there be enough of 'em to make a stand?

What if it wasn't those hicks from town? What if it was the law, and what if' they had army troops with 'em? They would follow his friends back up here, for sure.

Rooster's heart was pounding in his chest as he stepped away from the back wall of the barn. On trembling legs, he stumbled over to see how deep the hole was and realized it was deep enough to hold all four of the kids. By now, he was convinced that he should shoot the two boys where they stood, and then bring the wounded girl out and get rid of her. He would leave the black girl to the last. After he had his way with her, he just might bury her alive; that is unless Walt had already had his way with her and had already killed her. It would be just like him not to share.

Rooster was so wrapped up, his mind didn't take the time to consider how long it would take before his friends got back and how little time he had to do all the things his mind was conjuring up.

Rooster was raising his shotgun and pointing it in the direction of the boys as Joe-Bob came running around the corner of the barn. Rooster reacted by spinning around and swinging the barrel of the shotgun around to defend himself. When he saw it was only Joe-Bob, he let out a sigh of relief. He was trembling from head to foot and his shirt was wet with sweat.

"Hey, hold on, Rooster, it's just me, Joe-Bob. I've come ta give ya ah hand. Have you noticed, the shootin' and explodin' has stopped?"

"Of course I noticed, you idiot. Anybody who ain't deaf would have noticed."

Joe-Bob's cheeks turned red. He looked around and asked, "Where's Slim and Walt? I thought they was around here with you."

"I don't know and don't care," Rooster said as he lowered the shotgun and stood up a little bit straighter. "Walt left me in charge."

"Well what'cha gonna do? You gonna just shoot'em where they stand? And what about them two girls? Can we have ah little fun with 'em first?" Ain't had me ah woman in quite ah spell. Think we got time?"

Rooster took a moment to let his mind calm down and think. "Been thinkin' bout that my own self and at first it sounded like ah good idea, but since I ain't sure who won the shootin' match, I ain't sure how much time we have? We just might could have the law or maybe the army come drivin' down the driveway any minute now. No, I reckon we'll just half'ta get rid of'em as quick as we can. And after we gett'em all planted, I'm headin' inta the woods ta wait ta see who shows up. If'n it's the law and they get whoever is left, maybe they'll think they got us, all, and won't come lookin' out in the woods. Then I can wait 'til they've gone and sneak outta here when it gets dark. Surely, they'll leave at least one or two of the trucks behind. If not, I guess I'll half'ta walk."

Joe-Bob shook his head in admiration. "Rooster, you sure are smart. Why ain't they made you sergeant yet?"

Trace leaned close to Shaun and whispered, "I don't know about you, but I'm not gonna just stand here and let that idiot shoot me. I'm thinkin' we should make a break for the woods. You comin' with me?"

Shaun looked over at his friend as he wiped sweat from his forehead. "What about the girls? We can't just run off and leav'em to these imbeciles! You know what they'll do."

"I think the girls will be safe until Andy and whoever is with him gets here. Those nit-wits will be too busy chasing us to worry about the girls," Trace said with confidence he wasn't totally convinced he had.

"Yeah, maybe you're right," Shaun said. "We're younger and faster and I'll bet we can circle around and lead them right back here when Andy and the others show up. And if it isn't Andy and them men from town, I guess we'll try and figure out something then. Let's do it. I'm ready when you are."

"And if it isn't Andy, we're right back to what to do about the girls," Trace said.

"Well, we can't stand here and wait to see who shows up, can we?" Shaun said matter of factly.

Trace shrugged his shoulders and nodded. "Yeah, you're right. Maybe we could find Talltree and get him to help."

Shaun felt his jaws tighten. Ignoring Trace's idea about finding Talltree, he said, "No more waitin'. We need to go. It's now or never."

As Shaun and Trace began to crawl out of the hole, a small stone fell and hit the metal part of one of the shovels, causing a pinging noise.

Rooster and Joe-Bob both spun around at the same time and saw Shaun and Trace climbing out of the hole.

Rooster threw his shotgun to his shoulder and sighted down the barrel.

Trace and Shaun were still only halfway out of the hole when seemingly out of nowhere, an arrow drove itself through Rooster's throat.

Rooster dropped the shotgun and grabbed at his throat, which was now gushing blood. He sank to his knees, looked up at Joe-Bob with pleading eyes and then toppled over, dead.

As Joe-Bob stared at his comrade, something came over Shaun. He grabbed his shovel, climbed out of their would be grave, then raced over and swung the shovel as hard as he could at Joe-Bob's head, Joe-Bob moved just in time. The shovel slammed into Joe-Bobs arm so hard that the sound of bone breaking caused Joe-Bob to scream and drop his rifle. He stared at his broken arm for a moment then looked up just in time to see Trace's shovel as it smashed against the side of his head.

Wide eyed, Joe-Bob stood there, then like a tree being felled, he toppled over in slow motion and landed on the ground with a thud, blood oozing from his head.

Shaun and Trace turned toward the trees and saw Rafe Talltree come trotting out of the woods with a bow in his hand.

"Man, am I ever glad to see you! Those bastards were gonna shoot us," Trace said as Rafe hauled up just in front of them.

"I know," Rafe said. "I was standing over there behind a tree, checking things out." He nodded to Trace and said as he pointed toward Joe-Bob, "Maybe you should check and see if that one is still breathing."

"You got it," Trace said as he knelt down next to Joe-Bob and leaned close.

Rafe turned and faced Shaun. "You okay, Hot Shot?"

Shaun just stared at Rafe, unwilling to answer him, even to say thank you. After a moment, he said, "We were about to escape when you showed up. I'm not convinced you were needed."

Rafe shook his head in disbelief. When Shaun Tilford held a grudge, he held it forever.

Trace was down on one knee, next to Joe-Bob, looking to see if his chest was moving or not when Joe-Bob's eyes opened and he reached up and grabbed Trace by the throat and began to squeeze as hard as he could.

Rafe heard the scuffle and turned his head and in one fluid motion, he pulled his K-Bar Military knife from its sheath and threw it at Joe-Bob.

Joe-Bob felt the big knife strike his throat and sever the jugular vein. With the last of his strength, he reached up and jerked the knife free, which allowed blood to squirt in an arc as it spewed all over the front of Trace.

Joe-Bob's hand released its grip on Trace's throat and his arm dropped to the ground as his eyes glazed over and his heart stopped.

For a moment, Trace was paralyzed and then he jumped backward and stood up. With his left hand, he wiped Joe-Bob's blood from his face as best he could.

Rafe walked over, reached down and took his knife from Joe-Bobs hand, and then wiped it on Joe-Bob's shirt. When the blade was clean, he stood up and looked at Trace.

Trace was staring down at Joe-Bob and he was beginning to tremble. Rafe put his hand on Traces shoulder and said, "Animals like him don't deserve to live."

Stepping back, Rafe looked around to see if there were any other supremacists to deal with. Satisfied they were alone, he said, "We don't know who won that shootout down there and we can't take the chance it was the good guys, so grab their weapons and follow me. I'm sure we've got some anxious females wondering what's going on. And put some zip into it before any more of those crazies come back here to check on things."

That said, Rafe headed for the trees as Shaun and Trace stared at each other for only a heartbeat, then picked up the shotgun and rifle and hurried after Rafe.

"Guess the girls aren't still in the shed," Shaun said as they entered the trees.

Trace glanced behind him to make sure none of the bad guys were behind them, and then ran after Shaun. "He must have hidden them somewhere before he came for us."

Rafe was waiting a short distance ahead of them and when he saw them, he motioned with his arm for them to hurry.

CHAPTER FIFTY
Melissa and Jonas

JONAS MAYFIELD was one of the younger supremacists who had been left behind and happened to be leaving the barn when he saw the black girl racing across the yard and up to the back door of the lodge. Next, he saw who he perceived to be the man they were looking for, just a few steps behind her. He was carrying the white girl who'd been shot.

Jonas stepped behind the door so he wouldn't be seen and watched through a crack as they disappeared behind the lodge.

"What the devil is goin' on?" he asked himself.

He wanted to go after the Indian fella, but he'd seen and heard too much about him to try it alone, so he just stood there wondering whether to tell Rooster or Joe-Bob, or wait and maybe get a clear shot at the Indian fella if he came back out. They would sit up and take notice of him then. He'd be somebody. He'd be known as the one who got the Indian, single-handed. He was standing there wondering what he should do when Mother Nature made the decision for him.

The three cups of coffee Jonas had earlier were now making a strong request. As Jonas stood behind the barn door, relieving himself, he watched through a crack as Rafe exited the back door and disappeared into the woods.

"Damn," he muttered as he buttoned up his pants. "Well, I ain't gonna be stupid enough ta go chasin' him inta the woods and get myself killed. Guess I may as well tell somebody what I seen."

But he didn't like that idea because they'd want to know why he hadn't said something as soon as he saw them go into the lodge.

Suddenly, another thought struck him that had nothing to do with the Indian. The girls were all alone inside the lodge. A wide grin spread across his face, exposing a lot of brown, uneven teeth. He stepped from behind the door and looked around to make sure none of the others were nearby. When he was satisfied the coast was clear, he trotted off toward the back door of the lodge.

Melissa had been standing at the edge of the French doors, looking down into the yard, hoping to see Rafe and the boys, but the only ones she saw were a few of the ones who were left behind, standing out beyond the barn, talking and pointing in the direction where the sounds of gunfire and explosions had come from.

After a few minutes, she turned and walked over and looked down at Kristi who was asleep, but breathing heavily and groaning every now and then.

Melissa laid the pistol on the bed, then sat down next to Kristi and began wiping the perspiration from her forehead, neck and face.

Kristi let out a long groan and Melissa patted Kristi's arm, which seemed to help and she quieted down. When Melissa heard footsteps in the hallway, she jumped to her feet and rushed over and reached for the key to unlock the door just as the footsteps stopped.

Instead of unlocking the door, Melissa tiptoed back to the bed and picked up the pistol. She had chills running down her arms. Something was wrong.

Except for Kristi's breathing and low groans, the room was quiet. Melissa looked toward the door expecting to hear Rafe's voice, but there was only silence.

"Cautiously, she heard herself call out, "Rafe, Is that you?"

The only response was the doorknob turning slowly, but since she had not unlocked it, it didn't open.

There was another pause, then a loud noise filled the room when the door was kicked. Wood splinters around the lock area and door jamb flew into the room and the door swung open, pushing the chair off to the side.

Standing in the doorway was a very ugly young man who needed both, a bath and a shave. He was chewing a wad of tobacco and spit a long stream onto the hallway rug, then looked at her with a wicked grin on his face as he stepped into the room.

"Hello missy. I see that you two young ladies is all alone. And I reckon you might be in need of some manly companionship about now. I've heard stories 'bout how randy you black girls get when there ain't no man around. I ain't never been with no black girl before, but I'm looking forward to us havin' ourselves ah good time afore I have ta kill ya. . . Has nuthin' ta do with me. Captain's orders ya see."

He chuckled as he stepped further into the room. "If it's any consolation, at least you won't have ta die ah needin a man and you'll get ta go to the great beyond with ah smile on yer face, knowin' ya died ah full-filled woman."

Melissa could hear what the young man was saying but her brain shrugged it off. At this point in time, she was only reacting to the danger facing her just a few feet away. She raised the pistol and pointed it at her would be rapist-executioner, and said, "Hold it right there! Stay right where you are mister, or I'll shoot you full of holes and never lose a wink of sleep because of what I've done." Her insides were doing flip-flops and she hoped her voice sounded menacing enough to make him go away, but doubted it. She was having trouble keeping her voice from croaking and her hands from shaking.

Jonas grinned and took another step toward her. "You ain't got the stomach for it, Missy. Plus, you know you want the prize I got for you," he said, putting his hand to his groin.

Four shots rang out in rapid succession. All four bullets hit the young supremacist in the chest. The young man was driven into the hallway, where he landed flat on his back, dead as dead could be. Blood gushed from his chest, staining his clothes and the carpet.

The smell of gunpowder filled the room, causing Melissa to cough. She wanted to open the French doors and let it escape, but first she had to make sure the man was no longer a threat to her or Kristi.

She made her way to the door, cautiously; holding the pistol in front of her, ready to fire again if he even twitched. At the doorway, she saw the man lying flat of his back, blood dribbling out of the four gunshot wounds. Other than that, he was not moving. His eyes were wide open but they were glazed over and staring up at nothing.

Satisfied that he was dead, she looked up and down the hallway to make sure there were no others nearby. Other than herself and the dead man, the hallway was empty. She moved back into the room and closed the door, putting a chair against it so it didn't swing open on its own accord, then walked over and opened the French doors to let the gun smoke out.

She looked down and saw that the men out beyond the barn were still there but now were looking around, wondering where the shots had come from, but not coming to investigate. She watched as several other men came rushing out of the barn. They too, were looking around and when they saw no bodies lying about, they crossed the yard to where the others stood. Everyone was talking and pointing in several directions, but none of the newcomers made a move to come in her direction.

She eased back from the doorway before anyone saw her, then made her way over to the bed and sat down just as she felt her legs beginning to give out.

Her body felt numb. Not knowing what else to do, she just sat there, staring at the door. As best as she could remember, she had just shot a man who intended to rape her, and then kill her. She told herself that she had done what she did to protect herself from an evil man. She'd done what Rafe had told her to do. She'd never killed anyone before and didn't like the feeling. First, her mouth went dry and then, slowly at first, she began to tremble. Next, she felt the trembling spread throughout her body and she felt like she was about to throw up. She wrapped her arms around herself, wishing Rafe would come through the door and hold her and tell her everything would be all right.

As she sat there, trembling, she heard herself say, "I'm sorry, God, but it was either him or me. I never wanted to kill him, but I couldn't let him rape me and then kill me. I just couldn't do it. Who would look after Kristi? I hope you'll forgive me."

Tears began to run down her cheeks as she sat there, rocking back and forth.

After the young soldiers came running out of the barn, looking in all directions, weapons at the port, ready to shoot anyone or anything that wasn't supposed to be there and saw no threats, they went over to the men already outside and asked what had happened. The men shook their heads and admitted they too were in the dark. They'd heard the shots, the same as them, but saw no one. One of the men said the shots sounded like they came from the lodge, but that couldn't be, because no one was supposed to be in there. After a minute or so of discussion, they decided to check the back of the barn where the teenagers were supposed to be buried by now.

Rafe, Shaun and Trace were making their way slowly through the woods heading in the direction of the lodge when they heard the four rapid gunshots. Rafe hesitated for only a moment. "Melissa!"

All three broke into a fast run toward the lodge and in less than a minute found themselves creeping through the back door. Just inside the back door, Rafe held up his hand and whispered, "Be very quiet."

With Rafe in the lead, they crept up the stairs, looking in all directions, ready for anything.

The men from the barn found their comrades laying on the ground, dead, but no dead teenagers. They saw the arrow protruding from Rooster's neck and began to back up toward the front of the barn. At this point they're are all nervous and ready to shoot at anything that moved, and wondering if the Indian was somewhere close by?

"Has to be that Indian," one of them whispered as a wet spot appeared on the front of his pants.

Moving like she was in a trance, Melissa picked up the pistol and checked it. There were three shots left. Forcing herself to move, she stood up and walked to the open French doors and looked down. What she saw was a small group of men with weapons walking next to the side of the barn, looking in all directions. One of them stopped and stared in her direction. Melissa walked out onto the balcony and raised the pistol in both hands.

The boys had just reached the top of the stairs when they heard a shot and broke into a run down the hallway.

Rafe was the first to reach the bedroom door and saw the dead supremacist on the hallway floor and the splintered doorjamb. Without slowing down he rammed his shoulder against the door and went into the room, dropping into a roll that took him close to the bed.

Melissa swung the barrel of the pistol back into the room, ready to defend Kristi and herself. She had gone into shock and her eyes were glazed over. She was about to squeeze the trigger when she heard Rafe call out, "Melissa, it's me, Rafe!"

Melissa dropped the pistol and slumped to the floor of the balcony just as a bullet from below missed her head by mere inches.

Shaun and Trace raced out onto the balcony and began firing. Both, Shaun and Trace were nervous and were firing the weapons rapidly in the general direction of the men below. The men began shooting back, but neither Shaun or Trace was hit, but three supremacists went down from bullets and shotgun pellets coming from above.

Rafe stepped onto the balcony and aimed at the one who looked to be in charge, and then put an arrow dead center in his chest. When he went down, the rest ran for the protection of the barn.

Movement on his right brought Rafe's head around. Melissa was now standing close to him with the pistol in her hands. She was pointing it in the direction of the barn, squeezing the trigger over and over and continued to squeeze the trigger on an empty chamber. Tears were streaming down her cheeks.

Rafe realized she was in shock and had no idea what she was doing. He raised his hand in Shaun and Trace's direction and said, "Hold it. Hold it. They've gone into the barn." He then stepped over to Melissa and put his arm around her shoulders, and with his other hand, he gently took the pistol out of her trembling hands.

Ever so slowly, Melissa came back to the land of the living and looked up at Rafe for just a moment before burying her face in his chest as sobs erupted from her throat.

"Oh Rafe, it was terrible! He said he was going to rape me and then kill me. I had no choice. They're animals!"

Rafe held her tight and whispered, "It's alright now. You did what you had to do. I'm here now and I'll take care of you."

At these words, Melissa moved even closer to Rafe and felt herself begin to calm down. He was here now, and she was safe. She wondered if he could feel her heart beating?

He could and found that he was enjoying the feel of her.

Shaun and Trace, not far from being in the same condition as Melissa, stopped firing their weapons at Rafe's command and when they looked toward the barn, they realized the shooting was over, at least for the time being.

Shaun was the first of the two, to get his senses back, and rushed into the bedroom. Kristi was still on the bed with her eyes closed, issuing a groan from time to time. He reached over and touched her head. "She feels hot."

Melissa and Rafe moved up next to the bed and stopped. Melissa unwrapped herself from Rafe's arms and touched Shaun on the shoulder. "I know. She's still running a fever. We need to get her to a doctor, soon. She can't take much more."

"Melissa, why don't you go down the hall to the bathroom and see if there might be something in the medicine cabinet we can use to help break the fever; water, aspirin, or whatever you can find," Rafe said in a gentle voice.

Reluctantly, Melissa nodded her head, and then headed for the hall bathroom as Trace came in from the balcony.

Rafe watched her leave and felt a stirring inside him. 'She's not only beautiful, but she's also strong. She'll make some man a good partner, someday,' he thought to himself.

After she'd gone, he turned his attention to Kristi and began to undo the bandage on her leg. Looking over at Shaun and Trace, he realized they needed something to do. "Shaun, keep an eye on the barn and let us know if they come out. Trace, you watch the hallway and down below in case any of them come into the lodge."

Shaun started to protest, but was nudged by Trace, who walked him over to the French doors. "Let's just do as he says for a change. Okay, buddy?"

Shaun shrugged his shoulders and did as he was told, the same as did Trace.

All was quiet outside and inside. Both boys felt relieved. They'd seen enough of shooting and killing for a lifetime. Shaun glanced over his shoulder and watched as Rafe gently removed the bandage from Kristi's leg, taking great care not to hurt her. At that point, a bit of the rage he'd felt toward Rafe began to fade as he turned his attention back in the direction of the barn.

The wound on Kristi's leg did not look good. It was red and puffy and pus was oozing out of it. Fortunately, the smell wasn't rank, yet. Rafe knew he needed to get it cleaned and some medicine into her if she was going to survive.

Just then, Melissa walked back into the room with a small basket loaded with not only medicines, like aspirin, hydrogen peroxide and iodine, but bandage material, wash cloths for cleaning the wound and a bucket of hot water.

Rafe looked up at Melissa and smiled. "You are without a doubt, an angel."

Melissa blushed and set the basket on the bed and the bucket of water on the floor, next to him.

Trace followed her into the room; suddenly overwhelmed with a surge of energy he couldn't explain. "We did it! We actually killed some of those bastards!"

Melissa turned to Trace and reached out and slapped his face. "Shut up, Trace, just shut up, or I swear. . ."

Shaun rushed over and stepped between them, "Relax, Melissa it's all over."

She took a deep breath and nodded her head and turned back to see how Kristi was doing.

Rafe lifted Kristi into a sitting position and got her to take three aspirin, followed by swigs of water from his canteen. "I'll believe that when we're all back in Shortcut, safe and sound," he said to Shaun. "For now, we still have those guys in the barn to deal with, plus, we don't know who will soon be coming down the drive."

"What are you talking about, man? They're all gone," Shaun said pointing toward the outside. "Look for yourself, if you don't believe me."

"Are the trucks gone, too?" Rafe asked.

Shaun went to the balcony and looked out and saw that the trucks were still there.

Melissa had a troubled look on her face as she went to Kristi's side and began wiping Kristi's forehead with a wet washcloth.

Trace had a confused look in his eyes. "That means they're still here, hiding in the barn. You don't think they'll try to come up here, do ya?"

"Let 'em come! We'll kick their asses!" Shaun said, filled with a macho attitude.

Melissa looked at Rafe with hope in her eyes. "All that gunfire we heard, and those explosions, doesn't that mean help is on the way, for us?"

"You bet it does," Shaun said as he stepped closer to the bed. "What else could it mean? I'll bet the whole town turned out to come rescue us! Those scumbags never had a chance!"

Rafe washed Kristi's wound as best he could with hydrogen peroxide and then put some Neosporin salve he found in the basket over both wounds. When he'd done all he could do, he re-bandaged Kristi's leg and stood up.

"I don't know for sure what happened down there. And I believe you're right about one thing, Shaun. I think Andy and some of the men from town came looking for you. But don't forget, the men up here have been training for some time now with some heavy-duty firepower; probably a lot better than what the men from town have. The dynamite explosions; I guess that could have come from our guys, but we don't know for sure, do we?"

"You might be surprised at the firepower those old country boys have in their closets," Shaun said with a grin.

Rafe hadn't meant to get so long winded, but he wasn't finished, yet. He looked directly at Shaun and said, "Maybe you're right, I don't know. But there's one thing I do know for sure. We can't just sit around here and wait to see which side won."

About that time, Shaun glanced out of the French doors and saw something move in the far distance. He moved closer then grinned and said, "You gotta come and see this!"

They all moved up next to Shaun and looked to where he was pointing, and watched as what was left of the young supremacists were sneaking away. When they reached the road, they broke into a run; heading down the road as fast as they could. "The cowards didn't even bother takin' a truck!" Shaun yelled.

Rafe turned his attention to Trace. "Trace go down and collect all the weapons and ammunition you can find. Load everything into one of the trucks, and then bring the truck to the front door while Shaun and I carry Kristi down stairs."

Without a word, Trace spun on his heel and headed out the door.

As he left the room, he glanced down at the young man Melissa had killed. The front of his body was covered with blood and he still had a knife in his hand.

Trace shook his head in wonder as he hurried down the hallway and then took the stairs to the first floor. He marveled at the courage it must have taken for Melissa to do what she had done. She must have really been scared. For the most part, she was a quiet girl, a religious girl, who he doubted ever dreamed she could do something like kill someone.

Trace was half way down the stairs when Shaun walked to the door and for the first time, took a close look at the man Melissa had shot. "Whoa, Melissa, you did a job on this creep, four holes, dead center. You're like, Annie Oakley, or something."

Melissa began to shake. "I... I didn't want to shoot him."

Rafe walked around the bed and put his arms around Melissa's shoulders. "It's okay. You had no choice," he whispered in her ear.

Melissa put her arms around Rafe's waist and laid her head against his chest and instantly felt herself begin to calm down. She seemed to feel safe whenever he was close. "I know," she whispered back. She needed to blow her nose, but she didn't want to leave the comfort and safety of Rafe's arms. "I thought I was going to die."

Rafe tilted her chin upward and looked directly into her eyes and said, "Not on my mountain."

CHAPTER FIFTY-ONE

The chopper cometh

THE SUN was high in the sky when Andy turned his face toward the whoop, whoop, whoop sound the helicopter made as it approached the road behind where they were standing. He had to put his hand up to his eyes to shade them so he could see better.

Burns looked at his watch and said, "It's about time."

While the pilot was setting the chopper down, Andy and Burns were gathering weapons and ammunition from the trunk of Andy's police car.

Once they were aboard, the pilot lifted into the sky and easily took them across the river. Down below, they could see two men caring for the wounded FBI men and townsmen as best they could.

After the helicopter settled nearby, the two men ran over and were handed a bag with medical supplies in it. They waved and ran back to their patients as the helicopter rose into the air and moved on up the road.

Jacobs and the rest of the men heard the approach of the helicopter and looked up and waved. At the sound of Burn's voice over the walkie-talkie, Jacobs lifted it from its case hanging on his belt.

"Jacobs, this is Burns, come in."

"Yeah, I read you loud and clear. Go ahead."

"As you can see, the chopper finally got here. Andy and I are headed for the lodge. What's your situation? Over."

"Did you drop off the medical supplies?" Jacobs asked.

"That's a ten-four on the medicine. The pilot is calling his people now. He said they have a medi-vac team with their own chopper, and they can air lift the wounded to a hospital and the army is bringing an e-vac helicopter or two to airlift the rest of you out when this mess is cleaned up. Over."

"Thanks. They're headed back to the lodge. Be careful, those guys are crazy and well-armed. We'll get there as fast as we can. Over."

"Ten four. We're gonna take a fly-by up to the lake first, to make sure the kids aren't stuck up there. If not, we'll head for the lodge. Over and out"

Andy and Burns waved as the helicopter lifted up over treetops and headed in the direction of the lake.

As they left the area, Burn's walkie-talkie cackled and Jacobs voice came through. "If we don't get there in time, nail those bastards and get the kids."

Burns grinned and pressed the talk button on his walkie-talkie. "We'll do our best, but you guys shake a leg. You don't want to miss the fun. Over and out."

Jacobs watched as the helicopter disappeared over the trees.

CHAPTER FIFTY-TWO

A coming of age

TRACE DID HIS BEST to pick up all the weapons he could find and he even removed the ammo belts from the dead bodies. Being so close to the blood and gore of their handiwork, with flies swarming over the wounds was more than Trace could endure. He turned and headed for the barn, but before he could get there he emptied his stomach on the ground. After a long moment, Trace recovered somewhat, tied his handkerchief over his nose, and finished his task.

Rafe took the lead, with a pistol in his hand as they descended the stairs. Shaun was only a couple of steps behind, with Kristi cradled in his arms.

Kristi was in and out of consciousness and in a confused state when she was conscious. She asked so many questions in rapid succession that Shaun didn't know which one to answer first. "What's going on, Shaun? Are we home yet, Shaun? Shaun, help me, my leg hurts. Did we lose the baby?"

Shaun tried to comfort her as best he could with soothing words, but then it came to him that she hadn't heard a word he'd said. Frustrated, he turned and whispered over his shoulder in Melissa's direction. "I'm wastin' my breath. She doesn't understand a thing I've said."

Melissa was only a step behind Shaun and Kristi and said, "That's okay, Shaun. We don't know if she can hear you or not, but I think she can, and the sound of your voice just might be what helps her pull through this ordeal."

By now, they had reached the main floor and Rafe made his way over next to one of the front windows. He pulled one of the curtains back slightly, just as the sound of automatic weapons being fired filled the room.

From his military training, Rafe dove for the floor, and at the same time, yelled, "Down!" as he motioned with his hand for the others to take cover. They dropped to the floor just as bullets embedded themselves in the walls and furniture.

Shaun moved quickly and laid Kristi behind a large couch for protection as bullets whizzed over his head, striking a picture of Hitler hanging on the wall. The picture burst into several pieces and dropped to the floor. Shaun pumped his fist and said, "Yes."

Melissa dove in a different direction and found herself laying flat on the floor near the front wall.

Melissa looked over at Rafe, who was now crouched near the edge of the window, peering out. "They're back, aren't they?" she whispered.

"Yes, but they're not rushing the house. They're not sure where we are and don't want to take any more chances than they have to."

Trace had just come out of the barn and was carrying an automatic weapon and a bandoleer of ammunition when he saw them coming down the long driveway. One of them must have seen Trace because suddenly bullets began kicking up the dirt all around him, which sent him into action.

Trace fired a quick burst in their direction as he ran for the back of a truck and reached in, pulling out two rifles and a sack filled with bullets. Then, using the truck as a shield, he moved toward the front of the house, waving his arm to get their attention.

Rafe saw the signal and said to Melissa, "Melissa, Trace is about to make a break for the house. As soon as he reaches the front porch, you open the door. Shaun, you cover him from the window."

As Melissa moved to the front door, Rafe grabbed his bow and quiver of arrows and headed for the kitchen.

Shaun was belly crawling toward the window and saw Rafe leaving. "Hey, where are you goin'?"

"To try and even the odds," Rafe said as he disappeared into the kitchen.

Shaun crawled up to the window and picked up the rifle Rafe left propped against the wall. He checked to make sure it was loaded, and then peeked through the window. Melissa was staring at him, waiting for him to give her the signal to open the door.

The supremacists were now coming down the drive at breakneck speed. Trace knew he had to make a move before they got much closer or it would be too late to run. They would shoot him down and then storm the house.

Trace took a deep breath, and then headed for the front porch - running a zigzag pattern as bullets slammed into the ground all around him. Carrying three weapons and a sack of ammunition was not as easy as he thought it might be.

"Com'on buddy, com'on," Shaun said as he sprayed the area with cover fire for Trace. He saw one man go down at the same time he felt the wind of a bullet whizzing past his head. He jumped up and ran to the door. Pushing Melissa backward, he yanked it open and began firing as fast as his finger could squeeze the trigger. He could see his bullets strike the incoming trucks and one bullet smashing through a windshield and hitting the driver, who swerved into another one of the trucks.

Adolph stuck his arm out of the window of the vehicle he was in and waved them to a halt. The trucks stopped and the men jumped out and ran behind their vehicles as they continued firing at the lodge

By now, Rafe had made his way through the back of the barn and was near the front doors when he spied a missed case of dynamite. Rafe tucked several sticks into his pockets and then rushed to the front doors as the sound of gunshots continued to fill the air. He was just in time to see the trucks come to a stop, some twenty yards or so from a truck parked in the yard, which left them a good fifty yards from the lodge-house. Men with guns were jumping out and taking cover wherever they could find it.

Off to his left, Rafe saw Trace alongside the truck on the side nearest the lodge. He was holding several weapons and what appeared to be a sack of ammunition and looked to be about to make a dash for the lodge. Before he could yell a warning, Trace stood up and ran toward the lodge.

Midway between the truck and the front porch of the lodge, a rifle sounded and Trace was pitched in the air and came down hard on the ground. "I'm hit!" he yelled out.

From his hidden place behind the front door of the barn, Rafe saw the whole thing and knew that Trace had been shot in the right thigh. Rafe also heard Shaun's reply. "Hang on buddy, I'm comin'," as he came running out onto the porch, firing at the supremacists.

In a hail of fire, Shaun dropped his rifle and jumped off the porch and ran in a zigzag pattern towards his friend, grabbed him and jerked him to his feet.

Rafe watched as Melissa appeared in the doorway, pistol in hand, firing in the direction of the men shooting at Shaun and Trace.

When the supremacists saw the young woman come rushing out of the front door of the lodge with a gun in her hand and began to pepper them with hot led, they ran for cover, back behind the trucks.

She will be a woman to be reckoned with, Rafe thought as he stepped just beyond the front door and fired an arrow in the direction of the supremacists. The arrow arched high into the air and fortunately for him the afternoon sun was at an angle that kept the enemy from seeing the stick of dynamite with a burning fuse taped to it.

By the time the arrow landed in the back of one of the trucks, and a man standing next to the truck saw it, it was too late for him to even call a warning.

Rafe had timed it right and less than a second after the arrow landed in the bed of the truck, the dynamite exploded, which caused the gas tank on the truck to explode, causing a small chain reaction. The trucks on either side also exploded.

Debris, hot metal and burning gas flew in all directions; bringing death to eight of the supremacists. The rest hit the ground and covered their heads.

The three trucks exploding distracted the supremacists long enough for Shaun to assist Trace back to the lodge. Just as they reached the top step of the porch, one of the supremacists who was lying under the lead truck saw the two boys about to enter the lodge. He raised his rifle and fired.

Shaun felt sharp pain in his left shoulder and was spun around, landing hard on his butt on the porch. Trace was barely able to remain in an upright position and was about to help Shaun to his feet when Melissa came rushing out and grabbed Trace and hurried him into the lodge, then returned and helped Shaun to his feet and shoved him inside as bullets slammed into the front wall of the lodge; one coming so close, Melissa felt the hot air close to her cheek. She slammed the door just as a dozen more bullets ripped up the walls on either side of the door. Fortunately, none of the bullets hit the door.

Even with the pain caused by the bullet in his leg, Trace hobbled his way to the window and was able to see the wreckage Rafe's arrow with the stick of dynamite had done. He grinned at Melissa. "I do believe Mister Talltree just lowered the odds."

Without waiting for her to answer, he raised one of the rifles to his shoulder and took aim just to the left of a shadow next to one of the trucks. He took a deep breath and squeezed the trigger slowly. The sound of the shot reverberated throughout the room as one of the supremacist stepped from behind the truck with his hand to his head; blood running between his fingers and down his arm.

The man dropped to his knees, then toppled over, landing face down in the dirt. The man's body gave one short quiver and then, nothing.

Trace felt bile trying to fill his throat and his stomach was beginning to churn, but he swallowed several times and looked away from the man he'd just killed. It was like Talltree had said, "They had no choice. It was either - them or us - kill or be killed.

Trace swallowed again and wiped the sweat from his forehead, realizing how lucky he'd been being too young to go to Viet Nam. Being a soldier had sounded so glorious, but when it came right down to it there was not one thing that was glorious about killing another human being.

Melissa was tending to Shaun's shoulder when something caused her to turn and look at Trace. His face was the color of cotton and he looked like he was just about to pass out. She jumped up and went to him, putting her arms around him to keep him from slumping to the floor.

"It's okay, Trace, you had to do it. We have to stay alive until help can get here. Take a deep breath, then let it out slowly."

Trace took a deep breath and shook his head. "Thanks Melissa. I'm okay, now."

She smiled. "Can you hold out until I finish working on Shaun's shoulder? He's in a lot of pain, and losing blood.

Trace turned back to the window and looked out. Everything was quiet. Talltree was nowhere to be seen and the supremacists were waiting to see what was going to happen next. He looked back at Melissa. "I'm okay for now, but hurry. I understand now what Kristi has been goin' though."

At the moment, everyone was being cautious. No one wanted to show himself for fear of getting shot.

As Trace reloaded his rifle, he said over his shoulder. "It's too quiet out there, gives me the creeps."

"Be thankful," Melissa said. "Gives us time to get reorganized. You two are in no condition to do much fighting right now," she said. Shaun was holding his shoulder and looking down at Kristi, and for the first time, truly understanding how she must feel.

"Where's Talltree hidin'?" he asked. "Isn't he supposed ta be helpin' us?"

Melissa's eyes had fire in them. "Don't ask stupid questions, Shaun. Who do you think blew up that truck?"

Trace limped over and stood close to them like a referee at a fight. "Okay, you two take a break. We know Talltree is out there. And he's helping us the best way he knows how, which is better than we've done. He's not stupid enough to put himself in harm's way to show how brave he is. He knows if something happens to him we're in deeper trouble than we already are. Now, I don't want to hear no more crabbin' about Talltree. We need to concentrate on stayin' alive until our folks get here. Got it?"

Shaun looked at Trace and nodded his head.

CHAPTER FIFTY-THREE
What to do about the Indian

Adolph was confused as he looked around and saw the destruction and the dead. He did a head count which didn't tally like he thought it should have. He was losing men faster than he could count because of four kids and a heathen Indian.

From his position behind one of the trucks, he raised his arm and motioned for what was left of his men to gather around him.

Very slowly and using great caution, each of the remaining supremacist inched his way to where Adolph was standing. As they came up behind the truck, they gave a sigh of relief for still being alive and not to have a bullet or an arrow penetrating his body.

As the men gathered around him, Adolph took another head count and when they were all there and he finished the count, he said, "There should be more of us. Where are the others? Where's Rooster and Walt and Joe-Bob?"

One of the men who had been left behind stepped up and said, "They're all dead. That guy we been chasin', that Indian feller, he raised ah bunch of hell while you were gone. About the time they got the graves dug, he come out of the woods and begun ta put arrows into everbody he could see. Didn't even use ah gun, jest ah bow and arrow, like one of them Apaches ya see in the motion pictures. I jest barely got away," he said, shaking his head.

The truth was, he'd been peeking through a crack in the back wall of the barn and had seen what happened to his friends and panicked. He had hotfooted it to the old out-house toilet and hidden there. He was sitting on the throne, shaking in his boots when he realized he hadn't even brought a gun with him. He hadn't come out until he heard the trucks returning. But now he wasn't sure he shouldn't have waited until it was all over.

Adolph didn't believe even for a moment that this idiot had engaged in any kind of warfare with the man they were after. When it came right down to it, this man was a coward. He was only brave when he was standing at the back of a crowd, or when they were just play acting, during practice. But to his credit, the man was loyal to the cause; or at least he pretended to be and he had taken the pledge.

Adolph sighed and asked, "Does anyone know where this ghost of a man might be at this very moment?"

A tall, gangly looking man with a chaw showing in the right side of his jaw by the name of Earl spoke up. "I'm pretty sure he's in the barn, Captain. Right before the truck exploded, I saw ah man step out of the barn and fire an arrow in our direction. I doubt if any of the kids can shoot like that. I reckon that would take ah man experienced with ah bow – which in my opinion would be, the Injun we been tryin' ta catch."

Adolph gave that some thought and had to agree. The man who was destroying his troops was probably in the barn, and it was more than likely the Indian they'd been trying to catch. And it made sense that that's where he would have gotten the dynamite.

Adolph lit a cigarillo and drew in a lung full of smoke as he pondered their situation. If they could take down this man who had become such a thorn in his side, and then exhibit the body, he was sure the kids would give up. He would take them hostage and then use them as bargaining tools with the people chasing them, to get out of this mess. The main problem was - this man seemed to be experienced in warfare. He'd already proven that - probably a recent veteran of that catastrophe the US government had been involved in over in Viet Nam.

Plus, there would soon be the problem of the men from town. Even though they were on foot, and had no automatic weapons, they wouldn't give up, and from what he'd seen, they were crack shots. Their strongest weapon would be the dynamite, if they still hand any. He looked back toward the road, expecting to see them turn down the driveway at any moment. After grinding out the butt of the cigarillo with the toe of his boot, he looked around. He had to do something and do it quick if they were going to get out of this mess alive.

He moved to a position where he could see both, the barn and the lodge without becoming a target. The sun had climbed high into the sky, causing sweat to run down the middle of his back. In the corner of one of the front windows, he could see a small portion of a male face peeking out from behind a curtain. The young man must have not been injured too badly if he was still up and about – another bad sign.

Next, he directed his attention toward the barn, but he could see nothing moving.

The Indian was there, he could feel it in his gut, but the problem would be getting to him without getting himself or any of his men killed. In the end, he knew it would come down to a fight to the death between him and the man who had caused him so much trouble. They were both professionals, which made it impossible to send any of his men to do the job. That would be like sending a child in to do combat with an experienced warrior.

CHAPTER FIFTY-FOUR
Kristi returns

Since he had been the first one to get his wound attended to, Shaun stood next to one of the front windows and stared at the trucks standing like roadblocks in front of the lodge. What was left of the three trucks was lying on their sides, flames and smoke lifting up and disappearing into the sky. Everyone had moved to the back of one of the larger trucks. He couldn't see enough to get a shot, but he knew they were there. In a way, he was glad. Firing a rifle would be very painful.

"I wonder what they're up to?" he said, turning his face toward Melissa. "It's too quiet."

For some unknown reason, the bullet that hit Trace in the thigh had gone in no more than a short way and stopped. Getting the bullet removed was more painful than getting shot, Trace figured, but Melissa was able to remove the chunk of lead without him passing out. She was in the process of cleaning the wound when she heard Shaun. She turned in his direction and looked at him for only a moment, then went back to her chore. She had no idea what they might be up to, so she said nothing.

After rinsing blood out of the cleaning rag from the pan of water sitting next to her, she dabbed the wound again, and again until the blood stopped and she was satisfied.

Before putting a bandage over the wound, she picked up a bottle of medicine she had found in the medicine cabinet, and said, "Bite down really hard on that rag I gave you because this is going to burn like blazes."

"What is it?" Trace asked.

"Iodine," she answered as she removed the top from the bottle.

Before Trace stuck the piece of cloth in his mouth, he asked, "How bad is it?"

Melissa smiled and said, "I'm no doctor, but I'd say both of you were extremely lucky. Shaun's bullet went straight through without hitting anything vital. And I was able to remove the bullet from your leg and the wound looks clean. Now bite down on that rag."

Trace held up his hand, trying to prolong the stinging pain he knew was coming. "Where'd you get the medicine and the bandages?"

"Don't be a baby. You know very well the medicine is from the cabinet in the bathroom, and the bandages are clean rags I found in the kitchen. Now bite down on the rag and quit being such a sissy. I'm not waiting any longer. I need to get this wound dressed so I can look after Kristi - her bandage needs changing."

"Who do you think you are, Florence Nightingale?" Trace said with a wide grin.

She gave him a look, as she poured the Iodine directly into the wound. Trace bit down on the rag, clinched his fists, made a face and gave a subdued groan as the first wave of pain raced to his brain. The Iodine also hurt worse than being shot had. For the second time, he thought he might pass out.

Melissa quickly bound up the wound and stood up. "You'll be alright now, I think." Wiping her hands on one of the clean rags, she turned to Shaun, who was still standing watch out of the window.

"What are they doing now?" she asked.

Shaun pulled the curtain back just enough for him to see the yard. "I'm guessing they're holding a pow-wow; trying to figure out what to do next. They all seem to be over behind that large truck next to the one that got blown up by Talltree's dynamite arrow." He let the curtain fall back into place and looked over at Trace. "How you doin'?"

Trace grinned. The pain had subsided and he could breathe again. "I'm good now that Miss Nightingale did her magic." He looked at Melissa and said, "Seriously, I don't know what we would have done without you. Thank you."

Melissa was blushing and batting her eyes to hold back the tears. "I'm just trying to help."

"I was wonderin' if maybe you might be up to covering the other window?" Shaun asked Trace, trying to change the subject.

Trace nodded and used one of the rifles as a crutch to help himself to his feet. After just a moment to get his balance, he hobbled over to the window on the opposite side of the front door and leaned against the wall, taking a moment to catch his breath. He hadn't realized how much being shot took out of a guy. After a couple of moments, he peeked out from behind the curtain. "Yeah, man, I can cover this side."

His body was covered with perspiration from no more movement than it took to go from where he'd been sitting, to the window. He stood there trying to will his body to stop shaking as he realized how close he'd come to death. He felt weak and wondered if he would be able to hit any of them if they decided to attack.

Trace took several large breaths of air to help slow down the shaking, and after a few minutes, he felt the shaking begin to disappear. He peeked out of the window again and saw that everything was still quiet. He looked over at Shaun and grinned.

As Melissa knelt down next to Kristi, she felt a certain amount of pride in the two boys she hadn't felt before. They were finally standing up for themselves. She was also worried about Rafe and wondered if he was ok. What was he planning to do next? She knew he could take care of himself, but there were so many of them and she didn't know if he had a weapon besides his bow and quiver of arrows, which wouldn't last forever. There was the dynamite she thought to herself as she gave a little chuckle. Blowing up that truck with a stick of dynamite tied to an arrow was not only genius, but a huge surprise. "It sure made those men out there put a halt to their surefire attack," she whispered to Kristi as she knelt down next to her.

Melissa was just beginning to remove the bandage from Kristi's leg when Kristi opened her eyes and said, "I'm awake and have a clear head, now. We're in a mess, aren't we?"

Melissa ignored the question and asked a question of her own. "Are you in much pain?"

"Yes, it hurts a lot," Kristi said, "but there's not much I can do about that, is there? I wonder why haven't our folks come to take us home?"

Melissa gave Kristi her best smile and said, "I wouldn't know about that, but I firmly believe they'll be coming soon. I found some medicine in the bathroom and I'm going to clean your wound and re-bandage it. That should make you feel a lot better."

Kristi stared hard at her friend. "Maybe temporarily," she said, giving a big sigh. "I could hear you guys talking. Those evil men out there are going to kill the boys, and then rape and kill us before anyone can get across the river. So, what is the point of bothering to patch up our wounds? Why not just let the wounds kill us?"

Melissa said, "Hold that thought for just a minute. I need to get a fresh pan of water. With that she picked up the pan and hurried to the kitchen, wanting to give her- self some time to think of what to say. It wouldn't be easy because a couple of times she had had similar thoughts. But, then there was Rafe and he'd told her, "Not on my mountain," which, as far as she was concerned, meant he wouldn't let her die up here.

Kristi whispered in the direction of Melissa's retreating back, "I don't want to die at the hands of those filthy creatures violating me and killing my baby. I'll kill myself, first."

In the kitchen, Melissa dumped the bloody water in the sink, and then refilled the pan with hot water from the large pot sitting on the stove. Her hands were shaking and she felt sick to her stomach. She took deep breaths, trying to overcome the feelings she was having. She had heard Kristi's parting words and it had shaken her to the core of her being. "We will not die today!" she whispered to no one. "Of course not! Not with Rafe out there. He won't let anything happen to us. He promised me. And what about our fathers and the other men from town, they'll be coming soon, won't they?"

She fought down the fear that had begun to take possession of her. She had to be strong, not only for herself, but for the others as well. She knew Rafe would not want her to be weak. She wiped her face with one of the towels and took several more deep breaths, wondering why Rafe Talltree's thoughts should concern her. Deep inside, she knew, but wasn't sure Rafe was aware of how she felt. She wasn't even sure, herself.

With a steady hand, she marched back into the front room, carrying fresh water and towels to dress Kristi's wound.

Kristi gave Melissa a weak smile as she kneeled down next to her. "I'm sorry for being such a. . . baby. I think getting shot, being in pain and stranded up here with those lunatics out there made me a little crazy for a while. I think I'm okay now. Can you ever forgive me?"

"There's nothing to forgive," Melissa said as she began to clean Kristi's wound. Pointing at herself and then Shaun and Trace, she said laughingly, "We've all had our times of being scared, and now with those two also being wounded. Don't think you're alone, because you're not. You and I just have to believe that Rafe, Shaun and Trace can hold them off long enough for the men from town to get here."

"Do you really believe they'll come?" Kristi asked.

"You bet I do. And so should you," Melissa replied.

"And none too soon for me," Trace said as he surveyed the area in front of the lodge, hoping one of them would raise his head long enough to take a shot at.

He had come to the conclusion that Rafe was right when he said it was either them or those crazies out there. He had never been faced with death before, but while he and Shaun were digging their own graves, something inside of him changed, and then when he and Shaun had been shot, he realized they could no longer depend on Rafe Talltree alone to defend them. He wondered if that was the way the guys who went to Viet Nam felt? He bet they were just like him, young and scared, knowing they could be killed at any moment.

His thoughts were broken at the sound of Shaun's voice asking him a question. "What?" Trace asked, coming out of his reverie.

Shaun grinned and said, "I was asking you if you'd seen anything? It's too quiet out there. It's kind of spooky. And where do you think Talltree is and what's he doin'?"

"I'll bet they're wondering the same thing. I mean, arrows flyin' through the air with sticks of dynamite tied to them would scare the be-Jesus out of me. I think they're just bein' real cautious right now. And, as far as Talltree is concerned, I believe he's up to something. I don't know what. But I don't see him sittin' out there in the barn, quiverin' in his moccasins."

Shaun nodded his head. "Yeah, you're probably right. I just wish I knew what he was up to so we'd know what to expect. Just sittin' here is drivin' me nuts."

"I know what you mean," Trace said, blowing out a puff of air, "but we just have to be patient and stay ready."

"Why don't you two start making a plan of your own," Kristi said, talking rationally for the first time since she'd been shot.

Shaun, Trace and Melissa, all stared at her with surprised looks.

"What?" she asked. "Okay, okay, I know I've been a mess, but I'm alright now. Now, what are we going to do to help Rafe Talltree until Andy, our folks, and the other men from town get here?"

Melissa held out a rag in Kristi's direction and said, "Glad to see you're back, but right now, bite down on this rag and brace yourself. I'm going to pour some medicine on your wound and I won't lie to you, it's going to sting like the dickens. But it will help your leg heal."

"The iodine, I know." Kristi smiled and took the rag and wadded it up and then stuck it in her mouth and bit down as she closed her eyes and clenched her fists.

Since Rafe had cauterized the wound earlier, the pain wasn't as bad as she thought it might be.

By the time Melissa began to wrap Kristi's leg with the new bandage, the pain had subsided.

Kristi unclenched her fists and removed the rag from her mouth. "That wasn't as bad as I thought it was going to be," she whispered to Melissa.

Both, Shaun and Trace marveled at how well Kristi managed the pain of having iodine poured onto her wound - never realizing the cauterizing Rafe had done earlier made things far less painful for her.

"I'm glad. You did good. Now, I need to dump this dirty water, and then see if there's anything I can do to help Shaun and Trace hold those maniacs off, in case they start something," Melissa said, as she stood up and headed for the kitchen.

"Is there anything I can do?" she called in the direction of Melissa's back.

"Just stay put and rest," Shaun said. "If things get rough, we'll see. But for now, just think about getting well, okay?"

"Whatever you say," Kristi said, pulling herself up into a sitting position to give her leg and back some relief. She looked at Shaun's back and felt proud of him for the way he was coming around and helping. She knew it was a coming of age thing for him and knew that accepting Rafe as one of the good guys had been hard. But she was happy to see that he had done some growing up while she'd been under the weather, so to speak.

Rafe had been busy searching the barn for anything else he could use against the supremacists, and after a while he began to feel a quiet all around him, which raised the hackles on his neck. First, he checked the back and sides of the barn in case they were trying to sneak up on his blind side. When he saw no one, he eased up next to the front doors of the barn and peeked around the corner and immediately saw three rifles staring back at him.

Even though the three supremacists saw only a small portion of Talltree's head, their nerves being strung tight, they began firing as fast as they could.

Bullets slammed against the wall of the barn and kicked up dirt near the bottom of the door.

Rafe jumped to the side and away from the door, then grabbed another stick of dynamite and arrow combination from the small pile he'd put together earlier. When the firing stopped, he lit the fuse and stepped into the open doorway and let the arrow fly. The three men were reloading their weapons and didn't notice the arrow until it was already in flight.

One of the men happened to look up and saw the arrow arching its way across space between them. He yelled and all three, as one, turned and ran for cover.

However, they could have stayed where they were because in his haste, Rafe missed his target and the arrow landed some distance away in the dirt and exploded without doing any damage, except for the large hole in the ground it made.

All of the supremacists breathed a sigh of relief when they realized the dynamite had done no harm, and the Indian was no Robin Hood, but they continued to keep a wary eye on the barn anyway. There was no way of telling when he might fire off another shaft of death in their direction. The next one might not miss.

Inside the lodge, both Shaun and Trace had been watching through the windows and were saddened when the arrow landed some distance away from the trucks.

"Well, at least that helps to keep 'em pinned down and not shootin' at us," Trace said with a grin.

Shaun had been checking his rifle and said, "Crap!"

Melissa looked at him and asked, "What's wrong?"

"This rifle only has one bullet in it!"

"Great. Maybe we should ask them if they're ready to surrender?" Trace said with a chuckle.

"Not funny, Trace. Not funny at all. What are we gonna do if they decide to charge the lodge?"

Trace got serious and said, "Try to take down the leader, I reckon. Maybe that will cause the others to back off."

"What if he stays in the back behind one of the trucks, like most generals do?"

While the banter was going on, Melissa checked the other rifles and found two with full cartridges. "Here," she said, "These two are loaded, and handed one to Shaun.

"Look in that sack on the table," Trace said. "It's full of bullets."

Melissa went to the coffee table in front of the couch and found a medium sized gunnysack full of bullets. She gave a thumbs up in Trace's direction and sat the sack on the floor in back of the couch so it would stand less of a chance of being struck by a stray bullet.

Shaun looked from Melissa to Trace. "Are you serious? We have ah whole sack full of ammunition?"

"That's right ole buddy. With you, Melissa and me all shootin' at them bastards, I think we've got enough firepower to hold 'em off until the Calvary gets here. Besides, they've still got Rafe out in the barn to worry about."

Shaun got red in the face and said, "Why didn't you tell us you had a bag full of ammunition?"

"Guess with both of us bein' shot and all the excitement, it just slipped my mind. Plus, nobody asked me."

"Well, it would have been nice to know," Shaun said in an offhand manner.

"Okay, now that you know, how do you want to go about defending this place?" Trace asked, still allowing his friend to feel like he was in charge.

While the boys were busy making plans, Melissa helped Kristi into a different sitting position behind the couch and showed her how to load a rifle, and then the two of them checked the other rifles and made sure each one was loaded.

"Do you really think we're going to have to use these?" Kristi whispered to Melissa as Melissa set the bag of shells within Kristi's reach.

"I sure hope not, but we can't take any chances," Melissa whispered back. "But we really do need to be able to defend ourselves. Just pray that our folks will get here before anything happens."

"Should I be learning how to shoot one of these things?"

Melissa shook her head from side to side. "If it comes down to it, keeping the rifles loaded will be a major help, along with keeping you busy."

Kristi cocked her head and gave Melissa a look.

"Okay. Just in case, I'll show you."

CHAPTER FIFTY-FIVE

Adolph goes forth

Adolph could feel his nerves dancing around inside his stomach like Mexican jumping beans. Time was running out and he knew it. He had to finish this thing once and for all before those farmers came charging down the driveway, along with any other help they had been able to get ahold of. This was not turning out like he had planned and it was all because of that dammed Indian.

He lit a cigarillo to help calm his nerves and he gave the situation more thought. The kids were trapped in the lodge and at least three of them were wounded, which was in their favor when the time came to storm the lodge. But they couldn't do it while that Indian was running around blowing people up with sticks of dynamite. He'd lost enough men already. If they could show the kids a dead Indian, maybe they would surrender.

He stubbed out what was left of the cigarillo with the heel of his boot and looked at the blazing sun for a moment, then reached for the Uzi one of his men was wiping with a cloth.

After checking it to make sure it had a full clip of ammunition, he raised his arm and said, "You men cover me while I make my way over to the side of the barn. I've got unfinished business with that redskin who's become a thorn in our side. I'm going to take care of that bastard, once and for all."

The men shook their fists and weapons in the air and shouted, 'Seig Heil! Seig Heil!

When they heard the men cheering, Trace and Shaun looked out of the windows, wondering what was happening behind the trucks. They held their rifles at the ready in case they decided to attack.

"Get ready, I think they're about to do something," Trace said as he peered from behind the curtain on his side of the room.

Shaun looked over at Melissa and asked, "Melissa, can you shove extra rifles to me and Trace, then cover the other end of this big picture window?"

"You got it," Melissa said as she slid the loaded rifles to Shaun and Trace and was about to make her way to the window with two rifles for herself when all hell broke loose.

The men were in position with some of them facing the lodge, while the others pointed their weapons in the direction of the barn. When the leader saw they were in place, he took a deep breath and yelled, "Now!"

CHAPTER FIFTY-SIX
Charge!

The men from town stopped dead in their tracks as the sound of gunfire reverberated throughout the forest all around them. They'd already heard the two blasts of dynamite and wondered if the kids were all right.

An old man from town, who looked like he'd just come straight out of the hills of Tennessee with his bib overalls, clod hopper shoes, worn thin shirt, floppy hat, long white hair and beard, and was carrying a double-barreled shotgun, yelled, "Jumpin-jee- haus-ah-fat, what the heck's goin on up there now? Sounds like world war three jest broke out. I sure hope them kids are still all right. You think Talltree is with 'em?"

"I'm not sure, brother Jim," Andy yelled, "but we better do our best to double-time it the rest of the way and pray he is and we're not too late."

Andy started off at a fast trot, running side by side with the FBI men. The others were not far behind. Most of them hadn't done any real running in a long time and some of them were pushing their endurance to the limit for fear of what may be happening to the kids. Their nerves were keyed up and they were anxious to meet up with the enemy, again. They were angry and ready for a fight, so, with knees, hips and feet that ached, they ran, sucking in great gulps of air.

Andy's bad leg was sending waves of pain to his brain as he ran. He gritted his teeth and willed his brain to ignore it. As he ran he silently prayed Rafe and the kids were still all right. He was sure Rafe would be doing everything he could to keep them alive and hoped they weren't like the sheriff, back in the ravine with the two FBI men.

As they ran, Jacobs threw out the question Andy had been thinking about. "You don't suppose that Indian fella, that, Rafe Talltree, you talked about; you think he might of decided to take them people on, single handed?"

"Kinda been wonderin' along those same lines," Andy said. "I reckon he might if the situation got serious enough. He is an ex-Viet Nam vet. Came home with a medal of honor and three silver stars, and he lives up here alone. Knows this mountain better'n anybody. And he's tough. If anybody would have the guts to stand up to them alone, it would be him."

CHAPTER FIFTY-SEVEN
Meanwhile, back at the lodge

Inside the lodge, Shaun and Trace dropped to the floor and hoped they would not be hit by flying lead. Melissa dragged a stuffed chair over next to Kristi who was already behind the couch and then covered her with her own body to help protect her.

Bullets tore through the windows and slammed themselves against the back wall and any furniture that got in their way, along with turning pictures into small pieces of glass that scattered the broken pieces in all directions.

"Are they coming for us?" Kristi asked.

"I don't know. I think right now they're just shooting at the lodge, hoping to kill us with some lucky shots," Shaun said, trying hard to sound positive.

"If they do get in, I want a gun," Kristi said, very matter of factly. "I won't allow them to rape me."

"We'll worry about that if they get in here, but for now, just stay as close to the floor as you can," Melissa said, having the same kind of thoughts. Her first time would not be with some redneck white supremacist.

At the same time the lodge was getting bombarded with bullets from automatic weapons, the front of the barn was taking a beating as well. Chunks of lead ripped holes in the doors and wall, leaving it looking like a hunk of Swiss cheese.

Rafe grabbed the rest of the sticks of dynamite taped to arrows and headed for the hayloft where he could get a better look at what was going on. Maybe from up there he would have a better chance to send some damage in their direction.

Rafe was so intent on getting to higher ground that he did not see the leader of the supremacists run in a zigzag pattern toward the side door of the barn. Nor did he see the man enter the barn, quickly and quietly.

Once he was inside the barn, Adolph stepped into a nearby shadow and let his eyes adjust to the dimness of the barn, while listening for any sound. To conceal himself even more, he knelt down behind an old wooden crate. He didn't know if the man had seen him enter and was just waiting for him to make a mistake and show himself.

After several minutes of seeing and hearing nothing but the sound of gunfire from outside, Adolph moved stealthily to a new place of concealment where he could see the interior of the barn more clearly. Not even a mouse moved, and after several moments, Adolph made a foolhardy decision and decided to become the stalker.

It was evident the man was not on the ground floor, so that meant he must have found a hiding place in the hayloft. In his deranged mind, Adolph could see the Indian crouching in fear, knowing he had lost and was hoping they would give up and go away. But he was not going to go away, not until he did what he came to do. He was going to kill the man who had ruined his plans.

Although Rafe had not seen Adolph running for the side of the barn, he had, through his peripheral vision, seen light enter and then disappear when the side door had been opened and closed. It had been no more than a flash of light, but it was enough to alert him of someone entering the barn, and his gut told him it was not Shaun or Trace. They would have called out. Whoever had come through that door had only one thing in mind - to kill him. That's what all the shooting was about - to distract him so one of them could sneak into the barn. If they took him captive, or killed him, the kids wouldn't stand a chance. And if the kids were taken prisoner they would be used as a bargaining tool so these idiots could get away.

With all of the shooting going on, very few men would have noticed the brief stab of light, but Rafe Talltree was no ordinary man. His father had begun teaching Rafe things like tracking and hunting when he was barely ten years old.

His father had taken him to the mountains many times and taught him to see the movement of a leaf, or hear the sound of a twig breaking when many others would have missed it. He taught Rafe that every movement or sound meant something. He also taught him how to distinguish what it was. "The eyes and ears are valuable allies," his father had told him. And as he grew older, they had played roles in surviving everything from bear attacks in the woods, to saving his and other men's lives in Viet Nam.

After blindfolding him, Rafe's father had walked away, leaving him alone in the forest, sometimes for hours at a time before trying to sneak up on him. Rafe had lost the game only twice. And because of all of the training his father had given him, along with his military training, those instincts were serving him once again.

Rafe moved to a place of concealment that would allow him to see the lower part of the barn, but not be seen by anyone below. He kept his breathing shallow and made no sound as he watched - waiting for the slightest movement, never allowing his eyes to linger on any one thing in particular, but keyed on any movement, be it ever so slightly.

Several minutes passed before he saw the man move from his hiding place to a different spot; a place the man foolishly believed would hide him, but still allow him to see everything but not be seen.

The man had been quick and efficient in his movements and Rafe had not been able to get a clean shot at him, nor did he try. Giving away his own hiding place was the last thing he wanted to do until he was ready to strike.

Suddenly, as quickly as the shooting had started, it stopped and a huge quiet fell over the area. The wind stopped blowing, the birds stopped flying and sat silently on the limbs, wondering what was going to happen next. The men behind the trucks turned and stared at one another, also wondering what to do next. Without the Captain to tell them what to do, they just stood there and waited. Most began reloading their weapons, while others lit cigarettes and smoked.

The only thing that moved was the sun as it crept ever so slowly toward the west, leaving a trail of heat.

After a short time, Adolph's patience began to run low. The silence was killing him. He wanted action and he wanted it now. He wanted the Indian dead.

While his eyes took in as much of the barn as he could, he called out, "You're pretty good with that bow, Redskin, but how are you at fighting a man face to face, man to man. Fists or knives, whichever you prefer; just you and me, boy. What'ya say?"

Rafe smiled and said nothing. He knew the non-action and silence was getting to the man who he now realized was the leader of the supremacists. Like his father had trained him, he remained silent as he moved to a better location and waited.

Adolph was not the only one lacking in patience. A relatively newcomer to the group by the name of Murphy, was dancing back and forth on the balls of his feet. After only six months in the US army he had gone AWOL. [Away Without Leave]

Two months after he'd deserted - on a tip, the military police trapped him in his apartment. He'd climbed out the second story window and jumped into a swimming pool and escaped into the night. A week later, he joined up with Adolph and his small band of cutthroats who were planning to overthrow the US government, which was more to his liking. The man had said there would be plenty of action.

Murphy turned to the others and saw they were becoming as jumpy as he was. "Hey guys, listen up. I got an idea. While the captain is taking care of that Injun, why don't we take the house?"

They looked at each other as if they were pondering the idea, but not totally committed to the plan. After all, who was this new guy to be giving orders? But, on the other hand, what else did they have to do?

He looked at the three men closest to him and said, "You boys cover me while I make a run up onto the porch. I'll take a look-see and we'll go from there. What do you say?"

The three young men looked at each other, then one of them said, "Sure, why not. Beats just standing here. Besides, there's a couple of females in there and it's been awhile, if you know what I mean."

Murphy nodded and said, "On my signal," and raised his hand as high as his shoulder, took a deep breath while he assessed his chances. Finally, he was satisfied and dropped his arm, then lit out for the porch as the three men peppered the front door with lead.

Just like he'd been taught in the army, Murphy zigzagged his way across the opening hoping no one inside the lodge would get a clear shot at him. He leaped onto the front porch and flattened himself against the outside wall.

Because of Rafe's lack of response, Adolph was gaining confidence, believing for sure now that the Indian was a coward and was hiding in the loft. It was time to get rid of him, once and for all.

Moving with great caution, just in case, Adolph moved from the open space to a place under the loft, not far from the ladder. Once he was in place, he calculated where the man might be hiding and then fired a burst into the floor of the loft before hurrying to the ladder and climbing up to the loft and crouching behind some bales of hay.

Rafe remained where he was, wanting to get a good look at the man who was a cold blooded killer; a man who would execute anyone who got in his way - even young men and women who had nothing to do with him or his crazy war.

Silence settled over the loft and the waiting began once again.

Murphy eased his way over to one of the windows and peeked inside. The kids were all grouped together behind the couch. He figured he could get at least one of them, maybe two, if he was on the opposite side of the window. He signaled for his comrades to hold their fire, then went to his hands and knees and scurried to the other side of the window and stood up.

His view from that side was excellent. He figured he couldn't miss as he slowly lifted his pistol and took aim on the nigger loving white boy.

Just as he was about to squeeze the trigger, he heard a whoop, whoop, whoop sound and looked back over his shoulder and saw the helicopter moving into a hovering position above his comrades.

"This is the FBI. Lay your weapons on the ground, now!" a voice coming through a bullhorn, commanded.

Murphy watched as his comrades dropped their weapons and raised their hands in the air. "Fools!" he yelled and lifted his pistol and began firing at the helicopter.

At the sound of the helicopter, Shaun ran to the window, where he saw a man standing on the porch with his back to him, shooting at the helicopter.

Shaun grabbed his rifle and eased to the door and opened it as silently as he could, then peeked around the doorsill and saw the man had just reloaded his pistol and was about to start firing, again.

Without thinking about it, Shaun leaped onto the porch and yelled, "Hey!"

Murphy's head came around and he saw one of the boys standing on the porch with a rifle in his hand. "What the hell?"

he yelled as he swung the pistol in the direction of the young man with the rifle.

Just as he squeezed the trigger, the young man moved wide of his shot and pointed the rifle at him. Murphy saw the flash from the end of the barrel at almost the same time he felt something slam into his chest and felt himself being driven off the porch.

Before death took him, he saw the young man run back inside the lodge and slam the door, never knowing the bullet that brought him down was the last one the young man had in his rifle. His body landed with a thud and lay with blank eyes staring at the sun. The score was now, one less lunatic to deal with.

From his place in the open doorway of the helicopter, Andy watched the scene on the porch between Murphy and Shaun and was blown away at what he saw. "The boy has grown up some," he muttered to himself.

"What?" Burns yelled over the sound of the helicopter.

"Nothing. Just talking to myself," Andy answered as the helicopter began to descend to an area between the supremacists and the lodge building.

"We'll secure these guys, then I'll watch 'em while you check on the kids. The others should be here soon," Jacobs yelled over the noise of the helicopter.

Andy nodded his head in the affirmative, as the helicopter sat down, throwing debris into the air.

While everyone was distracted by the helicopter landing, one of the supremacists who went by the name of Herman Smith, which wasn't his real name, bent down, picked up his rifle and rolled under the truck he was standing behind. He decided he would not go to jail. His father had died in prison. His mother had dragged him there for visits and he had watched as the years ate away at the man. He'd vowed to himself that he would never let that happen to him. It would be better to go out in a blaze of glory than to rot away in some prison, just waiting to die.

Herman crawled to a place near the center of the truck and waited for his chance to come out shooting. He hoped it would be the Indian, but in truth, any of them would do.

From inside the lodge, Melissa watched from the window as the helicopter sat down. Andy and a man she didn't recognize, who was dressed in a suit, stood in the doorway with their weapons trained on the men who had been trying to kill them.

Beyond the helicopter, she saw the supremacists with their hands raised in the air and their weapons lying on the ground. Excitement flowed through her and she wanted to sit down and cry. They'd come, and it was over! They weren't going to die!

But instead of sitting down, she turned and ran over to where Trace was sitting and took him by the arm and helped him to his feet. "They're here! We're saved!" she said and gave Trace a hug and a kiss on the cheek.

Shaun was already next to Kristi. He was fighting back tears of joy as he gently touched her face with his hand and said, "It's all over, sweetheart. The lunatics have given up, and Andy is here with a helicopter to take us home!"

Tears were running down Kristi's face as she looked at Shaun and nodded her head. She was too happy to speak.

After embracing Trace, Melissa turned and walked over to the window and stared in the direction of the barn, wondering why Rafe hadn't appeared? She longed to see him come walking out of the barn, alive and unhurt.

CHAPTER FIFTY-EIGHT

A time of reckoning

INSIDE THE BARN, the game of hide and seek was still going on. Adolph had long ago decided the Indian was a coward and hiding. Maybe he was out of arrows and had no other weapon, he wondered as his eyes sought his prey.

Feeling brave and sure of himself, Adolph stood up and waved the barrel of his automatic weapon around, searching for even a glimpse of the Indian, so he could fill him full of lead.

As his eyes searched the inside of the loft, the sound of the helicopter filled the inside of the barn.

Adolph backed toward the double doors where hay was loaded into the loft and with great stealth, he pushed open one of the doors just enough to see the helicopter sitting down and his men with their hands in the air.

A wave of anger raged through him, which caused him to want to see the Indian dead, all the more. All his work and planning was disappearing before his very eyes, and it was all because of that damn Indian.

Calmness washed over Adolph as he turned his attention back to the issue at hand. And when he spoke, it held no malice, no anger, just one man talking to another.

"So, you somehow radioed for help. And as you can hear, they have arrived. But it will do you no good. If they're not dead already, the kids may have a chance, but it's too late for you, boy. You're never going to leave this barn alive. I'm going to kill you for what you've done to spoil my plans."

Through a small space between two bales of hay, Rafe watched this man slowly loose his mind; reality had become a thing of the past. The man was even crazier than before and just aching for the chance to kill him.

Rafe took his eyes off the man for just a moment to check the stick of dynamite that was taped to the arrow he had just notched in his bow.

"Come on out and face me like a man instead of hiding like a woman, and the sniveling coward you really are," Adolph said, as he took a quick glance out the open door, then turned his attention back to the inside of the loft, waiting for the Indian to show himself. He was getting anxious. He'd seen only two men and the pilot out there and in his mind he could see himself saving his men. He would rush out of the front doors and open up on the three men, taking them by surprise and killing them before they had time to react. His men would put him on their shoulders as he gave the orders to capture the kids inside the lodge. He would hold them as hostages until they were free, then he would kill them, too.

Rafe had grown tired of the game and hiding behind bales of hay. The man was what his people would call, a demon from hell who needed to be destroyed. The man was brazenly standing in clear view as though he was taunting Rafe to make a move. "Well, if that's what he wants," Rafe whispered to himself. He would not have a better opportunity than now. With his knife, Rafe cut off most of the fuse and pulled a match from his pocket and lit the short fuse and stood up, calling out, "Hey, big mouth, you lookin' for me?"

As Adolph turned in Rafe's direction, Rafe let the arrow fly, then ducked behind the bales of hay and on hands and knees, scrambled toward the edge of the hayloft.

When Adolph saw Rafe, he swung his weapon in Rafe's direction and squeezed the trigger, spraying the loft with bullets that ripped into the roof of the barn and tore their way into the bales of hay.

The sound of an automatic weapon being fired filled the air, forcing its way out through the open hayloft door and across the space to where Andy and the rest were standing.

Rafe slid over the edge of the loft and dropped to the floor, running as soon as his feet touched the hard surface.

The sound of the gunfire caused everyone to look in the direction of the barn. The supremacists were grinning, believing their leader had done what he'd gone to do; kill the Indian. In unison, they all cheered, "Seig Heil! Seig Heil!

By now, the helicopter pilot was standing next to Andy and Burns, with a pistol in his hand. Burns looked at them and said, "You two keep an eye on those yahoos. I'm gonna check out the barn and find out what's goin' on down there."

Andy nodded his head and called after him, "Be careful."

As Burns moved away, Andy wondered if whatever was going on in the barn had anything to do with Rafe Talltree. He had seen neither hide nor hair of him since they'd showed up. As an afterthought, he wished he'd warned Burns that Rafe might be in the barn and not to start shooting at him.

By now, Andy was getting annoyed with the chanting and yelled, "Quiet!" And like a switch being thrown, the chanting stopped.

Andy looked at the helicopter pilot and smiled.

The pilot grinned at Andy and said, "I wish I could do that with my kids."

Everyone inside the lodge had also heard the gunfire coming from the barn and wondered if it was Rafe or the leader of the lunatics.

"It would be insane if, after all we've been through and all the stuff Talltree has done for us, that those idiots out there happen to kill him just when the Calvary arrives."

"Don't even think like that, Shaun!" Melissa shouted.

Shaun looked down at the floor and said, "Sorry about that, I didn't mean it like it sounded."

Trace stared at his friend in awe. Shaun was talking nice about Rafe and even apologizing to Melissa. Now, that was something to take notice of. Suddenly, he felt very proud of his friend.

Andy commanded the supremacists to lay face down on the ground with their arms and legs spread wide so as not to be a threat when the pilot came by to retrieve their weapons.

Adolph felt a pain in his stomach and looked down. His eyes grew wide when he saw an arrow embedded in his stomach with a stick of dynamite taped to it! The stick of dynamite had a very short fuse that was hissing at him and burning very fast.

Out of desperation, Adolph grabbed the arrow and tried in vain to yank it from his stomach, but all he got for his effort was gut-wrenching pain.

As the pilot jumped to the ground, the explosion took off the top of the barn. Wooden shingles and other debris came raining down on them, including body parts.

Stunned by what they were seeing; no one spoke a word as flames leaped out of the upper part of the barn.

The supremacists realized their leader was gone and the fight was over. As a unit, they dropped to their bellies and spread their arms and legs. That is, everyone but Herman, who was hidden under one of the trucks. He kept his eyes on the front doors of the barn, waiting for his enemy to appear - and he didn't have to wait long.

Simultaneous with the explosion, Rafe came racing out of the barn, not more than twenty feet directly in front of Burns.

Burns immediately went into a firing stance. With two hands gripped on his pistol, he pointed it at Rafe and yelled, "Hold it right there! FBI! Hands in the air where I can see them!"

Herman saw Rafe come out of the barn and stop and raise his hands in the air.

"Perfect," he whispered to himself as he scrambled from beneath the truck and stood up, and then began running toward Rafe, firing his rifle as fast as he could and yelling, "Die, you filthy Injun bastard!"

Burns stared in horror as he watched Rafe being lifted off the ground and thrown backward as several of Herman's bullets struck Rafe's body.

Burns and Andy both reacted by turning in Herman's direction and began firing their weapons at him.

Herman was struck in the head, the heart and several other spots on his chest, at almost the same time. He was in hell before his body hit the ground.

From their positions on the ground, Herman's comrades witnessed the death of the Indian by one of their own, and together, they chanted for their fallen comrade, Seig Heil! Seig Heil! Seig Heil!

They kept it up until they heard Andy yell; "Quiet!" and they went silent, again.

Melissa was standing at the window, wondering when they would be allowed to get on the helicopter and go home, and watched in horror as Adolph's body pieces flew from the upper part of the barn and flames began to climb out of the holes in the roof.

A movement from the front of the barn caught her eye and she saw Rafe come running out of the barn. Immediately, her heart began to race as a smile spread across her face, only to be replaced with a look of terror as she watched Rafe being shot down by someone who had climbed out from under one of the trucks and was running toward him and firing a gun at him. She saw the bullets slam into Rafe's body and toss him into the air and then fall to the ground.

"Nooooo!" she screamed at the top of her lungs.

Trace raced to her side and asked, "What? What's wrong?"

Melissa turned and looked at Trace with vacant eyes. "He's dead. One of those maniacs killed Rafe."

Everyone in the room was stunned, to say the least, but it was Shaun who spoke first. "Are you sure? Not Talltree, he's invincible! He can't be dead; not because of what I just said about him."

But Melissa heard not a word of what Shaun had just said. Her adrenaline was coursing through her veins like the raging river that had washed away the bridge. Her legs were moving her out of the lodge, off the porch and in the direction of Rafe's body lying in a heap on the ground.

Burns was kneeling next to Rafe as she ran up and looked down. Rafe was bleeding from several places. His eyes were closed and she knew he was dead, until she saw his chest rise, slightly.

Burns looked up at the young black girl whose chin was quivering and had tears running down her cheeks.

"He's alive, but just barely," Burns said to her. "Do you know him?"

Melissa swallowed and blew out a long breath of air. "Yes, his name is Rafe Talltree. He's the one who rescued us from these awful people," she said, waving her arm in the direction of the supremacists.

"Is he going to live?" she asked in an almost whisper; wanting to know, yet not wanting to know. Her breathing was raspy and her hands were shaking so bad she had to put them behind her back so the man couldn't see what bad shape she was in.

"I honestly don't know," he said as he began stuffing his handkerchief into one of the holes that was spurting blood. "I need more rags," He said.

Without a word, Melissa turned and sprinted in the direction of the lodge. As she ran past Andy, she yelled, "He's badly wounded, but he's still alive!"

The chopper pilot looked at Andy and said, "We don't have time to wait. I'll fly him and the kids in as soon as we can get them loaded. The e-vac chopper is on its way."

Andy nodded his head in agreement as Melissa went flying past with an armload of rags.

When he turned his attention back to his captives, he felt the bile in his throat. Never in his life had he ever wanted to commit murder more than he did right now. It took all of his control to keep from executing each and every one of these murdering, low life scum.

His concentration was broken by the sound of men coming down the drive. He looked up and saw Jacobs leading the rest of their small army in his direction. He let out a breath of air and was glad to see them. They just may have saved him from making the biggest mistake of his life.

Without being told, some of the men from town surrounded the supremacists and pointed their weapons at them, just daring them to move, while three of the others ran to the barn. One of the men turned off the electricity while the other two, hooked up hoses and began spraying water on the fire.

Jacobs walked up to Andy and said, "Is everyone ok?"

Andy looked at him and said, "Not sure, yet." He nodded toward Burns, Melissa and Rafe. "You remember me mentioning an Indian that lived up here by the name of Rafe Talltree?"

Jacobs nodded his head, "Yeah, what about him?"

"I don't know much, except that he rescued the kids, and took on these guys single handed and just before you got here, one of these lunatics loaded him with more lead than he can likely carry. Burns and one of the girls are with him now. I'm told he's alive, but barely. He's got multiple gunshot wounds - at least six. The chopper pilot is going to take him and the kids to the hospital in town and then he's coming back to do what he can to help. He said the e-vac helicopter is on his way."

"Sorry about Talltree. Let's hope he pulls through. And the kids?"

"Two leg wounds and one of them took one in the shoulder."

Trace and Shaun came out the front door of the lodge with Kristi between them. Her arms were around both their shoulders to keep weight off her leg.

Kristi's father was the first to notice them and yelled at the others. "Hey, it's the kids and they're alive!"

Even as tired as they were, the kid's fathers ran toward them and stopped when they saw the bandages. Kristi's father was the first to speak.

"Are you kids all right? What' happened? Who did this to you?"

Kristi almost leaped into her father's arms, talking a mile a minute. "Oh daddy, it was awful. I was shot in the leg and so was Trace; and Shaun was shot in the shoulder, but Melissa fixed us up, but we still need to see a doctor. Rafe

Talltree saved us and cauterized my wounds, and, and, and I'm so glad you're here!"

By now she was sobbing into his shoulder and he was patting her on the back. "It's going to be all right. We'll get all of you to the doctor as quickly as we can."

Andy ran up and said, "We need to get you kids aboard the helicopter, now! Rafe and Melissa are already on board. There's no time to waste, Rafe is hurt real bad."

As they rushed toward the helicopter, Melissa's father called out, "Why is Melissa in the helicopter? Is she wounded?"

Not wanting to get involved, Andy called over his shoulder. "You'll have to ask her, but I don't think so."

While Kristi, Shaun and Trace are being loaded into the helicopter, Thomas Walker rushed up and saw his daughter tending to Rafe Talltree, tears running down her cheeks.

"Melissa? Are you all right?"

Melissa looked up and smiled. "Thank you for coming, daddy. Yes, I'm all right. I was the only one who didn't get shot."

"Then what are you doing in the helicopter?"

"I'll explain later. Please trust me. We have to go now. I'll see you at the hospital. I love you."

Melissa's father stepped back and stood with the others as the helicopter lifted into the air.

As the helicopter headed toward Shortcut, Andy called out. "Okay, somebody get some rope so we can get these people secured and ready to travel."

CHAPTER FIFTY-NINE
One year later

A COOL BREEZE wafted through the city park of Shortcut, Utah. Rows of picnic tables were sitting behind thirty rows of benches, which sat in front of a newly painted stage. The stage contained ten chairs, a microphone on a tall stand, and two large speakers; one sitting at each end of the stage.

People were seating themselves at the picnic tables, while others found places to sit on the benches in front of the stage.

An air of excitement filled the park as Shaun's father – the mayor, Andy, now dressed in a sheriff's uniform, and the two FBI men, Burns and Jacobs, mounted the stage, followed by Shaun, Kristi, Melissa and Trace. Everyone found a chair and sat down, conversing quietly while waiting for the rest of the town to arrive and find seats.

After close to half an hour, Shaun's father was beginning to get nervous. He looked at the one empty chair, then turned his attention to the crowd and saw the whole town patiently looking back at him. "We can't wait any longer, Andy, I'm sorry."

Andy sighed and nodded his head as the mayor stood up and approached the microphone.

The mayor raised both hands in the air and waited until they quieted down. As he stood waiting, he looked down at the front row of chairs and smiled at his wife, who was holding their first grandchild, a bright-eyed little boy. Kristi was staying with them until Shaun could get an apartment down in Texas where he would be attending Texas A & M on a football scholarship. Thomas Walker and his wife were sitting on his wife's left, while Big Mike and his wife sat on her right. Big Mike was on top of the world. His son, Trace, would be playing football for Kansas on a full scholarship and had been accepted into the University's law school. Next to them, sat Tracy Babcock Singer, the wife of Andrew Singer, the sheriff of Shortcut. She was wearing a pink maternity outfit.

The mayor was grinning from ear to ear. This was the biggest thing to ever happen to the people of Shortcut. When all was quiet except for the sound of the wind blowing gently through the trees, he began.

"Thank you all for coming. Well. . ." he said in a booming voice, "this is a big day for all of us, as many of you well know since you were a part of it, so I won't bore you with a lot of details on why we're here, today."

From somewhere toward the back of the park, a voice filled the air. "Thanks!" followed by laughter.

"I thank you for your appreciation for my speechmaking," the mayor said to more laughter and applause.

"So, without further ado, it is my pleasure to turn the microphone over to a man who informed me, he hates speaking in public, our new sheriff, Andrew Singer."

On his way to the microphone, Andy shook hands with the mayor as laughter and applause filled the air.

Andy looked down at his wife and smiled, then back at the large crowd of people.

"Thanks, but I only have a couple of things to say."

The same voice from the back of the crowd, called out again. "Don't you always."

"Thank you, George. I'll remember that the next time I see your pickup parked in the no parking zone down next to the pool hall."

Hoots and hollers filled the air.

"Seriously folks," Andy continued, "I want to thank you for making it official and electing me sheriff."

Before they could applaud and cheer more, he raised his hands. "And Tracy and I want to thank you for all the wedding gifts and the shower. We now have three baby cribs and two strollers, and to the best of my knowledge, we're only expecting one baby. Right, honey?"

More hoots, hollers and applause filled the air. When they finally quieted down, Andy took a deep breath and spoke seriously. "I also want to thank you for letting me run my own show, so to speak. Your trust in me means a lot."

He turned and looked at the two FBI agents, who nodded their heads. "At this time, two men you already know, agents Burns and Jacobs, have something to say that I think you'll all be interested in hearing. So, with that said, I'll turn the microphone over to them."

Andy shook hands with both men as they approached the microphone, and then went back to his seat.

Jacobs stepped up to the microphone and said, "We thought you folks would like to know that those people we encountered up on the mountain last year, were in fact, a group of fanatical white supremacists that had plans to kill the president, vice president and all the other people at the debates down in Salt Lake City – in an attempt to take over the United States of America. But. . . he let the word hang there for a moment. "Because of your help, it didn't happen."

As one, the people stood up and cheered and applauded.

Jacobs stepped back and gave Burns his turn to speak. When the people were seated and quiet, again, be began. "The FBI in conjunction with the President of the United States are proud to present to you with a token of esteem for your help in this most dangerous and touchy situation. . . Normally, the FBI doesn't allow civilians to become involved in their operations, but in this incident, you didn't give us a choice and taught us what it means to be, both a parent and a patriot."

Roars of applause and yelling erupted as Andy made his way down off the stage to a large statue covered with a piece of cloth. Burns pointed in Andy's direction and when they looked his way, Andy pulled the cloth away to expose the statue of a man resembling Rafe Talltree. He had a bow and had a quiver of arrows hanging over his shoulder. Four teenagers and a crowd of people holding weapons surrounded the man.

The people were amazed at the size of the statue. It stood nearly twelve feet tall and the base was ten feet wide.

As Andy turned and walked back toward the stage, the people took their seats and waited for Burns to continue.

Burns drew in a breath and spoke into the microphone. "I know that each of you who risked your lives or got wounded, have already received your special citation from the President. Will you please stand up?"

It seemed like half the men from Shortcut stood up and many with embarrassed looks, stood while the people applauded and cheered.

Burns stepped back and Jacobs stepped in front of the microphone, again. And, when they finally sat down, he said, "Along with the citations and the statue, Burns and myself are privileged to present special FBI awards to those young people who showed above normal courage in the face of danger and even though they were injured, they still found the courage to stand up and fight against overwhelming odds. Please step forward when I call your name. Kristi Lange Tilford, Melissa Walker, Trace Bozeman and last but not least, Shaun Tilford."

As each one came forward, Burns placed a medal hanging from a wide ribbon around their necks and shook their hands. Jacobs was next and handed them a piece of rolled up paper, tied with a ribbon, as he shook their hands.

Again, the air filled with applause and shouts and whistles until the kids returned to their seats.

Jacobs walked back to the microphone and cleared his throat. "And finally, it is my honor to present a special award to a man who, unfortunately, isn't with us today, though I wish he was. This man's courage exemplifies American patriotism to its fullest. When he could have. . ."

Jacob's speech was interrupted by the drone of an airplane flying overhead as it buzzed the park, then circled back around. The people watched as a man jumped out of the plane and fell in their direction. The parachute blossomed and the man drifted into the park, landing not far from the statue.

Andy limped off the stage and hurried over to where Rafe Talltree was taking off his parachute. He's dressed in a police uniform with a deputy's badge pinned to his shirt.

Andy grinned and slapped him on the shoulder. "Well, you cut that close enough. Jacobs was just talking about you. Glad you made it – and in grand style, too."

Rafe looked at Andy and said. "I got your message and the head of the academy gave me permission to come up, just like you said he would. What's going on? And why was someone talkin' about me? And what are all these people doing here?"

Andy said, "Just follow me, Chief."

As they passed the statue, Rafe gave it a questioning look, and as they mounted the steps to the stage, the crowd went into a wild uproar.

CHAPTER SIXTY
The following day

MELISSA'S SUITCASE sat next to her feet as she stared up at Rafe Talltree. In the background, a train was rumbling and bellowing smoke, waiting to be called into action. People were already boarding.

Rafe took his time before stammering, "You know we're doing the right thing."

Melissa put her hands on his arms. "But it seems such a long time."

Rafe gave her a boyish grin and said, "Hey, we'll see each other during breaks and on holidays. Going to college, then nursing school is very important to you. I would never forgive myself if I did anything to hinder that. Plus, I still have to finish my time at the Police Academy."

"But I could still go to school, even if we were married."

Rafe reached up and scratched his ear. "Trust me, this is the best way. If you are meant to be the wife of a deputy sheriff, then it will happen.

"What do you mean, if?" Melissa said with panic in her voice. "I love you, Rafe Talltree and I want to be your wife."

"And I love you, too. And I want you to be my wife and have a whole passel of kids if that's what you want. But right now, you're going to get on that train before I change my mind. We can talk about this later."

Melissa reached up and put her arms around his neck, drawing him close, and kissed him passionately.

When the train began to move, Rafe pushed her away and reached down and picked up her suitcase and handed it to her. He then turned her around and swatted her on the rear end as she ran for the train and stepped aboard.

Just as she turned and waved goodbye, Andy's voice came over the walkie-talkie Rafe had hanging on his belt. "Okay, lover boy, time to get back to the academy. The plane is gassed up and the pilot is getting' antsy.

Rafe waved goodbye as he pulled the walkie-talkie from its holder.

THE END

THANK YOU FOR READING

"NOT ON MY MOUNTAIN"

By

Jared McVay

LIKE THIS BOOK?

Look for more titles by Jared McVay at

www.CreativeTexts.com

THANK YOU!

MEET THE AUTHOR

At the current time, Jared McVay lives in the great northwest, where he writes his stories and does storytelling. Many consider him a Master Storyteller. Jared is also a three-time award-winning author. He writes several genres, which includes - westerns, fantasy, and action/adventure. But mainly, he writes about people and their struggles with everyday life.

Before becoming an author, he was a professional actor – on stage, in movies and television. As a young man he was a cowboy, a rodeo clown, a lumberjack, a power lineman, a world-class sailor and spent his military time with the Navy Sea Bees where he learned his electrical trade.

When not writing you can find him fishing somewhere, or traveling around and just enjoying life with his girlfriend, Jerri.

ALSO BY JARED McVAY

Jared is the author of five novels, two children's books, a long list of short stories and several television and film screenplays. So far, Jared has been blessed by having three of his books win awards.

CHILDREN'S BOOKS:
Bears, Bicycles & Broomsticks
Santa's Magic Ring

NOVELS:
Stranger On A Black Stallion – Western – new – book one – Clay Brentwood series
The Legend of Joe, Willy & Red - Historical Fiction – Chaucer Award
Hacker's Raid – Western – Laramie Award
Not On My Mountain – Contemporary – Laramie Award – Grand Prize Award

SCREENPLAYS:
The Hobos – Action Adventure
Jared and the Warden – Western
Talltree – Action Adventure
Santa's Magic Ring

PILOT: TELEVISION SERIES:
Acute Care Transport – ACT – Drama/Comedy about an Air Ambulance Service
McClusky – Action – Human Interest – Six Episodes

COMING SOON:
Unjust Punishment – Western – Book two of the Clay Brentwood Series
The Legend of Silent Runner – Fantasy
Bears, Bicycles & Broomsticks, Volume 2